Praise for Olivia L

'A witty, fluent writer, Lichtens[...] mother and daughter, Cape Tow[...] of-the-moment comedy puts the world to rights in the way good popular fiction can' *Independent*

'Lichtenstein is a fine writer ... if you recognise the sentiment behind the words "I hate you. When I'm a mother, I'm never going to be like you ..." then you will adore this funny, touching tale' *The Lady*

'A moving tale told with humour and warmth' *Bella*

'Olivia Lichtenstein's first novel is full to bursting with good things ... succinct, witty and often funny enough to make you hoot unbecomingly on public transport ... [an] accomplished, enjoyable and surprisingly moral fable'

Independent on Sunday

'A deliciously funny and frank first novel which will strike a hidden chord with so many women and should be read by just as many men if they truly want to know what drives a loving wife into someone else's arms' Meera Syal

'Simultaneously witty and poignant ... Lichtenstein has cleverly plotted the thrills – and pitfalls – of having a bit on the side ... seamlessly blending the erotic with the comic, this story is full of very funny (but oh so valid) observations'

Jewish Chronicle

'*Mrs Zhivago* is like a script for the perfect comedy drama. And, reading between the jokes and comic situations, there's a real message about what keeps a marriage alive' *First*

'Both poignant and darkly amusing, we heartily recommend'
Irish Tatler

'A deliciously compelling read that tells enduring truths'
Nigella Lawson

Olivia Lichtenstein's first novel, *Mrs Zhivago of Queen's Park*, won the *Good Housekeeping* Award for Most Entertaining Read and was shortlisted for the Melissa Nathan Award for Comedy Romance. Olivia works as a TV producer, director and journalist. She lives in West London with her husband and two children. For more information about Olivia Lichtenstein and her books, see her website at www.olivialichtenstein.com.

By Olivia Lichtenstein

Mrs Zhivago of Queen's Park
Things Your Mother Never Told You

Things Your Mother Never Told You

Olivia Lichtenstein

An Orion paperback

First published in Great Britain in 2009
by Orion
This paperback edition published in 2010
by Orion Books Ltd,
Orion House, 5 Upper St Martin's Lane,
London WC2H 9EA

An Hachette UK company

5 7 9 10 8 6 4

A CIP catalogue record for this book is available
from the British Library.

ISBN 978-1-4091-0348-6

Typeset by Deltatype Ltd, Birkenhead, Merseyside

Printed and bound in Great Britain
by Clays Ltd, St Ives plc

The Orion Publishing Group's policy is to use papers
that are natural, renewable and recyclable products and
made from wood grown in sustainable forests. The logging
and manufacturing processes are expected to conform to
the environmental regulations of the country of origin.

www.orionbooks.co.uk

For my mother, Leonie
August 1930–May 1989

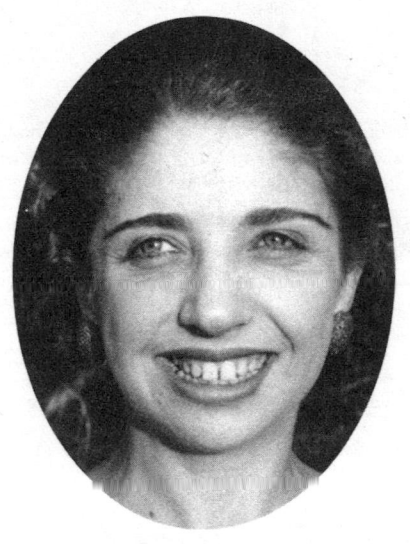

Ubuntu ungamntu ngabanye abantu

Xhosa proverb
A person is a person through other people

Gumbaggley */guːm.bægliː/*

Anything pertaining to or redolent of Eastern mysticism or
alternative therapy, medicine or philosophy. Often
used pejoratively. Thought to have been coined by
musician, Michael Townsend in London in the
early 21st century.

First of all ...

'I'm your best friend, Ros,' her mother, Lilian, always told her. 'No one else will tell you the truth.'

The truth was that Ros didn't want, or need, a best friend; she had one at school. What she wanted was a mother, not someone who felt she had a constant duty to give it to her straight, to tell it like it was, nor indeed one who raised a disapproving eyebrow murmuring, 'A minute on the lips, Ros ...' before patting her own slim hips silently to finish the sentence '... a lifetime on the hips,' when as a hungry, growing teenager Ros reached for yet another potato.

'Your mother is such fun,' her best friend Debbie said. She'd come over for the day and they were listening to Ros's new Bee Gees single in her bedroom. 'I wish my mum was like her.'

Ros nodded doubtfully. She loved her mother. Of course she did. And she *could* be great fun, but she could also be quite tricky. In fact, trickiness was in the air right there and then. Ros could almost taste it.

As so often happened, that particular day had started well. The three of them had passed an enjoyable afternoon, Ros, Debbie and Lilian, trying on Lilian's clothes from when she was young and doing each other's make-up. Encouraged by Lilian, Ros and Debbie had chatted about the boys they liked and the teachers they hated and Lilian had joined in with stories of her own, of when she herself had been thirteen and living in Cape Town with her parents.

'I think I loved our servants, Diana and Josiah, more than I 'loved my parents,' Lilian said, her fingers trailing through the clothes that lay discarded on her bed: strapless satin evening gowns, fur stoles, high-heeled shoes, African print dresses that she had designed herself, the bodices artfully darted to obviate the necessity for a bra.

'I certainly preferred spending my evenings with them, sitting on the steps of their outhouse sharing the *mealies* they had roasted on a small fire ...'

'Corn on the cob,' Ros explained to Debbie.

'Sometimes we'd have *sudsa*, with a gravy they said they made from the juice of grasshoppers,' this time Lilian paused to allow Ros to translate.

Ros shook her head, she didn't know.

'Don't you remember?' Lilian looked at Ros critically.

No, actually, funnily enough Ros didn't remember every detail about Lilian's bloody South African childhood. What was this, an exam?

'*Sudsa*? It's a sort of porridge made from *mealie* meal,' Lilian clarified, running a brightly coloured silk scarf through the circle she'd made between her thumb and index finger. 'I don't know whether they were teasing or not, about the grasshopper gravy, I mean, but it tasted far more delicious than the meals my mother made Josiah prepare for me, which I always had to eat on my own in the kitchen.'

'Gosh,' said Debbie, looking admiringly at Lilian, 'you're so much more exciting than my mum. The most interesting thing she's ever eaten was powdered egg during the war.'

'We had such exotic food,' Lilian said, the faraway look of Africa in her eyes, 'mango, pawpaw, grenadilla, sugar cane ... I used to chew on a stick of sugar cane for hours, until it was dry and stringy. I never wore shoes and the ground was so hot I had to hop, scorching the sole first of one foot, then the other.'

'I had mangoes once,' Debbie said, 'when we went to an Indian restaurant on my birthday.'

'They were probably tinned,' Lilian said dismissively. 'They taste completely different. When I was a child, mangoes were so succulent that Diana made me eat them sitting in the bath, the sticky juice running down my face and arms.'

Debbie was watching Lilian with an expression of rapt admiration.

I wonder if they'd even notice if I left the room, Ros thought, feeling thoroughly excluded.

'I'm just going to fetch something,' she said. Debbie didn't even look up, lost in a story Ros had heard many times before about how Lilian, on her way home from school, dragging her small brown leather satchel in the dusty earth behind her, would search the ground for the red and black lucky beans that had fallen from the trees to give to her nanny, Diana, who would thread them into necklaces for her. The necklaces were Ros's now, although you wouldn't think so judging by the state Lilian had got into only the week before when Ros had accidentally broken one of them. Lilian had shouted at her and made her scour the floor for ages until satisfied that Ros had found every last bean.

Ros went to her room and sat on the bed. It wasn't that she minded her mother talking to her friends. On the contrary, she liked the fact that Lilian was interesting, clever and fun. It was just that she never knew when to stop and always ended up being the centre of attention. Sometimes Ros felt there was no room left for her to have a personality of her own. Maybe it would be different if she had a father who lived at home. All the other girls did, but Ros's mother and father were divorced and her dad had remarried and now lived in Australia. It was the first thing she'd told everyone when she started secondary school just to get it out of the way, blurting it out to almost the entire class at milk time. After she'd said it, she'd punched her straw into the small milk carton with too much force and spattered her brand new uniform.

'I hate these stupid cartons,' Debbie had said, squeezing Ros's arm. 'I wish we still had those little bottles, don't you?'

Ros had smiled at her gratefully and they'd been best friends ever since. She hated it when people were sorry for her, but Debbie managed to communicate sympathy without pity. There was only one other girl in their class with divorced parents and her dad lived nearby. Ros only saw her father once a year. How could anyone be a proper dad when he hardly ever saw his daughter?

'Don't worry, baby, I'm your mother and your father,' Lilian said, whenever Ros got upset about not seeing him. 'You mustn't mind being different; it makes you special. You learn to think for yourself rather than blindly following the pack.'

'But I want to fit in,' Ros said.

'The trick is to fit in while standing out,' Lilian said.

'Is that what you did, Mommy?' Ros asked. (She always called her Mom or Mommy; that's what they did in South Africa.)

Lilian had laughed. Ros thought it was a sad laugh, which was strange because laughing was meant to be happy.

'I certainly stood out,' Lilian said, 'but I didn't ever fit in.'

Ros still couldn't understand what could possibly be good about not really having a father, but she liked the way Lilian made her feel special. Sometimes she thought that Lilian, with her unconventional clothes and loud voice – its clipped vowels still betraying her origins – was a beautiful, exotic and noisy bird, at once compelling and terrifying.

'Stop showing off, Mommy,' she used to say, when she was little and felt that Lilian was flapping her wings too loudly. Like that time when Lilian had sung 'Day-O' loudly with the conductor on the bus on the way home from school. Sophie, one of the prettiest girls in the class, had been on the same bus with her own mother and they had giggled and stared at Lilian and Ros until they'd got off.

Ros could hear Debbie and Lilian laughing in the other room. She should be pleased that her mother liked her best friend. Today, that was. Lilian was inconsistent and blew hot and cold. It was like living in an unstable microclimate. She looked at herself sideways in her dressing table mirror to see if her tummy was sticking out like Lilian had told her it was earlier. She sucked it in and decided to eat nothing but apples for the rest of the day.

She went back into her mother's bedroom just as Lilian started dancing. Ros thought she might die of embarrassment; Lilian was moving around in a circle wriggling her bottom and shaking her hips.

'It's an African dance called the *kwela*,' Lilian said. 'Miriam Makeba taught me herself.'

'Who's she?' asked Debbie.

'Don't you know?' Lilian said. 'She's Mama Africa, the queen of African music. Come.'

Lilian took Debbie by the arm and led her into the living room. She put a record on the gramophone player and soon Makeba's voice filled the room singing in her native Xhosa.

Sat wuguga sat ju benga sat si pata pat pata pata …

Oh God, it was so embarrassing; Lilian was singing along and making all those weird clicking noises that the Xhosa language demanded. Ros glanced at Debbie who was watching Lilian and trying to copy her dancing. She felt cross and left out all over again, a familiar lonely feeling that seemed to start at the ends of her toes and work itself all the way up her body. She didn't want the feeling to reach her stomach and leave her with that big empty hole she never knew how to fill, so she joined in. Soon all three of them were singing and dancing together. Ros felt a little better, but she now had an uncomfortable feeling that something unwelcome was biding its time in the shadows of the small flat she and her mother shared.

Sure enough, Ros felt Lilian's mood shift at the precise moment when, the dancing over, Ros was winding a length of batik fabric around her head like the African woman in the painting on their living room wall. Ros could see her mother's reflection behind her in the mirror and witnessed her face appear to darken. It was hard to pinpoint how emotion changed expression. Was it the eyes? A tightening of the facial muscles? A change of colour in the complexion? Lilian suddenly looked completely different. If it didn't sound so silly, Ros would almost have said she had turned into someone else.

Lilian left the room soon after, telling Ros to hang all the clothes up, her message clear: the party was over. There was an edge to her voice that only Ros noticed.

'Ask your mum if I can stay the night,' Debbie said, struggling into a pair of tight shorts and oblivious to the change in atmosphere. Ros felt anxious; she knew Lilian would go mad if she came in and found everything hadn't been tidied away and now, to top it all, she had to ask her mother to agree to Debbie staying over. She hated having to ask Lilian for things. All too often the answer would be an emphatic and implacable 'no' that would leave Ros with the embarrassment of having to invent a reasonable explanation to offer others.

She found her mother in the kitchen, standing by the window, her gaze resting distantly on something Ros couldn't determine. Ros tiptoed up to her, preparing herself.

'Mommy,' she began.

'You gave me a fright!' Lilian said, jumping. She smiled.

Ros laughed uncertainly. Maybe it would be all right; perhaps Lilian's mood hadn't changed after all.

'Is Debbie still here?' Lilian's voice was cold.

'Yes, um, canshestaythenight?' The words gushed out like water under pressure.

'No,' Lilian said.

'Why, Mom? Please let her stay.'

'Not tonight.'

'Please, Mom.' Ros wondered how she was going to tell Debbie she couldn't stay.

'How many times do I have to say it, child? The answer's no.' Lilian was shouting and Ros was afraid that Debbie would hear her. Her accent always got stronger when she was angry. Ros had read something in her history book only the week before about a Russian woman who was a spy in Germany during the war. Her German was so good that no one suspected her, but she gave herself away by shouting out in Russian, her mother tongue, when she was giving birth. Ros thought it was a bit silly of a spy to get pregnant in the first place, but they'd had an interesting discussion in class about something her teacher called *primary identity* asserting itself in times of stress. What she couldn't understand was why her mother was stressed and so ... so ... fucking unreasonable. There, she'd said it. After all, she just wanted her friend to stay the night.

'I hate you,' Ros said, looking at her mother's taut expression.

'When I'm a mother, I'm never going to be like you.'

She left the room and went out onto the small balcony that led off the living room. In the near distance, she could see the Post Office tower and wished she could go to the top and stay there all night, high above everything and everyone, the lights of the city carpeted beneath her. Angry tears coursed down her cheeks and she took big gulps of cold spring air in an attempt to compose herself. She didn't want Debbie to see she'd been crying. Why was it always the same? Fun and laughter followed by anger and tears, pleasure always having to be paid for with pain? Was everyone else's mother like hers? She didn't think so.

'Can I stay?' Debbie asked, when Ros returned, her expression anticipating agreement.

Ros couldn't meet her eye. She tried to sound casual. 'Oh, sorry, no, listen, I forgot, we have to go somewhere later, to see some relatives.'

'I thought you didn't have any relatives here,' Debbie said. 'I thought they were all in Africa.'

'One of my cousins has come over.' Ros hated lying.

'Ros,' Lilian's voice called loudly from the other end of the flat.

Ros's heart jumped and she hurried to Lilian's room before Lilian could shout out anything Ros didn't want her friend to hear. Her mother lay on her bed, looking straight ahead.

'Has she gone yet?' she asked. Her voice was flat and sounded deeper as it always did when she turned into the other Lilian.

'Not yet.'

'I want her to go,' Lilian said, 'NOW.'

The next morning, Lilian brought Ros breakfast in bed. A freshly cut daffodil lay on the tray, the first of the season, picked, no doubt, from the window box on the balcony. It was Lilian's way of saying sorry. Ros didn't want to look at her mother, and looked instead at the yellow of the flower, which matched that of the scrambled eggs exactly. The green sprig of parsley decorating the eggs echoed the daffodil's stalk. Yellow and green. The colours of spring, of new beginnings. Would things be better now? After Debbie had left the day before, Ros had sobbed in her room, her core a well of misery that no amount of weeping seemed able to drain.

'You're crying to be heard, Ros,' Lilian had called out from the hall. 'You have to learn you can't always get what you want.'

Now, Lilian sat on the edge of Ros's bed while she ate her breakfast.

'How come you hardly ever talk about your parents?' Ros asked her.

'There's not much to say,' Lilian said. 'They weren't members of my tribe.'

'What do you mean?'

'Well, there are people you find in life, the ones who you know at once will be your friends, who share your beliefs and see the world as you do.'

'Like me and Debbie?' Ros asked.

'Yes, like you and Debbie, and your gang at school, and you and me.' Lilian stroked Ros's hair.

Were Ros and Lilian in the same tribe? Ros supposed so, although all too often it felt like Lilian metamorphosed into its scary witch doctor or despotic chief.

'Let's go to Brighton for the day,' Lilian said. 'I'll make us a picnic.'

Ros was reluctant to be won back so easily. It was all very well Lilian being jolly and pretending nothing had happened.

'Come on, darling, get dressed and we'll get an early train. The sea air will do us good and it'll be fun.' Lilian pulled at Ros's mouth until Ros smiled. 'Stop being cross.' And then she laughed and said that thing that made Ros's breath catch in her throat, leaving her feeling sick and dizzy.

'You'll be sorry when I'm gone.'

The thought of life without Lilian, however demanding, made Ros feel as though she was standing on the edge of a very high building about to fall off. It wasn't a good feeling but, if she examined it closely, there was something flaring at its edges that felt strangely, if not quite like relief, then perhaps like liberation.

Then ...

Ros had taken a day off from the school where she taught, carefully planning her absence for when she had fewest lessons, and giving the Head plenty of notice. A Day of One's Own, she called it: one day a year when she could do what she wanted out of radio contact with the rest of the world generally, and her husband, twin sons and mother specifically. The telephone had caught her just as she was leaving the house and she'd come running to the hospital. Angina, they'd said when she'd got there, nothing to worry about; Lilian should be home by the weekend.

She sat by Lilian's bed, watching her mother's motionless form. Lilian's breathing soothed Ros in a way Lilian herself had rarely been able to. Ros contemplated her mother's sleeping face, still beautiful even at seventy. A curl, its vibrant red now dusted with the small amount of grey she allowed to show, had worked itself loose from the rest of her hair and hung in the centre of her forehead, a poignant reminder of a time, only hours before, when Lilian had been up and about, busily getting on with her life, instead of lying frighteningly and uncharacteristically inert in a hospital bed.

> There was a little girl,
> Who had a little curl,
> Right in the middle of her forehead.

The childish verse went round and round in Ros's head. It could have been written for Lilian: mercurial, unpredictable Lilian who could be, from one instant to the next, first funny and brilliant and then angry and vituperative. Ros reached out a hand towards her, to smooth the curl away. Her action surprised her; she didn't usually initiate physical contact with her mother, didn't like it much on the rare occasions when Lilian hugged or kissed her. Ros had learnt early on to hold herself apart in order to preserve her own identity and to prevent Lilian from overwhelming her. And, Lilian, for all her involvement and interference in Ros's life, retained an elusive, separate quality that placed her curiously out of reach.

Lilian opened her eyes and turned her head to look at her daughter.

'What's that?' Lilian asked, staring at a spot on Ros's chin.

'It's a spot,' Ros answered shortly, her finger tracing the source of Lilian's enquiry.

'You know how I hate you to have blemishes,' Lilian said, smiling.

She may have been joking, but, thought Ros, it was typical of her mother to find something to criticise. Ros remembered how, whenever she'd dressed up to go out, Lilian would stop her at the door, look her up and down and ask, 'Are you going out like that?' Ros's confidence would seep from her, like the juice from one of Lilian's African mangoes, leaving her limp and drained, any excitement she might have been feeling for the evening ahead quite gone. When Ros had become a mother herself, she was careful to keep the promise that she'd shouted at Lilian all those years earlier: to be a different sort of mother. She looked at her watch.

'I'd better go, Mom, I've got to fetch the boys.'

'Can't Mike get them?' Lilian asked. 'There's something I want to tell you.'

'Tell me tomorrow, you look tired.' Ros was suddenly impatient to be gone, to exchange the fetid atmosphere of the hospital for the familiar doggy smell of her twin teenage sons' unwashed hair.

'But it's important, I've been meaning to tell you for years; it's something I should have told you a long time ago,' Lilian said.

'Well, I'm sure it can wait a bit longer, can't it?' Ros said absently. Although still seated, she could already see herself walking to her car, breathing the welcome air of a cold January day, driving back to her life with Mike and the boys and away from the discomfort that Lilian so often aroused in her.

'The book ...' Lilian said.

Ros took from the bedside table the novel that her mother had been reading earlier and placed it on the bed beside her.

Lilian shook her head sleepily, 'No, not that one. I mean, my book.'

Ros looked around impatiently. She couldn't see any others.

'I'll come back later,' she said, trying to pace her departure, lest Lilian see how eager she were to be gone.

In the event, there had been no later. Ros hadn't gone back to visit Lilian that night – she'd sent Mike instead with a mendacious note.

Dear Mommy, I thought it best if I didn't come in this evening as I'm getting a cold and I don't want to give it to you. I'll come in on the weekend with the kids. Hope you're feeling better. Love you, Ros.

The telephone woke her in the early hours and Mike had answered it. Ros, her heart pounding, had watched his face, only too aware that ringing telephones before daybreak rarely bring happy news.

'I'm sorry,' Mike said, shaking his head and replacing the receiver carefully in its cradle as though fearful of breaking it. In the numb contemplation of the irrelevant that often follows death, Ros had wondered at Mike's caution. After all, wasn't everything already broken?

'I wasn't there to hold her hand,' Ros said, over and over. 'She was on her own.'

Later, while retrieving Lilian's effects, Ros had found her note folded into the zipped compartment of her mother's handbag, where she always kept anything precious. Next to it, she'd found a small black and white photograph of a young, smiling Lilian sitting on the crossbar of a bicycle, a young black man in the saddle behind her.

It had taken a post-mortem to reveal the cause of death. A

ruptured aortic aneurysm. Lilian's heart had broken. Literally. Ros felt that her own was about to as well.

Just because a relationship is complicated, doesn't mean you don't mourn it when it's gone.

Chapter One

'Shave it,' Ros said.

'Pardon?' Luis glanced up, moving around her as she sat in the hairdresser's chair, his small, tight bottom attracting covert glances of longing from the other customers, both female and male, as he pushed and pulled her shoulder-length, tawny, highlighted hair this way and that.

'My head,' Ros said, 'I want you to shave it.'

Luis swivelled her chair around to face him and looked hard into her eyes.

'Ah,' he said at last, comprehension dawning. 'So, you and Mike have split up?'

Ros nodded, annoyed by the lump that had suddenly formed in her throat. She tried a careless laugh; it didn't really work and she sounded more like a goat being strangled than a woman happy to have parted from her husband of twenty years.

'Yup. New Year, new look, new me,' she said.

'I think shaving may be a little extreme, but we'll certainly do something different; a proper end-of-the-relationship haircut,' Luis said soothingly, and he pushed some strands of hair out of her eyes with a tenderness that made Ros want to cry.

'Let me give you a "new beginnings", it's very popular with all my just-out-of-a-long-relationship ladies.'

Ros watched her hair drop to the ground as Luis snipped. Since Lilian's death the year before, scenes from her childhood replayed in her mind more and more often, like scratched film turning on the sprockets of a home-movie projector. She had a vivid memory of childhood when her mother had taken her for her first proper haircut. She'd sat dwarfed by the big chair, her small plump legs dangling high off the ground, and cried as her baby curls had been cut away. At the end she'd marvelled at her reflection: no longer a baby, but a big girl.

While Luis was working, Ros admired her new emerging self in the mirror as this time the effect was reversed: no longer an ageing woman in her forties, but a woman who could, in good light, still pass for a girl. The words of the bereavement counsellor Ros had seen briefly after Lilian's death drifted through her mind, like a whisper of smoke escaping through an open window. 'After the death of a parent, people often change careers and marital partners.' Was it a case of either/or? Ros hoped so; now that her marriage was over, she wondered whether she'd manage to hang on to her job.

Two chairs down from her, Ros could hear a woman filling her hairdresser in on the details of her own recent break-up. Her long dark hair was being savagely chopped into a short back and sides, which seemed to suggest that she might have been driven to change her sexual persuasion in *her* search for a new beginning.

'I keep asking myself why,' she was saying, 'why did he leave me and go off with her?'

The woman's hairdresser wore the glazed expression of someone who has been punched repeatedly about the head.

'Do they make you do a course in psychotherapy at hairdresser's school?' Ros whispered to Luis.

Luis followed Ros's gaze and smiled.

'They should,' he said. He leant forward and continued softly in Ros's ear. 'There are two types of woman: one who beats her breast and complains like the Ancient Mariner repeating his tale of woe, and the other, like you, who although she feels as deeply, makes light of the situation and is able to laugh about it.'

'Is that why hairdressers always express such an unusual interest in their clients' holiday destinations?'

Luis laughed, 'Yes, it's the safer option, we never know which one the woman may turn out to be.'

Ros could see what he meant. The woman two chairs down was weeping now, fat tears leaking from her eyes as she spelled out the ways she would like to hurt her former husband. Her hairdresser stoically cut on, her face impassive as she snipped, and chewed gum, hoping, perhaps, by her silence, to encourage her client to follow suit.

'Sometimes I wonder whether I should have been an undertaker after all,' Luis said cheerfully.

Ros looked at him questioningly.

'My father always told me to consider two options,' he explained. 'Hairdressing or undertaking. That way, he said, you can always be assured of employment. After all, people always need their hair cut and we all die at some time or another.'

He stood back to admire his work and held a mirror up so that Ros could see the back of her head.

'Tell her to sew prawns into the hem of her husband's new curtains,' Ros said, nodding towards the Ancient Mariner woman. 'I believe it's the standard punishment for infidelity. The prawns soon go off and stink the place out and the source of the smell is almost impossible to find. That should contaminate his new love nest quickly enough.'

Luis shook his head in disbelief. 'Hell hath no fury ... Is that what you're planning to do to Mike?'

'No,' said Ros, 'Mike's crime doesn't warrant the prawn treatment; he hasn't traded me in for a hotter number. He just seems to have had a personality transplant. I believe he's been gathering material for a new handbook for husbands, you know, *How to be a Complete and Utter Cunt.*'

'I'd better give you Tattoo Tony's number,' Luis said, laughing. 'You'll be needing to pay him a visit.'

'Oh no,' Ros responded, pushing the piece of paper he proffered away. 'It may be part of your starter pack for newly single women, but I've never liked tattoos much.'

Luis had pressed the number into her hand anyhow and she'd

rested against him for a moment, enjoying the comfort of his warm hand against hers. She experienced a brief moment of despair; her life had unravelled in the year since Lilian's death – did she have the energy for a whole new era?

Chapter Two

Ros was woken by the sound of dogs barking from next door. Even though she was a dog lover, indeed was coming to terms with having to share her own dog, a giant black poodle called Ruffy, as a result of a recent custody battle, it was the kind of barking that made her wish she had a gun so she could go and silence the beasts summarily with one round of ammunition. She wasn't normally given to thoughts of violence, but after the events of the past few months, indeed the past year, she was discovering an entirely new range of emotions. She was, in a sense, rediscovering herself. Sometimes it felt good to be an 'I' again, no longer a sanctimonious 'we'. But sleeping alone was hard, one half of the bed flat and lonely without the second body that had filled it for the past twenty years. Most nights she hugged a pillow in an attempt to fill the void and get to sleep, which was why the dogs hadn't helped, rousing her, as they had, from hard-won slumber. What was Mike doing now? she wondered. Was he enjoying the emptiness of the divorcé bed? Or planning to fill it with a woman twenty years her junior, the secretary at the school where he worked perhaps, or some other such clichéd replacement? Men hardly ever stayed single for long. Particularly not men as attractive as Mike. Single women, hovering like vultures over the road kill of another woman's marriage, would make off with their prize in their predatory beaks in no time. In fact, two weeks was apparently the length of time an eligible man remained available.

'It's called the two-week window,' her friend Charlie had explained over a glass of wine the evening before. 'When a man comes back on the market, a woman has two weeks to snaffle him up. Everyone assumes that women are the ones who can't hack it on their own, but in fact it's men who behave like amputated limbs in search of a torso.'

Charlie should know; although gay, he was a divorce lawyer and well versed in the customs of wedded heterosexuals.

'It's been more than two weeks,' Ros said. 'In fact, it's over three months.'

'Well, the two-week thing is more of a metaphor,' Charlie explained. 'The point is, men don't tend to stay single for long.'

Mike had moved out of the marital home and rented a flat a few streets away so that Sid and Jack, their eighteen-year-old twin sons, could come and go between them. ('Sid? Honestly, Ros, what sort of name is that for a child?' Lilian had said when the twins were born.) When the boys were with Mike, Ros found herself rattling around in the house they'd shared since the children were born with only the ghost of her marriage for company; a temporary state which was soon to become permanent in just a fortnight when the boys went off travelling on their gap year.

'Try and marry a rich man,' her mother had told her repeatedly when she was a teenager.

'That's such a horrible thing to say,' Ros had retorted. 'I want to marry a man I love, not a bank balance. How can you even say such a thing?'

'I simply think it will make you happier and it's as easy to fall in love with a rich man as it is a poor one.'

'You didn't, so why should I?' Ros had replied. Her father had been far from rich although he appeared to have found relative prosperity since in his new life in Australia.

'Do as I say, not as I do!' Lilian had answered, smiling to show that she acknowledged her double standards.

But Ros's heart always went to penniless would-be poets, musicians and writers. She'd tried to make herself fancy a millionaire once. He had his own swimming pool in the basement of his house and everything. She couldn't do it; although he was personable enough, she simply wasn't attracted to him and no amount of money could persuade her otherwise.

The dogs were still barking – in fact, they seemed to be having a competition to see who could bark the loudest. Men were like that too when one came to think of it. Mike had taken to barking rather too loudly and too often in their last months together, his voice booming complaint at the boys' and her perceived misdemeanours until it had seemed he might begin to bite as well. Ros looked at her clock. Five forty-five. Bloody marvellous. She wished Ruffy were with her, but it was Mike's turn to have her. Ruffy was an entirely appropriate barker, giving voice only in moments of extreme pleasure or possible danger, and Ros hated being in the house without her. Since the separation, Ruffy had slept on the bed with her. Lately, she'd even taken to sleeping like the person she believed herself to be, her head on the pillow next to Ros's and her body under the duvet. Ruffy, who had spent years campaigning for this privilege, couldn't believe her luck and her black eyes seemed to shine with smug satisfaction. Ros comforted herself with the thought that Ruffy, at least, had benefited from the end of the marriage.

Ros had taken up yoga after Mike left and now tried some deep breathing in an effort to calm down and block the noise out. She repeated to herself the words that Joti, her yoga teacher, had spoken in class the day before.

'Let awareness stand like a gatekeeper at the entrance to your nostrils, letting nothing in or out, just breath.'

The yoga was part of a general makeover and reinvention programme that Ros had recently undertaken. Well before the obligatory haircut, she'd embarked on a campaign of alternative therapies and had been filling Charlie in on her latest foray when he'd popped over the night before.

'You did what?' he'd asked.

'I sent my spit to California.' Ros noted Charlie's incredulous expression and stopped herself from reminding him of his almost obsessive tidiness. 'We all have our foibles,' she remarked mildly.

'Look, I've been feeling really tired and I think I'm on the brink of the menopause.'

Charlie looked bemused.

'You spit into little bottles at four different times of the day and they analyse it at their lab to find out whether you're suffering from adrenal fatigue and if your hormones are all up the spout,' Ros explained.

'And how much does this little experiment cost?' Charlie had asked, settling back into the sofa and lifting his feet onto the coffee table in one graceful motion.

'One hundred and twenty-five of your English pounds,' said Ros, 'but since I no longer seem to eat, I figured that it's money I'd normally spend on food.'

'Why pay someone to tell you what you already know?' Charlie said. 'You are exhausted from going through a separation and, at forty-five, it's quite possible that you're menopausal.'

'Ssshh', Ros said. 'Someone might hear.'

'What, that you're forty-five, or menopausal?'

'Both, sshh.'

'Ros, we're alone in your house.'

'It could be bugged.'

Ros had met Charlie through the school where she taught before the boys were born. She had been a teacher-governor and Charlie was then chair of the governing body. Charlie's one regret about being a gay man was that he didn't have children of his own, but he had been keen to have some involvement in children's lives and his logical, legal mind had proved invaluable. Whenever meetings had seemed set to stagnate in petty squabbles or irrelevant detail, Charlie used smoothly to sum up and move matters forward. He'd tried to talk Martin, his then boyfriend, into adopting a child or finding a surrogate but Martin's heart had never really been in it. The years had passed, the holidays had become more exotic, Charlie and Martin had parted company and when Charlie took silk at the age of forty-four and became a QC, he reluctantly accepted that children were not to be. Not biological children in any event.

Years ago when the boys were still babies and Mike, Ros and Charlie had been out shopping, she'd passed the buggy over to Mike, saying, 'Take your sons.' Charlie had taken her arm and turned her towards him, his face serious and intent. 'Can they be my sons a bit too?' he'd asked. 'Of course,' Ros had said, hugging him. She'd asked him to be godfather to Jack and Sid and he'd agreed on the condition that he could be a fairy godfather and spoil them. In the intervening years he had made good his intention with lavish gifts and the institution of special 'Charlie Days' when he would take the boys on outings to the park and to West End shows. By the age of twelve, they knew all the songs from the most recent musicals. Ros and Mike referred to the three of them as 'The Showgirls'.

Charlie laughed. 'So what other gumbaggley nonsense are you spending your money on?' he asked.

'Gumbaggley' was Mike's word for anything alternative or smacking of Eastern mysticism. It had entered the vernacular of all those around them and it was so onomatopoeic that Ros was certain it would eventually find its way into the *Oxford English Dictionary*. Mike had always teased Ros about her predilection for alternative therapies and once, when she was on one of many detoxes, he'd presented her with glasses of mineral water, chanting, ringing a small, silver bell and kneeling before her all the while, her very own temple boy. The recollection of this made her miss him sharply and she could feel tears sting her eyes. The memory, however, was of a time before his anger had taken hold and the associated transformation had occurred from amiable loving husband into Jekyll and Hyde. Ros had felt awful in the final year of their marriage, increasingly unhappy and anxious. She'd found herself tiptoeing around Mike on eggshells, uncertain how he might react to anything.

One morning, a few weeks before they had parted, Ros was sitting in the staffroom of Woodville High, the co-educational state school where she taught English and was Deputy Head, having a coffee with her friend, Jaime Rockley, Head of History.

'What's up?' Jaime had asked, noticing Ros's unhappy expression.

'Husband,' Ros said shortly. 'Ill-humour emanates from him like steam off newly laid horse manure; it permeates the whole atmosphere.'

Jaime nodded knowingly. 'Ah yes, grumpy husband syndrome. Do you think it's an extra chromosome that men have?'

'Must be.'

'He can't be as grumpy as Tony, though. He's like a tinderbox, the slightest thing seems to ignite him.'

'At least he's still Tony.'

'What do you mean?'

'Well, the trouble with Mike is that he's become two different people. If something annoys him, his face contorts and he transforms from a pleasant-looking man into some kind of rage-filled monster rather like the Incredible Hulk. I actually expect to see him turn green. If he wants to transform into someone else, why can't it be into a superhero like Superman, or one called Niceman or something, instead of rage-filled Pig-Fuckman?'

Jaime covertly added a spoonful of sugar to her coffee and Ros pretended not to notice. Jaime was on a permanent diet and had appointed Ros head of food intake police. Ros had reluctantly assumed the role, acutely aware of how cross she used to get when Lilian monitored her own food intake. Ever since, Jaime had become as unskilfully devious as a secret drug user, eating and drinking extra calories behind Ros's back while constantly, and with feigned astonishment, bemoaning her failure to lose any weight.

'Has Mike changed since your mother died?'

Ros considered the question. It hadn't occurred to her that her mother's death and her husband's inability to control his temper could be connected, but then, she supposed, the death of someone close can affect the ecology of all one's relationships.

'You mean he can behave badly now that I've no longer got a mother to run home to?'

'Sort of,' said Jaime. 'I don't mean he's doing it consciously, but I remember when Tony's mum died; I felt a demonic surge of power. He couldn't tell on me to her any more and get her to drop insinuating remarks to help him win battles like he'd done in the past.' Jaime sipped her sweet coffee with obvious satisfaction. 'Mind you,' she continued, 'since he's always been the absolute dictator in most areas of our relationship, I welcomed a bit of power. Not that it's done me much good. I'm still not allowed to have curly hair.'

'What on earth do you mean?' Ros asked.

'Tony won't allow it and I have to spend hours straightening it.'

'Are you serious? I didn't even know your hair was curly.'

'Precisely,' Jaime said. 'Or, as the French might say, *je reste mon valise*.'

Ros, who had just taken a gulp of her tea, laughed, snorting hot liquid over her top.

'Don't let Madame Sauvage hear you say that,' she said.

'Why?'

'Because it's *ma valise*, not *mon* and I'm not sure you can *reste* it, I think you may have to *repose* it.'

'Honestly, you're as annoying about French grammar as you are about English,' Jaime said, pretending to slap Ros. 'I'm not allowed to dance either,' she added.

'God, Jaime, I never realised you were such a doormat. What about tapping your feet in time to music, is that permitted?'

'Only just.'

'That could be construed as an infringement of personal liberty,' said Ros.

'Yeah, but when you think about it, so could the whole of marriage.'

She had a point; cleaving one's life to someone else's usually meant the curtailment of any number of activities in the name of compromise. Ros and Jaime became engaged in a contest as to whose husband was the most unreasonable. The anti-curly hair and dancing laws did strike Ros as quite extreme, but at least Tony didn't have Mike's temper and tendency for shouting and swearing at the people he professed to love the most. Ros was feeling less and less like herself when with him. Fearful of triggering his transformation, she was in danger of becoming a timid creature that she neither recognised nor liked. This troubled her deeply; how she felt about herself in the context of a relationship was almost as important as how she felt about her partner.

'I've married my mother,' Ros said, recalling Lilian's changeable nature. 'They say women usually marry their fathers, but we don't, we actually marry our mothers.'

'I'm not sure that's true,' Jaime said, surreptitiously removing a wine gum from its wrapper in her handbag with one hand. 'Perhaps it's that we marry the person most like our more difficult parent in the hope of repairing that relationship. The trouble with unreasonable behaviour,' she continued, 'is that the person being unreasonable always wins because you can never make them admit that they are behaving unreasonably.'

'Yeah, Jonathan Swift had a point, you know. He said: "It is useless to attempt to reason a man out of a thing he was never reasoned into,"' Ros agreed.

She sat back and looked through the window. Outside in the playground a tall maple tree stood stripped bare of its leaves. Ros remembered how it had been a few months before, ablaze with autumnal pinks, golds and browns. The leaves had been so vibrant and beautiful it was difficult to believe that they were dying; one final glorious conflagration before they fell and crumbled to dust. It was like the strange euphoria she had heard sometimes precedes death.

'Mike spent the entire weekend screaming at the boys for leaving dirty mugs and glasses around the house,' Ros continued. 'You'd have thought they'd been smoking crack the way he went on. Naturally I took their side and so he shouted at me too. Then he said he was going to break every cup or glass he found that had been left lying about. And he actually grabbed a glass and smashed it against the wall, leaving me to pick up all the pieces. I think that classifies as pretty unreasonable behaviour, don't you?'

Jaime's eyes widened. 'Glass-smashing is a bit excessive,' she said. 'I can't see Tony doing that. Perhaps Mike needs anger management?'

She gave Ros a considering look as though realising for the first time that her complaints were more than the usual competitive grumbling about husbands that women enjoy and, hoping to make Ros feel better, she protested a little more about her own life.

'On Saturday night, I sat at home with my freshly straightened hair, watching old episodes of *Who Wants To Be A Millionaire* after the kids had gone to bed, with Tony snoring on the sofa beside me. I felt like a Chekhovian heroine, in mourning for her life.'

'Well, next time you feel like that, you can always come over to Grumpy Towers and walk on broken glass and eggshells,' Ros said, thinking that a little boredom would be infinitely preferable to Mike's unpredictable rages.

It was a relief to laugh and joke about their husbands together, but it didn't disguise the fact that when, as the boys put it, Mike 'went off on one', a fist of pulsating misery took root in Ros's gut. Despite her attempts to make light of his moods, they poisoned the atmosphere and were impossible to ignore. She was on the point of confiding this when Jaime interrupted hastily, alerting Ros to the direction and approach of Peter Seers, Head of Physics and general know-all.

'Angel of Death at twelve o'clock.'

Peter Seers was the staffroom bore and the frequent and gleeful bearer of bad tidings, hence the Angel of Death sobriquet. Ros and Jaime shot out of their chairs in an attempt to look busy. Bitter experience had taught them to devise all manner of ploys to avoid getting trapped in conversation with him. On the occasions they failed, how they wished they could fast-forward through his relentless outpourings and get to the heart of what he was saying in the quickest time possible. Always supposing, of course, that such a heart existed. Ant Slinger, the music teacher, was the unlucky man who fell into Peter Seers's path in this instance and Ros and Jaime steadfastly ignored his silent, anguished appeal for rescue.

'I'm your friend,' he mouthed at Ros, 'help me.'

Ros gave a small helpless shrug and turned her head away with a ruthlessness that surprised her. Ant looked like a cat that had got its head stuck between railings and Ros was certain she'd be made to pay for her cruelty in ignoring his mews for help at some later date.

Jaime's obvious surprise at Mike's glass-smashing made Ros realise that all really was not well and, that morning in the staffroom, she had understood for the first time that she wouldn't be able to live like this much longer. In the weeks that followed, Mike's increasingly frequent outbursts had left her feeling more and more isolated. It didn't help that she could remember every detail of all their conversations and arguments, a talent she had inherited from her mother, who appeared to recall verbatim every important conversation she'd ever had. The night when Mike had sworn at her, calling her a 'stupid fucking bitch' and telling her to 'fuck off' over and over again, replayed itself in Ros's head. She had simply and mildly asked him if he could turn his music down and he had turned on her, his features contorted with rage; the words he'd spat at her had felt like blows. She'd felt strongly that the violence of his language could just as easily escalate into physical violence. The following day, when she'd said as much to him, Mike had replied that he would never hit her and had accused her of being a drama queen. Although he'd been contrite a day or two later, the abusive language had somehow severed the cord that bound them. Ros had found herself separate yet miraculously still whole, and, after so many months of unreasonable behaviour, she'd asked Mike to leave. The day he moved out, Ros was mugged in the street on her way home from buying milk.

'I lost my husband and my mobile phone on the same day,' she told Jaime the next morning in the staffroom.

'To lose one is unfortunate, but to lose two, as Oscar Wilde might have said, is careless,' Jaime said, hugging her.

They'd laughed. It had seemed the only possible response under the circumstances.

'Just think,' Jaime said with a touch of envy, 'now you can be in charge of the remote control. If I were you, I'd curl my hair and go out dancing.'

Ros smiled, although she had never felt less like dancing in her life.

'And,' Jaime continued, 'you don't have to give Mike a standing ovation every time he empties the dishwasher or takes out the rubbish.'

Ros laughed and felt a little cheered. It was true; men seemed to expect tumultuous applause whenever they performed the smallest household task. They were like small children holding up paintings for their parents' approval. Ros remembered the time when Mike had come back from the supermarket, his face quite pink with pleasure.

'The woman at the supermarket said that I'd done a lovely shop,' he said.

'What on earth do you mean?' Ros had asked.

'Well, when I got to the checkout, the woman looked at all my stuff piled up on the belt and said, "Your wife's a lucky woman; you've done a lovely shop." Then she turned to the queue of people behind me and said, "Look everyone, hasn't he done a lovely shop? Isn't his wife a lucky woman?" They all looked at me and examined my shopping, oohing and aahing over my selection of fruit and vegetables and a couple of women actually clapped.' Mike laughed as though amused, but Ros could see that he was actually bursting with pride. She had generously refrained from reminding him that his choices had been dictated by her shopping list.

How would Mike feel now, she'd wondered, with no lucky wife at home to boast to? Thinking of this incident saddened her, a reminder of all the jokes and nonsense that give a relationship texture and paint the details of a life shared. She'd forced herself to remember Mike's temper and bad behaviour in order that her resolve wouldn't weaken. She knew Mike hadn't wanted to go, but had been too proud to beg to stay. The children couldn't see any immediate advantages to their parents' separation and were furious with them both; Jack in particular.

'You and Dad didn't try hard enough,' Jack had told Ros recently. 'You're always telling Sid and me not to be quitters, never to give up no matter what. I know we all hate it when he's grumpy, but you married him. Remember the fuss you made when I wanted to give up the piano? Now look at you two; you haven't set much of an example. When I'm older, I'm going to work harder at my relationship than you and Dad did.'

Was he right? Ros wondered, feeling thoroughly told off. Had she and Mike given up at the first sign of trouble? Should they have subjugated their own needs and dreams of happiness to those of their children even though they were poised to fly the nest? Probably. But Ros had felt that she had no option but to excise the relationship and move on. It was unlike her as generally she held on to things even after they were broken. As a child, she used to hoard books with tattered pages, damaged dolls, teddies with torn ears and missing eyes.

'Come on, Ros,' her mother would say on discovering her stash of fragments and remnants, 'surely we can throw these away?' Lilian was herself a hoarder and would painstakingly glue shattered crockery together, but even she sanctioned the disposal of Ros's 'treasures'.

'I don't care,' Ros used to say, crying. 'I still love them. You can't throw things away just because they're broken, you can fix them.'

Was that what she'd done with her marriage, she wondered, parted with tradition and thrown it away because she felt it was beyond repair? Had she tried hard enough to fix it?

Mike was Head of Music at Mount View, a private girls' secondary school. He'd played violin in an orchestra for the first few years of their marriage, but after the children were born he went into teaching thinking that he could use the long school holidays to spend more time with the boys and to seek fame and fortune with his own music. A few years ago, he wrote a song that the then hottest girl-band, All Girls Together, came within a whisker of recording before they broke up. The near miss broke his spirit, he didn't have the fortitude to cope with the vicissitudes of the music business and he'd scarcely written a thing since. When Ros came to think of it, that was when the angry stranger she had finally asked to leave had first begun to assume Mike's form.

All those hopes and dreams we once had, Ros thought, as she lay sleepless in bed trying to concentrate on her breathing. Images of their life together came to her as though summoned with the intake of each separate breath, reminding her of the Mike she'd lost. Mike's face when he first held their newborn twins, the way he explained things to her, the pleased little smile he gave when he made her laugh, his talent for getting to the heart of an argument, the notes he left in obscure places to remind her he loved her, the carefully assembled colourful platters of food he would bring her when she was ill or in bed.

Ros turned over and tried to get comfortable. One minute you're young with your future ahead of you, the next it's behind you and you're staring fifty in the face. Well, perhaps not quite the face, but certainly in the neck. And, talking of necks, she wasn't too happy with the state of hers. Her bathroom shelf was littered with products that promised to lift and revitalise it, but the only impression they'd made so far was on her bank balance. She felt in danger of becoming a cliché in her quest to stave off the ravages of time.

Six thirty a.m. It was no use, she wasn't going to get back to sleep. She got up and went to the kitchen and started the laborious business of lining up her supplements. Six omega-3 capsules, two multi-vitamins, one vitamin E, two different sorts of B, one magnesium tablet, one digestive enzyme, three amino acids and a partridge in a pear tree. (Well, she might just as well add the latter as she wasn't sure what all the other pills did anyhow.) She was merely following Hari's instructions. Along with Joti, Hari, who ran a homeopathic chemist round the corner on Shepherd's Bush Green, had recently become another of her gurus. Ros was surprised she didn't rattle like a pill bottle when she moved as she couldn't bring herself to eat much. At least, she supposed, the supplements were giving her some kind of nourishment. She put the kettle on and looked around the kitchen, half-expecting Mike to come stumbling in, wearing only his boxers, to begin the business of making his porridge; a morning task he enacted with as much brouhaha as a sorcerer conjuring a particularly complicated spell.

Ros made a cup of maté cocido, a South American herbal tea with all manner of health-giving properties. It was an acquired taste with its faint odour of damp wood. Che Guevara used to drink it and, she reasoned, he was a doctor. She took her cup into the living room and sat in a large armchair. As she looked around, her old life seemed to rebuke her in the form of pictures, mirrors and armchairs. Ros's and Mike's scrupulous desire to be fair and share their belongings equally meant that items had been separated from their partners: where once two candlesticks had stood on a mantelpiece, now one kept solitary vigil. Next to it stood a photograph of Ros's mother, Lilian. Ros found it hard to look her mother in the eyes. The photo had been taken in her mother's native Cape Town in 2002; two years before her death and on her one visit home since leaving in 1957. She was wearing a blue cotton summer dress, her red hair framing her still-beautiful, heart-shaped face with its piercing blue eyes. Sitting on a rock with her knees drawn under her chin like a young girl, Table Mountain and a bright blue African sky rose in the distance behind her. In this photograph, Lilian was the nearest to looking at peace that Ros had ever seen her. With her colouring and her dress, she seemed to form part of the landscape and appeared at home in a way that she had never managed to in England.

'I told you Mike wasn't right for you,' she heard her mother's voice say. 'You should have married Robbie; he'd have made you happy. He could have supported you and you wouldn't have had to go straight back to work after the children were born.'

Ros spun round, expecting to see her mother in the room with her. She must be going mad. But surely it was simply her mother's voice, increasingly present in her own head with advice and instructions? The voice had been growing louder since she'd parted from Mike and sometimes it seemed to her that her mother had returned to look after her now that she was on her own. Last she'd heard of Robbie, some twenty years after their relationship had ended, he'd retired, presumably to sit in his counting house counting all his money made from stockbroking.

The day before, Sid and his girlfriend Liz had been going through some of Lilian's belongings that Ros kept in a pine chest that loomed, Gulliver-like, in her living room. Motes of dust tumbled in the sunlight as the familiar colours, patterns and smells of Ros's childhood cascaded out of the chest, punctuated by Liz's cries of delight as she pulled one item after another out of this unanticipated Aladdin's cave.

'Your mother was so cool,' Liz said, holding a short lace mini-dress up against her and turning this way and that as she admired her reflection in the mirror, 'and so tiny. I can't believe this stuff even fits me.'

Liz wriggled her nineteen-year-old hips into a tight satin skirt with a slit up the side and stuck out a leg provocatively. Ros could clearly see her mother wearing the red, crêpe Ossie Clark skirt that Liz held up next. She had a memory of herself as a young child with her mother leaning over her, as she was about to go out for the evening. Ros would reach up for her, her small arms encircling her mother's neck, and smell her perfume, Ma Griffe by Carven. As she bent down to kiss her daughter, Lilian would cite her farewell mantra, 'Careful of my lipstick, careful of my hair.' Ros, who had been aiming for her mother's mouth with her small, wet puckered lips, would find herself kissing a powdered cheek instead. When she became a mother herself, Ros had made sure to apply her lipstick after kissing her children goodbye so they wouldn't feel as rebuffed as she had. When Sid and Jack were small, Jack had insisted on hearing the lipstick and hair story over and over. When he was dressing up, pretending to be the Mummy to Sid's Daddy and putting Ros's make-up on, he'd say, 'Tairful of my liptick, tairful of my hair' as Ros tried to scoop him up in a kiss and hug.

The day before, she'd watched Liz as she wrapped the red skirt around her waist, like a matador flourishing a red flag in front of a bull, and caught the scent of Ma Griffe in her nostrils. In the first months after Lilian's death, when Ros had opened her eyes each morning, her first waking thought had been that Lilian was no more. With the months the sharp pain had lessened into a constant dull ache. In the cold dawn of this January day, Ros once again felt the loss of her mother with all the acuity of those first days. She could vividly imagine Lilian in front of her, could hear her voice, and experienced anew the painful incredulity that she was gone as though her death had occurred only hours earlier. Opening the chest seemed to have conjured Lilian into being and, since then, Ros had felt her mother's presence around her ever more intensely.

Eight o'clock. Ros sorted through one of the many piles of paper that appeared to follow her wherever she went, like ducklings resolutely waddling in their mother's wake. She came upon the crumpled piece of paper with Tattoo Tony's number and was about to throw it away when she noticed that it was written on the reverse of a flyer, fuchsia pink and edged with blue, a garish advertisement for the apparently acclaimed talents of Clare Voyante, medium to the stars, as seen on breakfast television. She shivered suddenly in the chill of the early morning. The path of gumbaggley, once undertaken, gathers its own momentum and leads the unwitting traveller onto unimagined highways and byways. Ros looked at the woman on the flyer: bottle-black hair, high cheekbones and golden hoop earrings, an archetypal Gypsy Rose Lee.

Getting up, Ros felt something beneath her bare foot. She looked down and saw a playing card sticking to the bottom of it. It was the Queen of Diamonds. Ros smiled at the seemingly portentous nature of this discovery and was further amused when a closer examination of the card revealed that the Queen depicted was none other than a smiling Marge Simpson, wearing a wimple and bearing a candle. Turning the card over, she saw that it came from a novelty *Simpsons'* deck. What did this find signify? The need to approach life with humour, or a sign that she should contact Clare Voyante? Both, Ros decided. She was surprised it hadn't occurred to her to go to a medium earlier, especially in the first months after Lilian's death when she had been unable to bear the deafening silence of a world without a mother as voluble and opinionated as hers had been; when she had felt insulted by the ability of the earth to go on turning with Lilian no longer in it. The abrupt cessation of her mother's frequent phone calls, a source of irritation during her lifetime, had left her with the uncomfortable sense of a conversation curtailed mid-sentence.

'Now she's dead, you're complaining about the absence of the very things you used to complain about,' Mike said in exasperation when he found Ros weeping yet again nine months after Lilian had died.

Ros had cried every day for almost a year and was still crying, although less often, and now, with her marriage over, she wasn't always clear what it was she was crying about. Sometimes it felt as though crying was simply another chore to be fitted in to her day like feeding the dog. Wake up, wash face, brush teeth, cry, carry on with the day ahead. It was curious how bereavement divided instead of uniting and stranger still that so few people understood how long it took to come to terms with a parent's death; it was almost as though they felt that mourning were simply self-pity. Grief was not a country anyone would choose to visit and you had to be a member of the adult orphan club before you could begin fully to comprehend what it was to lose a parent.

'You seem to have forgotten how Lilian drove you mad. I know it's an awful thing to say, but isn't it just a little bit of a relief that she's gone?'

'If it's so awful, why did you say it?' Ros had answered. 'Can't you see, it's worse because my relationship with her wasn't perfect and now I've lost the chance to put it right, for ever?'

Mike had shrugged. 'That's how it is, relationships with parents are rarely perfect.'

It was all very well for him, his parents were both alive and he wasn't nearly as involved with them as Ros had been with Lilian. They lived in Scotland and he saw them once or twice a year at the requisite births, marriages and deaths. Would she and Mike still be together if Lilian hadn't died? Although she had often been a source of conflict when alive, she had become even more of one after her death. The thought made Ros smile; it was typical of Lilian to continue exerting her influence even after she'd gone.

If only Ros could talk to her and benefit from the insight of the good Lilian, the Lilian who offered wise counsel, the Lilian with whom she had sometimes stayed up late into the night talking and laughing, the Lilian who, in spite of her anxiousness and foibles, had encouraged Ros to travel and told her she could do and be anything and anyone she wanted.

Ros waited until a little later to call the medium and quickly dialled the number on the flyer before her courage failed her.

'This is the number of Clare Voyante,' a female voice intoned, pronouncing the surname to rhyme with 'auntie'. 'It is no accident that you are calling me today. Please leave your first name and your telephone number and I will get back to you as soon as possible. Thank you.'

Ros felt compelled to put the phone down without saying anything. She resisted, and in a rush left her details and hung up. No sooner had she done so than the phone rang.

'With who might I be speaking?' asked a woman who, while attempting an upper-class accent, wasn't fully mistress of the grammar required.

'With whom did you wish to speak?' Ros answered archly, unable to resist flaunting her own grammatical dexterity.

'With Ros.'

'I'm Ros.'

'This is Clare-Voyante-Medium-to-the-Stars.' The words came out as one, as inextricably bound together as those that combined to form any aphorism.

A medium in time saves nine, thought Ros. She caught sight of the playing card glinting on the edge of the sofa. She must have placed it there after peeling it from her foot, although she had no memory of so doing. Marge, the Queen of Diamonds, seemed to wink at her, one large white eyeball obscured for an instant by the flutter of an eyelid.

'Listen to the queen, dear,' Clare-Voyante-Medium-to-the-Stars whispered in Ros's ear.

Ros shivered again and wondered whether video phones had become a reality that she'd failed to be informed of, or whether

her home were not, in fact, some kind of *Big Brother* house where her every movement was under scrutiny.

'I'd like to make an appointment to come and see you,' she said.

The medium said she was in luck as it usually took months to get an appointment, but she'd just had a cancellation for that very morning. Could Ros get to Milton Keynes for eleven thirty?

Chapter Three

Ros started her car awkwardly, her foot slipping on the clutch. The Queen of Diamonds was lodged onto the underside of her shoe and with a sigh of irritation she peeled it off once again and threw it out the window. If this were a movie, Ros reflected, she'd be exhorting the heroine to turn back now, shouting at the screen as she and the boys used to at the point where the protagonists enter the haunted house in spite of all the signs that they should do otherwise.

She glanced at the photograph of Lilian that she had brought with her, sticking out of her handbag on the floor beside her; a talisman to ease open the channels between this life and the next. She really was becoming the Queen of Gumbaggley.

Clare Voyante lived in a Barratt home on a modern estate. Row upon row of identical houses stretched out in front of Ros as she drove, stopping and starting as she tried to find the right one. It was a wonder any of the occupants could find their own home and didn't settle into someone else's and start living their life by mistake. Ros noticed a woman with bottle-black hair and black leather trousers making her way up the path of one of the houses. Instinctively, Ros knew that she was the person she sought; she parked and waited a few moments before following her in. She carefully pushed Lilian's photograph out of sight into the recesses of her bag, not wanting to give the medium any clues.

'I've got a lady here, dear, the one whose photo you've got in your bag. She's very anxious to talk to you,' Clare said as soon as they'd sat down.

A combination of surprise and fear surged through Ros. The room was still and white and quiet. A white, long-haired cat was sleeping, almost indistinguishable from the whiteness of the table on which it lay and made visible only occasionally by the intermittent opening and closing of its green eyes. A single candle burned on the mantelpiece. Clare Voyante hadn't asked Ros anything about herself, had merely set a tape-recorder running ('So you can listen to it all again at your leisure, dear'), settled back into her chair, taken a deep breath and begun to speak.

'Yes, I'll tell her.'

'Sorry?' said Ros.

'I was talking to the lady, dear. Is she your mother? Yes, I thought so. She doesn't think the red looks good on the walls of your bedroom, she says it's an unsettling colour for the children.'

Ros started to laugh and cry at the same time. It was the relief at hearing her mother's voice nagging her again. A few weeks before, Hari the homeopath had told her that red was the colour of health, strength and passion and that in heraldry it signified bravery and courage. Since these were all qualities that Ros aspired to possess, she'd painted her bedroom walls a deep, rich red.

Clare inclined her head as though listening to someone just behind her.

'All right, yes, of course.' She turned back to Ros. 'She's a bit of a worrier, isn't she?'

Ros nodded.

'Why does she keep saying South Africa, dear?'

'That's where she came from.'

'Now she's giving me the letter "S". Can you take that, dear?'

'Pardon?'

'Can you take the letter "S"?'

Take it? What did she mean? Take it where? Ros thought hard. Her father's name was Harold. It couldn't be him. Wait a minute though; his middle name was Stephen. Could that be it? Ros nodded uncertainly.

'Maybe.'

'Never mind, dear. She's saying something about an opal ring. It's an unusual setting, isn't it?'

It was a matter of pure chance that Ros wasn't wearing the opal ring. She'd taken it off before her shower that morning and forgotten to put it back on: a shimmering green African opal set widthways in white gold that her mother had taken from her own finger and put onto hers after Ros had given birth to the twins.

'She must have loved you very much, dear, as she keeps saying the word "daughter". She says her heart's better now and she's tapping her chest and smiling. What's that, dear? Yes, I'll tell her now. She says you're not to worry about the last night. She knows how hard it was for you.'

Clare Voyante's face contorted, she leant back in her chair and closed her eyes, emitting a strange guttural sound that seemed to come from the back of her throat. Ros started out of her chair: this was far beyond what she'd bargained for. When Clare spoke again, her voice had altered. It sounded familiar to Ros. Ros closed her eyes for a moment and realised she was hearing Lilian.

'There's something I want to tell you, but it's not the right time. I'd like you to come back another day.'

Ros was frozen, halfway between sitting and standing. She was struck by how similar her position was to the one she adopted when squatting over the seat of an unfamiliar lavatory. She wanted to laugh and cry all at once. Why was Clare talking in the first person?

'Don't be alarmed, dear,' Clare said. Her own voice had returned. 'I'm a transmedium, I channel people from the other side; they use me as a vessel.'

If Clare Voyante hadn't sounded so matter-of-fact about it, Ros might have fled screaming. Clare looked tired, as though the act of being Lilian had exhausted her. Ros wasn't surprised, Lilian used often to say how tiring she found it being herself and sometimes Ros would think unkindly that it wasn't half as tiring as it was being the person with Lilian.

'Can you see any ... um ... love in my future, you know ... men or anything?' Ros asked falteringly, thinking she might as well get her money's worth, a psychic two-for-one special offer, and sort her love life out while she was there.

'I'm a clairvoyant, dear,' Clare Voyante answered brusquely, 'I don't gaze into a crystal ball like some fairground fortune-teller.'

Ros apologised profusely for having unwittingly offended her, and after a certain amount of self-righteous sniffing, Clare told Ros not to drive too fast, to watch out for the post and that her mother would always be with her, was in fact always with her, especially in the mornings when Ros made her tea, 'Although in your case it's not ordinary tea, is it dear?' Clare added. 'It's that funny herbal tea.' She was certainly right about that, Ros reflected wryly, as she recalled Lilian's constant presence.

It was clever of the medium to ensure a continuing income by saying that she had to come back, and using Lilian's voice to say it, Ros reflected, as she wrote out a cheque for seventy-five pounds. Had the voice really sounded like Lilian's or was she, Ros, merely imaging it? Hearing voices was, after all, one of the first signs of madness.

'Yes, I see what she means now,' Clare Voyante said as she showed Ros out.

'I beg your pardon '

'You are pretty, but she's right, you should make a bit more of an effort. Bye, dear.'

Ros walked slowly to her car. Now that really must have been Lilian's voice, she thought.

The boys were in the kitchen when she arrived home, draped untidily over chairs in the manner peculiar to teenagers; mess, in the form of dirty coffee cups and scattered crumbs, mushrooming around them. Any irritation Ros might have felt was quickly offset by the awareness of how much she would miss them once they were gone. Sid was trying to pretend he wasn't rolling a joint and Ros that she hadn't noticed he was. She contemplated the top of his head with its twin crown. Jack's was the same. Two swirling patches of hair on each head that further reinforced the fact that they were twins. Ros had always taken care to dress them differently and had done all she could to ensure each boy developed a distinct and independent personality.

She went up to the attic, eager, for the first time since Lilian's death, to go through the box of photographs of herself as a baby that she kept there. Sitting cross-legged on the floor, Ros sifted through the gallery of her early years, pausing when she came to a picture of herself, aged three, sitting in her mother's lap. She had a dummy in her mouth and she remembered the day only too well. It was perhaps her earliest memory, the day when she had taken a final, hard, loving suck before relinquishing her dummy once and for all and throwing it into the lavatory, running immediately, on small purposeful legs, to her parents' room (her father still lived with them then) to report on her bravery in a voice caught between victorious laughter and regretful tears. She studied Lilian's face; she looked so young, her hair held up in a bun, her blue eyes seeming to challenge the camera and her legs stretched out before her, long and shapely in their sixties' miniskirt.

Ros had the uncomfortable sense that she was being watched, and turning round, found that she was caught in the unblinking gaze of a single eye. She gave a short involuntary shriek, immediately collecting herself and laughing at her silliness when she realised that the eye belonged to Big Mouth Billy Bass, the battery-operated singing fish she had given Lilian as a joke the Christmas before she died. It hadn't worked since Lilian's death, however many different batteries they'd tried. Ros picked it up and remembered that last Christmas together, a happy day when she and Lilian had found peace with each other. Lilian had, as always, thrashed everyone at Scrabble, triumphantly scoring seventy-eight points with one word alone: 'quixotic', with the 'x' falling on a double letter score and the 'c' on a triple word score.

'What does it mean,' Sid asked, 'is it even a word?'

'Of course it is,' Lilian said firmly, taking seven new letters from the velvet Scrabble pouch. 'It means "motivated by an idealism that overlooks practical considerations".'

'How do you know all these words, Granny?' asked Jack, cursing himself for having made the 'q' available to Lilian on his go (his word, 'queen', had earned him a measly fourteen points).

'Because I'm too clever for my own good,' Lilian answered. 'That's what my mother always told me anyhow.'

'What do you mean?' asked Ros, keen to hear more about this mother Lilian mentioned so rarely.

Lilian rested her back against the wall. (They all agreed Scrabble had to be played sitting cross-legged on the floor.)

'I remember once arguing with her that apartheid was an evil and that white South Africans would get their come-uppance one day; she told me that I'd never find a husband if I went around expressing such stupid liberal views and that, as it was, everyone thought I was too clever for my own good. She said her friend, Marion Du Toit, had told her at bridge only the day before, that, when she had asked her son Keith why he didn't take me to the bioscope – that's a drive-in movie,' Lilian had explained seeing Sid and Jack's puzzled expressions. 'Anyhow, Keith had laughed and told her all his friends thought I'd swallowed a dictionary. Boys, my mother told me, don't like clever girls.'

Lilian's words came out in a rush as though the incident she were describing had taken place only recently. Ros remembered thinking at the time how powerful parents are, their idle utterances reverberating through the years and burning themselves into their offspring's memory. She had understood then why Lilian always made such a point of telling her it was good to be clever and that girls could do anything boys could, that they were equal but opposite.

'Never trust a man who doesn't like clever girls,' Mike had said, coming back into the room with drinks for the last part of Lilian's story and planting a kiss on Ros's forehead. 'Me, I love 'em, this one in particular.'

'Did you just wink at me?' Ros had said.

'Yeah, baby, you know you love it.' Mike had winked at her with the other eye then, knowing full well Ros's opinion that there was nothing like the wink of a handsome man for loosening a girl's knicker elastic. A handsome man who could wink with both eyes, well, everyone knew that caused knickers to drop clean off.

'Puh-lease,' Sid and Jack said in unison, disgusted by the obvious chemistry between their parents.

'Since when did you become a black American?' Ros teased Mike.

'Since I saw you, pretty mama,' Mike said.

'You shouldn't say that, you should say *Afro*-American,' Jack said.

'Oh, potato, potato,' Lilian said and they'd all laughed. 'Mind you,' she'd added darkly, 'don't call black people "kaffirs", or I'll knock your block off.'

'What do you mean?' asked Sid.

'That's what white South Africans used to call them,' said Lilian. 'It's an Afrikaans word and very disrespectful. Either that or "boy". Can you imagine calling a grown man, "boy"? That's what my mother called Josiah, our cook. I don't think I ever heard her use his name.'

'Are you quixotic, Granny?' Jack asked.

Lilian laughed. 'Exceedingly idealistic and unrealistic? My parents would have said I was.'

Ros looked at her curiously, reflecting that Lilian's past and present appeared somehow to have kaleidoscoped, bringing her life as a child into the forefront of her mind. This perception had made Ros uneasy. Was her mother's unusual reminiscence of a childhood she claimed not to have enjoyed a portent of something?

They'd eaten turkey sandwiches cosily ensconced in front of the television later that evening, Mike's fingers lazily stroking the back of Ros's neck and almost lulling her to sleep. She caught Lilian watching her, flanked by her grandsons, and the women had exchanged a smile that seemed to say, 'this is what family means'. It was possibly the closest Ros had ever felt to her mother. Two weeks and an ugly collision over the matter of a small roast chicken later, Lilian was dead.

Ros found a dusty cushion that had once been Lilian's and, putting it behind her head, leant back against the wall of the attic and closed her eyes, the photographs spread out on her lap. She wished that she could travel back in time and once again be that small child in her mother's arms, safe and protected. Everything had seemed simpler then. Perhaps Lilian had preferred being the mother of a young child?

After a few moments, disturbed anew by the dogs barking next door, she opened her eyes and looked around. She felt something under her hand. The damned playing card yet again. Marge Simpson looked coyly up at her. Ros tore the card into several pieces and threw them in the air. As she did so, a small suitcase precariously perched on the edge of a larger one caught her attention. She couldn't remember having seen it before. Her mother's distinctive handwriting marked the outside. *Lilian Block, 23 Roland Street, Sea Point, Cape Town, South Africa.* She could just read the faded writing on a torn baggage sticker, *Athlone Castle.* It was the ship her mother had boarded to emigrate from South Africa to England almost fifty years before.

Lilian's father's family had come from Lithuania, her grandfather, Meir Bloch, sailed from Libau to England and thence to South Africa on the mail boats of the Castle line in 1896. When Lilian made the return journey from South Africa to England some sixty years after his voyage on the same shipping line, she'd had a strong sense of travelling backwards in her grandfather's footsteps. Meir, like so many both before and after him, had high hopes of prospecting for gold in South Africa's rich mines, he had ended up as a shopkeeper in the Karroo instead. A pursuit that hadn't made his fortune and after he died, when Lilian was thirteen, her grandmother had found piles of promissory notes from those who owed him money on which he had scrawled, 'Too poor to pay, don't ask'. His son, her father, Hymie Bloch had changed his name to James Block and done all he could to become assimilated to white southern African society. He'd moved to Cape Town and married an Afrikaans woman and together they'd done everything in their power to persuade Lilian to ignore her Jewish heritage.

Although Lilian spoke little about her parents, she used often to put her 'story' voice on and paint the picture of her grandparents for Ros, who, ever hungry for a larger family, would store Lilian's memories in her mind, like a collector hoarding jewels in a trinket box.

'I remember Grandpa Meir standing in the middle of the street in a striped suit with a waistcoat, the sitting creases clear in the groin of his trousers,' Lilian told her. 'A smiling man shading his eyes with his hand from the dazzling sunlight that cast a long shadow by his side. "Look, Grandpa, I'm jumping on you," I would shout with delight as I jumped on and off his shadow.'

(Ros had spent hours the following day struggling to catch her own shadow, jumping and circling like a dog trying to catch its own tail.) Lilian loved her grandparents and often went to stay with them as a child and learnt the customs of the old country. Moreover, it suited her rebellious nature to lay claim to her Jewish roots and she had embarrassed her parents by studying the religion and adhering to the dietary laws, even taking her own kosher food with a paper plate and plastic cutlery out to friends when they were asked to lunch. By the age of eighteen, she'd abandoned these rules, but a sense of her Jewishness had remained with her for the rest of her life.

'Some people would argue that we're not even Jewish because the religion passes from mother to child,' Lilian told Ros. 'But, when I was young, I found evidence of an ancient Jewish law that states that the religion originally passed from the father to the child.'

'What about me?' Ros had asked. 'My dad's not Jewish, so does that mean I'm not either?'

'No,' Lilian said firmly, defying logic as she frequently did to suit her own ends, 'you are, because I am, and I'm your mother.'

Ros knew better than to argue and accepted her Jewishness as further evidence of her 'specialness', although, sometimes, when she felt particularly dislocated, she couldn't help wishing she weren't so special.

Mike had brought many of her mother's belongings to the house after her death. When someone dies, Ros reflected, looking around her at Lilian's boxes, their possessions take on a sacred quality. After sorting her mother's clothes and storing those most precious in the living room trunk, Ros had not been able to bring herself to go through her papers and they had lain untouched in the attic for the past year. Well, almost a year – the anniversary of Lilian's death was only a few days away.

Ros lifted the suitcase down and tried to open it, working her fingers against the rusty buckle. She hurt a finger and broke a nail.

'Bugger,' she said, sucking her index finger. She'd had a manicure two days before – part of her reinvention and grooming regime – and now it was ruined. She shook the suitcase; it didn't make much of a noise, more of a dull thud, which didn't give any real clue as to its contents. It was probably full of old letters or paper. She put the suitcase back and knocked over a box, spilling some of the contents. A picture of a kangaroo caught her eye, a birthday card from her father sent on her fourteenth birthday. Ros could still remember how babyish she'd found it at the time, evidence, if more were needed, of how little her father knew his own daughter. As a child, she had spent a few summers in Australia with her father and his new family, but had always felt out of place. A gooseberry. She still kept in touch with him as one might an acquaintance one had made on a holiday abroad: light, inconsequential letters; emails and the odd phone call. Australia was an early destination on Sid and Jack's gap year itinerary and they would be staying with him. For some reason, Ros found the thought comforting, as though it rounded a circle she herself had failed to complete.

'Don't talk to anyone from Australia,' Lilian said jokingly whenever Ros travelled abroad in the years before she met Mike.

'Why on earth not?' Ros had asked her when she said it the first time.

'Because you may go out with them, fall in love, get married and then you'll go and live in Australia and be far away from me and I won't see my grandchildren.'

That was Lilian's problem; she lived her life in the expectation of loss and played out the consequences of any action, no matter how trivial, until they reached the point of disaster or despair. She said it was in her genes, part of her Jewish heritage.

'It's like that Jewish joke,' she explained to Ros, 'about a young man asking an older man the time on a train in Eastern Europe. The old man refuses him the information. "If I tell you the time," says the older man, "we'll get talking. You'll come home with me. You'll meet my beautiful daughter. You'll fall in love with her, marry her and take her away to your *shtetl*, which is far from mine. So I'll never see my beloved daughter any more. And anyway, I don't want her marrying a man who can't even afford a watch."'

Ros couldn't very well tell Sid and Jack not to talk to any Australians when they were in their country and she had a sudden pang of fear that they would both fall in love and settle far away from her. She could see what her mother meant now. It was, she reflected, something of an irony that Lilian's ex-husband had ended up there, but at least he'd gone after Lilian had stopped loving him.

Ros tugged gently at a piece of paper sticking out of the pile of stuff on the floor until it came free. It was covered with her mother's handwriting. She smoothed the dry, yellowing sheet with her fingers. It was one of her mother's many lists. Lilian's need for control meant that her life had been full of rituals. She was particularly careful to keep evil spirits at bay and was forever touching wood – both palms flat on wood or it didn't count – throwing spilled salt over her left shoulder, chewing cotton when being sewn on, or making Ros chew cotton when she sewed on her (if you didn't, it implied that you were dead and your shroud was being sewn on you), making sure that neither she nor anyone else stepped over anyone – if you did you had to step back (again, something to do with dead people). It must have been exhausting to be her mother, Ros reflected. She'd tried as hard as she could not to replicate her mother's obsessive behaviour, but some habits die hard and she often found herself surreptitiously touching wood when she thought no one was looking. She had another habit – that she'd managed to keep secret from Mike and her children – of having to make things even. So, if she turned off a light switch with one hand, she had to repeat the action with the other to even it up. Or else … Or else what, exactly? She wasn't precisely sure, but some terrible misfortune would be bound to befall her or one of her loved ones.

Ros looked again at the faded, yellowing list in front of her.

Eggs, milk, sugar, cod (cheaper at Mac Fisheries than Sainsbury's). Tell Ros: Mayo clinic diet (NB: Mona lost ten pounds in ten days); O levels start three months today.

Ros had hated going food shopping with her mother. You could never talk to her while she shopped; she was too busy adding up the price of items as she went along.

'Why do you add up anyway? They'll do it at the till,' Ros asked.

'They make mistakes and overcharge sometimes,' Lilian answered.

Was it worth it, she wondered, if it made you as tense as her mother looked? Lilian was biting her lip in concentration as she added the cost of the last item she'd dropped into her basket to the amount in her head.

'Two pounds, six and threepence,' she muttered, moving along the shelf to reach for some tinned guavas. Pink fruit, rough like a cat's tongue, in heavy syrup that reminded Lilian of home. When would that have been? It was before decimalisation, so probably when Ros was ten, when her mother gave her a shiny shilling every Saturday morning for her pocket money.

A ringing telephone pulled Ros back to the present. She hurried down the ladder to answer it, resolving to deal with the boxes later.

'Ros, it's Charlie. Listen, I just had to tell you about my latest case.'

'What?' Ros asked, sitting down, ever eager to hear about Charlie's real life courtroom dramas.

'I've got a client who is being sued for child maintenance. You'll never guess what the mother did?'

'What?' asked Ros once again.

'Had sex with him, he used a condom, then when he was asleep, she crept into the bathroom, retrieved the used condom from the bin, syringed out the contents and syringed them into herself. Nine months later, bingo! Baby! DNA tests show it's his and now she wants his money.'

'He's wealthy, I suppose,' said Ros.

'Oh yes, as wealthy as a shmealthy.'

'Was he her boyfriend at least?'

'Well, they'd been seeing each other for two weeks. Fourth date, I think.'

'Can he really be expected to support a child when he took every precaution to avoid having one? I mean, how was he to know that she'd turn out to be a sperm burglar?'

'Bodily fluids carry all sorts of information, don't they? There's you with your spit in California, and here's my client with an ejaculate he thought he had safely disposed of, a father out of the blue.'

'He needs to learn the art of having an orgasm without ejaculating. Joti, my yoga teacher, was telling me about it. Apparently the semen circulates around the man's body and is a source of enormous energy to his brain or something. If your current case proves to be the beginning of a sperm-stealing craze among baby- and maintenance-hungry women, it could be the only safe way for men to go.'

'Interesting notion, but a little too late for my current client, I fear.'

'Keep me posted,' said Ros.

Sex, thought Ros as she hung up, was a thing she barely remembered for herself. More than the sexual act itself, it was being touched that she missed. Sid and Liz had been at it constantly, exuberantly celebrating the end both of A levels and of school. It had been Sid's principal activity for the past six months. But then, that's what gap years were for, Ros had thought, all too painfully aware, as she tried daily not to hear his headboard thumping rhythmically against his wall, that his and Jack's departure date was rapidly approaching. While Jack was still deciding what to do with the rest of his life, Sid would be taking up a place at Manchester University in September to read heavy drinking, recreational drug taking and too much sex with a little English and Philosophy thrown in. Ros remembered her and Mike's early weeks together when she had jokingly complained to him that they were having too much sex.

'There's no such thing,' he had said. 'There are only two quantities when it comes to sex: *enough* sex and *not enough* sex.'

It had certainly been a case of the latter in the final year of their marriage. The only time Mike had made advances towards her was when he'd had too much to drink and Ros, repulsed by the alcohol-soaked tongue that Mike tried to force into her mouth, had found herself unable to respond to him.

Some of her friends thought she was crazy for allowing Sid to sleep with Liz in her home. She disagreed. Obviously she'd rather not hear them actually at it, and the familiar and frequent creaking made her cover her ears and move as far away from Sid's room as possible, but she much preferred knowing where he was and with whom. In her experience, the kids who had to keep their lives secret from their parents were often the ones with behavioural problems at school. Forced to be angels at home, the bad behaviour had to erupt elsewhere. Like muffin tops spilling over tight jeans, the fat had to come out somewhere. Anyhow, Ros reasoned, what was so bad about sex? Although she was suddenly struck by the alarming thought that she was only a broken-condom away from being a grandmother, a thought that shocked her profoundly. Grandmothers were old people, weren't they? People who idled in God's waiting room as they bounced babies on their knees and pinched plump cheeks. Was her life almost over?

She thought of her children's firm young skin and considered her own forty-five-year-old body. It's a cruel trick of nature, she thought, to have such blossoming fruit growing beside produce that is withering and threatening at any moment to drop from the vine. It felt only seconds ago that she had been admiring her own ripening body with its newly grown breasts. She had been later than her classmates in acquiring them and when they'd finally arrived, seemingly overnight, a month after her fourteenth birthday, Ros hadn't been able to take her eyes off them.

'You're obsessed with your bosoms,' Lilian said sharply one day as Ros stood in front of her bedroom mirror turning to admire her new shape from all angles.

Ros had turned to her with a shy, pleased look and said, 'They're new.'

Her mother had frequently had the knack of deflating her when she felt excited. Couldn't she see that bosoms like Ros's that cocked such a magnificent snook at gravity should be celebrated?

It had been three months since she and Mike had separated. At first her other friends had been attentive, phoning daily to see how she was coping, taking her out, cooking her meals. With time, their care and concern had diminished to be replaced with an unspoken admonishment that she should be over it by now and getting on with her life. Not that she blamed them, they had their own lives and she certainly didn't want to be one of those women who spent the next twenty years getting over a divorce. She hated that expression, 'newly single'. It was usually uttered in hushed tones as if someone had just been diagnosed with a terminal illness or had died. Which in a way they had, for what her still-married friends didn't know, and she had only recently discovered herself, was that the end of a marriage *was* like a death. The savage pain of the loss was succeeded by the long, dull, ache of bereavement. The death of her mother had segued into the death of her marriage and Ros felt she'd been in a state of continuous mourning for the past year.

Some friends did still phone to ask her over for dinner, stating brightly, 'It'll be just us.' At first she'd gone, had dreary dinners à trois where she was discouraged from talking about Mike or their life together. Married couples, Ros had discovered, are nervous in the company of newly single friends; they're afraid divorce is contagious. Husbands fear that their wives will be infected by the heady scent of freedom that they imagine exudes from the single woman's every pore, and wives fear that their husbands may want to sleep with her now that she's available. Wives also catch the aroma of her dread that she'll be alone now for ever and worry that proximity may taint them with the same fate. That's why inclusion in dinner parties is prohibited, whittled down to 'just us' dinners, and finally fades away altogether. Ros felt a new sympathy for Lilian, who had remained single after her divorce from Ros's father during years when a divorcée was an object of curiosity. She'd had several boyfriends, but had taken great care not to impose them on her, and Ros could only dimly recall a couple of them, just glimpsed as Lilian swept them away from the front door and out of sight when they called to collect her.

Ros had taken to having dinner out either with Jaime or with Charlie, just the two of them. Charlie was pushing her to start dating, to get back out there, but Ros wasn't sure where 'there' was any more. Last week she'd walked through Soho late one evening on her way to her car. The streets had thronged with noisy people and cars and she'd become acutely aware of a life she was no longer part of. 'Out there' for her certainly wasn't in the loud, heaving clubs and bars she'd passed.

Ros had a secret; one that she had not confided in anyone, not even in Charlie or Jaime. She'd discovered Internet dating. Well, not actual dating as yet, but certainly flirting. StartingOver.com was a site specifically geared towards those coming out of long relationships. She'd first heard of it a year or so before when Anthony Slinger, the music teacher at her school, had come round for supper. (She was ashamed now to recall that it had been a 'just us' supper with her and Mike.) It was after the summer holidays and Ant, newly single, had lost two stone and bought new clothes.

'You look gorgeous,' Ros had exclaimed on opening the door to him.

'Life after divorce,' Ant said, 'less money, but more sex. Much, much more sex.'

'Stop it,' Ros joked, little realising then what her own future held, 'you'll give Mike ideas.'

'All these women out there gagging for it, lining their wares up on the Internet.' Ant went on, turning to Mike, 'It's like being in a sweet shop, mate. StartingOver.com. It should be called pick 'n' mix for grown-ups.'

Ros punched him in the arm. 'Hardly, since as you've just demonstrated, men never grow up.'

Looking at Ant's smug expression, Ros had understood for the first time the phrase 'to smile fatly'. She could never have supposed that all too soon she would come to use the site herself. A couple of months after Mike moved out, on a lonely evening when winter was impatiently gusting the last remaining leaves off the trees, Ros had recalled Ant's Internet adventures and, feeling faintly dirty, as though she were watching porn, she had trawled the web to find StartingOver.com. With mounting terror, she'd explored the goods on offer: Hungry4love; Adventurer7; AsoftenasUlike and had initially chickened out of leaving her own profile on the site. Beneath the extravagant boasts of sexual prowess and film-star good looks, Ros caught the whiff of desperation that seemed to spiral through the speakers of her computer. She'd thought no more about it until a few weeks later when she heard Pam Woodhall, the drama teacher, talking openly in the staffroom about the successful date she'd had the night before with a man she'd met on the Internet.

'Don't tell me, he had such a nice smile that it enabled you to overlook both his third eye and his halitosis,' Jaime said.

'Ha ha, very funny,' Pam said, 'trust me, the man is delicious. I'm seeing him again tonight.' She had actually smacked her lips at the prospect, causing Ros to wonder what it was about Internet dating that made people give life to hackneyed figures of speech. The point was, thought Ros, looking at Pam's beautiful face, you clearly didn't have to be a sad loser to look for men on the Net.

Ros enrolled that very night, almost stumbling once again at the starting block when prompted to write her profile. What, asked the questionnaire, were her hobbies? Do women have hobbies? Ros wondered. There wasn't time, not if you worked, and had children. A woman, Lilian had always told her, could do two things, but not three. Ros couldn't remember what she liked doing. There was yoga, she supposed. Yes, that was good, it made her sound lithe and bendy; men liked that. What else? All her gumbaggley; her constant questing for answers to the enigma of life? No, too New Age, it would attract men in socks and sandals with a passion for naturism or tantric sex. Tantric sex might be good, though, what girl would mind that?

The house was quiet. Sid and Jack were working on a building site to earn the money to go travelling and Liz was a waitress in a hotel down the road. Somehow they'd survived Christmas. In fact, they'd spent it together as a family. It had seemed the best thing to do for this first Christmas living apart. Ros had cooked a turkey and Mike, keen to prove how well he was coping, had made a Christmas cake, meticulously feeding it with brandy since early November. He'd searched her eyes, looking for approval when she'd taken her first mouthful and Ros had felt a visceral pang for their early years together when she would lie in his arms while he made her laugh by singing nonsense words to the tune of well-known songs. Nothing lasts for ever, Ros had thought sadly as they'd pulled crackers and worn silly hats and pretended everything was fine. Ros and Mike had even bought each other presents: an emerald green shirt to go with his eyes for him and a DIY book for her; a not so subtle reminder that she'd have to do things for herself from now on. He'd intended it as a joke, but she hadn't felt much like laughing when she'd unwrapped it. Sid and Jack had spent the day looking from one parent to the other for signs that they might be reconciled. After lunch, she'd caught Sid pulling a strange face in the hall mirror.

'What on earth are you doing?'

'Friling,' Sid said.

'What?'

'Frowning and smiling at the same time,' Sid said. 'You try it.'

Ros did. It looked peculiar. It was as if the top half of one's face were contradicting the bottom half.

They both laughed.

'That's how I feel when I see you and Dad together,' Sid said, simultaneously furrowing his brow and grinning.

They'd stopped laughing.

Later that night as Mike was leaving, he and Ros had agreed it would be better not to see too much of each other for a while – they didn't want the kids to get false hopes. She'd spent New Year's Eve quietly at home, unable to face a 'just us' evening with Jaime and Tony.

'I promise it's not a "just us" dinner,' Jaime said. 'I mean it is, but not for the reasons you think. It's simply that we hate New Year's Eve and always spend it at home alone.'

Ros didn't want to be a gooseberry. She'd spent a lesson teaching the derivation of idioms and sayings to her Year Seven pupils the term before and discovered that gooseberry, in times past, had been one of many euphemisms for the Devil, who was, not surprisingly, unwelcome in most company. So when she turned down Jaime's invitation, she'd simply waggled her fingers on top of her head to represent horns.

'You won't be a gooseberry, or a Devil for that matter,' said Jaime. 'Do come.'

But Ros had stayed at home instead and gone to bed at eleven thirty in a 'Bah! Humbug' sort of way.

It was January 4th, a few days into the New Year and time to start her new life in earnest. Ros turned on her computer to check her emails. Junk mail invited her to take up the offer of a bigger penis and other messages recommended Viagra to help her use her new, bigger penis to its best advantage. She'd often wished she could be a man for a day purely to have sex and see what it felt like. Such a thought was a luxury these days, as sex from any perspective, male or female, still felt out of her grasp. Or was it? Ros clicked onto StartingOver to see if anyone had noticed her profile. She'd used a pseudonym and hadn't posted a picture of herself, unable to face the shame of anyone she knew seeing that she was shopping for a mate. She knew that Ant wasn't on the site any longer having married the last woman he'd met on it six months earlier, but that didn't mean that other friends and acquaintances weren't.

What was Ros's name now, anyhow? She'd taken Mike's

surname when they married, a very unfashionable thing to do at the time, but her maiden name was Alcock; not the sort of name best-suited to a teacher. She'd had quite enough of all the jibes it had provoked as she was growing up. Since she'd been a late developer, one of the boys favourite taunts had been, 'Oi, no tits, are you all cock instead?' Struggling to maintain dignity, she'd said, 'Gosh aren't you clever, no one's ever said that before.' She used to take out a small notebook and, licking the tip of her pencil, make a great show of writing it down, saying, 'No tits and all cock, very good.' Her mother had taught her that cleverness was the best route out of trouble. It usually worked; eventually the boys tired of their jokes and laughed with and not at her. But this didn't solve the problem about what she should do now. Continue using Mike's name, or revert to her maiden one? It seemed sensible to remain Mrs Townsend at school. Perhaps outside school and in her new life, she should use her mother's maiden name instead of her own.

Block. Rosalind Block. That had a certain ring to it, it sounded strong, a name for the sort of woman who was in charge of her life. 'Nice to meet you,' she practised, 'I'm Ros Block.' It still wasn't what she'd put on the StartingOver questionnaire. For Internet dating purposes she'd stolen the heroine of *Cabaret*'s name – Sally Bowles.

Someone had whistled at her – this was StartingOver speak for being sent a message. It was from a man calling himself UpForIt24/7.

Hey Sally, your profile looks interesting. Whatcha say we hook up and get to know each other? I'm a sexy, fun guy (lol) recently out of a looong marriage and looking for that special lady to spend time with.

Men, she suspected, used the Internet in search of sex, while women wanted to form relationships. Not that she was in a rush to get involved with anyone, she simply wanted to go on a few dates and open herself to new possibilities. She shuddered, pressed the delete button and turned off the computer. UpForIt24/7 had depressed her with his hackneyed cyber-speak.

Chapter Four

It was eleven o'clock in the morning on the second to last day of the school holidays. Ros would have to hurry or she'd be late. She ran out of the house and bumped into Dogman coming out of his front gate. Two of his five dogs flanked him.

'Good morning,' she said, bending down to pat one of the dogs on its head in a neighbourly fashion. She drew her hand back abruptly when, snarling, it bared its pointed yellow teeth. It was more wolf than dog. Ros cleared her throat nervously.

'I wonder if there's any way you could keep your dogs a little quieter at night.'

'What do you want me to do, sing them a fucking lullaby?' Dogman looked her up and down. 'You're that teacher, innit? Well, I can tell you this for nothin', this 'aint no bleedin' class-room, you can't tell us what to do, can she, boys?' One of the dogs growled in confirmation.

Nice. So much for neighbourliness. Dogman clearly hadn't graduated from charm school, in fact, by the looks of him, he'd barely gone to any school at all. Now she would indeed have to treat him like a recalcitrant pupil and find a way to make him yield to her. In the meantime, Ros added earplugs to her mental shopping list. She thought nostalgically of Jim and Ethel Collins who used to live next door. Jim used to bring them vegetables from his allotment and let the children eat his blackberries over the wall when they were little and Ethel would regale her with stories of her racy past.

'I almost shut the Windmill Theatre down with a sneeze once,'

Ethel told her. She'd been one of the first girls to pose nude there during the war. The theatre had been granted a licence on condition that the girls didn't move a muscle: they were to present a motionless nude tableau and be a living work of art. Once the feather in Ethel's hair had fallen onto her nose tickling her. She'd had to muster every ounce of self-control not to sneeze and, by moving, contravene the terms of the licence.

'What did your parents think of your job?' Ros once asked her.

'Goodness, dear, they'd have had a heart attack. I wore a red wig on stage so no one would recognise me.'

Ros's secret mission this morning was as nothing compared to Ethel's antics all those years ago. She took the bus to Notting Hill Gate and walked quickly up Portobello Road where, casting a quick, furtive glance over her shoulder, she disappeared through a doorway. The windows were blacked out save for a drawing in red of a Chinese dragon and she felt as though she were entering a dodgy sauna parlour. The front of the shop had been fashioned into a waiting room of sorts with two red padded plastic chairs; the seat of one looked as though it had been slashed by a knife and the padding oozed from the tear like pus from a sore. Ros was about to turn and run when the proprietor appeared from behind a curtain, naked to the waist and brandishing an implement. A modern samurai warrior who, in place of a sword, wielded some kind of drill, the tool of his trade, the nature of which became only too apparent after an examination of his body. Never mind the naked Windmill girls of yesteryear, here indeed was an example of art made flesh; the man's torso was entirely covered in tattoos. It was impossible to tell where one started and another ended. Ros could just make out barbed wire, Chinese symbols, the face of a beautiful woman and, here and there, flowers in vivid blues and reds curling around sweeping tendrils of green foliage.

'Piercing? Tattoo?' his gruff voice interrupted her. She slowly raised her eyes to meet his. 'Didn't your mother tell you it's rude to stare?' he asked.

'My mother told me many things and gave me many instructions,' said Ros, 'but, curiously, that wasn't one of them.'

He smiled, a sweet smile, strangely at odds with the spike sticking out of his chin and Ros wondered what his own mother might think of his appearance.

'Come on then,' he said, gesturing through the curtain to the room beyond. 'You'll be wanting a tattoo on the ankle, I suppose.'

'How did you know?'

'I'm Tattoo Tony and I've been doing this for twenty years. There's not much I don't know about human nature. Getting divorced are you?'

Ros said nothing. She stared at her feet like a schoolgirl and blushed. How could he see into her soul?

'Thought so. Don't worry; getting a tattoo is an involuntary psychological reaction to change and women often come to me when they throw off the shackles of marriage. A tattoo marks the prelude to a new phase in their lives. You'll be wanting a butterfly, no doubt, it's a common symbol of freedom.'

Just her luck, a bloody philosopher. What was it with hairdressers and tattoo artists these days? Ros had decided that since she'd seen the medium, what the hell, she might as well get a tattoo as well; in fact, she'd suddenly felt a strange compulsion to get one, as though this ritualistic marking of her flesh would punctuate the end of one era and open the door to another. She did want a butterfly, but she was damned if she was going to tell him that. She had proven herself to be enough of a living cliché.

'Actually,' she said, thinking on her feet, 'I'd like a small bluebird.'

Tattoo Tony looked at her disbelievingly and led her into the little room at the back of the shop. He took a pad from a shelf and began sketching with rapid, sure strokes. Ros looked around. The walls were covered with photographs of tattooed body parts. One picture showed a man's bald head inclined forwards and covered with an intricate swirl of abstract patterns. Now that she was here, she shuddered involuntarily and was wondering whether it was too late to back out when Tattoo Tony thrust his pad under her nose. It showed an aerial view of a bluebird in flight. Ros reached out a finger to stroke it, half expecting to feel warm feathered flesh.

'It's beautiful,' she said. 'Why aren't you an artist?'

'Who says I'm not?' Tony said. 'Art comes in many different forms. Granted it's not what I dreamt of when I was at the Royal College, but how many artists make a decent living? Besides, I like etching on flesh; it makes my artwork live and breathe and I like the interaction with people, suiting the right design to their temperament and aspirations.'

He moved about the room as he spoke, pinning his sketch to the wall beside his chair, pulling out another chair for Ros to sit on and drawing up a small stool on which she could rest her leg as he worked.

'Ready?' he asked, gesturing her to sit down.

Ros hesitated. She liked the bluebird, but she really did want a butterfly. She'd always been beguiled by them and, as a child, her mother had lulled her to sleep with stories of how, when she was growing up in Africa, she would nurture caterpillars and silkworms in a shoebox lined with mulberry leaves from the large tree in her parents' garden. The lid of the box was punctured with holes to allow in air and every morning Lilian would open the box, leave a fresh leaf for them to feed on and place the box carefully back in the darkness of her cupboard. Later, when they changed into chrysalises and cocoons, she would peep beneath the leaves and smell their distinctive musky odour. When the time came and they showed signs of disintegration, she'd leave the box open and lie on her belly with it in front of her until the butterflies and moths emerged and took flight. She never tired of marvelling at how a small ugly worm could metamorphose into a beautiful butterfly.

Tattoo Tony was watching her.

'You do want a butterfly, don't you?' he said.

'How did you know?'

'I told you, twenty years' experience. Butterflies represent change and growth, they're the classic metaphor of transformation and ultimate freedom and that's what you need to express at the moment. Don't be ashamed of it, just because you're not unique in wanting one doesn't make it any the less significant.'

He pulled a pad from a shelf above his head and invited Ros to look through it. She leafed through, admiring his drawings of swallowtails, monarchs, whites, admirals and coppers. What intricate patterns they formed and what variety there was; it was almost enough to make a person believe in God.

'I want this one,' she said finally, pointing at a pale yellow butterfly edged with black, with dark striations on its wings and a flash of blue at the wings' apex.

'The eastern tiger swallowtail. Good choice,' Tony said, nodding his head appreciatively. 'How do you want it, in flight, or wings folded as though resting?'

'I think sort of halfway between the two, if that's possible,' said Ros, 'poised for flight. Can you do that?'

'Your wish, Madam, my command.'

Ros sat down and stretched out her leg. Tattoo Tony anchored his thigh against her foot, cleaned her ankle with alcohol and then placed his hand on it and closed his eyes.

'I'm getting in tune with your energy,' he explained.

Ros smiled; trust her to have found a gumbaggley tattoo artist. She liked the feel of his hand on her skin and his trousered thigh against the sole of her foot. It had been a while since anyone had touched her and it really did feel as though his energy were flowing into her and hers into him. It was an intimate position to find herself in with a stranger and she had a sudden image of his tattooed flesh and her unblemished soft white skin meshing together. What an arresting picture they'd make.

'OK,' said Tony, breaking her reverie. 'Let's get started. Now this might be a bit uncomfortable because it's right on the bone.'

It *was* painful; Ros practised her yoga, breathing deeply through her nose into her diaphragm and out through her mouth and filling her head with clear golden light as she said to herself over and over like a mantra, 'not as bad as childbirth, not as bad as childbirth'. And it wasn't. Few things were. What would Mike think when he saw it? Or the children for that matter? She hadn't told anyone that she was going to get a tattoo. Why should she? She was spreading her wings, just like her nascent butterfly and wasn't accountable to Mike any longer. She carried on breathing deeply until the gnawing pain in her ankle became something dimly felt and separate from her.

'Why don't you have a bone put through your nose while you're at it?' Her mother's voice, louder than ever, shattered her yogic trance.

Ros started.

'You OK?' asked Tony, looking up at her. 'I need you to keep really still.'

'Sorry, I'm fine, just an involuntary twitch,' Ros lied. She couldn't very well explain that her dead mother seemed to have taken up residence in her head. Ros remembered when she was sixteen and she'd had her ears pierced without asking her mother's permission. Lilian had been furious.

'Are you mad, child?' she'd shouted, in that angry South African accent. Lilian thought ear piercing was mutilation and had actually cried when she saw what Ros had done.

'It's my body,' Ros had retorted, slamming doors and retreating into her bedroom.

That's what getting the tattoo was all about too, reclaiming her body and asserting her ownership of it. Maybe she'd get her belly button pierced while she was at it.

'No,' Tattoo Tony said unequivocally when she asked him about it. 'You're too classy for that.'

She was flattered, but here was someone else telling her what she could and could not do. Still, perhaps she'd leave the belly-button piercing for today and see how she felt in a week or so.

Tony had finished and sat back to admire his work. The area was red and raised, but for all that, a butterfly now rested on the outside of her left ankle, its wings half-open, ready for flight. Ros admired it, turning her leg this way and that. The butterfly seemed to move as she did so, a living, breathing creature, symbolising a new incarnation. She recalled something Lilian had once told her that had moved her profoundly. At the end of the war, soldiers had found butterflies etched onto the walls of the children's barracks in a concentration camp. Each one a message of hope left by a child who knew he was going to die.

'Do you ever get unusual requests?' Ros asked.

'Sometimes,' said Tony. 'I won't do faces, necks or hands. That bloke there was my one exception.' He gestured to the bald head Ros had been looking at earlier.

'And I won't do knobs,' he suddenly retorted with some passion, as though she had suggested he might. 'I'm not holding some bloke's knob in my hand for half an hour. I'll do lips, though.'

'Lips?' Ros said and then blushed, 'Oh, those lips.'

As Ros was counting out the sixty pounds she owed him, Tony took her hand.

'Fancy a drink one evening?' he asked.

Ros was about to decline politely and explain that she was a married woman, but then she remembered she wasn't and that she could no longer use matrimony as her Get Out of Jail Free card.

'I bet you ask all newly tattooed, divorcing women that,' she said, thinking fast. 'But I'm not really ready for dates yet – I'll call you when I am. OK?'

He scribbled his mobile number down on the back of a leaflet and handed it to her. There was something alluring and forbidden about him, but Ros's need to rebel didn't extend as far as going out with someone who was half-man and half-tattoo. Besides, how could she possibly kiss him without impaling herself on his chin spike? And who knew what other piercings might be revealed by further intimacy. No, she wasn't quite modern enough for all that.

Chapter Five

Ros turned the corner into Devonport Road, giving her a clear view of Mike's new flat as he ushered an unknown young woman in through the front door. Ros caught sight of his hand in the small of the girl's back when he closed the door. She'd decided to pop in on her way back home, ostensibly to make some arrangement about Ruffy, but actually to see if Mike would notice her tattoo. She wasn't yet out of the habit of needing to share each new event in her life with him. She stood frozen on the pavement, her heart pounding and a terrible feeling of desolation rising in her stomach. The corpse of their marriage had barely had time to grow cold before he'd invited another woman over for a spot of lunchtime nookie. The two-week window. Charlie was right; it hadn't really taken all that much longer for Mike to fix himself up with someone new.

Ros fumbled in her bag until she found what she was looking for. She wished she had a hand grenade; that she could tear the pin out with her teeth and hurl it through the window to explode the, doubtless, naked copulating bodies of her soon-to-be-ex husband and his new girlfriend. In the absence of one, her fingers curled instead around a small glass bottle. Bach Flower Remedies: Elm.

'Take a few drops under your tongue when you are feeling overwhelmed,' Hari the Homeopath had prescribed.

'Is that because overwhelmed has elm in it,' Ros had quipped. 'Would you take Wild Oat if you were hoping to sow some?'

'Wild Oat is for uncertainty over one's direction in life,' Hari had answered impassively.

Ros had felt chastised; humour and homeopathic remedies were apparently mutually exclusive.

From her position behind an evergreen shrub, Ros continued to watch the front windows of number forty-five Devonport Road as she unscrewed the bottle and squeezed the rubber end of the pipette. She drew the flower remedy up into the glass dropper and felt the tang of the elm essence as it hit the delicate flesh under her tongue.

'It's your own fault, Ros.' It was her mother's voice again, loud and clear in her ear. 'You threw away a perfectly good marriage.'

'What are you talking about?' Ros answered. 'You're the one who always said he wasn't good enough for me.'

'Nonsense,' said Lilian. Her memory could be selective. 'You made your bed and you should have continued to lie in it.'

'That's so typical of you, you always move the goalposts.'

A woman walking past carefully steered her young child in a wide arc to avoid any proximity to Ros, a look of concern on her face. How could she know that Ros was having a perfectly rational argument with her mother when all she could see was a well-dressed, middle-aged woman hiding behind a bush and shouting at herself like a care-in-the-community madwoman? Ros smiled in a reassuring manner, but this only made the woman quicken her step and gather the child up in her arms. She hurried away, glancing back over her shoulder as if to make sure that Ros wasn't following them. She looked familiar and Ros realised that she was probably a mother from school. She'd better get a grip or word would soon get out that she'd gone mad.

Her newly tattooed ankle was throbbing in time with the dull aching beat of her heart and she felt like crying. Of course Mike was perfectly entitled to see other women – they were separated, soon to be divorced. In fact, she decided, she would ask her lawyer to serve the papers and get the whole business under way. The sooner it was all resolved the better. She wished Charlie could have handled it for her, but he said it wasn't fair since he knew Mike too. It stung to see for herself how easily replaceable she was. She hadn't had a chance to get a proper look at the girl, just a flash of long dark hair and a slim, tight body. She must be young. Ros tried to comfort herself with the thought that she could have been ushering a man through her own front door if she chose. Perhaps she shouldn't have deleted UpForIt24/7 so summarily.

The first thing she did when she got home was to turn her computer on and log onto StartingOver.com. Actually, it was the second thing. The first was to clear away the dog shit that had been left outside her gate in a neat malodorous package that she had initially and myopically mistaken for an express delivery from DHL. Matters were escalating with Dogman and she'd have to take action. But that could wait; at present there was the urgent matter of three new 'whistles' to be dealt with.

`Hey Sal, I've got what you want.`

It was UpForIt24/7 again and he was online NOW! – the word flashed at her in a seeming frenzy of portentous excitement.

`And what might that be?` she tapped out. Mike's apparent betrayal had made her less dismissive of UpForIt than she had been before.

`What are you looking for?`

`Tell me about yourself first`, she wrote.

`I'm six foot tall, dark hair, all my own teeth and I work in IT. I like walking, going to the cinema and the company of an attractive woman with a sense of humour. Now you.`

This was fun she decided. The anonymity was emboldening; it allowed her to be more brash than usual and to assume whatever personality she chose. She'd heard numerous stories about cyber love affairs and had always been sceptical of them, believing it was ridiculous to fall in love with someone you'd never met. But now she was beginning to see how it might be possible to form a relationship with a stranger that turned him if not into a lover, at least into a friend.

`OK. I'm five foot five, curly brown/blonde hair and blue eyes. I have two children and am adjusting to being on my own after almost twenty years of marriage.`

Do you have a photo?

Too early for photos, let's talk more first.

What are you looking for on here?

What are you offering?

A nine and a half inch cock all for you to play with, baby.

Ros was dismayed; her foray into cyber dating at once rendered tawdry and shameful by UpForIt's reduction of flirtatious interchange to a crude bartering of body parts. How should she respond? Should she lay her own poker hand in front of him with a flourish? I'll see your improbably long penis with good legs and a trick pelvis. Ugh. She clicked on the block button instead. This meant that UpForIt could no longer contact her or see when she was online.

The house was quiet and it had started to rain. The branches of the chestnut tree outside the kitchen window fractured the sky. It was a typical, dreary London winter afternoon and all too soon it would be dark. Ros dreaded the short winter days. Each autumn she felt herself spiralling into gloom as the evenings drew in, and by January, like a child charting the arrival of Christmas with an advent calendar, she marked the time until late March when the clocks would go forward. Her mother had been the same, unable to adjust to the bone-chilling British climate and forever yearning for the bright African sunshine of her youth. No wonder Finland had the highest rate of suicide and alcoholism in the world, Ros reflected, there was so little light in winter there wasn't much else for it except to drink to excess and plan your own demise.

Ros contemplated pouring herself a glass of wine but it felt too sad to drink alone on a Tuesday afternoon. Should she phone Mike? She imagined the jangle of the telephone acting as coitus interruptus; the thought gave her a certain grim pleasure and she reached for the receiver.

She was saved from herself by Jack coming through the front door. Some instinct made Ros hide her ankle from him. As soon as she'd heard the front door open, she'd rushed to her bedroom and pulled on a pair of thick socks, the first thing she saw, trying not to yelp with pain as the wool came into contact with the skin of Tattoo Tony's latest canvas. The unforeseen flaw in her strategy became apparent as soon as she joined Jack in the kitchen.

'Mum, those are my socks, take them off,' said Jack.

He was scanning the fridge for something to eat with fewer than fifty calories. He'd become obsessive about food in the past few months and knew the calorific value of everything. Ros watched him like a hawk; terrified that Mike and her separation would send Jack hurtling into the vortex of teenage anorexia. She'd read all the articles about the rise of the illness among teenage boys and realised that she wasn't setting a very good example herself. Always slim, apart from a few years of plumpness at puberty, she was now in danger of becoming too thin.

Ros looked down at her legs. In her haste she had indeed pulled on Jack's socks, which, for some reason, he had abandoned on Ros's bedroom floor.

'Well, if you will leave your things in my room,' Ros countered in an attempt to keep the socks on.

'Off. Now.'

There was nothing for it. Ros pulled the socks off, turning her body away from Jack so that her ankle remained hidden from view.

Jack picked up a natural yoghurt. Fifty-two calories. Even he wasn't going to quibble about the extra two calories. He fumbled as he took a spoon out of the drawer, dropping it on the floor. As he bent to pick it up, he found himself staring his mother directly in the ankle.

'What have you done? I don't believe it. Oh my God, you've got a tattoo.' Jack seemed about to burst into tears. 'Now you won't have the same Mummy leg ever again.'

Was he joking? Ros looked at his face and saw genuine sorrow in it. It was the same expression he used to wear when she left him at nursery school – stricken and abandoned. Ros bit her lip as she felt the tears start in her own eyes.

'How could you have just gone and done it without discussing it with us first?' said Jack.

All she'd wanted was a symbol to mark some sort of end-of-marriage rebirth, an assertion of ownership of her own body. But, she realised, as she looked at Jack's tearful face, as a parent, one could never truly own one's body. In fact, it turned out one could never own it at all: as a child, one is answerable to one's parents, and as a parent, it seems, one is answerable to one's children.

'Why didn't you have a bone put through your nose while you were at it?' Jack said.

Ros started. This was exactly what she had heard Lilian's voice say to her earlier when she was at the tattoo parlour. Not only was she back in Ros's own head, but apparently in Jack's mouth too.

'I'm having my eyebrow pierced then,' said Jack, 'and don't you dare try and stop me, that would be hypocritical.'

In the course of this confrontation, Charlie had turned up, his arms full of lever arch files and bundles of documents tied up with pink ribbon.

'And I'm having my nipples pierced,' Charlie said promptly on observing Ros's tattoo.

Ros should have thought this all through properly. Of course Jack would use the situation to his advantage and get the piercing he'd been nagging for these past two years, as would Charlie, whom she'd spent the last six months talking out of nipple piercing on the grounds that it was wholly inappropriate at his age. Now, of course, she didn't have a leg to stand on. The irony wasn't lost on her, as it was a leg, or at least an ankle, that had caused all this trouble in the first place.

Chapter Six

Ros was dreaming. She had murdered someone and hidden the body under the floorboards. Years had passed and so far she'd got away with it, but now the police had arrived and were starting to take her house apart. It wasn't a house she'd ever seen before, but it was hers nonetheless. They started by opening drawers and overturning tables and then, her breath quickening as a policeman tapped his boot over the floor of the hallway, she watched as he listened carefully to how the reverberating sound changed in one particular area; on the very floorboards beneath which her victim lay hidden. The policeman raised his head and looked at her. Time hung suspended in that moment of perfect stillness when a predator observes its prey immediately prior to the final merciless attack. Ros was only dimly aware of who it was that lay beneath the floorboards. She thought it was Barbara Williams, a girl in her class at school, who always used to beat her by two marks in Latin and French. In the logic of dreamland, the only way for Ros to assume her rightful place as top linguist was to take Barbara out. Ros felt no guilt about the murder, only terror at its imminent discovery and at the certainty of the long jail sentence that would take her away from her children. She could hear the terrible clanging sound as the cell door shut behind her, the jangle of the warden's circle of keys and the finality of metal scraping on metal as the lock turned. It was the searing pain of loss that woke her and found her panting with relief in the dark bedroom. She sat in the lotus position on top of her bedclothes and tried to calm herself. Her eyes closed, she could see a large metal key in front of her, shrinking gradually, becoming smaller and smaller. Keys, locks, suitcases, secrets. Ros opened her eyes with a start and felt her way into her slippers.

She would never have dared go up to the attic in the middle of the night if she were alone in the house, but the sound of Sid and Jack's even breathing as she passed their rooms gave her courage, while simultaneously making her aware that they wouldn't be at home much longer. She took the added precaution of painstakingly touching the banisters on her way up, first with one hand, then with the other, and was careful to ensure that her right foot was the first to tread on each stair, rendering her ascent both slow and awkward. She knew this behaviour was absurd and bordered on the obsessive, but she persuaded herself that it was the only way of guaranteeing her sons' safe return from their imminent travels.

A pale moon shone through the small skylight in the attic, illuminating Lilian's small suitcase. Ros shivered and wished that Ruffy were still with her and that Mike hadn't taken her back the day before. She held the knife she had taken from the kitchen and inserted the tip of the blade into the lock. She felt unaccountably nervous, like a burglar in danger of being surprised by the owners at any instant as she rifled through their possessions. Ros remembered how much she used to love rummaging through her mother's jewellery drawer when Lilian was out, basking in the pleasure of the unique pieces – valuable only in sentiment – that had been collected over a lifetime, and admiring her reflection as she tried things on. Now that Lilian was dead and the jewellery belonged to her, she rarely wore it, save for the opal ring that her mother had brought with her from Africa. Each piece had somehow absorbed the sadness of her passing and seemed to ache, as she herself did, for Lilian's neck, wrist or fingers.

The lock wasn't budging. Was this a sign that Ros should leave well alone or that she should simply try harder?

'Never give up,' Lilian had always told her, 'anything worth having takes effort.'

Ros went to fetch a hammer. She drew it back over her shoulder and brought it down hard on the suitcase's rusty buckles. Her dream came back to her like a bad taste repeating, a hammer on the skull of a soon-to-be buried body. Ros shuddered and struck again. The locks shattered and sprung open.

Ros hesitated, caught between curiosity and uncertainty, and then carefully opened the suitcase. The lid was lined with photographs. They were faded by time and peeling from the corners. She smoothed down the ends and angled a lamp onto them. She could see a young Lilian smiling from the safety of her grandfather's lap. She looked much like Ros herself had at the same age, the same quizzical tilt to her brows, the same penetrating stare. A larger photograph dominated the collection. It showed stern-faced matrons in black dresses edged with white lace seated next to white-haired, rabbinical patriarchs. Lilian's ancestors. At the bottom she could just make out a date: eighteen ninety-five. A family portrait taken before Lilian's grandfather set sail from Lithuania? Elsewhere, the smiling face of a young black man in a trilby caught Ros's eye. He was standing beside a bicycle, his fist raised in a gesture of defiance. Someone had drawn a caption underneath the photograph and Ros could just make out the faded writing. *Amandla! Ngawethu!* It was the same man whose photograph Ros had discovered in Lilian's handbag after her death.

Ros turned her attention to the contents of the case. It held a notebook, bound in pale blue leather with the words Five Year Diary embossed on the cover in gold. In addition, there was a beaded necklace, a small African basket with a lid and some other papers. Ros picked up the diary and weighed it in her hand.

The night was unusually quiet. Even the Uxbridge Road, whose distant rumble could always be heard, seemed to hold its breath as though waiting for Ros to open the diary. She almost felt a sense of relief when one of the dogs started to bark in the house next door. It was quickly joined by others.

Ros noticed a single, loose piece of paper at the bottom of the case, covered in Lilian's dense, forward-sloping handwriting. She picked it up.

It's 2 a.m; that quiet time of the night when I can't help wondering what my life's been for and whether I could have lived it differently. Well, I know I could have and often ask myself whether I should have. The dark English winters oppress me more than ever now and my thoughts turn more and more to the distant years of my African past. Could it be that Mandela's release from prison after twenty-seven years has broken the dam that has contained my recollections for all these years? I feel my memories have been frozen like so many images on a roll of film, which, after decades lying dormant and hidden in a tin can, are now projected onto the screen of my mind in vivid Technicolor. I can smell the African earth, particularly after an unexpected summer rainfall, feel the warm air of a rare summer breeze and see the bright light and vibrant colours of a familiar landscape undimmed by the passage of time.

It was curious this voice of Lilian's that Ros had chanced upon, captured on a brittle piece of paper and different from the one that she heard in her head. This was a voice full of yearning; the voice of a person whom Ros felt she didn't know. The beauty of writing, she reflected, and its almost unbearable poignancy was that it allowed the voices of those who had died to vibrate into the future. Autobiographies should not be solely the provenance of the notable, she thought. All families should have a book, a journal in which each generation writes; their words twisting like a vine to bind them to their ancestors whose thoughts and experiences form part of their own past. As Ros held the paper to her face, the faint whisper of her mother's scent caught her senses and she pressed her lips to it before carefully returning it to the suitcase. She got up and went to the living room where she lay down; her head propped up by one end of the sofa, the unopened diary on her lap. Not for the first time, she wished she had a brother or sister. It was lonely being an only child, particularly when your mother was dead and your father far away in another country. She recalled the imaginary friend she'd had as a small child; a girl to whom she'd talk for hours in her bedroom in the still night hours.

She hadn't thought about her for years; Ros had named her Kosi and she came from Africa, just like Lilian. Ros couldn't remember when she'd relinquished her, although she had a distant memory of a bad fight with her mother that seemed in some way associated with her imaginary friend's demise.

Although she had her own family now, Ros had never got over the loss of her primary family, the one where she had been the child. Other people seemed able to replace the family of their childhood with one of their own creation, but there was always a part of Ros that felt forlorn and adrift, perpetually astonished to find that she was the parent and not the child. No one else seemed to understand this, not even Mike; she could see it in his puzzled expression when she tried to explain. It was, she supposed, an immaturity in her, a case of arrested development. Perhaps it was born of the fact that for so long it had been just the two of them, Ros and Lilian?

Ros felt dislocated, unsure where she was in space and time. She wedged herself into a corner of the sofa as if to anchor herself, took a deep breath and opened the diary.

Chapter Seven

The first page gave Lilian's contact details, her full name and address in Johannesburg and the dates the diary spanned: 1952–1957. Lilian would have been twenty-three in 1957. It was the year she had left Africa. Ros fanned the pages and found, to her disappointment, that the diary was largely empty, annotated only here and there by Lilian's handwriting, with seemingly irrelevant dentist and doctor appointments and reminders to collect dry cleaning, write letters and make phone calls. Various and frequent dates had a small black cross in the top right-hand corner with the single letter 'm'. January 12th 1955 carried the enigmatic entry, *three years today!* On February 9th of the same year, Lilian had written: *Black Wednesday.* December 5th 1956 carried the single word *Arrest* and under May 10th of 1957, Lilian had drawn a small heart. On June 16th of the same year, the same heart was drawn, only this time in two halves as if broken. Ros felt frustrated, as though Lilian were teasing her. Why keep the diary in a locked suitcase if it said nothing? She went back to the attic to fetch the suitcase. She examined the lock; had it been locked or simply rusted shut? It was impossible to say. She looked again at the photographs that lined the lid. The one of the young black man seemed padded. Ros carefully peeled away the yellowing tape that held the picture in place. Behind it she found a piece of paper folded into a small square. Ros unfolded it. It was dry and brittle; the writing in blue ink had faded to purple.

My life seemed both to begin and to end the day that Sipho was knocked off his bicycle. I knelt beside him and held his head

in my arms and urged him to hold on to life. The car that had
knocked him over drove off, the driver shouting, 'bloody kaffir'
out of his window and shaking an imprecating fist into
the shimmering heat of a Johannesburg afternoon as he acceler-
ated ...

Ros read the page again and Clare Voyante's words suddenly reverberated in her head, 'She's giving me the letter "S". Can you take that, dear?' S for Sipho?

Ros walked slowly back into the living room and took her place once more on the sofa. She looked out the window at the first signs of the city awakening from a night's sleep. Across the road, she could see the smoke wafting up from the brazier that Chris, who owned the junk shop on the corner, lit at first light every morning. His shop was always open; its contents taking up much of the pavement, a television blaring from morning to night, the brazier positioned at right angles to it and Chris's armchair, the stuffing leaking out here and there, placed at its side, a position that allowed him both to watch television and to observe the local population's comings and goings. Ros watched the smoke climb and settle above the shop, hovering like a cloud in the lightening sky and heard her mother's voice in her ear. Not her everyday voice, but the voice of Lilian the storyteller who would weave exotic tales of faraway places to lull Ros to sleep.

'Every summer, Cape Town's Table Mountain is shrouded in a white south-eastern summer cloud,' she could hear Lilian say. 'It's known as a "tablecloth" and the legend goes that in the eighteenth century, a Dutch pirate, Captain Van Hunks, having retired from a lifetime of sailing the seven seas, liked nothing better than to sit in solitude on a rock beneath a tree at the mountain's summit to smoke his pipe.'

Ros sat back and closed her eyes, listening.

'One day, he was surprised to see a man wearing a black cloak and hood sitting in his spot. He bade him good day and, seating himself beside him, took out his pipe and began boasting about his ability to smoke great quantities of tobacco. The stranger replied that he could easily smoke as much as Van Hunks. Stung, Van Hunks challenged him to a smoking contest. He placed a large mound of tobacco between them and they lit their pipes and began to smoke. Far below, people marvelled at the cloud of smoke they observed hovering above the mountain, growing ever bigger until the entire top of the mountain was obscured from view. Finally, overcome by the heat of the day and the tobacco, the stranger keeled over, the hood of his cloak slipping off to reveal two horns protruding from his forehead. Van Hunks's smoking companion was none other than the Devil himself, who, piqued at having been beaten by a mere human, soon summoned a clap of thunder, causing the two of them to disappear in a puff of smoke. Ever since, each summer, in perpetuity, Van Hunks is forced to re-enact his smoking duel with the Devil and the "tablecloth" reappears over the mountain.'

Ros's eyes felt heavy and she allowed herself to drift off to sleep, cocooned, or so it felt, in her mother's embrace. She was awoken by Sid twisting her foot and whispering loudly, 'Bloody hell, I see what you mean. Liz, come and have a look at this.'

Through half-closed eyes as she feigned sleep, Ros could see Liz, Sid and Jack standing next to the sofa and staring at the tattoo on her ankle.

'Well, I think it's cool,' said Liz. 'I'd like to get one.'

'It's all right for you,' Sid said, 'it's not your mother who's going bonkers. She'll be wearing a kaftan, waving incense around and bloody chanting next.'

'She's doing that already, innit,' said Jack. 'She's doin' yoga and sittin' like a lotus.'

It was obvious that Jack had been talking to Dogman next door. He always unwittingly adopted the accent and mannerisms of the last person he'd been speaking to. When he was younger, Ros used to worry that it would prevent him from having a personality of his own but he managed always to retain a sense of himself, in spite of the fact that his outward manifestation of that self was unstable. He hadn't realised it yet, but there were only really two alternatives open to him for the future: acting or espionage. Of the two, Ros felt that espionage was marginally less perilous.

Ros sat up and looked at her watch. 'It's ten o'clock, what are you still doing here? You should all be at work. Go on, you'll be late, hurry up.'

'You didn't wake us,' Sid complained.

'You're meant to be old enough to wake yourselves up now.'

'Oi 'as Dad seen yer tattoo?' asked Jack.

'For God's sake, Jack, why on earth have you been talking to Dogman?'

''Ow d'ya know?' Jack continued fiercely to deny his habit of involuntary mimicry and was perpetually astonished that Ros always seemed to know whom he'd been with.

'It's the way yer talkin', innit?' she said, ruffling his hair. 'Now, for heaven's sake go and look into drama schools or MI6 or something and don't waste your time smoking dope with Dogman.'

It was handy being a teacher; rather like being a detective in some ways, years of reading guilt in the eyes of the young meant that she always knew when her boys had been up to no good.

'You always do that, Mum,' Jack complained, his own voice abruptly restored, 'it's so annoying. You're the one who's in trouble for getting a tattoo and now you're blaming me for being bad.'

'Yeah,' said Sid, 'like, what's the tattoo all about?'

Ros shrugged, 'Don't you like it?'

'Yeah, on a girl, but not on my mum.'

And that, of course, was the crux of the matter. Ros wanted to be a girl again with her life ahead of her. The future of a girl was full of possibility while that of a mum felt predictable and preordained. Not that she didn't love being a mother, she did, and indeed had only become one thanks to the wonder of modern science. Mike's sperm were lazy and Ros's Fallopian tubes were blocked. (It had helped somehow that the fault lay with them both; it evened things out so that neither had to feel a burden to the other.) Sid and Jack were IVF twins. Ros and Mike had been lucky; unlike the majority of couples, they'd scored on their very first try. The two little embryos that had been implanted in Ros's womb, after the hideous business of daily injections and egg harvesting, had taken a firm hold and after a textbook pregnancy, Sid and Jack had seemed to leap into the world, distinct one from the other. Sid was big and blonde, Jack, smaller and darker. She'd have liked one more child, a daughter to even the household up a little. But, having been so fortunate the first time, neither she nor Mike wanted to tempt fate and Ros had an instinctive antipathy for the drugs that would once again be required to produce another child. They'd decided to leave it to nature and when nature hadn't delivered they'd decided to get a dog instead. It wasn't quite the same thing, but a consolation of sorts and Ros had insisted that their dog, when they chose one, was female.

The tattoo on Ros's ankle was itching and had turned crusty. She cleaned it carefully with one of the antiseptic wipes that Tattoo Tony had given her and sought a reason for her nagging sense of unease. She was grateful it was almost the start of the school term; she wasn't good without a framework and it was no accident that she had chosen as structured an environment as a school where her days were ruled by the bell. For Ros, freedom was anything but liberating and now that the boys were older, the holidays, formerly pleasantly constrained by their needs and routines, had lost their shape. That wasn't the cause of her unease, however. Two things troubled her: the first was her mother's diary – its lack of detail irked her and the unresolved clues to her mother's early life had intruded on her own with a nudging insistence that demanded her attention and presaged something unknown. The second was Mike. The image of the slim, dark woman entering his front door replayed itself in her head. She tried to slow it down to observe more detail, but it was no good, the girl remained nothing more than fleeting film frames of dark hair and slim, trousered hips.

> *Underneath the baobab tree*
> *I see you, but you don't see me.*

Ros hummed to herself, or was it Lilian's voice she could hear singing gently in her head? It was a song Lilian used to sing to her.

'Now I know where the dead go,' Ros realised with an unexpected certainty. 'They move into the heads of their loved ones.' Lilian had undoubtedly taken up occupancy in hers.

The dogs next door were barking again.

I'll go and get Ruffy and take her for a walk, Ros decided.

On her way out, she went next door to talk to Dogman about the persistent barking issue. She raised her hand to knock on the door and heard one of the dogs growling on the other side, a low sound that threatened to rise in cadence until it erupted into the kind of full-blown barking that heralded an attack. She didn't have the energy for a confrontation and let her fist drop before turning away meekly, her tail, she couldn't help feeling, firmly between her legs as she let herself out of the gate and into the street.

Minutes later, her hand was raised again to knock on a different door. Mike's front door was as unfamiliar to her as her husband himself was becoming.

'Ros,' Mike said unnecessarily as he opened the door.

Ros studied him. Did he have the look of a man who had recently had sex? His hair was certainly dishevelled; his face covered in designer stubble and was that the beginnings of a deliberate moustache that she could see? He'd never been permitted to grow facial hair when they were together; Ros was suspicious of it. She liked to see the structure of a man's face and all too often beards both hid weak chins and served as food containers. Ros felt that people should use Tupperware like everyone else and that if, as Mike did, a man had a handsome well-formed jaw, why on earth would he choose to disguise it? Similarly, moustaches of the variety that Mike had favoured in his youth, the big handlebar Village People sort, were strictly *verboten* on the grounds of sheer ridiculousness. (There were clubs for people with such moustaches, Ros had read about them in a magazine called *Moustache Monthly* – or something very like that – in the doctor's waiting room: ordinary people in an effort to appear extraordinary grew walrus moustaches and, united by nothing more than their hairy appendages, met with each other on a regular basis to celebrate their lifetime's achievement. It was like that housewife in Chorley Wood who'd devoted her life to growing long, twisting, turning, eat-your-heart-out-Howard-Hughes fingernails that trailed ape-like along the ground and meant she couldn't pick her nose, let alone dress herself. She'd achieved a certain amount of fame certainly, but Ros couldn't help feeling there were nobler and more meaningful ways to distinguish oneself from the crowd.) Throughout their marriage, Mike had tried to trick Ros into signing a piece of paper stating, 'I, Rosalind Townsend, give permission for my husband, Michael Townsend, to grow a moustache.' He used to insert it among legal papers that required her signature, and between the lines of shopping lists. She'd almost signed it early on in their relationship when she thought she was signing the marriage register. They'd giggled like schoolchildren while the registrar had looked at them sternly over his reading glasses to remind them of the importance of the occasion.

Ros and Mike faced each other over the threshold. It was strangely quiet.

'I've come to get Ruffy to take her for a walk,' Ros said.

Mike stood aside, running his fingers through his unruly hair, and ushered Ros in. She walked into the living room. He'd had what he called the drinker-decorators in and, true to form, they'd drunk all his beer except for one can, which he'd had the foresight to hide on his bedroom windowsill (an old trick from his student days when he hadn't had a fridge.) As they had drunk, they'd painted the living room a bright Mediterranean blue (Ros had always favoured plain white walls), which gave Mike the pleasurable illusion he was in a villa in the south of France rather than in a small flat in a residential street off the Uxbridge Road. Ros noticed that he'd bought himself the Bose digital music system he'd always wanted. Modern jazz was playing loudly, which Ros always referred to as angry fly music, a cacophony of discordant sounds that made her feel simultaneously anxious and irritated. When Mike used to play it, she would turn the volume down whenever his back was turned. The television was on, a forty-inch plasma screen that dominated the room and the black box squatting toad-like on a shelf on the wall above it indicated that he'd installed satellite (both things he'd similarly always wanted and which Ros had forbidden on the admittedly snobbish grounds that they didn't live in suburbia, so why behave as if they did?). The television was tuned to Sky Sport and the footballers on the screen seemed to be dancing in time to the music, their movements frenetic. Now that he lived alone, Ros realised, Mike could play his music as loudly as he wished, watch TV anytime he wanted, belch and scratch his balls to his heart's content, a state near to ecstasy that many married men could only dream of.

Ros understood that this technologically enhanced gingerbread house was Mike's attempt not only to express his newfound freedom, but also (and principally) to entice the children into spending more time in his flat with him. It was a cheap trick, but an effective one: Sid and Jack spent at least as much time with him as they did with Ros. Who could blame him? Ros considered. After all, he was the one who'd had to leave the family home. There were some compensations to being newly single, she thought ruefully, remembering the new crisp white sheets and over-abundance of pillows on her bed, which were her equivalent of Mike's digital nirvana.

It was odd for Ros and Mike to be standing so close together while feeling so far apart. Once they'd been inseparable, but life had steadily pecked at them like a flock of birds until only a few crumbs of their earlier contentment remained. Something was different, something beyond Mike's awkward stance in the living room door and the strange food on a plate in his hand that resembled a pale severed breast. Where was Ruffy and why hadn't she bounded to the door as she usually did?

'Ruffy's gone out,' Mike said.

'What do you mean?'

'One of the language assistants from school came to take her for a walk. She said she was missing her own dog in Spain.' Mike couldn't seem to meet her eyes.

Ros watched his face carefully. So that's who the girl was. Letting *Her* take their dog out felt like the worst sort of betrayal. Mike looked shifty.

He could feel Ros's eyes on him and looked down at the ground.

'What's that?' he asked, his eyes drawn to the tattoo on Ros's ankle.

'Nothing,' said Ros, covering the tattoo with the toe of her other foot. 'What's that?' she asked, pointing at Mike's nascent moustache.

'Nothing,' said Mike, his hand flying up to cover his top lip.

They both felt they'd done something wrong. It was odd how couples made parents out of each other and felt the need to seek permission for their actions. Ros's and Mike's newfound freedom sat uneasily on them, they still felt beholden each to the other, and naughty for doing things without asking. Ros had wanted to tell Mike about Lilian's suitcase, but she suddenly felt too alienated from him to do so.

'Well,' she said, 'you're clearly very busy, growing moustaches and things, so I'll leave you to get on with it.' She'd meant it jokingly, but it had come out rather acidly. 'Give me a call when Ruffy's back.'

They kissed each other clumsily on the cheek, noses bumping like uncomfortable acquaintances; this physical awkwardness yet another indication that they no longer danced in step to the same tune.

'Intimacy is an illusion,' Lilian's voice told Ros as she walked away from Mike and down the few steps that led to the front path, 'it's entirely dependent on the agreement of two people; once that agreement ceases to exist, it vaporises.'

Ros felt that her head was buzzing like a hive full of angry bees. Was she on the verge of a nervous breakdown? And if she were, would she know that she was? She hesitated on the pavement, fighting the desire to hide behind a bush and wait for the Spanish trollop to return with her dog. She sensed that Mike was feeling both guilty and furtive. The threads of a long marriage could not, it seemed, be severed all at once; they stretched out over the years to form an invisible umbilical cord between husband and wife.

Chapter Eight

Ros forced herself to walk away from the house and down the street. She matched her footsteps to the rhythm of Lilian's voice, which continued to reverberate in her head.

'You've too much time on your hands, darling,' Lilian told her. 'You'll be fine when you get back to work. You need a project, everyone does, human beings need projects; it's as simple as that. As the philosopher Immanuel Kant said, we are purposive beings.' Lilian too had been a teacher, a lecturer in English at a sixth-form college. Ros used to get irritated when Lilian used her teacher's voice on her, but now she felt glad of it. She had a sudden longing to be a child again and to have someone tell her what to do. Being a human being didn't always come naturally to Ros; she often felt unsure of what she should be doing or saying and had to remind herself to do the things that others seemed to do naturally; things like eating, enjoying the sunshine or sitting on a park bench and reading a book. That was why she lost herself in busy-ness and why she felt drawn to the world of gumbaggley. In the absence of religion, alternative therapies and New Age thinking gave her the order and meaning she craved. She worried that the break-up of her marriage might lead to a further fragmentation of her world and culminate finally in her own personal disintegration. Even now, it felt as though pieces of her were flaking off and that she was holding herself together only by a sheer effort of will. She looked at her watch. If she hurried, she could get to her yoga class. That would surely help glue some of the parts of her back together.

She was a few minutes late. The room had the stillness and hush peculiar to the yoga practice studio. Joti sat in the lotus position at the front of the class, his long dark hair piled on top of his head and fastened into a bun. He was, as always, shirtless, eyes closed and the *ujjayi* breath that he practised and encouraged them to learn, noisily washing his body with strong clear energy. Ros suddenly noticed that Joti wasn't wearing his customary white yoga trousers either. He was, in fact, naked, as were many others in the room. Naked Yoga. Ros froze and then began to tiptoe back out of the room. Joti caught up with her at the door.

'The class decided to create a sacred space for those who wanted to do a naked session here today,' he explained. 'We discussed it at the start of the lesson. It allows greater freedom to get deep into the poses and tap into our multi-dimensional energies.' He held her back by the arm. 'Stay and join us, Ros – you don't have to undress but you might find it liberating.'

Ros felt she had no option but to obey and found a place to roll out her mat near the back. Her eyes fixed on the floor, she started to take off her T-shirt; she hesitated and then quickly pulled it back down again. She wasn't ready for naked yoga and doubted that she ever would be. She had taken her position next to José, a bearded Mexican from Guadalajara. Except that he wasn't any longer. Bearded that is. And his chin was weak, which, thought Ros to herself, rather proved her point about beards. It was a shame as he was one of the few men that should be permitted a beard; with it he'd been handsome and Ros had overlooked his hirsuteness to the extent that she'd allowed herself the odd improbable sexual fantasy about him. She quickly averted her eyes so that he wouldn't think she was staring at his body.

'Sanskrit is the language of the heart,' Joti was saying from the front of the class as he rose from a cross-legged position in one fluid movement. 'Before we start with the sun salutation, the *Surya-namaskar,* let us say our prayer to focus our attention and offer up our practice.'

Ros always had a childish inclination to giggle when Joti used Sanskrit words in yoga. Especially since she knew that his real name was Darren and that he came from the White City Estate. She knew this because his younger brother Gary was a pupil at her school who thought that his older brother was a right fuckin' poofter. But Ros admired Joti; he'd gone off to Goa when he was seventeen because he'd heard the spliff was good and had discovered yoga and the path to enlightenment. He'd stayed in India for seven years studying with various spiritual teachers until, reborn as Joti, he'd returned to England to teach yoga himself.

'It means "flame",' Joti explained to Ros the first time he met her. 'My third teacher, Swami Niranjananda gave me the name; he told me that I burn bright and have a duty to warm others with my fire.'

You couldn't fault Joti, he'd opted out of the family business that his brother Gary, at sixteen, already seemed certain to join: armed robbery.

Joti stood now; his hands in the prayer position, his head bent down and began to chant, stopping at the end of each line so that the class could echo him.

>'Vande gurunam caranaravinde
>Sandarsita svatmasukhava bodhe ...'

Apparently, it was something to do with bowing to the lotus feet of the guru who would awaken insight into the happiness of pure being. Ros wasn't entirely sure what lotus feet were or what any of it actually meant, but it sounded preferable to the buzzing of her current febrile mind where thoughts of Mike entwined with the Spanish assistant twisted and tumbled like garments in a washing machine. It also helped to deflect her attention from the fact that many in the class were stark naked. She felt self-conscious and fraudulent when uttering these incomprehensible Sanskrit words and so she silently mouthed them rather than saying them out loud, just as she used to (and still did) with hymns at school assembly. She watched Joti's face – it seemed the safest place to rest her gaze under the circumstances. His eyes were closed and the beginnings of a smile pulled his mouth upwards. She sensed that he had something that she wanted; a kind of peace and certainty that she wished she could siphon out of his head and into her own. The chanting over, they began the sun salutation.

'As you move, feel all the stress flow away out through your breath and your anus,' Joti said.

Ros breathed deeply, willing herself to exhale her anxiety. It must feel strangely liberating to move in the nude, she thought, although the woman on her right appeared to be in danger of being suffocated by her own breasts. Next to her, José took Joti's words literally and farted loudly. Ros wrinkled her nose at the smell and stifled a giggle. It was an altogether too earthly reminder of his naked state. A few moments later, she started as she felt Joti's hands on her wrists correcting her position and increasing the stretch of her arms over her head. She watched his face through half-closed eyes and matched her breathing to his. For an instant, she had the briefest inkling as to what this yoga business might really be about, but it was elusive, somehow always just beyond her grasp, if she could only reach out her hand and catch it. Joti smiled at her and gave an encouraging nod that suggested that he knew what she was thinking. He silently moved on to the large-breasted girl next to her and straightened her hips. For the rest of the lesson Ros tried to recapture the feeling, but her busy head intruded. The boys were with their father this evening and the house would be empty when she went home. She felt a mounting sense of panic at the thought of being alone and wished now that she'd planned something to fill the time. How had her mother managed all those years after Ros had left home, alone in her flat?

'Inner life,' Lilian's voice said. 'You have to have an inner life to sustain you so that you're not entirely dependent on others for your entertainment.'

'That's why I'm doing yoga, isn't it?' Ros answered petulantly inside her head, 'To get a bloody inner life and replace my hidden shallows with depths.'

When the class was over Ros gathered her things together quickly and as they were rolling their mats up, José offered her salvation.

'Would you like a drink?' he asked. 'Well, not alcohol of course, it doesn't go with yoga, but how about a shot of wheatgrass?'

It was the first time he'd asked her out; perhaps his nakedness had given him courage. She might have agreed if it had been just one strike against him, but the farting and the weak chin taken together discouraged Ros from spending any more time in his company, empty house notwithstanding. After all, she was a woman who had once chucked a boyfriend for committing the sole crime of wearing purple socks. Anyhow, wheatgrass tasted disgusting and she had decided that she would spend the evening having an inner life while drinking half a bottle of wine and sorting through Lilian's papers, a job she'd avoided since her death. She thanked José and said she had to get home.

José nodded solemnly and said, 'You know, in a former life, I was a warrior princess who was brutally executed.'

Ros wondered whether he intended to link this information in some way to her refusal to have a drink with him. She wasn't sure how to answer him and mumbled that she hoped he was finding his current life rather more enjoyable. As she was leaving, Joti came up to her and slipped a folded square of paper into her handbag.

'Look at this later, you might find it useful.'

They stood talking for a few minutes and by the time they'd finished, Ros had forgotten all about it.

'Did you see the size of his cock?'

'I'm sorry?' Ros turned round to face Sally-Ann, the yoga class's answer to Chaucer's Wife of Bath.

'I'd give him one,' Sally-Ann said.

You'd give anyone one, Ros thought.

Sally-Ann was a bawdy, lascivious, forty-something divorcée, more male in her attitude to sex than any 'cor look at the tits on that' man Ros had ever met. Ros was sure it was insecure over-compensation, but Sally-Ann with her over-bleached hair, toned abs and too-tight clothes was the living embodiment of mutton dressed as lamb. The jewel at the centre of Sally-Ann's midriff glinted as she raised her arms to pull on her coat and Ros was suddenly grateful that Tattoo Tony had vetoed her own piercing.

'All this yoga makes me horny,' Sally-Ann was saying. She looked at Ros consideringly. 'You're single, right?'

'Um ... well ... yes, I suppose I am ... now,' Ros answered.

'Me too.'

Doh, Ros thought but didn't say. (Teenage speak was very appropriate in certain circumstances.) 'Really?' was what she actually said, affecting surprise as though unable to believe that someone like Sally-Ann *could* be single.

'I could fuck all night after a yoga session,' Sally-Ann continued.

Ros thought she must have been watching too many re-runs of *Sex and the City*.

Sally-Ann leant towards Ros conspiratorially. 'You and I should go out on the pull together one of these days.'

'Oh, I don't ...' Ros began.

'We'd have a great time, find a couple of young guys and teach them a few tricks, eh? They love us older women. Know why?' Sally-Ann hoiked one of her forty-something-year-old breasts further up in the cup of her bra.

'No ... I don't really ...'

'Because,' said Sally-Ann, with all the solemnity of Buddha delivering words of infinite wisdom, 'we know exactly what we want in bed.'

Ros gave an involuntary shudder at the image that had presented itself of Sally-Ann barking orders at a young man in bed much as a sergeant might at a new recruit on a tough assault course.

That's it then, Ros thought to herself, I can never have sex again. What if I become like Sally-Ann?

She finally made her escape when the sight of a young man's peachy buttocks tightly encased in Lycra deflected Sally-Ann's attention. Looking at her face, the image that came to Ros was that of a giant lizard preparing to catch a juicy fly with a single flick of its lethal, sticky tongue.

*

It was dark when she left the building. The streets were busy with office workers making their way home, their heads bent against the damp chill. Ros decided to walk part of the way rather than take the bus. She told herself that it was for the exercise, but really it was to put off arriving home. She'd have to get a grip. If she felt like this at the prospect of one evening alone, how on earth was she going to cope when Sid and Jack went off travelling?

'You have to learn to be happy in your own company, Ros.' Lilian's voice intruded once again.

'Earlier you told me I needed a project, now you're saying I should be happy on my own; it doesn't make sense.'

'They're not mutually exclusive,' Lilian said. 'Yes, of course you should have a project, something that keeps you busy and engages you on your own.'

'Oh shut up, just shut up and leave me alone.'

A young man walking level with her gave her a strange look, which made Ros realise that she was talking aloud again. She hummed and sang, 'Oh shut up, just shut up and leave me alone,' snapping her fingers and trying to pretend that she was singing a song. She was about to explain to him that she was a songwriter and often composed as she walked, but managed to stop herself. What did she care if he thought she was crazy; why shouldn't he, when even she was beginning to think she was? He continued past her and on down the road, glancing back at her once or twice. The incident lightened her mood. Ros walked on past the busy late-night supermarkets with their cornucopia of fruit and vegetables that reeled prospective customers in from the street. She paused for a moment to admire the displays; the seeds of halved pome-granates glittered like rubies and fresh dates shone like lustrous cockroaches, remaining inviting nonetheless. Closing her eyes, she inhaled the powerful aroma of fresh herbs – dill, mint, coriander and parsley – and let the sounds of various languages wash over her. The Uxbridge Road was a modern-day tower of Babel. You could travel the world in London and sample the cuisines of myriad cultures in a mere square mile. Who would want to live anywhere else? She could make out Polish, Arabic and Amharic and was that Xhosa she could hear? She only recognised it because Lilian had spoken it, not fluently, but she'd had a collection of eclectic expressions that she'd produce now and then with a flourish. One such came back to Ros suddenly. It was the summer she had turned thirteen, that age when, seemingly overnight, parents become an affliction. She had just taken to wearing her long hair parted down the middle so that two curtains obscured her face almost entirely, leaving only the tip of her nose visible. It was partly the fashion of the seventies but also an expression of acute awkwardness not only in response to her own existence, but also to her mother's. By any stretch of the imagination, Lilian was an embarrassing parent; she had a habit of speaking her mind and would loudly say to someone's face what others would say only behind their back. She was a vigilant consumer and let it be known when things failed to meet her exacting high standards. Coupled with her flamboyant appearance (Lilian's clothes always looked like fancy dress; she wore high heels and satin skirts with slits up the sides to show off her shapely legs even when shopping in Mac Fisheries), the effect of her frequent complaints was, for Ros, buttock-clenching discomfort. On this particular occasion, Lilian had marched into a shop to take back a dress that Ros had bought a few days before, along the seam of which Lilian's eagle eyes had discerned the tiniest of tears. The sales assistant's insolent lethargy had provoked Lilian into raising her already loud voice further and calling for the manager. Ros tensed her whole body and tried to shrink into herself in the hope that she might disappear altogether.

'Mommy, for God's sake,' she'd muttered.

'Ros, this is an important lesson in life. There's a Xhosa expression you should know: "*usana olungakhaliyo lufel' embelekweni*". It means, "a baby that does not cry out, dies on its mother's back".'

'What the hell's that got to do with anything?' Ros said, made even more distressed by her mother talking stridently in an African language with unfamiliar and resounding clicks where consonants should be.

'If you don't complain about something, nothing will happen

and the problem will persist. It's something you should consider when making choices in your life.'

The loud beep of a car horn brought Ros back to the present and she went into the shop, made suddenly hungry by the aromas she had been inhaling. She hadn't eaten all day, but once inside, her appetite left her again. She passed the halal meat counter and saw that there were faces for sale. Really. Whole skinned sheep's heads, with unblinking, staring eyes. A movement caught her eye, the turn of a shoulder as someone disappeared around the corner of an aisle. Lilian? A sudden rush of adrenalin propelled Ros forward. In front of her, she could see the familiar hurried movements and red hair of her mother. She felt the relief of the small child who thinks she is lost and searches among the skirts at eye-level, terror mounting, until she finds the one that means home to her. Ros was reaching out, on the point of tapping the woman on her shoulder and calling her name, when the woman turned and gave the quizzical, tight smile of someone surprised by the unnaturally close proximity of a stranger. Ros let her hand fall and hurried out of the shop. Is this what it feels like, she wondered, to lose your grip on reality? She forced herself to walk briskly past the turning into Mike's road, although she felt drawn to hurry up it and stand vigil outside his house to check if he were alone or whether, through a gap in the curtains, she might be able to make out his silhouette as he held the Spanish assistant in the close embrace of a future that excluded her.

Her own house was in darkness and for a moment she wished that everything was as it had once been: the boys tiny again and safely asleep in bed, her husband reading on the sofa waiting for her to return home. As she turned the key in the door, a figure emerged, causing her to jump. It was Charlie.

'You gave me a fright,' Ros said, her heart thumping with fear.

Charlie stood in front of her.

'I thought I'd drop by,' he said, 'I know how you hate being alone.'

Ros hugged him gratefully.

She told Charlie about her visit to Mike earlier and her certainty of his liaison with the Spanish girl.

'Right,' Charlie said, 'enough moping about; you need to find the equivalent of Gaydar.'

'What's that?'

'It's the online shopping mall for homosexuals.' Charlie turned Ros around to face him, suddenly earnest. 'You have to stop thinking about the past and concentrate on the future.'

'You're right,' Ros said, 'I am mired in the past and every time I try to move forward, I'm sucked back.'

'I'm worried about you. It's time you got out of the quicksand and looked forward. I think it might help if you indulged in a little sexual retail therapy.'

'I already have.' The words came out before Ros was aware of forming them.

'You have what?'

'Shopped a little,' she paused. 'Well, window-shopped that is, without making an actual purchase. On StartingOver.com, the site for the newly single.'

'And?'

'And nothing … so far. But I was considering the possibility of trying some meaningless sex at some point in the near future.'

'Don't be silly,' said Charlie, 'you're a woman, women can't do meaningless sex.'

'Yes, we can,' Ros said, remembering Sally-Ann.

'You can't, you know you can't.' Charlie paused. 'God knows, even I'm getting a little tired of it, but only a little.'

'Perhaps we should both try girls,' Ros said.

Charlie laughed and he and Ros pulled faces at each other, both queasy at the thought.

'I wonder if anyone's life unfolds in the way they envisage,' said Ros. She felt a great wave of sadness engulf her. 'That's probably a good thing as well as a bad one.'

'What do you mean?'

'Well, if one knew how the story ended, would one have the energy to embark on the journey?' Ros said. 'The thing about making choices in life is that you're not always aware that you're making them or what their significance is and by the time you become aware, it's usually too late.'

They spent the rest of the evening drinking and talking. Ros was about to tell Charlie about her visit to the clairvoyant and Lilian's seemingly constant presence, but he had borne the brunt of so much of her grief over the past year that she remained silent.

'I met a gorgeous twenty-nine-year-old last week,' Charlie said, refilling their glasses. 'He was six foot five with size thirteen feet. I woke up to feel his foot moving over my face like a giant squid. It completely covered my face and was surprisingly erotic.'

'Are you going to see him again?' Ros asked.

'Might do, but there are so many other molluscs in the sea. He wasn't much of a conversationalist.' Charlie settled more comfortably on the sofa. 'Although you don't satisfy my carnal desires, Ros, I can't think why we aren't married. It's so much nicer being here with you than it is being alone in my own house. I may have to move in.'

'The door is always open,' Ros said, wishing he would and trying not to think how Mike was probably curled up in bed with La Española.

We're all frightened of being alone, she reflected, thinking that the fear of loneliness might be truer for men generally than for women. The so-called two-week window wasn't solely due to women snapping up available men, but also to men's terror of being on their own. And another thing; she couldn't help feeling that men, straight or gay, were less forgiving of their partner's ageing than were women. Perhaps it was too potent a reminder of their own mortality. She felt renewed rage at Mike's predictability in falling into the taut, smooth arms of a younger woman. Although, she was forced to remind herself, their parting had been precipitated by her rather than by him, which meant, irritatingly, that she had no one but herself to blame for the fact that she was now alone. Perhaps Sally-Ann wasn't so foolish, perhaps she really should try meaningless sex and, by way of revenge, choose for her partner a much younger man?

'What's your handy tip for life after marriage, Mrs B.?' Ros asked. She was feeling a little drunk and lying on the sofa with her feet on Charlie's lap. Charlie was an encyclopaedia of household tips, a twenty-first-century Mrs Beeton. So much so that Ros had given him the nickname Mrs B.

'Surprisingly, it's not quite as easy to erase the pain of heartbreak as it is a red-wine stain from a carpet,' Charlie said, 'but the strong arms of a handsome man might help to lessen it a little.'

Ros started crying and couldn't seem to stop, so later Charlie said he'd stay the night and he climbed into Ros's bed where they curled around each other like animals seeking warmth.

'I suppose a shag's out of the question?' Charlie asked.

Ros laughed and put her head on his shoulder. It felt nice to have a warm male body in her bed again and to be lulled by the steady breathing of another.

'I love you being my gay husband,' she said. 'And I won't even mind if you use other men for sex.'

She was joking, but as she drifted off to sleep, there was a part of her that couldn't help feeling that a gay husband might just be the ideal solution.

'Me too,' Charlie answered, 'you're the perfect secret wife.'

Chapter Nine

The start of a new school term. She'd been longing for it, but as soon as Ros walked into her office and looked at the neatly typed note of things to do that had been left for her by the school secretary, she found herself yearning for the freedom of the holidays. It was eight a.m., but there'd already been an 'incident' and the offender was waiting to be summoned in. The girl started talking before she was in the door.

'You know I don't normally hit girls I don't know, right? If I know a girl, I might hit her like, you know.'

Ros wasn't entirely sure of the logic of this statement, but found herself nodding nonetheless.

'But this girl, right, she was comin' up to me and smilin' in my face and I was like, I don't know you, why you comin' up and smilin' in my face?'

'What's wrong with someone smiling at you, Versace?' Ros asked.

Versace Porsche Brown kissed her teeth and tossed her ponytail over her shoulder. She looked Ros up and down. Ros was tempted to see what would happen if she, Ros, smiled in her face.

'It's not acceptable behaviour,' Ros continued. 'I thought we'd agreed at the end of last term that this term would be different. I know you're leaving this summer after GCSE, but try and make an effort for the rest of your time here. I expect to see you in detention tomorrow.'

'Yeah, well you tell that girl if she ever come near me again with her cheesy little grin, I'll smack her up big time.' Versace hitched her skirt up so that it just skimmed her bottom and strutted out without looking back.

Ros sighed and looked out of the window. In the playground, she could see Versace walk over to the group of girls who made up her 'crew'. Aaron, who was in Year 12, the class above, joined them and put his hand on Versace's bottom in a lazy gesture of possession. One of the other girls started shouting at him and drew her hand back as if to strike him. He must have appeased her somehow as she allowed her hand to fall. Ros never ceased to be amazed by the incipient violence that simmered in these young boys and girls, ready to erupt at the slightest provocation. Versace, Ysatis, Chanel, Hollywood: the names given to many of the pupils were an indication of their parents' aspirations and represented designer lifestyles where material success was everything. Nowadays, Ros reflected, the power of the name was all and displayed everywhere; on the back pockets of jeans, stitched onto breast pockets and on the front of baseball caps and glinting on the sides of trainers. In former years, names like Hope, Liberty, Happiness and Joy had similarly conferred unreasonable levels of expectation on those who bore them; but they were at least states worthy of ambition, to do with *being* rather than *having*. These days, everyone wanted to be rich and famous, so much so that it had become one word, 'richnfamous' and was the central ambition instead of the occasional and accidental by-product of being good at your job. When Ros was at school, no one would openly have admitted to so crass a purpose, but that was in the seventies when they were still busy trying to make the world a better place. Perhaps she remembered wrongly and it was the fate of each generation to recollect their youth as somehow better and nobler. In any event, Ros couldn't help feeling that there should be a law against giving children silly names.

At break, Ros locked her office door and logged on to StartingOver. Her inbox held an email.

Dear Sally, I like your profile. I too am just out of a long relationship. It's strange isn't it to be talking to strangers and hoping to form some kind of connection? I'm not really sure what I'm seeking, at this point perhaps nothing more than to reach across cyberspace and make contact with someone who feels as I do. What can I tell you about myself? Any kind of description feels like I'm offering second-hand goods for sale. I'm forty-six, my wife and I have parted and I'm not quite sure why. I think we both felt that there could be more to life and if there was, we'd better find out before it was too late. You know how you lose your joy both in yourself and in each other? Well, that's what happened to us. I hate it when people use the words of others instead of making up their own words, so I apologise in advance, but you know that song about piña colada and getting caught in the rain? Well, I guess that's what I want, romance and the delight of discovering someone new. Shall we talk? Write back if you'd like to. Jimmy.

Ros smiled. This one didn't sound like a sex-crazed imbecile; between the lines of his simple letter she could discern the presence of someone real and he correctly used the tilde above the letter 'n' in 'piña'. Ros liked good grammar and linguistic accuracy in a man.

Hi Jimmy, I'm at work and shouldn't be on here at all, but I liked your email. Let's talk on line; I'll check later to see whether you're here. About 8 o'clock tonight? Must dash. Sally.

Ros was just about to log off when someone called Pleasure4U 'whistled' at her.

Sally, you sound gorgeous. I'd like to take you to a desert island and tie ribbons in your hair ...

Ros looked at her watch. She had five minutes until her next lesson.

Mmm, that sounds nice, and what would you expect in return?

Well, why shouldn't she flirt – he couldn't see her after all and she need never appear from behind the screen of virtual reality if she chose not to.

`I'd expect you to lie naked in my arms and let me make love to you with the waves lapping at our feet.`

Corny, but somehow arousing.

`I bet you say that to all the girls.`

`Only to exciting older women whom I dream of possessing.`

'Whom' and not 'who', that was a good sign. But, older? God, how old was he?

`How old are you?`

`Does it matter?`

`No, but tell me.`

`I'm thirty-five.`

The bell rang, startling Ros.

`Got to go. Talk later? I'll be back on here at eight tonight.`

She had a date with two different men at eight and could 'see' them both at the same time without fear of discovery. The Internet was a marvellous thing; it was hard to tear herself away from her computer, she felt like Alice in Wonderland; she'd chanced upon a magical world where everything seemed to be labelled 'eat me' and she felt a small frisson of delicious fear at what the consequences might be.

There were only six in her A level English class and they were studying *Bleak House*. The previous term, Ros had taken them to the Inns of Court, where, within the winding alleyways close to a hundred and fifty years later, it was still possible to imagine that the lawsuit of Jarndyce and Jarndyce rumbled on. Matt, a tall and clever sixth-former with light blue eyes and hair painstakingly hand-twisted into corkscrew curls had been reading his essay aloud to the rest of the class.

'... In conclusion, secret lives and their consequences form the central theme of Dickens's novel juxtaposed with the tortuous workings of the British legal system, which feeds on the lives of the interested parties with an appetite that will not be sated any time soon.'

It had all gone so well and suddenly Matt had spoiled it. He'd been unable to resist lapsing into what Ros called '*Heat*-speak', the ubiquitous, lazy prose of the magazine generation. 'Any time soon'. What was wrong with the word 'never'? '... with an appetite that will never be sated'. She was aware of how precarious Matt's confidence was and didn't want to pull him up on this in front of the rest of the class. At the same time, she felt bound to uphold what she considered to be certain absolutes of the English language and she could hear Lilian's voice urging her to correct him. The two of them had shared this zeal to preserve the written word. She hadn't thought of Lilian at all today and her renewed presence in her head both pleased and dismayed her. She'd been glad of the excuse afforded her by Charlie's appearance the previous night not to return to sorting Lilian's papers. After the episode in the shop on her way home, she'd begun to fear for her sanity. Now, once again, it felt to Ros as though Lilian were hovering on the periphery of her vision, a shadow just barely discernible at the side of the cupboard next to the blackboard. Matt was looking at her expectantly; only the repetitive action of his thumb and forefinger worrying at the edge of his essay belied his apparent self-assurance.

'Excellent, Matt,' Ros said. There was plenty of time to take up the issue with him in private. After all, the lazy use of colloquial phrases wasn't a matter that was likely to disappear 'any time soon'. Ros indicated to him that he should sit down.

'It's clear that you've understood the book's central themes and the importance of the past to the present, how people's actions in the past can resonate into the future and change the lives of others. Very good work indeed.'

Matt blushed with pleasure while managing to settle his body into a position that announced to his classmates that he was still cool: hands in pockets, legs wide apart and head slightly flung back with his chin raised in what, if Ros didn't know him better, one might assume was a gesture of insolence. Jamila, the pretty Asian girl seated next to him, threw him a speculative glance that signalled a certain promise and caused Matt to sit up a little straighter and smile, anticipation lifting his mouth at its edges. What do you know, his expression seemed to say, this being clever business might even get me laid.

Ros addressed the whole group. 'I'd like you all to think of something in your past that has come back to haunt you. Or in the past of someone you know, or make it up if you like, it doesn't have to be true. Play with it, create a character and a scenario that you think could have repercussions on your, or your character's, present life, or find someone real or imagined that you think you know and see whether new information about their lives or circumstances changes the way you think about them.'

Chantelle, a heavy blonde whose body, Ros couldn't help thinking, seemed to be awaiting the earliest opportunity of the pregnancy and birth of a first baby before inflating into obesity, was texting her boyfriend on her mobile phone. She paused and looked up at Ros and her expression changed. Ros could see that she had awakened Chantelle's interest and imagination and was reminded of why she loved her job; it was something that she had forgotten over the past few months. She regretted her sneering appraisal of Chantelle's destiny of only a moment before and reminded herself that what she did could make a difference. But if she, their teacher, fell into the trap of easy stereotyping, what hope was there for these kids? So, in the staffroom a few minutes later, she answered more sharply than she intended when Melanie Booker, the Head of Science, asked her mockingly how tomorrow's captains of industry were shaping up that morning.

'When were these taken?' Jaime asked Ros. She was holding the photos that Ros had found in Lilian's suitcase.

'This one was taken in nineteen fifty-five,' Ros said, handing her the photo that she'd found in Lilian's handbag.

Jaime looked at it carefully. They were sitting in the staffroom. It was lunch break and the laughter and shouts of the pupils in the playground below could still be heard through windows that had been tightly closed against the January cold.

'This is amazing,' Jaime said, 'look, he's got his arm around her.'

'Where?' Ros leant over, squinting at the small black and white photograph. Jaime was right, the man's arm encircled Lilian's waist and Lilian was laughing, her head thrown back against his shoulder. She hadn't registered the intimacy of their pose before now.

'Do you realise how extraordinary this is?' Jaime said. 'I mean, the picture was taken at the height of apartheid, soon after the National Party had passed a whole bunch of new laws stating that whites and blacks couldn't live in the same areas or have any sort of sexual relationship with each other, you know, actually criminalising it and making it against the law.'

'Yes, of course,' Ros was bemused.

Jaime pointed to the writing below the picture of Sipho that had been taped to the lid of the suitcase.

'*Amandla! Ngawethu!* It means power to the people, the call and response of the ANC.'

'Oh my God . . .' Ros said.

'What is it?'

'I've just realised; today is the anniversary of her death. It's odd, I mean, I've been dreading it and have felt terrible the past few days, you know, really thinking about her a lot and seeing and hearing her everywhere and then today, January the ninth, the actual day she died, I forgot all about the fact that it's the actual anniversary.'

'You've already marked the anniversary over the past week, it's not really the day itself that's important, is it?' Jaime laid a comforting hand on Ros's arm.

'Don't be nice to me or I'll cry,' Ros said.

'Well, I must say these photos are amazing.' Jaime changed the subject. 'She was active in the ANC, wasn't she?'

'Yes, I don't know to what extent. She didn't speak about it much, but she was definitely part of that whole anti-apartheid set.'

'Will you have a look and see if there's anything else among her stuff?' Jaime asked. 'It would be great to have some primary source material to show my Year Elevens. They're doing a project on South Africa from nineteen forty-eight.'

Ros promised to look while wondering whether she'd really have the stomach to go through Lilian's papers.

'You're so lucky not to have to live with your husband,' Jaime said, sinking her teeth into a piece of bread and butter pudding that she didn't even pretend to hide from Ros. 'I've been having fantasies about being single. I'd opt for crisp white sheets on my bed too, wouldn't have to account for my every action and could do exactly what I wanted on the weekends the kids were with their father.'

'It's funny, isn't it,' Ros said, 'when you're single you want to be married and when you're married the reverse is true. There's something perverse in human nature: we always want the opposite of what we have.'

She glanced over and saw Ant sitting by the window, his head buried in a book.

'I think Ant must be regretting his new marriage,' Ros said.

'What makes you say that?' asked Jaime.

'He told me that he only gets sex in return for odd jobs.' Ros nodded towards the weighty book Ant held in his hands, its title, *Assembling Flat-Packs Made Easy*.

'Not really?' Jaime asked.

'Fact.'

'Wonder what he has to do for oral sex?'

'I'd have thought *that* would require major building work,' said Ros.

'A conservatory?' Jaime and Ros giggled.

'What?' said Ant, looking up, disturbed from his careful study.

'Remarrying. Who was it said it was the triumph of optimism over experience?' Ros said.

'Samuel Johnson,' said Ant, 'but I think it was hope.'

'What was?'

'Hope, not optimism.' Ros couldn't help thinking that for a newly remarried man, Ant seemed markedly lacking in either.

'Are you sure it wasn't Wilde?' Jaime said.

'No,' Ros shook her head. 'He said, "Marriage is the triumph of imagination over intelligence."'

'I think both of them may have been right.' Ant's smile didn't quite reach his eyes. He got up and joined them.

'Living gladly apart, that's the answer,' Jaime said.

'Meaning?' asked Ros.

'It's the new craze, I read about it in a magazine, so it must be true. Living gladly apart, or living apart together – you're married or whatever, but you have separate houses.'

'Two houses?' Ant looked even more bleak, 'That would mean even more flat-pack assembly.' He looked longingly at Lola, the pretty Spanish language assistant who was standing by the window and giggling into her mobile phone. His expression seemed to say, now there's a girl who wouldn't make you put up shelves before she let you touch her.

'I've found a better solution,' Ros said. 'A gay husband. That way you still have someone to empty the rubbish and lift heavy objects.'

'*No me digas*,' Lola was saying, '*quiero saber todo, nos vemos a las cinco*.' She hung up and approached the others 'My girlfrien', Marie-Carmen, she have new boyfrien'. Is bery funny,' Lola said, 'is ol' man, but she like her.'

'Him,' Ros said automatically, 'she likes him.'

Lola brushed away Ros's correction of her grammar as one might a troublesome fly.

'She say me, she go in his house with a cheese we have in Espain to give like a present, is look like this,' here Lola patted one of her breasts, matter-of-factly and rather vigorously, 'and also name is same, we call *tetilla* and then she take off the sweater. She is without the bra. English man is very strange; he only look at her *tetillas* and not do nuffing.'

Ros, overwhelmed by so many grammatical transgressions, was about to wade in, but Ant held up a hand like a policeman stopping traffic, eager to hear the rest of the story.

'What do you mean?' he asked.

'He say he too ol' for her and tell her to put the sweater on.'

'You mean she offered him naked breasts unconditionally and he turned them down?' Ant was incredulous.

'So he's not her boyfriend after all?' Ros said.

'Maybe no now, but he will be,' Lola said, with the twenty-two-year-old's confidence in her sexual power. 'She tell him he will make sex with her, even if not this day, then soon.'

'What does she do, this friend?' asked Ros, the kernel of a suspicion forming within her.

'Marie-Carmen? She also the language assistant like me and also from Sevilla, same town like me.'

'Did she say what the man's name was?' Ros tried to sound casual.

'Is Miguel.'

Well, thought Ros. Yes. Of course. It would be. Miguel, Michael, Mike. That's how small the world was. Her very own husband the target for Lola's friend's sexual advances. She was sure of it. Ros realised that the peculiar object on the plate Mike had been holding, dome-shaped and ending in a nipple-like point, must have been the very cheese of which Lola spoke. (And, one part of her mind thought distractedly, she'd like to see the Spanish assistant cope with that particular grammatical construction.) Mike, after all, was a DILF. Liz, Sid's girlfriend, had explained the phenomenon to her only last week over a late-night glass of wine. DILFs, MILFs, SILFs, BILFs: Dads, Mothers, Sisters, Brothers I'd Like to Fuck; easy teenage shorthand for assessing the desirability of a friend's relatives. Although, in this case, Mike was more accurately a TILF, Teacher I'd Like to Fuck. She knew that Mike was free to do as he pleased, to partake of whichever sexual fruits were on offer, as indeed was she, but that didn't mean she had to be happy about it.

She could just imagine the scene, Marie-Carmen pushing her long dark hair up against her head with both hands so that it framed her face, leaning over to Mike and kissing him on the cheek or perhaps the lips, her mouth lingering; allowing his senses to fill with her, persuading him he would surrender soon. He feeling himself begin to harden and bustling her out of the front door before his resolve weakened, wondering all the while how her naked skin would feel and how her mouth might taste. She could imagine Mike worrying about how he should behave with her now, when he saw her at school; whether he should ignore her or be polite and friendly, while, somewhere in an area just above his groin, he would perhaps feel the flicker of desire and certainly something else, very like possibility. Should he part his hair behind? Did he dare to eat a peach? Was Mike a modern-day Prufrock growing bolder by the second as gradually he understood why Marie-Carmen was so sure that it was only a matter of time before he succumbed to her charms and, really, did it matter so very much if he were older than she? That was the trouble with knowing someone so well, Ros thought, swallowing hard in an attempt to clear the nut of misery that obstructed her throat, you could imagine all too well how they might behave in any given situation. And then, yesterday, Marie-Carmen must have called on Mike again on the pretext of taking Ruffy out for a walk. Did she think that the way to a man's heart was through his dog? If so, she was probably right.

'Are you OK, Ros?' Jaime asked, looking at Ros with concern.

Ros dug her fingernails into her palms and forced a smile. ''Course, I'm fine, why?'

She was saved from further scrutiny by Peter Seers's arrival. He had caught them unawares.

'The Headmistress wants to see you, Ros,' he said, with the satisfied expression of someone imparting bad news, 'she looked rather stern.'

Ros felt a pang of terror, had she been caught out by the IT police for flirting on the Internet?

'It's about your tattoo,' Peter said smugly, 'she told me.' He cleared his throat as he always did when about to embark on a lecture and continued, 'Tattoos started in Egypt between 2800 and 2600 BC and travelled with the centuries in all directions throughout the world. But approval and disapproval of tattoos has ebbed and flowed: at times the mark of an aristocrat, at others, of savages, sometimes with religious connotations, where even priests have borne them, sometimes with magical meaning and used to differentiate tribes.'

Ros, Jaime and Ant exchanged desperate glances.

'I'd better hurry if the Head wants me,' Ros said, fleeing.

'Where, last century, tattoos became the trademark of the sailor in the western world ...' Ros could hear Peter's voice booming after her as she fled from the staffroom. Jaime searching frantically for her own salvation, picked up the first pile of books she could see, which happened to be French textbooks. Mme Sauvage, who had just come in to collect them herself, was about to protest.

'*L'Ange du Mort*,' Jaime whispered.

'Oh, *mais, dis-donc, bien sûr, tout est compris*,' Mme Sauvage answered, quickly turning on her heel, lest she be trapped herself.

Ant made a show of looking at his watch and left the room briskly, immediately followed by Jaime, Peter's voice trailing after them.

'... and in some countries of the convicted criminal. Tattooing in Soviet prisons, for example, was elevated to an art form and there are books dedicated to the science of decoding prison tattoos.'

Ros found Versace sitting outside the Headmistress's study.

'What have you done now?' Ros asked, joining her on the bench of shame, the area where recidivist pupils took their seat to await their fate.

'Belly-button piercing,' Versace said. She looked Ros up and down. 'What about you?'

'Tattoo,' Ros said, showing the girl her ankle.

'Is that some kind of a mid-life crisis thing, then?' the girl asked, not unkindly.

'Yes,' Ros answered, too bemused by finding herself in the same situation as Versace to do anything other than tell the truth.

Versace nodded in an understanding sort of way. 'You go in first then, get it over with, I'll wait,' she said kindly.

'Thanks,' said Ros, wondering whether she should offer to meet her for a fag in the cloakroom later to compare notes.

'You're hardly setting a good example, Ros,' Penny Shields, the Headmistress, said a few minutes later, pulling vainly at her navy blue suit jacket in an effort to make it meet over her ample bosom. Were there special shops, Ros wondered, particular outfitters that provided the ubiquitous sensible dress that every headmistress appeared to favour? No one else she knew outside the school system wore these judicious skirts and jackets with flowered blouses and stout low-heeled shoes.

Ros tried to explain that she'd been having a difficult time and was getting divorced. Penny Shields seemed to wince; she found the personal details of her staff's lives distasteful.

'Yes, yes,' she said, 'well, don't do it again or if you do, for heaven's sake get it done in a place where no one else can see it; although why anyone would willingly mutilate their flesh is beyond me.'

She waved Ros out. Versace gave Ros a sympathetic look as she passed her and Ros whispered 'good luck' as the girl got up to take her turn in front of the Headmistress.

It was a relief to have the first day back at work under her belt. Ros cried in her car on the way home that afternoon. Lately she had come to think of her small Renault Clio as the Weepmobile. Nor was she the only car-weeper: on more than one occasion she'd seen other women crying behind the wheel, wiping away steady streams of silent tears as they waited at traffic lights. Even though one was plainly visible to others, the tangible metal parameters of a car nonetheless created the illusion of immunity from anyone else's vision. The end of Ros's marriage, her two sons on the brink of leaving home, the loss of her mother, and her own inevitable descent from her prime all combined to create a sadness that seemed to seep from her as though she were saturated in it and could no longer contain it within herself. She carefully touched the dashboard of her car with both hands, palms outstretched, to ward off any evil spirits that might be lurking unseen.

I'm turning into my mother, Ros thought, a potent memory infusing her of Lilian stretching her own hands towards the dashboard of her car in pagan ritual to ensure her and Ros's continued safekeeping. (Dashboards used to be made of walnut wood and Lilian had been insistent that this earlier incarnation conferred magical properties on the moulded plastic that had replaced it.) Lilian and Ros were both a curious blend of fearfulness and courage, both happy to travel alone and talk to strangers, but afraid of burglars and reluctant to sleep in empty houses. 'We're where the old world meets the new,' Lilian used to say, laughing at their shared superstitious nature.

The recollection that Charlie would be joining her for supper later and her Internet dates cheered Ros briefly and she rummaged in her handbag for a tissue. Her eyes on the road, Ros drew out the piece of paper Joti had put there the day before and which, until now, she had forgotten. She waited until she'd pulled up at the lights at the junction with Bloemfontein Road before glancing at it.

Shepherd's Bush Buddhist Centre invites you to learn the peaceful art of meditation. This month's practice will begin with the Fire Sermon; the Buddha's famous teaching to the matted-haired fire worshippers. With Vilananda who has recently returned from the Himalayan retreat.

She crumpled the piece of paper into a ball and would have thrown it out of the window, but years of lecturing Sid and Jack on the evils of, what they called, litter-buggery prevented her. The brief interval of time that elapsed between the traffic light changing, Ros's failure to move and the wrath of the motorist behind her was as accurate a definition of the split second as one could hope to find. The angry honking made Ros slow down and the driver behind accelerated to overtake her.

'Fuck off, wanker,' she shouted, displaying the relevant attendant hand gestures and taking refuge in rage rather than in the fresh tears that threatened to fall.

The window on the passenger side of the car next to her glided down electronically as the driver drew up alongside her.

Leaning over, Penny Shields said, 'Steady on, Ros, I was only trying to tell you your door wasn't closed properly.'

'Oh gosh, I'm so sorry,' said Ros. Carpeted by the Head twice in one day. She could feel the heat suffusing her and had no doubt that her face had turned red. 'I thought you were a road-rager.'

'No,' the Headmistress said wryly, 'it would appear that that honour is all yours.' She gave Ros a final disapproving look and drove off.

Ros couldn't help laughing at herself for being caught swearing by Teacher. The laughter changed her mood, making her feel like a teenager and she examined her face in her rear-view mirror. She felt, for the first time in ages, oddly accepting, even approving, of what she saw there: an older woman certainly than the image of herself she carried in her head, but an attractive one nonetheless with clear almond-shaped blue eyes, weeping notwithstanding, and a still youthful complexion. Her sadness had been extinguished. Sometimes she felt that danger had just passed her by, had grazed her or whispered in her ear like a warning and that if she'd been a moment earlier or later, it might have caught her. Ros felt the sudden and urgent need to come back to life and re-enter the world. If Mike could take a lover, why then so could she. She felt as full of expectation as the nascent butterflies in Lilian's African shoeboxes might have felt all those years before, or indeed as her own tattooed swallowtail might, poised for flight on her still gently throbbing ankle.

Ros stopped off at Hari's, the homeopathic chemist, on her way home. A candle was burning on his counter and the atmosphere was suffused with a musky odour.

'What's that?' Ros asked.

'Sandalwood,' Hari answered.

He was squeezing drops into a bottle. A woman stood in front of the counter with her dog, a greyhound, nervously pacing beside her. Hari turned to her, holding the bottle up for her inspection.

'I have put six drops of lavender, one drop of neroli and four drops of marjoram. Place a few drops on the tips of his ears and rub a little on his head and spine. It works very well on greyhounds and should help calm him down and bring him to a place of acceptance.'

Ros thought this was rather missing the point of greyhounds.

After all, wasn't their nervy nature the very thing that made them good at their job? Why else would they bolt out of hatches and chase mechanical hares?

'He's retired,' the dog's owner said as though reading her thoughts, 'and he needs to calm down.' The dog moved up and down, anxiously turning its head this way and that as though to reinforce her words.

Ros gave a friendly talking-to-strangers-in-shops laugh, 'Yes, well, don't we all,' she acknowledged, wondering whether she should buy some to massage not only into her own ears, but also into those of Dogman's querulous hounds.

'Take one of these candles, it brings peace and acceptance,' Hari said to Ros, indicating the sandalwood. 'The flame of a candle has always been a metaphor for the soul. It reflects the spiritual and ethical changes we would like to bring about in ourselves and burns as a reminder and symbol of our desires.'

'Gosh,' Ros said, 'a small burning flame can do all that?'

'Sometimes we have to hand our dreams over to a force more powerful than ourselves,' Hari said sternly.

Ros felt sad that the small flame of a candle could be more powerful than her, but bought it anyway, and some lavender oil to place on her pillow in order that she might sleep more peacefully.

Arriving home, she examined her post: the usual bills and declamatory mail offering her untold wealth provided she filled out forms of immeasurable complexity. The house was quiet, a premonition of her childless future. Ros picked up an A4 manila envelope and glanced at it briefly, noting that it carried an American postmark. She was certain the bin would be the final resting place for all her mail. (Sometimes she didn't know why she bothered to open it at all, it was just like when the boys were small and wouldn't eat their vegetables – she'd thought then that she might as well cut out the middleman, simply take the vegetables out of the fridge and throw them straight into the bin without all the unnecessary nonsense of peeling, cooking and putting them on the boys' plates before scraping them away minutes later as so much garbage.) She stuffed everything into her handbag to deal with at a later date, a habit that had always infuriated Mike, which she was now free to indulge.

It was six o'clock. The boys were still staying with Mike and Charlie wouldn't be over for at least an hour. Ros made herself a cup of oolong tea (magical green tea fermented on the plains of China that promised to see off cancer and weight gain) and carried her cup gingerly towards the sofa.

'How many times have I told you not to walk with liquids?' It was her mother's voice again, loud and clear. Ros jumped, spilling some of her tea onto the beige carpet.

'You see,' the voice scolded, 'you've done it again.'

Walking with liquids was forbidden, especially with hot ones. It had been one of Lilian's many house rules and was absolute. It didn't deal with the issue of how to get a cup of tea or coffee from one room to another and when Ros had raised this, her mother stated that eating and drinking should take place only in the kitchen area.

'What about when you have friends over and you all drink coffee in the living room?' Ros had asked with a child's faultless logic.

'That's different, we're grown-ups,' her mother answered. Ros hated it when she took refuge in that 'I'm a grown-up' stuff. In any event, as a child, Ros had disobeyed the liquids rule (and countless others) constantly, but no matter how carefully she tried to carry her tea or coffee from one room to another, walking slowly, both hands gripped around the mug, she was sure to trip or miss her footing and some of the drink would inevitably fall onto the carpet, leaving tangible evidence of her disobedience. In order not to replicate with her own children her mother's strictness in matters pertaining to walking with hot liquids, Ros had opted for varnished wooden floors throughout except in the living room, which Mike had insisted should be carpeted.

Ros looked down at the beige carpet. Setting her cup down carefully on a coaster – no hot liquids were allowed straight onto surfaces without protection (she hadn't been able to free herself from her mother's instructions on this point) – she went to get some kitchen paper and dabbed at the carpet to absorb the liquid. The carpet was already covered in stains, the result of years of spillage, but this didn't stop Ros from using sheet after sheet of kitchen towel, trampling the paper with her bare feet as people once trod grapes to yield wine, her objective, unlike them, to absorb liquid and not to release it. She realised that she was now free to replace the carpet with wood, or this way madness lay.

When Charlie arrived, she was reading a book on meditation and wondering whether her situation would benefit from an examination and understanding of her chakras; the centres of subtle energy in the body. He laughed at her, saying that she was a sucker for every charlatan in the land. He was excessively cheerful and was on his hands and knees, still in his sombre lawyer's suit, his tie loosened and his top shirt button undone. He was first sponging small quantities of water onto the dark stain left on the carpet by the oolong tea and then meticulously soaking the water up moments later with kitchen paper.

'Handy tip for tea removal – soda water with half a teaspoon of vinegar,' he explained.

Ros watched him from the small kitchen where she stood cooking a mushroom omelette.

'How come you're so happy?' she asked.

'I had sex on the way home,' Charlie said.

'You didn't really?'

'Yup, stopped at a little bar I know in Soho and was made a fuss of by several lovely young men who all thought I was gorgeous. I disappeared into a back room and had a little frottage with one of them.'

Ros looked at him closely. He wore the obvious look of recent sexual fulfilment.

'I can't believe it; you stop off for a shag like people stop for a pint of milk on their way home. Mike and I split up over three months ago and I'm nowhere near being in a situation where sex with another man is even remotely possible.'

'Meaningless sex,' Charlie said smugly. 'See, I told you women couldn't do it.'

'Did it make you feel good?'

'Fabulous,' Charlie said resolutely, 'it perked me up enormously. I feel just like Ruffy after she's been chewing on a bone; spring in my step, coat all glossy and eyes a sparkle. Can't recommend it highly enough.'

It was well after quarter past eight before Ros logged onto her computer. She could feel the beginnings of an Internet addiction, as all through supper while Charlie had filled her in on his latest job, namely the remarkable case of the sperm burglar, Ros had been aware of the laptop beckoning to her from her desk in the corner of the living room. She'd been deflected when Charlie told her that Angelique, the sperm thief had 'previous' and for the same offence. But in the prior instance, her date (it would be unjust to call him a boyfriend as it was only the second time they had seen each other) had actually caught her in the act of syringing up his sperm with a turkey-baster in preparation for the act of self-insemination. He too was a wealthy man, a venture capitalist who specialised in biotech companies. On that occasion there'd been an ugly tussle between the two of them, which had ended with the contents of the turkey-baster being spilled onto a Persian carpet and two charges of assault. Not so much walking with liquids, more fighting over them, thought Ros, wondering what Lilian might have made of such a thing.

'I still can't believe that a man is financially responsible for progeny he has been tricked into producing,' said Ros. She was eating her omelette and salad with an appetite she hadn't felt for months, although their topic of conversation caused her to push that part of the omelette where the egg whites had not fully cooked to the side of her plate.

'I told you,' Charlie explained patiently, 'the court's duty is to the well-being of the child, irrespective of how he or she came into being.'

'Don't go all lawyerly and pompous on me,' Ros teased. She could just see Charlie in court, bewigged and handsome, holding forth fulsomely with his 'm'lords' and his 'if my learned friends'.

'What about if the man had locked his sperm in a safe and she'd cracked the safe and stolen it, then, whoosh, up her fanny and bingo, baby?'

'Same deal,' said Charlie, 'although,' he added, an idea dawning, 'I wonder if we could then counter-sue her for robbery? In fact, why couldn't we do that anyway since she took the sperm without his permission, which could be construed as theft.'

He'd started pacing up and down, running his hands through his thick blond hair and becoming quite agitated.

'Mind you, she took it from the dustbin, which might imply that he, having thrown it away, had relinquished ownership of it. Hmm, I'm just going to make a couple of calls,' he said.

It was then that Ros had noticed the time and realised that she was late for her Internet dates.

There you are, wrote Jimmy, I was just about to give up on you.

Sorry, Ros typed, I got caught up.

Hi gorgeous. Pleasure4U jumped onto the screen.

This should be interesting, Ros thought. Could she juggle two conversations?

Sal, let's not get into all the 'what do you do' and 'where do you live' stuff. I just want to find out about you as a person, Jimmy wrote.

Does that mean you're the director of a funeral parlour or work in an abattoir or something and you're afraid your occupation will put me off you?

I'm laughing - I would write LOL, but I hate that kind of easy text speak, it makes me want to punch people.

Hmm, aggressive as well as a slaughterer of animals, Ros teased.

Are you there? Pleasure4U was feeling neglected.

Yes, sorry. Can I call you Plezh for short? How's the desert island? How many maidens have you taken there?

LOL, you can call me anything you want baby and none, you're the only one I want to take there.

How do you know? Why did a complete stranger calling her 'baby' excite her so?

I can sense it. I've just sent you my photo.

Sal, have you vanished? It was Jimmy. Ros was finding the juggling quite tricky. Luckily, she typed faster than either of them, but she'd have to take care not to write the wrong thing to the wrong person.

Still here, Jimmy. So, what shall we talk about?

Her mailbox beeped and Ros opened it to find Pleasure4U's photo. He was gorgeous. If a single image could encapsulate a meaningless fuck, Ros thought, then this would be it. Taken on a beach, Plezh stood looking directly into camera. He was tanned with brown hair flecked gold by the sun. She couldn't see the colour of his eyes, but they were fringed by dark lashes so long that they cast a shadow on his cheek. His build was slim but athletic and his swimming shorts revealed a promising bulge. There are few things more disappointing in life, Ros reflected, than the discovery of a penis rather smaller than the one you had hoped for, especially when such a discovery is made beyond the point of no return.

You're gorgeous, Plezh.

Your turn now.

Ros didn't feel confident enough to send him her photo now that she'd seen his. She wasn't even sure if she had one. She sifted through the photo library on her computer and came across a picture of herself taken sitting on a playground swing, aged six. She was wearing a yellow and lilac checked dress that went in at the waist before falling into a gathered skirt that reached to her knees. A matching ribbon caught up her long hair, the ends of which fell in carefully arranged ringlets. Lilian used to curl them painstakingly round her fingers after she had completed the excruciating business of brushing Ros's hair and tying it back. Ros would poke her index finger up the centre of a ringlet until it disappeared from view. Her legs, in their short white socks, were neatly crossed at the ankles and on her feet she wore a pair of black Mary Jane shoes. It was the summer of 1968, the year that Russia invaded Czechoslovakia, French students rioted in Paris and the Beatles released *Revolution*. Ros remembered Lilian sitting by the window in their flat later that same day singing 'Where have all the flowers gone'. The laptop beeped loudly bringing her back to the present. It was Jimmy.

Let's talk about things that have made us happy. For me, a summer's day in the '80s, lying on the grass in a field, laughing and feeling that life was a gift to be enjoyed. It's possible that some kissing may have been involved. Now you.

Ros quickly sent the photo of herself as a child to Plezh and considered how to answer Jimmy. His words threw her back to the eighties and conjured up the memory of how she and Mike had first met. Mike had been Oxford Circus tube station's most popular busker. ('At least he's top of his field,' Ros had explained to a horrified Lilian.) She used to drop a fifty pence piece in his cap every evening on her way home from work. As soon as Mike saw her approaching, he would start a new song, always a love song that he seemed to sing directly to her, following her with his eyes long after she'd disappeared from sight. Once she'd looked back to see if he were still watching and had tripped up over the person ahead, grazing both knees and landing sprawled with her pants showing. The next day, they started talking. Mike was studying music as a mature student at the Guildhall. Ros was working as a junior account executive at an advertising agency that she privately called Bollocks, Baloney and Bullshit. She didn't see much of a future for herself there. (Neither did they, it seemed: they let her go three months later and she went into teaching instead.) Ros and Mike were both twenty-five. Talking turned into coffee and later that night he'd kissed her and, gently stroking her wounded knees, had asked her to come back to his place, student digs around the corner from the British Museum.

'I never sleep with a man on the first date,' Ros said firmly.

'Can't you make an exception for the man you're going to marry?' Mike answered.

Ros looked at him speechlessly.

'It's rare that you so instantly know what you want,' Mike explained, holding her eyes with his own, 'but when you do, you have to seize the moment.'

Ros had looked intently at his handsome face. He had dark green eyes and brown curly hair, and when he laughed a deep dimple appeared in his left cheek. He wore a single gold hoop earring in his left ear and looked like a gypsy. Hard to resist.

'We can have a second date tomorrow if you like,' she said.

Ros shook her head with irritation; she kept getting dragged back to the past when she was trying her best to focus on the present and create a future.

Kissing is often involved in memories of happy times, she wrote, although waterfalls make me joyous too, particularly ones that have a shelf of rock that allows you to stand and watch as the water gushes in front of your face. Every now and then you can put your head into it and feel icy mountain-fresh water wash your head in an action that feels like a ritual cleansing.

Where can we go and do this?

Brecon Beacons is the nearest place I can think of in this country.

Let's go now.

Much more talking needed before I can possibly contemplate undertaking such a sacred act with a stranger. You could be the waterfall murderer for all I know.

Groovy, but I told you, I like older women, not younger ones and certainly not ones as young as this. Nice legs though.

It was Plezh, responding to her photo. Did anyone actually say 'groovy' any more? Charlie appeared suddenly at her shoulder.

'Nice,' he said, pointing to the photograph of Plezh that was still on her screen. 'Ask him if he goes both ways.'

'Get off, he's mine,' said Ros, 'although I've also got a rather nice chap here called Jimmy who gives better conversation.'

'You see you just don't get it.' Charlie held out his hands on either side of him and moved them up and down as though weighing something. 'Conversation, meaningless fuck, which is it that you want? Conversation you've got, I can give you that, that's what a gay husband is for. But what you need is a good old-fashioned seeing-to and much as I love you, that, I'm afraid, is way beyond my remit. This guy, on the other hand, looks perfect for the job; in fact his photo looks like it could appear in a Meaningless Fuck mail-order catalogue if such a thing existed.'

'That's all very well, but now he wants to see a photo of me.'

'So send him one, you're gorgeous.'

I like talking to you, waterfall woman; I'll think of you when next I'm in the shower. Have to run now. Jim x

That just left Plezh for now. She chickened out.

Got to go, will sort out a photo and send next time.

Not fair, Plezh pouted, I showed you mine . . . you know how it goes.

Will send one tomorrow, kiss kiss, Sal.

The weather had cleared and a pale moon shone in through the sitting room window. Ros and Charlie curled up on the sofa and shared the remains of the bottle of wine they'd had for supper. Charlie had linked his iPod to Ros's old stereo system and the soundtrack to *Cabaret* played softly in the background.

'You're such a showgirl, Charlie,' Ros said, nudging him affectionately with her toe.

'I feel very happy,' Charlie said.

And so, Ros realised, with a start of surprise, did she.

*

She got up early on Saturday morning. The boys were at home for the weekend and Charlie had gone to Amsterdam for a weekend of libidinous homosexual revelry. Perhaps he was right, it was a male thing and sex for women was necessarily loaded with meaning. Ros hadn't ruled out the possibility of having sex with Plezh, or indeed with Jimmy. Of the two, Plezh seemed least complicated and she was tempted to try it out. She'd been talking to them both online again and had sent Plezh a photograph of herself that had been taken a year ago on Brighton beach. Her face had been fortuitously backlit; the rays of a sun that seemed to sigh with satisfaction at the end of a good day's work illuminated her hair in such a way as to provide a perfect frame for her heart-shaped face. Although her face was slightly turned away from the camera, her eyes were turned back towards it and her lips were parted in a half-smile. Ros didn't usually like photographs of herself – she rarely recognised herself in them – but this one pleased her and seemed to go some way towards expressing who she was. Plezh had been impressed.

He'd written, Not just ribbons, baby, I want to rub coconut oil in your skin, every inch of it. When can we meet?

Soon, she had answered, but not yet.

She let herself out of the flat quietly, taking care not to wake the boys. The dogs began their low snarling as she walked past their gate. Ros snarled back and felt a sudden pang of longing for Ruffy. It was her turn to have her and Mike had been evasive about when he would return the dog. She drove to Chiswick and settled herself in an armchair in a coffee shop. There was only one other person there, a woman, sitting reading a magazine. She looked up briefly as Ros passed and smiled. Ros emptied the contents of her handbag on the table and prepared to embark on its long over-due ritual cleansing. She pulled out the mail she'd been carrying around unopened and looked more closely at the manila envelope and its postmark. Boston, USA. She didn't recognise the hand-writing, but it seemed to belong to a different era and reminded her of Lilian's. Clare Voyante's words, spoken towards the end of their session, echoed in her head: 'She says you're to watch out for the post, dear.' Ros felt uneasy and placed the envelope to one side while she continued to sort the rest of her bag's contents. Carefully, she arranged items into piles and wrote a list of bills to pay and things to do, reflecting as she completed it how much it reminded her of all the many lists Lilian used to draw up. She collected the pile of rubbish that her sorting had generated and looked around for a bin. She was procrastinating, uneasy about the unknown envelope that hovered on the periphery of her vision whichever way she turned her head; certain that its contents were somehow connected to Lilian. Finally, she glanced through the window at the awakening High Street, opened the envelope and began to read.

Dear Ros,

My name is Gloria. I am an old friend of your mother's from South Africa. I last saw you when you were a very young child but Lilian sent me photos of you over the years and I have followed your progress always wishing that I could have been a part of your life. A few years ago, some of us were asked to write 'books' of our early years growing up in South Africa and of our involvement in the anti-Apartheid movement. The plan was that these accounts, commissioned by the Truth and Reconciliation Committee, would be held in an archive in South Africa. Ten days ago, I had a vivid dream about Lilian. She was standing at the end of my bed and she said, 'Show my book to Ros. Perhaps she will understand my actions and forgive them, as I myself have never been able to.' The following morning, I received a letter from a publisher in South Africa, who has decided to publish our accounts of those years in an anthology. Your mother did not expect to die when she did and I feel sure that one day she would have wanted you to know about this part of her life. The publishers have asked me to contact you on their behalf and have sent me the first part of Lilian's contribution, which I enclose. They are currently editing our

*writings and will send the remaining parts to you directly
as and when they become available. Ros, I hope this is not too
alarming for you. Forgive this hasty letter, but my brother is
unwell and taking up all my time. I will be in touch when you
have read and learned the whole story.
Much love, Gloria*

Ros's heart was beating fast. She'd always wished that Lilian
had left her a letter, a final goodbye, something to fill the terrible
silence after her death, and now it looked as though she had. Ros
turned the pages in her hands and hesitated, unsure whether her
unwillingness to confront evidence of Lilian's life was born of the
desire to keep Lilian somehow within reach for as long as possible
or whether it were actually the reverse; a need to hold her and
anything she might have to say at bay.

Ros paused for a moment. In the distance, she could hear
the roar of a plane taking off from Heathrow and the honking
of car horns on the high street; everyday sounds resonating in a
world that she unexpectedly felt wholly removed from. She placed
Gloria's note on the table and smoothed it with an accuracy that
belied her unease. What, she wondered, did her mother have in
store for her now?

Chapter Ten

Lilian

I took the train to Johannesburg early one Friday morning in late January of 1951; I had turned seventeen the week before and had won a scholarship to Wits University to study English. My parents saw me off at the station and Josiah loaded my trunk onto the train, sweating with exertion in the summer heat and mopping his face with a large white handkerchief while Diana fussed around me with the snacks she had prepared for my journey.

I had always found it strange that Diana and Josiah were our 'servants' when they felt like family to me. I hugged them both tightly, more tightly than I had hugged my parents. My mother in any case did not like to be hugged and would always fold her arms against her chest to prevent me from getting too close. I hung my head out of the window as the train pulled away to watch the four of them growing ever smaller as the train accelerated. My parents turned away and began to make their way from the station, my father looked suddenly stooped, his silhouette reminding me briefly of Grandpa Meir's and I felt a sharp longing for the intimacy I had shared with my grandfather, which had always eluded me with my own father. Diana and Josiah remained on the platform. As the train gathered speed, I could soon make out only two spots of blue and white, like small flags fluttering, as Josiah waved his handkerchief in farewell and Diana her headscarf which she had hastily untied, before the train curved north-east on the track and lost them from view. The bracelet that Diana had given me as a parting gift was made up of small blue and white beads, the same colours as the fabric she and Josiah had been waving. It was an echo of their farewell and I twisted it around my wrist as I stood suspended between the past and the future: my new life about to begin as my old one visibly receded behind me. I looked at the water in Table Bay, magnified and made iridescent by the sudden tears in my eyes, and made my way down to the observation coach at the end of the train. I sat in one of its deep brown leather armchairs, smoothing down the gathered skirt of my summer dress. I was a young woman now, no longer a girl, and to enhance my sophistication I lit a cigarette and smoked with Van Hunks and the Devil as I watched Table Mountain and the white fluffy 'tablecloth' that shrouded it disappearing from view through the large picture window at the rear of the carriage. Then, like the child I was trying to suppress, unable to wait until midnight for her feast, I took out one of the small logs of sugar cane Diana had packed for me and chewed on it. I must have dozed, as I was awoken by an alteration in the train's rhythm when it slowed to a halt to wait for a signal change. A group of Africans appeared from the bush to run alongside our train and tout their wares. Amidst the sudden clamour of their cries, one voice rose above the rest.

'Two little threepenny baskets,' it sang, 'who will buy two little threepenny baskets, just one tickey each.'

I opened the window and saw a man below with two small Zulu baskets woven from Ilala palm with looped handles and lids. He was walking to and fro, swinging the baskets, his eyes darting here and there in search of a prospective buyer.

'I'll take one,' I called, reaching into my handbag for the small silver threepenny coin.

He handed me the basket, thanked me and continued up the train.

'One little threepenny basket,' he called, 'who will buy one little basket for a tickey.'

The guard blew the whistle and the train began to move again, steam billowing from the chimney at the front as the Africans ran alongside to complete their sales of Zulu beadwork, wood carvings and basketware, while passengers hung out of the windows to pay for their purchases. White hands extended eagerly towards the black ones reaching upwards to meet them, touching briefly as they exchanged goods and money. I ran my fingers over the basket in my own hands.

'Curious, isn't it,' said a familiar voice beside me, 'how we rush to buy their art and fill our homes with it and yet treat them like dogs?'

I spun round. It was Lenny Bloomstein, the muscular, tousle-haired law student I'd had a crush on the year before. He was even more handsome than I remembered and I had to fight to keep my breathing steady. He smiled, all too aware of the effect he had on me.

I used to pass his house on my way to school, circling on my bike until he asked me in. My interest in him amused him and we began to spend some time together. One afternoon the previous May, as I sat in his lounge while he played the piano, a tapping at the window had interrupted us. The anxious face of a young black man appeared between the bars at the window, his hands cupped around the side of his face to block out the last rays of the bright winter sunshine so that he could see inside. Lenny glanced at me.

'Stay here,' he said, 'I won't be a minute.'

The forced casualness of his tone aroused my interest and I watched carefully as he went out on the stoep to join the black man.

'Afrika,' said the stranger, holding his arm against his chest with his thumb pointing upwards.

'Mayibuye,' Lenny answered quietly, looking around carefully.

Night was beginning to fall and the first of the crickets, lazily rubbing its legs together, was making itself heard, a car drove down the road raising the dust on the dry earth and Lenny and the stranger withdrew into the recesses of the verandah and conducted their conversation sotte voce. I was able to make out only the occasional word. The new laws … strike … too far this time. It was enough to make me realise that Lenny was involved in African politics. Afrika. Mayibuye. Africa. May she return to us. I felt a sudden surge of energy flow through me with the realisation that the many uneasy and ill-formed feelings I had harboured for so many years could, at last, be about to find an outlet. Their conversation concluded, the black man got on his bicycle and rode off quickly. I resumed my position in the armchair and pretended to read a magazine that I found on the table next to me. Lenny looked at me carefully as he re-entered the room; I could tell from the expression on his face that he was composing a lie.

'That was a fellow from the township who has a problem with his pass,' he said offhandedly. 'I give a little legal advice to those people from time to time.'

'They're planning action against the new apartheid laws, aren't they?' I said quietly.

Lenny rubbed his hand over his face in a tired gesture. 'Listen, Cookie, why don't you just go home and get on with your homework, this isn't something you want to get involved in.'

How dare he call me Cookie, I thought angrily. Stung, I rose from my chair and pushed my face into his. 'Listen, man, I'm not some little kugel who wants to marry the first suitable doctor or lawyer she meets and become a lady of the house with servants. I can see what's happening in this country.'

Lenny looked at me, surprised by my passionate outburst.

'Please don't treat me like a child,' I said.

There was a long silence.

'What can I do to help?' I asked.

'OK,' he said finally.

He went over to the small wooden, fold-down bureau in the corner of the room next to the piano and, taking a piece of paper, quickly scribbled something down. He folded the paper and put it in an envelope, his eyes meeting mine as he licked it down. A flicker of excitement ran through me, a warm feeling that started in my stomach and, without thinking, I moved towards him and lifted my face up to his. He put the envelope in my hand, drew me towards him and kissed me hard. It was the first time he had touched me.

'Listen, Cook—' He stopped, seeing the expression on my face. 'Lilian, if you're sure you want to get mixed up in this business, give this to Josiah.' Lenny handed me the envelope, his eyes moving over my face as if assessing whether or not he could trust me.

'I didn't know you knew Josiah, what's he got to do with this?'

'That was his brother Paulie who came to see me. Just give him this letter.' He paused before adding, 'You're right, they're planning a May Day strike all around the country.'

When I got home, my parents were sitting outside on the porch, *as they did every evening, being served drinks by Josiah. My father looked at me over the edge of the* Cape Times.

'Why are you so late, child?' he asked.

I shrugged noncommittally.

'Have you been over at the Bloomstein place?' my mother asked. 'I don't want you mixing with that boy; he's a kaffir-loving commie.'

I winced at the derogatory word and glanced at Josiah, noticing his almost imperceptible hesitation before he continued pouring my father's whisky.

'You're not to go over there any more, you hear?' said my father.

'Marion du Toit says she sees your bicycle outside that house every afternoon,' my mother said. 'You'll get a reputation.'

'We're only talking, he plays the piano for me,' I protested.

My parents exchanged a look.

'Ja,' my mother said, 'well, I don't want you going over there and that's that, end of story.'

I'd have to find a way round that later; in the meantime, I needed to get Josiah on his own to give him Lenny's letter. I found him in the kitchen preparing supper and closed the door behind me quietly.

'For you,' I said, taking Lenny's letter from its hiding place down the front of my blouse and smoothing it out with my hands carefully before handing it to him.

Josiah looked at me questioningly.

'It's from Lenny Bloomstein. Paulie was at his house earlier.'

I felt the roughness of his work-worn hands briefly as he took the letter and quickly slipped it into a back pocket.

'I don't want you getting into trouble,' he said. His eyes were wide with alarm in his dark face and I noticed how white his hair had grown. 'Promise me you won't get mixed up in any more of this business?'

When I said nothing, he took me by the shoulders and looked me hard in the eyes. 'Promise me. This isn't a business for you.'

'I can't,' I said, 'if I did, I'd be lying.'

'Isala kutyelwa siva noolopu,' he said in Xhosa. 'A person who will not take advice gets knowledge when trouble overtakes him.'

'That's the risk we all have to take,' I said, and even to me my voice sounded sad.

My mother's voice interrupted us, querulously calling down the hallway to ask when dinner would be ready. Josiah looked at me and sighed, a heavy sigh that betrayed a lifetime of troubles and I let myself out of the back door quietly not wanting my mother to discover me with him.

'Nearly ready, Madam,' I heard him call out as I crept around the house and climbed into the lounge through an open window.

The next morning, I woke early and left the house before my parents were up. I rode my bike through quiet roads until I came to Ndebeni Street, less than a mile from the township of Langa. I stopped at a dusty petrol station and dismounted. The place had the quiet empty air usually associated with a Sunday morning. A bus stood by the side of the road and a man was remonstrating with the driver who was casually picking his teeth with a splinter of wood as he leant against the door, barring entry.

'I have to get to work,' the man said, pushing his brown trilby back on his head and wiping the unseasonable sweat from his brow with a handkerchief; he was clearly worried, as the morning was cool.

'No one's working today, brother, haven't you heard it's a strike?'

'How can I strike, my baas will take my job away from me quick-quick.'

A crowd was gathering around them. A few were grouped nearby around a single communal tap, the men warming themselves in the May winter cold at a small brazier while the women carried their burdens on their heads and their babies on their backs. To my left, a man wearing a tribal blanket lifted his head to the sky and began to sing a song that sounded like a lament. Some, like the man in the hat, were anxious to get to work while others remonstrated with them.

'I can't afford to get mixed up in this business,' said the man. 'I just want a quiet life, to keep my job and provide for my family.'

'No, man, it's time for us to stand together and protest or how can we get our country back?' said the bus driver. 'Afrika!' he shouted.

'Mayibuye!' *answered the gathering crowd.*

Suddenly, one of the men leant to the ground and placed his hand on the earth.

'Peri-Urban,' *he shouted, recognising the vibrations of distant horses' hooves. The crowd turned and began to run back in the direction of the township. After a few moments, I could hear the approaching sounds of the mounted police and shielding my eyes with my hand soon made out the dusty silhouette of the Peri-Urban as they drew near. I hid behind the corrugated iron lean-to at the side of the garage. The man who wanted to go to work stood frozen in an agony of indecision. The horses galloped past my hiding place and a policeman drew up on his horse alongside the man.*

'What are you doing, boy?' *the policeman asked him.*

'I'm walking to work, baas.'

'Show me your pass,' *said the policeman, holding his hand out for the papers that every African was required to carry at all times. He studied it for some time and finding it in order grudgingly handed it back.*

'Go on, voetsak, kaffir,' *he said and, almost casually, he raised his baton and with the easy swing of a polo-player, brought it about the man's head, felling him before riding on without looking back. I was shaking, immobilised by fear as the man himself had been only moments before, and, torn between the desire to hurry to his aid and to run away, I eventually managed to move and made my way to his side. He was groaning, his hand held to his bleeding forehead. I tore off my cardigan and, my fingers trembling, wrapped it around his head.*

'What's your name?' *I asked.*

'Tickey,' *he said. His hat had fallen off and lay on the earth beside him.* 'I'm OK.' *He picked up the hat and rising to his feet dusted it off with a carefulness that indicated how precious it was to him.*

'Why?' *I asked.* 'Why did he do that, you weren't doing anything wrong?'

'Why?' *he smiled ruefully, shaking his head to clear his vision.* 'This Why is what we are asking ourselves every day and every night.' He tipped his hat to me and turned away from the township and in the direction of Cape Town, to work.

I hurried back to fetch my bicycle from behind the bush where I'd hidden it and caught up with him further down the road.

'Get on my bicycle,' I said. 'I'll ride on the crossbar, that way you'll get to work quicker.'

After some persuasion, he agreed and we rode off, making our way unsteadily along the dirt road. He got off on Strand Street where he returned my blood-soaked cardigan and tipped his hat once more in farewell.

'Where do you work, Tickey?' I asked.

'Quality Bazaar,' he answered, 'I'm a delivery boy.'

My parents' department store; his baas was my father. I rode the rest of the way to school and buried myself in my work in an attempt to erase the morning's events. Later that day, after Diana had finished scolding me for going to the township, she soaked the blood from my cardigan and told me the police had made sixty arrests and that twelve people had been injured, Josiah's brother Paulie among them.

'How come you and Josiah didn't strike today?' I asked.

'Paulie told us not to in that letter you gave Josiah.'

'Why?'

'That's enough questions. Now go, your mother's looking for you.' Diana finished retying her pale blue headscarf and chased me away.

'I'm going to fire that boy, Tickey,' my father had said the day after the strike as he'd ushered me into his study. Of course, my parents had found out about my early morning visit to the township.

'What for?' I said. 'He was only trying to get to work on time.'

'Look here,' he said, 'what were you doing out there anyhow? How many times do I have to tell you to mind your own business?'

'It wasn't fair, Dad, he wasn't doing anything; he was just trying to get to work on time so I helped him. What's so bad about that? Anyhow, who told you?'

'Keith du Toit saw you on your bicycle with him and told his mother who told your mother. Lilian, you have to be careful; everyone knows everyone else's business around here and you're not making any friends with your attitude.'

I said nothing. My father reached into his desk drawer and took out a piece of biltong and a small sharp knife. He cut a few careful slivers of the dried beef and handed me one. We sat chewing in silence.

'Listen, Lili ...' I knew he was trying to be conciliatory; he hadn't called me Lili since I was a little girl. 'You're not doing yourself any favours. Try and fit in, hey? Look, let's do a deal; you stay out of trouble, get on with your schoolwork and concentrate on your matric and I'll let Tickey keep his job. I'll let you go out, but I want to know where you're going and with whom and on no account are you to go anywhere near that Bloomstein boy.'

'How can you be like this, Dad? Can't you see how unfair this country is?'

My father sighed, finished chewing his biltong and carefully wiped his mouth with a handkerchief, playing for time before he answered.

'All my childhood I felt like an outcast,' he said, 'I never fitted in anywhere. I hated that feeling, so I made myself fit in.' He shrugged as if to say that there had been no other choice open to him. 'You can't change things on your own, you have to try and fit in, it makes you much happier in the end.'

'Ja, but if everyone thinks like that then nothing will ever change. If other countries hadn't stood up to Hitler then all the Jews would have been killed.' I angrily wiped away the tears that my parents always had the ability to provoke when I couldn't make them understand how I felt and thought.

'Listen, girlie, I'm not going to start arguing world politics with you. Let's agree to disagree and when you're grown up you can do things your way.' He ran a hand over his face in a gesture at once of irritation and isolation.

I got up to leave and my father moved towards me. For an instant I thought he was going to hug me, but at the last moment he patted me awkwardly on the shoulder.

*

I chose the path of least resistance and did as my father had asked. In spite of everything, I was still a young girl who needed her parents' approval and so I no longer cycled past Lenny Bloomstein's house, I concentrated on my schoolwork and even forced myself to be civil when I bumped into Keith du Toit on the high board at the swimming pool at Sea Point a few weeks later.

'I'm sorry I told my mom I'd seen you,' he said.

I looked out to sea, out towards Robben Island and shrugged.

'It was only because I didn't want you getting into any trouble.'

'I don't need you to look after me, Keith.' I turned to look at him and couldn't avoid noticing his impressive physique, the blueness of his eyes echoed by the glittering blue of the pool beneath us.

He touched my arm. 'Will you come to a braaivleis *with me later?'*

My skin tingled where he'd touched me. I surprised myself by answering that I might and turned and dived into the water, a clean arc of a dive that sent a rush of delight through me. I wanted to enjoy myself and to stop worrying about the things that everyone told me I couldn't change. So I did go to the braai *with Keith and enjoyed the pleasures of a temperate Cape winter afternoon eating barbecued steak and sausages and laughing with people my own age. I didn't let Keith kiss me, even though I could tell that he wanted to, but I did find myself agreeing to meet up with him in Jo'burg where he too was going to study.*

Now in the observation coach of the Union Limited train, I wondered what had happened to Tickey, the man who rode my bicycle the day of the strike, and who had given him his name? Was that the worth he was held in, the same value as the small basket I held in my hands? I looked into the amused brown eyes of Lenny Bloomstein and recalled the taste of his warm lips from our brief kiss all those months earlier.

'So, I hear you left me for the Boers,' he said, presumably referring to my friendship with Keith.

'I didn't …' I began, but was prevented from finishing my sentence by the arrival of a slim, hard-faced brunette who entered the carriage and took Lenny's arm.

'Shirley, this is Lilian,' Lenny said.

I felt disappointment land like a stone in my stomach. Shirley gave me an appraising look and tightened her grip on Lenny's arm.

'I'm off to do my bar practice in Jo'burg,' said Lenny. 'Are you staying in the women's res? I'll look you up at varsity and introduce you to some people.'

I nodded eagerly and immediately wished I hadn't and that I'd acknowledged his words with a bored shrug or a half-hearted 'OK'.

'Nice to meet you, Lilian,' said Shirley in a tone that suggested otherwise. 'I've heard a lot about you.'

They turned to leave. Lenny turned back. 'Can you type?' he said.

'Yes, I can – a hundred words a minute.' I could hear the pride in my voice; I'd taken a course in the summer holidays and been best in the class. Damn, I'd been over-eager again.

'I always refused to learn,' said Shirley archly. 'I'm not spending my time typing for other people like a secretary.'

'Oh, I only learnt because I plan to be a journalist,' I said. We were like two cats arching our backs and preparing to spit at each other.

Lenny looked amused. 'Good,' he said to me, 'that might come in handy. I'll be in touch.'

Shirley whispered something in his ear as they left and I saw her hand rest briefly on his lower back, her fingers tracing circles of sexual promise.

To my dismay, Lenny and Shirley were in the same compartment as me. Not wishing to endure Shirley's condescension, I spent much of the evening in the restaurant car reading my book, returning only when the guard had made up our beds. Lulled by the rhythm of the train, I was on the point of sleep when a movement disturbed me. In the darkness, I could make out Shirley's silhouette as she moved from the bed beneath mine to join Lenny in his couchette. The sounds of their muted lovemaking kept me awake long into the night in a state somewhere between arousal and envy. Surely I should have been the one in Lenny's arms?

*

Johannesburg. It was everything I had hoped it would be from the moment I arrived: tall buildings, bustling streets and a welcome release from the confines of my parents' house. Not even the rules of the women's residence could compromise my initial sense of liberation, notwithstanding the fact that we had to sign in no later than midnight and gentlemen callers were strictly forbidden.

In my first term, I dated several men who took me to the cinema and bought me chocolates in the interval, dutifully fulfilling the requirements of dating protocol. One afternoon, I went on a picnic with Keith du Toit but, sensing his growing interest in me, I avoided his subsequent calls. For all the pleasure I was experiencing in my new life, I didn't have much in common with any of these men and felt constrained in their company; I continued to have the same strong sense of not properly belonging that had always troubled me. Grandpa Meir had often told me that you had to find your people to be happy in life, and the narrow-minded, suburban white South Africans that I met in my first few weeks definitely weren't my people.

Then I met Gloria Wiseman.

Gloria was a tall blonde with high cheekbones and dark green eyes who wore dresses that she designed and made herself in vivid African fabrics. Her signature was her generous décolletage.

'You're a Lithy, aren't you?'

These were her first words to me as we sat one evening on the verandah of the Waverley Hotel with our companions for the evening; two men who'd brought the four of us together for a double date: a fact which proved to be the beginning and end of these particular men's significance in either of our lives.

'What do you mean?' I asked.

'A Lithuanian Jew – I can tell just by looking at you.'

I was delighted that my paternal genes had won out over my questionable Boer maternal ones and that it was so easy for her to match me with the ancestry with which I most identified. It felt like a fitting tribute to Grandpa Meir and Granny Rebecca. I nodded.

'Takes one to know one.' Gloria raised her glass of Mint Fizz up towards me. 'You're at Wits, aren't you? Me too, I'm studying drama.'

She sipped her drink, tinted a lurid green by the crème de menthe that was its vital component. I marvelled at her sophistication and regretted my timid order of a small sweet sherry.

'Glorious,' a familiar voice called out, causing Gloria to turn around.

It was Lenny. I must admit, I'd been hoping to see him again ever since I'd arrived. Gloria jumped up to greet him.

'Lenny always calls me that,' she said, laughing over her shoulder to me.

'Good,' said Lenny who had come up to our table and was leaning down to kiss me, 'you two have found each other. Lilian, I've been meaning to get in touch. I need to talk to you, phone me tomorrow at my office.' He scribbled a number onto a piece of paper and handed it to me. 'Better still,' he said, swiftly changing his mind, 'Glorious, bring her over tomorrow night.'

I could see Shirley standing in the doorway to the restaurant inside. She looked irritated, but felt obliged to smile briefly as her eyes met mine.

The next day, Gloria led me to the bus stop. The intense fire of summer was beginning to surrender to early autumn's more muted flames, discernible only in the cooler temperature at night. It was dusk, the remainder of the day's flies were at last clearing the air in readiness for their night's rest and here and there a cricket began tuning up for its evening performance. Further up the street, a group of Africans stood at their bus stop waiting to return home to their township. They were laughing and talking loudly and now and then one of them sang a few lines from a song. Their apparent joie de vivre was, I couldn't help feeling, an eloquent expression of their defiance. By contrast, the whites at our stop stood mute and unsmiling, demonstrating their reluctance to express themselves in front of people they saw as little more than servants. For some reason, these two groups of us, separated by the colour of our skins and banned by law from riding the same bus home, imprinted an indelible picture of apartheid in my mind.

Gloria hadn't said anything about where we were going and I assumed it was to meet Lenny. We rode the bus to Hillbrow and *got off at Kotze Street from where Gloria led me briskly round the corner to a busy deli.*

'Harry, this is Lilian,' she said, introducing me to a man a few years older than us. He was wearing black horn-rimmed glasses and reading a newspaper. 'Harry's my brother,' Gloria said as she slid into the booth opposite him, 'he's a lawyer, at the bar with Lenny.' She patted the leatherette bench beside her to invite me to join them.

'Do you girls want a cup of coffee?' Harry asked, folding his paper and looking at me appraisingly.

We nodded. He looked around, trying in vain to get the waitress's attention.

'Let me go and get it from the counter, it'll be quicker,' he said.

As he made to stand, he put both his hands on the edge of the table and leant forward, his head thrust towards me and his elbows bent to form right angles.

'What am I?' he asked.

I must have looked bemused because Gloria laughed and said, 'A spider.'

I laughed; it was perfectly true, he had, with minimal movement, evoked not precisely a spider, but something very like a line-drawing of one.

'For God's sake, Harry,' Gloria said, 'Lilian doesn't know you well enough to understand your nonsense yet.'

He left to order our coffee and Gloria turned to me.

'Harry has a whole zoo of creatures he impersonates,' she explained. 'It's his way of flirting. By the looks of things, you'll get to see his repertoire very quickly.'

I blushed. Although Harry was funny and handsome, my head was full of Lenny; I was disappointed to find that he wasn't there and reluctant to reveal my interest by asking where he might be.

'So, Lilian, I've heard a lot about you, and Lenny tells me you're going to join us.' Harry settled back in his seat and looked at me intently.

'I am?'

'Ja, course you are. Now hurry, drink up your coffee and we'll get going; Lenny and the others are waiting round the corner.'

That's how my political life began in earnest. The meeting Harry took us to was held in Lenny's lodgings off Pretoria Street, which were owned by an ageing and apparently deaf Jewish widow called Marlie Greenburg. I believe she thought we were earnest young Zionists planning our eventual exodus to Israel. How she reconciled this notion with the fleeting glimpses of the young black men and women we smuggled into her premises, I do not know. Perhaps her eyesight was as selective as her hearing.

When we arrived, Lenny and Shirley were already there with several others. It emerged that they had all been Communist Party members, but when the government had declared the party illegal and banned it in 1950, they, along with many others, had gone underground. Since then, Lenny and his comrades had forged an alliance with the ANC, united by their shared aim to overthrow the apartheid system. They were jointly preparing for the Defiance Campaign.

What am I getting myself into? I wondered.

'The plan is simple,' Lenny explained, 'the ANC want as many people as possible peacefully to refuse to obey the laws that they consider unjust and discriminatory.'

'Like what sort of thing?' I was nervous, but also felt the first flicker of excitement bubbling up inside me.

'Look, the thing is to show the government this whole bloody system is unjust by disregarding their pass laws, staging strikes and boycotts and generally committing acts of civil disobedience.' Harry took over from Lenny.

'What will happen to the people that do this?' I asked.

Harry and Lenny looked at each other and shrugged. 'They'll probably go to jail,' Harry said.

'We'll probably go to jail,' Lenny corrected him. 'The point is, we have to take a stand,' he added.

Shirley, who had been looking at me with the beginnings of a contemptuous smile, implying that I wouldn't have the courage to join them, precipitated my own personal act of defiance right there and then.

'I'm in,' I said, 'what can I do to help?'

Lenny turned his head towards me sharply. Did he remember that I'd spoken these same words to him once before while standing in his lounge in Cape Town and that he'd kissed me shortly afterwards? The look on his face seemed to suggest that he might.

At last, I had found my people and I slotted into their company with all the satisfaction of someone who has, after many failed attempts, finally fitted the right key to a lock. I imagined I could almost hear the satisfying click as the bolt turned.

Why did they seek me out? Lenny knew I would be sympathetic to their cause, I could type fast and he could use me to make Shirley jealous – a game that amused him and, for a short while at least, tantalised me.

The following weeks and months became full with lectures and classes at varsity and secret meetings at night. Gloria and I revelled in our double lives and became close friends. On the weekends, we would travel into the townships, into nearby Sophiatown and Alexandra to disseminate literature.

My first visit to Sophiatown was with Lenny to deliver newspapers to an ANC activist. It was the first time Lenny and I had been alone since Cape Town and even though we were on political business, I pretended to myself that we were on a date of sorts. I dressed carefully in one of my favourite dresses and wore a pale blue mohair cardigan over my shoulders. Any thoughts of romance soon evaporated as I absorbed the stark reality that is the African township. We arrived at night; the police increasingly monitored visits by whites to the African locations. In the light of our car's headlamps, for there was no electricity, I saw shacks roughly fashioned from wood, cardboard, tin and hessian sacks teetering by the side of unpaved streets. Many of the houses, if one can call them that, had been built in the yards of grander brick and stone properties once intended for the use of the white man. Each yard had a single tap, and here and there barefoot and scantily dressed children ran in and out of the shadows. Men on bicycles wove through the streets on their way home from work, some carried friends who sat either on the crossbars or on the saddle forcing the riders to stand while *they pedalled. Dim additional light came from the glowing braziers in the yards and the overall smell was one of uncontained sewage and stagnant water. For all that, and without wishing to romanticise the lives of the so-called Natives, there was an inescapable vibrancy that arose from the men and women as they talked, laughed and called out to each other in groups.*

We drew up behind the burnt-out wreck of an old car and Lenny led me into a yard where he knocked quietly on the door of one of the shacks. It opened and we were quickly ushered into a single room by a young African. A newspaper curtain hung across one corner of the room to create the privacy of a bedroom and it was there that the man led us.

'Lilian, this is Sipho; Sipho, Lilian,' Lenny introduced us.

Sipho could tell instantly that it was my first time in a township.

'So now you see how we live,' he said, a warm smile softening the bitterness of his words.

I felt personally culpable and wanted to apologise to him, but I couldn't find the right words.

'Please sit,' he said, gesturing towards the bed and seating himself on an upturned crate. The bed was raised so high on bricks that when I sat down, my feet dangled above the ground like a child's.

'It's my mother's bed; she raises it to keep safe from the tokoloshe.'

The tokoloshe is a mischievous, sometimes malign, dwarf-like water sprite that can become invisible by swallowing a pebble; South Africans hold it in common belief. Even those of us who don't believe in it, believe in it a bit. Instinctively, I crossed my legs to lift them further away from the ground.

'I'm sorry I haven't got anything to offer you to eat or drink.' Sipho looked away as he spoke, his shame all too apparent in his discomfort.

'Ag, man please,' said Lenny, producing a half bottle of whisky from inside his jacket.

Sipho found a few glasses and filled them. 'Afrika!' Lenny and Sipho said quietly.

'So you've heard these rumours about the government planning to remove us from this place?' Sipho said.

'Ja, Harry told me all about it; he heard it from someone who works in the Native Affairs Department.'

'They can't stand having Sophiatown so near the white areas. You know, first they don't want the land, then they do and this way they can get rid of us by sending us back to our so-called homelands; never mind the fact that most of us were actually born here. We knew the implications of this Group Areas Act from the word go,' Sipho said, rubbing his face with his hand.

'We'll fight it, man,' Lenny said.

We sat in silence. We could hear voices in the yard outside and the distant sound of a tin whistle, which grew steadily louder signalling the player's approach. Through the window, I could see one of Sipho's neighbours dancing the kwela, a hip-shaking, bottom-swivelling African dance, in tune to the music as she brought in her washing.

'You people had better go: the drinking shebeen's going to open up and you don't want to be caught illegally taking alcohol with Africans if there's a police raid,' Sipho said.

'Be careful, my friend,' said Lenny, getting up and slapping Sipho on the back. 'You know what they say?' Lenny turned to me. 'The three things you shouldn't give an African: alcohol, a gun and the vote? Christ, man, I only hope we get them in our lifetime.'

'Even the gun?' I said.

'Ja, even the gun, either everyone should have one, or no one should.'

'Of course.' I felt embarrassed by my naïveté.

As we entered the yard, the woman who had been dancing came over, her washing balanced on her head.

'Hey, Bra Sirra,' she called out, using what I later discovered to be Sipho's Xhosa nickname. 'Aren't you going to teach your girl to dance?' She jerked her head in my direction.

She wiggled her hips suggestively and moved away from us, laughing.

'My girl,' Sipho said, shaking his head and laughing too, a rich deep laugh that made me feel happy and carefree. Lenny and I were infected by his mirth and started to laugh as well, although I could feel Lenny's hand, which had previously been in the small of my back, shift to hold me proprietorially around my waist.

We unpacked the newspapers from the car and stacked them in a corner of Sipho's kitchen.

'How on earth do you carry them all?' I asked, as we left the shack.

'I take them on my bicycle to Freedom Square to sell on Sunday mornings,' Sipho explained, pointing with undisguised pride at a battered black bicycle tied to a wooden post in the yard.

He patted its worn and patched saddle. Little remained of the leather that had once bound it; layers of cardboard and brown waxed paper fastened with sticky tape provided covering and beneath newspaper, used, no doubt, as upholstery poked through intermittent tears.

'Every bicycle has a story,' he added.

'Tell her,' said Lenny, taking out a packet of cigarettes and offering us both one. Sipho sparked a match against the wall. As I inhaled, I looked up at the stars that were stitched into the Johannesburg night sky.

Sipho dragged deeply on his cigarette and exhaled, blowing a perfect smoke ring into the night air. Without thinking, I put my finger through its centre, just as I used to when Grandpa Meir smoked his pipe. Sipho smiled and adjusted his position against the wall.

'My cousin Zakhele, the oldest boy of my mother's sister, was living here with us in Sophiatown and after he finished school he got a job as a garden boy for a family in Johannesburg. One day the Madam of the family made him stay late to move a rosebush. She kept on changing her mind about where she wanted it and he was planting and replanting this bush over and over again. Finally she let him go. On his way home, he saw a child lying sick by the side of the road. So he cycled some distance with this child on his bicycle to find the parents. It was late by the time he found the mother and he got back on his bicycle rushing to get home before the curfew. It was just eleven o'clock, maybe two minutes after the curfew, when the police stopped him for his pass; he didn't have it because he was supposed to relocate with his family to the Transkei after his father lost his job. The police took him to jail. When he was there, he tried to reason with them and ask for some time to sort out his pass, but they wouldn't listen and they beat him very badly. When he came out, he lost his job because the family said he was unreliable and they didn't want someone working for them who had all these pass problems. Zakhele was very upset and angry. A little time afterwards, he fell into some bad ways and joined up with the Americans.'

I nodded, I knew about the Americans. They were a gang of Tsotsis; gangsters who had earned their name because of their expensive dress: elegant American cardigans, brown and white shoes and narrow blue trousers called Bogarts.

'Zakhele always used to say the Americans were better than the Berliners or the Russians.' Sipho made a kissing sound with his mouth and teeth to express disgust. 'Those boys are vicious; they will take money from anybody. Zakhele said the Americans are the Robin Hood of the Tsotsis: they steal only from the white man and sell their goods in the locations at cheap prices to the Africans. Anyway, one night they were out at their work, stealing from a delivery trailer, when the railway police interrupted them. Zakhele had a gun and while they were trying to get away he slipped and it went off. Zakhele saw for sure that the bullet didn't hit anyone; it landed against the ground because Zakhele was falling and the gun was pointing down. But when the police heard the gunshot, they started firing and by mistake, one of the policemen was shot by one of their own stray bullets. Later on this policeman died. Anyhow, the police came here and took Zakhele to jail. He swore he didn't kill that policeman and I believe him.'

'How did they know to come for him?' I asked.

'We found out later that one of the gang is an informer of the police; he told them Zakhele was the one with a gun. So later on, the other boys in the gang killed him.'

Sipho paused and blew a final smoke ring, before crushing the cigarette beneath his foot.

'What happened to Zakhele?' I prompted.

'When he was in court, we all went along to try and help him. But they sentenced him to death anyway.'

We were silent. The shebeen, the illegal drinking house in Sipho's yard, was preparing for the night ahead. People had been arriving while we stood talking and the music, a steady beat that had accompanied Sipho's narrative, burst through loudly each time the door was opened to admit a new customer. A young boy stood by the corner of the building from where he had sight of the street to give early warning in the event of a police raid.

'Tell her about the bicycle,' Lenny said quietly.

Sipho took his hands out of his pockets and folded his arms as though preventing himself from unravelling.

'So when we were in the courtroom and the judge had pronounced the sentence, he asked Zakhele if he had anything he wanted to say. Everything was very quiet and we all were watching. So my cousin, Zakhele, he turned his head and looked all around the room, at each of us, his friends and his relatives who had come to see him. He looked at every one of us in turn, holding us with his eyes as if he were saying sorry for this trouble he had brought and then he looked at me again for a long time. "Bra Sirra," he said, "my bicycle, I want you to have it." He was very proud of this bicycle, he bought it with money that he earned before he went into the gang. He said it was the bike of Zakhele, the good boy, the one who used to believe the world could be fair.'

Sipho bent his head when he finished speaking and looked at the ground. I reached out and placed my hand on his arm.

'So, you see,' he said, forcing a laugh, 'this is the story of this particular bicycle. I am sure you can go anywhere in this township and you will find a hundred stories like this one.'

We stood motionless, the three of us, as though frozen in the aftermath of this tale of the unjust loss of a young man's life.

'One day it will explode,' Sipho said quietly, 'all the rage and the anger, that's all, it will explode.' He brought his hands together and pushed them up and apart to illustrate his point.

*

Lenny and I were quiet on our return to the city. Unlike the African locations that had been established further afield, Sophiatown was a suburb of Johannesburg, four miles west of the city centre, and it wasn't long before we exchanged its noisy, crowded dirt streets for the quiet tarmac-covered avenues of the white suburbs Africans were permitted to frequent during prescribed hours and then only to work. With their neatly manicured lawns, fiery explosions of bougainvillea and shiny automobiles parked in the driveways of large houses, it felt like we had travelled from one country to another and it was hard to believe that only a few short miles separated the two.

We drew up outside the women's res and Lenny caught my arm as I prepared to get out of the car. He pulled me to him and kissed me. For an instant, I lost myself in the urgent warmth of his mouth.

'What about Shirley?' I said.

'What about her?' Lenny asked, tracing the top of my breast with a finger.

'Have you broken up with her?'

'No, what's Shirley got to do with this? Come on, Lilian, don't be so bourgeois.'

I removed his hand from my breast and said, 'What a pity, Lenny, that your impeccable sense of moral right in political matters doesn't extend to your personal life. I will not be your plaything but am happy to continue as a comrade in our joint struggle for justice and equality in our country.'

(I can hear now how pompous this must have sounded, but I was a young and idealistic girl of seventeen.)

'Pity,' Lenny said lightly. 'You're so feisty and beautiful, Lilian, you can't blame me for trying. It's greedy of me, I know.'

He tried to pull me to him once again. I laughed and, getting out, slammed the door, the sound a satisfying punctuation to an infatuation drawn conclusively to an end. Where over the past few weeks I had been full of Lenny, watching him while he spoke, monitoring how often he turned his gaze in my direction rather than in Shirley's, awarding myself points for each small attention or smile that seemed to imply that I was winning the battle for his affections, now, with a few words, I was free of him and no longer *in his thrall. Perversely, his interest in me was heightened and in the weeks to come, it was he who watched me and craved my company. I would have derived satisfaction from this turning of the tables were it not for the fact that my own attentions were increasingly engaged elsewhere.*

Over the following year, Sipho and I spent more and more time in each other's company. My parents, on a rare visit to Johannesburg, had driven my mother's old Austin Seven up and given it to me as a belated gift both for winning my university scholarship and for my eighteenth birthday. Since then, I had assumed the task of delivering Sipho's newspapers to him each week. Often, after our meetings, we would take a long walk together in the veld surrounding Sophiatown and share the very different stories of our childhoods.

One day, we'd been at a meeting at Lenny's lodgings where we were finalising plans for the Defiance Campaign. I checked over the documents I had been typing, stacked them in a bundle and handed them over to Harry.

'Lilian, do stop initialling things,' he said as he leafed through them, 'this isn't an essay.'

'I can't help it,' I answered, taking out a rubber. Retrieving the papers from him, I erased the neatly pencilled LB in the top right-hand corner of the cover sheet. 'We have to do it with everything at varsity and I keep forgetting to leave it off.'

'What am I?' Harry said, poking the tip of his tongue out and swiftly pulling it back in.

'A snake,' I said, laughing.

'You know me too well, doll,' Harry said.

I'd been out with Harry a couple of times, and although I liked and admired him, I wasn't attracted to him. We had long since made a tacit agreement to be friends and Gloria had jokingly agreed that he could be my brother too.

More and more, I caught myself thinking about Sipho and looking forward to the time when we could be together. When we spoke, we stood too close to one another, as though magnetically drawn together and small flames of excitement ignited my forbidden desire for him.

'Come on, my girl,' he said when the meeting was over, 'I'll walk you to the bus.'

He'd called me 'my girl' ever since we'd met that night in Sophiatown. It was a hot afternoon and we walked slowly until we reached the corner of Catherine Street where I went to my Whites Only bus stop, and since Sipho couldn't wait with me, he mounted his bicycle and pedalled off, turning to give me a final goodbye wave. I waved back and stood admiring the kaleidoscopic heat-shimmer of the cars, bicycles and people travelling in front of me. To my right, I could see a rubbish cart making its slow progress along the road, the dustbin men forced to hurry to and fro emptying heavy dustbins before running to catch the cart up, for it didn't stop to wait for them. I remembered something Sipho had said earlier that day: 'Whites use us like extra limbs to fetch and carry for them.'

I followed Sipho's progress with my eyes and could see my bus approaching in the distance. My languorous contemplation turned to horror when a car drove directly into Sipho's bicycle, knocking him to the ground. The flow of everything around me appeared to decelerate, and as though in slow motion, I moved through the traffic until I reached his side, where I cradled his bleeding head in my arms. The driver, who had knocked him over, shouted at him and drove off.

'Call an ambulance,' I called to the crowd who had gathered at the side of the street. A couple of them, seeing that the injured man was black, turned and went about their business. 'Someone call a fucking ambulance, now!' I screamed.

A man held his hand up to indicate that he would and ran towards the nearest building.

I turned to Sipho. 'Hang on, Sipho, we'll get you to hospital.'

'I'm OK,' he said, opening his eyes. He closed them again and lay motionless. His bicycle beside him, the front wheel, crushed and misshapen, seeming to dangle from the frame while the back wheel continued to turn uselessly like the final futile twitchings of a hanged man.

The ambulance that soon arrived was for whites only. When the driver saw that the victim was black, he turned to leave.

'Please take him,' I begged, 'you can drop him outside Baragwanath hospital.'

'Ag man, look, you know I can't, it's against the law, I can only go to Jo'burg General,' said the driver, indifferently picking a piece of food out of his teeth with a matchstick.

'What about the Hippocratic oath, for Christ's sake, don't you ambulance people have to take it too? What kind of a man are you?' I shouted in vain over the sound of his engine; the ambulance was already pulling away.

We waited a further twenty minutes by the side of the road before a black ambulance appeared. By then Gloria and Harry had joined me, alerted by the noise I was making as they walked past on their way home.

'Look after Sipho's bike,' I told them as I scrambled into the ambulance behind Sipho, ignoring the protests of the ambulance men.

I stayed with Sipho through the long wait in casualty, through the short-staffed, short-tempered doctors, and all through a long night where he drifted in and out of both consciousness and delirium.

'The tokoloshe is here,' he shouted at one point, sitting bolt upright with terrible fear in his eyes. 'It wants to take me and kill me. Look at it; can't you see its sharp teeth? It's trying to bite off my toe.'

At last, in the cool pink dawn of the eventual morning, his breathing grew steady and he l ooked at me directly, took my hand in his and said, 'My girl.'

I realised then that I was his girl; I had been for months. I looked into his eyes and found there the sense of belonging that I had sought all my life. I knew that when he recovered, we would flout the inhuman law that forbade our union and be together.

'My boy,' I said as I bent to kiss him.

Chapter Eleven

Ros looked about her, confused for a moment by her surroundings, wrenched from the hot red earth of her mother's African past to the grey reality of her own present. It's disquieting for any child to imagine that their parents could have had lives of any significance before their birth and Ros had rarely considered how her mother's life might have been. How very grown-up Lilian seemed in her teenage years, how different from the girls of the same age that Ros taught and how solitary she appeared growing up with parents who felt like strangers. She was struck forcibly by how different the Lilian of these pages was from the one she remembered and whose voice she heard in her head. Images of her mother came to her: Lilian standing in her nightie ironing Ros's school blouse for the morning; Lilian with Pond's cold cream spread thick and white on her face; the late night click of Lilian's absurdly high heels in the stairwell outside their flat; Lilian's powdered cheek and the smell of her lipstick; the occasional sound of her mother crying alone at night in her bedroom. Once Ros had gone in to see what the noise was and had found Lilian curled up and alone in her big bed. Precociously Ros had told her that she should find someone to marry and Lilian had shaken her head and said, 'There's nothing more lonely than being with the wrong person' before sending Ros back to her bed. Ros understood what she meant; she had felt lonelier with Mike in the final year of their marriage than she did now that she was actually on her own.

Ros glanced at the woman at the table next to her, engrossed in a magazine, her lips moving slowly to spell out the words she was reading. One of the many celebrities who obsessed the nation smiled out from the cover, an ice-cream cone held tantalisingly to her lips. Hold the front page, Woman Eats Ice Cream, Ros thought, or rather clasps it, for it was unlikely that the calorie-rich confection would actually touch her lips. Famous for being famous, the celebrity in question had no discernible talent aside from her ability to wear clothing in child's sizes. In the absence of any gift, her body was her work of art: the perfectly golden limbs, surgically enhanced face, improbable breasts and changing hairstyles her very own work in progress. Ros stood up, pulling up jeans that were growing ever looser and reflected how pleased her mother would be to see her so slim. Lilian had always regarded excess weight in a person as a character defect. When Ros had been briefly plump, Lilian, the antithesis of a Jewish mother, had urged her to eat less. One might have thought Lilian's neurosis would have led Ros into defiant over-eating, secret stashes of empty chocolate wrappers and the scattered crumbs of furtive sandwiches. Indeed, for a while, she had eaten secretly, tiptoeing to the kitchen, soundlessly prising open the biscuit tin, kept full for visitors, and stealthily making her way back to her room with her forbidden booty. However, in the end, the need for Lilian's approval had won out and Ros had lost weight and remained slim ever since. Her mother's vanity, her meticulous attention to the details of her own appearance had always struck Ros as incongruous in a woman so concerned with matters of the mind. But, as Lilian always said, 'Just because you're clever, it doesn't mean that you can't look pretty.' The pages she had just read confirmed Lilian in Ros's mind as a complex character, full of contradictions. Why had Lilian never told her about Sipho or her involvement in the ANC? What further revelations lay in store and when would the next instalment arrive? Ros picked up Gloria's letter and read it again. She had made no mention of the publishers' name and had not given her own address.

Ros went to the Ladies and contemplated her face in the mirror. 'Put a little lipstick on, darling,' Lilian seemed to whisper in her ear, 'you look pale and approximate without it. As women grow older, they lose definition, their outline blurs. You should never leave the house without lipstick and mascara.' Without realising she was doing so, Ros reached in her bag and coloured in her face. She tilted her head back up towards the mirror, like a child holding up a piece of work for a parent to praise, and was rewarded by Lilian's voice. 'Much better, you see how much younger you look? Wait, what's that?' Ros sensed Lilian's face peering hard at her own as, eagle-eyed, like a mother ape grooming her young she homed in on a blemish on Ros's left cheekbone. Ros dotted concealer over it and, with a final glance at herself, made her way to the exit. En route, deflected by the sight of people mute in front of computer screens in the coffee shop, she paid for fifteen minutes of Internet time and, like a slot-machine addict in a gaming hall, took her place beside them. Her addiction was rewarded. Jimmy was online.

Sally, are you there? How can you miss someone you don't even know? I keep thinking about you.

Shall we meet? she typed recklessly, made adventurous by her recent knowledge of Lilian's daring relationship with Sipho. Not this week, but next?

YES! Tuesday week, 7pm, The Coach and Horses in Greek Street?

How will we recognise each other?

Shall I send you a photo? Jimmy wrote.

No, spoils the surprise. Ros felt reluctant to send him one of herself. She wanted it to be a proper blind date.

You don't want to know if I'm tall or short, black or white, or whether I have a horn growing out of the middle of my forehead? Jimmy asked.

Nope, although the horn's a given by virtue of your gender.

Oh, ha ha! Not all men are so stereotypical, I happen to have a sensitive soul.

I know, Ros wrote, that's why I've agreed to meet you.

OK then, I'll be reading a copy of the Guardian.

So corny, and I'll have a red rose between my teeth. Ros was enjoying herself.

Are you serious?

Of course not. But I'm sure we'll find each other.

The twins were leaving on Saturday. Ros needed something to look forward to, something to fill the void that threatened to overwhelm her once they'd gone.

Like a mother that can distinguish the cry of her own child amidst all others, Ros recognised Ruffy's bark as soon as she parked in her street. The dog bounded up to her as she entered the house and, placing its paws on her shoulders, licked her face, covering her in acrid doggy breath. Ros fell laughing against the wall.

'Ruffy is bery bery goo' dog,' Jack said, appearing in the doorway eating an apple. 'She love you bery much.'

For God's sake, whom on earth had Jack been talking to? He sounded like a Spaniard. Of course. The dog-and-husband-stealing Spanish assistant. Well, soon-to-be-ex husband.

'What's she like?' Ros asked.

'What's who like?'

'Your father's new girlfriend.'

Jack blushed and looked as though he might burst into tears. 'She's not his girlfriend,' he said, 'she just comes round to walk Ruffy.'

Ros wanted to press him further, but it didn't seem fair. Children, she firmly believed, should not be used as weapons in their parents' battles. She drew Jack to her and pulled his head onto her shoulder, feeling the hard strong muscles in his back where only yesterday, or so it seemed, she had felt soft and tender baby flesh. 'Where's Sid?' she asked.

Jack said nothing, merely inclining his head towards Sid's room from where the sound of wood knocking against plaster could be heard. He and Liz were at it again. Ros and Jack both blushed, finding it suddenly awkward to meet each other's eyes. They giggled, first Ros and then Jack, holding their fists up to their mouths to stifle the sound like naughty schoolchildren.

'Are you seeing anyone?' Ros asked, emboldened by their mutual guilty mirth.

She rarely pried, leaving it to her sons to choose when to share intimacies. Lilian had always cross-examined her relentlessly in her own youth, rarely patient enough to wait until Ros was ready to offer confidences. They were brutally torn from her and the assault often left her feeling sullen and resentful.

'Naa,' said Jack, 'I mean, I was, you know, this girl, yeah, but like, I'm not now. Anyhow, we're going away ...' he trailed off and Ros asked nothing more, saying only, 'Well, darling, any girl would be lucky to have you, you're gorgeous.'

She often felt the need to shore him up. Sid was the more confident of the two, he moved smoothly through life, while Jack was more hesitant, less certain of himself. More, Ros couldn't help feeling, like her.

Ruffy nudged Ros's leg with her wet nose and, looking down, Ros saw that she had her lead in her mouth, her eyes bright with anticipation.

'Will you take her?' she asked Jack. Pleased though she was to see Ruffy, she'd just come in.

'Oh, Mum, I've just come back from picking her up from Dad's. You take her; she's missed you. She needs some quality time with her mother or she'll think you don't love her any more.' Jack looked at her slyly, fully aware that by leaving Ruffy with Mike, Ros felt almost as bad as if she had, in fact, abandoned a child.

Dogman was by the front gate, a copy of the *Sun* under his arm and the post in his hand; he was looking at a letter upside down with a puzzled expression on his face. For once, he was dogless. It was fortunate since Ros was, on this occasion, with dog and the encounter could otherwise have proved ugly. Dogman jumped as Ros approached and then resumed his study of the letter in his hand. Ros glanced at it and saw her own name on it.

'Oh, that's for me,' she said, putting her hand out to take it.

'I was bringin' it to ya, innit? I know it's for you; I'm not stupid, I can read.'

Ros realised at once that therein lay Dogman's problem. She quickly glanced at the rest of the letters he held and pointed to the one that was addressed to him. It took her a moment or two as she was half-expecting it to be addressed to a Mr Dogman, and what she saw instead was his real name, Mr Terry Brice.

'I'm Ros,' she said, holding out her hand.

'Terry,' he answered, taking her hand but not quite meeting her eyes. His face brightened as he looked at Ruffy. 'Now that,' he said, his head nodding in approval, 'is what I call a poodle.'

Ruffy stood magnificent and proud as if she understood the compliment. Her fur was black and tightly curled, her very existence made nonsense of those miniature approximations that had the temerity to go by the name of poodle. Dogman too was dressed entirely in black. He and Ruffy looked good standing side by side, sleek and black and shiny. Dogman's black hair was artfully greasy and carefully oiled into an Elvis Presley of a quiff.

''Ere, Ros,' he said, blinking hard at Ros from behind black-rimmed spectacles. 'I've got sumfink in me eye, can yer read this letta to us?'

Ros took it from him and scanned it swiftly.

'It's from the council,' she said, 'the Noise Department, there have been complaints about your dogs from the neighbours.'

Dogman looked at her accusingly.

'It wasn't me,' Ros protested. 'They say that if there's another complaint, you'll have to get rid of the dogs or leave.'

'I bet it's that fuckin' old geezer from next door,' Dogman said broodingly. 'Fuckin' council stickin' their noses in, what they expect me to do about it? Dogs, they bark, don't they, I mean, that's what dogs do.'

Ros sighed; she could see that she was going to have to get involved in letter-writing and dog training on Dogman's behalf, not to mention gently steering him in the direction of adult literacy classes, and she wasn't sure she had the energy for it. 'Jack will write to them for you,' she said, a solution suddenly presenting itself to her. 'He'll draft a letter and we'll sort it out.'

'Fanks,' said Dogman, 'you're diamond. I'll 'ave a word wiv me dogs and see if I can keep 'em quiet.'

Ros tried to imagine how such a conversation might go as she and Ruffy made their way up the road. Ruffy seemed quite clear about the direction she wanted to take and so Ros, no longer sure which of them was on the end of the lead, allowed her to dictate their path. What, she wondered, should she wear for her date with Jimmy? Should she go the casual trousers with trainers route, or the little black dress with heels? 'Heels, of course,' said Lilian's voice loudly, making Ros jump. 'You must wear heels, they make one's legs look longer.' Ros sighed. Sometimes she wondered whether her memory of her adolescence as not quite happy was due largely to the fact that her feet had hurt so badly. In accordance with Lilian's high-heel rule, she'd always worn absurd stilettos, indeed had been famous for the inappropriateness of her footwear and, as a result, had spent most of her teenage years with the balls of her feet stinging. Could this physical state have been to blame for her general sense of discomfort when she recalled those years?

Ruffy was growing excited, pulling at the lead and leading Ros resolutely in the direction of St Mary-in-the-Fields, one of the many bleak red-bricked churches that proliferated in the Shepherd's Bush area. Her determination to lead Ros to the church suggested that she'd been there before. A grey pallor painted the street and it had begun to rain in a manner that felt almost apocalyptic. Ruffy drew Ros into the church's porch for shelter. Ruffy sat with the satisfied air of someone who has reached their destination and Ros waited for the rain to stop, passing the time by reading the parish notices pinned to a board. 'We are the us in Jesus,' she read and snorted with the disbelief of an atheist, although in the next instant, she glanced up towards the ceiling to check that she hadn't made God angry. A sudden bolt of lightning streaked the sky. Oh dear, God was clearly a little bit cross. She sighed again. She seemed to have been doing a lot of that these days, sighing that is, and wished that she could be more definite about her religious views and hedge her bets less.

Ruffy suddenly jumped to her feet, her head darting from side to side as though seeking something or someone. Ros followed its direction and was astonished to see Mike appearing from a small door at the side of the church. He was with two or three other people. Ros pulled Ruffy out of sight into the recesses of the porch. What on earth was Mike doing in a church? He really was a determined atheist and felt strongly that religion in any form was utter nonsense, the opiate of the masses. He'd said as much on numerous occasions to the various religious travelling sales-people who turned up periodically at their front door, their faces kind and pitying as they had nonetheless offered him salvation. He'd even told some Jehovah's Witnesses not to be so silly. Could he suddenly have found God? Should she approach him? Ruffy was certainly keen to and on the verge of barking a greeting, her mouth hastily stopped by the Good Boy chocolate drops that Ros had pulled from her pocket.

She observed Mike from their hiding place. His companions were unlikely: a man and a woman. The man looked like a tramp, unkempt, with grubby brown trousers too short in the leg held up by a striped tie belted around his waist. The woman looked like the sort of person who might be head of cakes for a fund-raising bring-and-buy sale to build a new church roof or belfry. A row of small pearls flashed white around her neck and she carried a patent leather handbag on one arm. Mike was laughing at something the man was saying and Ros noticed how happy he looked, his eyes bright and his characteristic laugh seeming to bounce off the grave-stones of the small yard they were traversing. She was struck by the ease that this unusual threesome shared in each other's company, their heads and smiles bent towards each other as they walked on, indifferent to the rain. Curiouser and curiouser, she thought, feel-ing once more like Alice, but this time like an Alice whose familiar world has abruptly and inexplicably transmogrified into not so much a Wonderland, but a dubious unknown country.

'Can I help you?' A deep voice interrupted Ros's thoughts. She looked up into the friendly gaze of a vicar or a pastor, she wasn't sure what the difference was, if any.

'Oh no, really, we're just sheltering from the rain, if that's all right.'

'There is always a place in God's house for you,' he said. 'He is always ready to give you shelter.' He bowed, a slight inclination of the head, and moved away as silently as he had approached.

Mike and his companions were standing by the gate continuing their conversation. Others who had straggled out of the same door joined them and seemed, from the odd word that floated across to her, to be debating where to go for a coffee. Ros was trapped and in urgent need of a pee and Ruffy was growing restless, the chocolate drops eaten and her master within sniffing distance. She poised as though deciding with whom her allegiance lay or which of the two was most likely to offer her further treats. Ros's mobile rang and she answered it quickly, fearful that the noise might give her away. It was Charlie.

'Amsterdam's amazing,' he said, 'I've met a lovely man called Rick.'

'Already?' said Ros. 'Lucky you. I seem to be in church, well not quite in, but hovering on the periphery.'

'Don't do it,' Charlie said, 'turn back, there's still time.'

Ros laughed. 'It's OK, I'm just sheltering from the rain.'

'Thank God for that. Get straight back onto the path of un-righteousness. Go and flirt with Pleasure4U and set up a hot date; I can't recommend meaningless sex highly enough.'

'It's all right for you,' said Ros, 'you seem to do it as easily as ordering a pizza. Anyhow,' she continued, keeping her voice lowered, 'my husband is mere yards from me, oh, thank goodness, he's finally leaving.'

'What is this, a happy clappy divorce convention or religious marriage guidance or something?'

Ros explained the situation.

'How odd,' said Charlie. 'I certainly never figured Mike out for the sort of bloke to turn to the Almighty. Must run; have to meet Rick at a coffee bar. See you next week.'

Ruffy could wait no longer, she jerked herself free of her lead and took off up the road in the direction that Mike had taken.

Ros hurried after her and caught up with them both at the corner. Mike's companions had continued down the road without him.

'What are you doing here?' asked Mike, automatically feeling in his pockets for a treat for Ruffy; his eyes darting nervously back in the direction of the church. He looked like a man with a secret. Ros noticed that his facial hair was no longer accidental unshaven stubble; it was maturing into a deliberate appendage, a moustache in its own right.

'I wasn't aware that I needed permission to visit certain areas of Shepherd's Bush, or that individual streets were part of our division of property and possessions,' said Ros.

As at their last meeting, she had intended her tone to sound light and amusing, but it had come out sounding bitter instead. Mike handed her Ruffy's lead, his mouth tightening. She noticed too that his nose hair was visible and wondered why he wasn't using the nose hair trimmer she'd given him for his last birthday. (Most men over the age of forty are certain to have received one from their wives at one time or another.)

'Listen, I've got to rush, but let's talk later about getting the boys ready and taking them to the airport next weekend,' he said.

'A perfectly good marriage and you've just thrown it away.' Lilian's voice echoed sadly in Ros's head as she watched Mike walk away.

Chapter Twelve

Sid was entwined with Liz on the sofa while Jack sat in a chair texting on his mobile phone. The little bleeps of messages sent and received sounded frequently.

'Here's a novel idea,' said Ros, walking over to them, 'try talking to each other on the telephone. It's much faster and means you will use whole sentences rather than text speak.'

'Probs madre, but gt 2 gt ready 2 go out,' said Jack.

'Yeah,' said Sid, 'we've got like a goodbye party at our mate's house.'

'Like a goodbye party? Or, in fact, a goodbye party?' said Ros, ruffling his hair.

As Sid was speaking, Ruffy jumped up and ran for her lead. Where previously she had fetched her lead whenever anyone said 'walkies', she had recently begun doing so whenever she heard any word beginning with 'w'. As far as possible they'd tried to ban the letter from their speech, but it was impossible not to slip up now and again. Ruffy was running round and round in circles; she'd become very excitable of late and Ros couldn't help feeling that the constant chopping and changing between her house and Mike's flat wasn't good for her. She needed some of Hari's soothing aromatherapy Doggie Drops.

Sid jerked his head from Ros's hand in annoyance and carefully reorganised the strands of hair she had disturbed into a precise arrangement discernible only to him.

The boys left soon after, taking the dog with them to drop with

Mike. They wouldn't be back until some time the following day; it was going to be, like, a real all-nighter.

Ros drifted around her flat, feeling like a stranger in her own life, picking objects up and placing them down as if she'd never seen them before. She could hear Lilian chastising her again for her lack of inner life and she sat with a glass of wine and thought about Lilian's story, picturing her mother in that faraway foreign land that felt so removed from her own experience and wondering why Lilian had spoken so little about her past and why she, Ros, had thought to ask so little. She wished she could read more. She felt restless and circled the room like Ruffy did when she was preparing to settle, before finally coming to rest in front of her computer. H-a-a-h! Another sigh; but this time one of contentment as Ros prepared for the easy escapism of cyberspace.

Sal baby, where have you been? I've got my ribbons ready.

Pleasure4U.

Where? Oh, here and there. What are you doing?

Waiting for you. Let's meet.

When?

Now!

Now? Ros's fingers paused over the keyboard. She couldn't now, her hair was a mess.

I can't.

Why not? Come on, let's be spontaneous. It's 7 o'clock; I'll meet you at 8.30. There's a bar near where I live in Clapham.

Ros sat frozen. Could she? Should she? She felt a flicker of excitement and stood up to look at herself in the mirror on the wall above. An hour to lick herself into shape, to wash her hair, de-fuzz and anoint. Why not? That or another evening at home alone with her thoughts and her mother's memories.

Well?

OK.

The wheres and whens decided, Ros hurried to prepare, pleased that her need for adventure had the power to overcome her intrinsically fearful nature. 'We're where the old world meets the new.' Lilian's voice sounded softly in her ear.

He was handsome. Young and handsome and, truth be told, more than a little dull. But, dullness notwithstanding, he had smooth golden skin that she ached to touch and she was not, she reminded herself, looking for meaning. She'd worn a simple black dress with heels; the very outfit she'd planned for her date with Jimmy the following week. Her hair was caught up in a loose knot with tendrils pulled down to frame her face. Her eyes were mascara-ed and her lips frosted with gloss. Lilian would have approved. Well, at least with how she looked, not perhaps with what she intended to do. She felt nervous and at the last minute, just as she was about to enter the bar, she'd almost turned back. It was her first date in over twenty years.

'So, you're like a teacher?' he said, his voice going up at the end as he handed her a second glass of wine. 'That's cool, I've never been out with a teacher before.'

His hand grazed hers and their eyes locked. If she hadn't been so starving hungry for the feel of a man's skin, she'd have made her excuses and left. But she was. Famished. She hadn't realised to what extent until now. Their lips touched and the kiss felt full of promise. Back at his flat, they barely made it through the front door before tearing at each other's clothes and falling naked onto his sofa. Ros marvelled at her own lack of inhibition, losing herself in sensation as she answered the hunger of his warm, hard skin.

And then he spoke.

'Now that Pussikins has met the Cock Rooster, she'll want to hear him crow,' he said, pulling her hand down towards his erection. How strange for a man to talk about his penis as if it were an individual, a mini-me that had a mind of its own. She tried hard not to shudder. There was no turning back now. Pleasure4U, whose real name was Steve, twisted her nipples hard as though searching for a remote radio station. Come in Tokyo, Ros thought as she winced. He moved his hand downwards and attacked her clitoris with a thumbnail as if he were scratching an itch and Ros sounded several loud notes of pain, which he mistook for an arpeggio of pleasure. Thus encouraged, he increased the pressure. Of the promised ribbons, there was no sign. Ros thought of asking for them but she'd already insisted that he use a condom and didn't want to sound too bossy. Foreplay quickly over, he thrust into her and this was the biggest surprise: his penis was simply too big. Not too big to fit; she managed that, although with difficulty, tilting her pelvis back and then moving her hips to ease him in, inch by inch, but simply too big for pleasure. Who would have thought such a thing were possible?

'Yeah, yeah, you like that, baby? Am I big enough for you, hard enough?' He leered at her, confident in the knowledge that he was. 'It's all for you, baby, pleasure for you.'

Pleasure4u, geddit? she thought, feeling strangely removed from her body.

Ros took refuge in politeness.

'Yes, thank you,' she answered, thinking, when will this end and that's another fine mess you've got yourself into and if this is meaningless sex, you can keep it; each thought punctuated by another thrust that pushed her further up the sofa so that her head was twisted into a position of almost excruciating agony. She thought briefly, longingly, of Mike and the safe contours of his familiar body.

'Let's come together,' Steve said, his breathing growing erratic.

In your dreams, thought Ros. The likelihood of her achieving orgasm with him was as remote as that of a Channel swimmer reaching her destination with legs and arms bound together.

'Come on, Steve,' he panted, 'go, Steve, go.' He pulled her hair hard with one hand, punched the air with the other as he crossed the finishing line, patted Ros's naked bottom and fell asleep. His body felt heavy and Ros was finding it difficult to breathe. She lay in the mournful aftermath of sex with a man who was destined for ever to remain a stranger, caught between laughter and tears. Inching an arm out from beneath him, she felt for her mobile phone in her bag. Putting it on silent, she texted Charlie.

Meaningless sex an unqualified disaster. You were right; girls can't do it. Now get me out of this mess.

Ros couldn't help wondering how her life had come to this: an unknown man's naked body lying beside her own forty-something one in an unfamiliar apartment far from home. That would teach her to indulge her long-suppressed adventurous spirit. There had been a time, before Mike – BM as he called it, when, he liked to joke, her life had been a barren desert – when, during a briefly promiscuous phase (and then only ever after a second date), her bra could have been found lying discarded and forgotten in any of several locations around London. She now felt as if she had lost her centre of gravity and was spinning out of orbit. Steve's body felt alien and foreign and she was trapped by its weight; not knowing what else to do, and with no succour yet from Charlie, she fell into an uneasy sleep. Later she was woken by his hands reaching for her, busying themselves, tweaking and pulling at her as he began his discordant lovemaking once more.

'I've got a present for you, baby,' he said as he hardened and started to pull her head down towards his groin. 'Some more Steve love.'

Not again, she simply couldn't. Ros sat up and looked at her watch. It was four a.m.

'Good Lord,' she said, 'is that the time? I must dash.'

Steve looked puzzled. Where on earth could someone need to *dash* at such an hour? Ros picked up her phone and pretended to read a message: 'I have to get back, my sons are ... um ... locked out. They've ... er ... just got back from a party and can't get in.'

Hastily gathering scattered garments, she dressed and leant over to give Steve a quick peck on the cheek, her body carefully arched away from his to discourage further contact. He pouted with disappointment, like a child that has been told he can't have pudding. Ros rehearsed the lies she would write him later: *It's not you, it's me. I'm not ready for a relationship ...*

Oh, the relief when she closed the door and breathed in the damp night air. She stood for a moment in the dark street in her black dress and high heels and felt like something left over from the night before; a working girl on her way home from turning a trick.

As soon as she got into her car, the tears began to fall. Her phone rang – it was Charlie, finally, and the tears turned to laughter as she recounted her evening to him. At least, she reflected wryly, like so many of life's disasters, it made good copy.

'Was it his dick?' Charlie asked. 'You know, like a penis, only smaller?'

'*Au contraire*, my friend, like a penis, only bigger. In fact, too big.'

'What do you mean too big?' Charlie said, his voice going high and squeaky. 'There's no such thing.'

'You'd have thought not,' Ros answered, 'but apparently there is. Where are you?'

'With Rick, he's asleep. We've had a fabulous evening.'

'What do you talk about?' Ros asked, mindful of how difficult it had been to talk to Plezh.

'Oh, we talked of cabbages and kings and all manner of things,' said Charlie.

'If he's going to cause you to talk in such appalling rhyming verse, I'm going to have to forbid you from seeing him,' Ros said.

Charlie laughed. 'He told me I have unhappiness in my eyes.'

'Honestly, Charlie, surely you realise that's shagmeisterese for "my big knob will soon put a smile back on your face".'

'What's got into you?'

'You know perfectly well, what's got into me, I've just explained in some detail.'

Charlie chuckled on the other end of the phone.

'That's it, I've decided to become a lesbian,' Ros continued. 'I've noticed that it's a career choice for lots of women. It's not like I want any more children and women are so much easier to get on with. Look at Sophie Bagshott, you know who I mean, Head of Chemistry, she left her husband when her kids had grown up and moved in with Emily Ball, the Head of Biology.'

Charlie laughed. 'You don't need to go that far, Ros,' he said, 'not when you've got me as your gay husband. Are you sure it was too big? Is that possible?'

'For God's sake, Charlie.'

'Listen, I've decided to take the week off work and stay here. I'll be back on Saturday in time to say goodbye to the boys before they go off.'

The reminder that her boys were leaving set Ros off again, her tears mirrored by the soft rain that fell on the windscreen as she drove through the empty London streets. As she crossed Wandsworth Bridge, she automatically undid her seat belt and opened her window; that way, if the bridge collapsed and she fell into the river, she'd stand at least a fighting chance of escaping from her car. She shook her head, amused by her ability to have sex with a perfect stranger while fearing the freakish collapse of a bridge that had been standing firm for over a hundred and thirty years.

Approaching home, Ros couldn't resist taking a detour down Devonport Road, slowing as she passed Mike's flat. It was in darkness and still, save for the flutter of a curtain at the open bedroom window. She liked to sleep with the windows closed, Mike liked them open. That, at least, was one advantage of separation, Ros reflected; you could do what you wanted again without reference to anyone else.

On Monday morning Versace Porsche Brown was outside her door once more at first break. Her crime? Attempting to pierce the nose of her best friend, Hollywood, in the girls' toilets when they should have been in a maths lesson. Ros felt she'd lost much of her authority with Versace since meeting her outside the Headmistress's office.

'Yeah, well she asked me to, right?' Versace said, her arms folded against a self-justifying chest. 'Like what's the big deal, it's her nose.' She shrugged and looked out of the window.

'There are two issues here, Versace,' Ros said. 'One is mutilating your friend's body, the other is missing maths.'

'Well, it 'aint no mutilation,' said Versace, 'it's art, innit? That's how I look at it, your body's your own and you can change it and make it more beautiful. Anyhow, Miss, you've got a tattoo, you should understand. And I was doing it real careful like, with a sterilised needle and everyfink. And anyhow, I don't need no maths for what I want to do.'

'What do you want to do when you leave school, Versace?'

'I'm goin' to be a beautician. Or,' she said, tapping her mouth with a forefinger as though the idea had just occurred to her, 'I might have a baby. Yeah, I think I'll have a baby next year, keep me busy. Who shall I have it with?' She started counting on her fingers evaluating her possible options.

'There are easier ways to be busy,' Ros said. She wrote a quick note to herself to ask the PSHE teacher to enrol Versace on a course where teenage girls were given robot dolls to care for.

On her way towards the staffroom, Ros bumped into Lola.

'How's your friend getting on with her new boyfriend?' she asked, affecting casual interest.

'Oh, she make sex with him, of course,' Lola said. 'She say is bery nice but is saying him, next time, don't be so quickly.'

Ros found it difficult to breathe; it felt as though Lola had punched her in the solar plexus. She could just imagine the scene. It must be unbearably exciting for Mike to have sex with someone new after so many years. Unlike women, men rarely seemed to have bad sex. She even remembered Mike saying there was no such thing. If there was sex, it was good; how could it be otherwise? He used to make her laugh when he was trying not to come, endeavouring to keep going for her pleasure by conjuring up distasteful images for himself and sometimes even describing them out loud, 'Fish heads, squashed pigeons, overflowing trash cans.'

'Don't be so quickly.' It was just the kind of phrase that Ros and Mike might once have adopted and incorporated into the private language every couple shares. Ros recalled a meal she'd had in a Thai restaurant some years before with Mike and the kids. She had been staring at him intently, moving her head this way and that as though trying to decide something about his face.

'Look at Daddy's nose,' she'd said to the kids eventually, 'is it me, or is it crooked?'

They'd pulled his face from side to side and both agreed that it was.

'Nonsense,' Mike had said, wiggling and wrinkling it.

'It is crooked, Dad, honestly.' Sid had reached his finger out and traced the length of Mike's nose.

Mike had gone cross-eyed trying to look down at his own nose and made them all laugh. The waiter came to take their order and just as he was turning to go, Mike had asked him, 'Is my nose crooked?'

The waiter had given him a long considering look; holding his hand up between his eyes like a spirit level before nodding his head and answering gravely and definitively, 'Li'l bi'.'

Ever since, li'l bi' had become a family catchphrase. Are you hungry? L'il bi'. Have you got homework? Li'l bi'. Do you love me? L'il bi'.

Apart from family sayings and words deliberately mispronounced the way the boys had said them as toddlers, which all contributed to the mythology of their relationship, they'd had numerous silly games. For instance, points awarded for Ruffy-like poodles spotted, men with elaborate moustaches and people who couldn't roll their 'r's. All the little details of a life built with someone over the years rushed into Ros's head and she felt overcome by an ache of intense loneliness. 'Don't be so quickly' was not a saying they would share, but the beginning of a private language Mike was inventing with someone else.

'So, what do you think?' Ros asked.

Jaime handed back the pages she'd been reading.

'Amazing,' she said. 'Do you suppose Sipho is that chap in the photo with his arm around her on the bicycle?'

'I think he must be,' Ros said.

'Have you contacted this Gloria?' Jaime asked.

'She hasn't given me her number and directory enquiries couldn't help since all I've got to go on is the postmark. I don't even know if Wiseman is still her surname and anyway, there are thousands of those.'

'You'll just have to wait for the post,' Jaime said.

'I know, it's terribly frustrating, though. Not to mention frightening. I feel like I'm sitting in a room with a ticking bomb waiting patiently for it to explode when I should be running for cover.'

They sat in silence for a moment enjoying the brief lull of the staffroom before the bell sounded for the next lesson.

'It's amazing to think she was caught up in the ANC in the fifties,' Jaime said.

'It certainly brings history alive when you realise it's your own history,' Ros agreed. 'Although I can't understand why she didn't simply tell me all this when she was alive; I've told my boys about the life I led before I had them. I certainly won't be able to leave them a story like this after I've gone.'

'Well, that's not necessarily a bad thing,' Jaime said. 'Although I think it's good that you're finding out about her. Until you make peace with your mother, you'll be trapped by the past and you need to be free to get on with your future.'

'When did you get so wise?' Ros said. 'That's what Charlie has been telling me too. Am I really so caught up in the past?'

Jaime nodded. 'It's not surprising really, first your mum, then Mike and now the boys leaving ...'

'Can one resolve a relationship after someone has gone?' Ros asked.

Jaime nodded. 'Yes, I think one can. One can come to terms with it, anyhow.'

Ros got up to make them a cup of coffee. 'I'll just have to watch out for the post,' she said, pretending not to notice Jaime eating a fig roll.

Ant came in talking on his mobile phone.

'Yes, darling,' he was saying, 'I think the purple suede will look lovely with that new black dress, I really do.'

Ros and Jaime exchanged a look.

'No, I don't think the heels are too high, they're just right and make your legs look terrific ... No, I'm not saying your legs *need* heels; they're always terrific … Yes, the grey ones were lovely too.' Ant wouldn't meet Ros and Jaime's eyes. 'Yes, of course … no, I'm happy to meet you in Oxford Street … OK, see you later.'

'It's obvious he wants to come in her mouth,' Jaime whispered to Ros loud enough for Ant to hear, 'there can be no other explanation.'

Ant glared at them. 'Ha bloody ha,' he said, after he'd hung up. 'Peter,' he called out to the Angel of Death whose recent entry into the staffroom had sent teachers scattering in a way that was reminiscent of the Red Sea parting in front of Moses, 'Ros wants to talk to you.'

Ros gasped, rendered speechless by this betrayal.

'Payback time for leaving me with him the other day,' Ant said.

Ros glanced at the clock on the wall. Three o'clock – her next class began at half past. Peter Seers made his way over to her, trapping her in a corner as he began to espouse his theory on the necessity of restructuring the school curriculum. Hours later, Ros glanced up at the clock once again. It was five past three.

'I have some marking to do before my next class,' Ros said and walked away quickly before Peter could stop her.

It was true. She did have marking to do that she should have done the day before. She'd intended to get started as soon as she'd got home from walking Ruffy but had kept putting it off.

First she had made the boys some supper.

Then she had done the washing.

Then she had cleaned the bath.

Then she had lined up the tins in the food cupboard so that all the labels were facing outwards.

Then she had put the washing in the dryer.

Then she had plucked the hairs on her upper lip thinking that just because Mike had a moustache, didn't mean there was any need for her to have one too.

Then she had shelled some broad beans.

Then she had neatly folded the now clean and dry washing and put it in the washing basket.

Then she had flirted with Jimmy online for a while.

Then she had peeled the outer skins off each individual broad bean.

Then it was too late.

As she was falling asleep, she had reflected that, were it not for the fact that she would never get round to it, she should write a little book on the art of procrastination. Now, she scuttled away from Peter Seers and reflected that completing unpleasant tasks was simple; all you had to do was find something you wanted to do less than the thing you were supposed to be doing. Marking felt like a treat when compared to listening to the Angel of Death and Ros read the first sentence of Ysatis Goodwin's essay on *Animal Farm* with a surge of emotion akin to joy. 'This book ain't really about animals at all ...'

There was a message waiting for Ros on her answering machine when she got home.

'This is Clare Voyante, medium-to-the-stars. I've had your mother back, dear. She likes to talk, doesn't she? She's not happy with the way your head is sitting on your shoulders, she says you should get it seen to. There's a lady in Wimpole Street, Jasmine somebody-or-other. Who? Yes, I'll tell her.' Lilian was clearly in Clare's other ear. 'Jasmine Thompson, that's it. Bye, dear.'

So, Lilian didn't think she had a good head on her shoulders. Ros tended to agree with her. Apart from the fact that her decision to have sex with Plezh at all was, she was forced to admit, ill-judged and an indication that her firmly held no sex on a first date rule should be adhered to at all times (he'd never have qualified for a second date), the experience had indeed left her with a very sore neck.

Directory enquiries gave the number for a Ms J. Thompson at 49 Wimpole Street, London W1. Ros was no longer surprised by spooky occurrences and had come to expect them. She did not seek rational explanations, choosing instead to submit to her fate. Obediently, therefore, she dialled the number and booked herself an appointment with the soft-voiced woman and mender of necks who answered the telephone.

The remainder of the week passed for Ros as the last days must pass for a condemned man as he approaches the day of execution. The boys had only ever been away for a week at a time before, and then, not often. Perhaps three or four times in their lives on school trips. Ros was always the mother who stood by the coach weeping as she saw them off while all the other parents waved their children off gaily professing their delight at a few days to themselves. It was her fear that she would never see them again that distressed her, her need to keep them safe and protected. She would take photos and torment herself with the thought that, she might, in the future, find herself looking at such a photograph, at the happy smiling faces of her two sons and thinking, *only a few hours later, they were dead.* Whenever she heard of a fatal accident, she was haunted by the notion that the victims had got out of bed that morning and gone about their business, unaware that they were beginning the last day of their lives, that within a few short hours it would all be over.

'You have to promise me to stay alive,' Ros always told the boys, 'it's the one thing I ask of you.'

'Yes, Mum, we'll do our best,' the boys would answer easily, confident, like all young people, of their immortality.

The day that Lilian died, Ros had gone to her mother's flat and found an onion chopped and ready for cooking on a wooden board beside the gas hob; a piece of sewing set aside temporarily on the arm of a sofa and, for some reason most heartbreakingly of all, a small pile of unwashed underwear in the African basket Lilian used for her dirty laundry. She'd put a wash on and when clean and dry had carefully folded the garments and put them away in Lilian's closet, hoping that the act would somehow conjure her mother back into being. Then she'd left the flat and had been unable ever to return, leaving Mike to pack it up and put it on the market.

Like Lilian, Ros lived in the expectation of loss and although careful to keep her fears to herself and not to burden her children with them, she spent the week nervously touching light switches with both hands, avoiding the cracks in pavements and touching wood whenever an anxious thought overcame her. 'You're as bad as me,' she could hear Lilian's voice telling her. Are we, Ros wondered, destined to become our parents, our teenage rebellions a vain bid to establish a separate identity, which ends in failure as we succumb to our inevitable fate some twenty or thirty years later and see our parents' faces staring back at us from mirrors and hear our mouths forming the very words that they once uttered? Are families little more than part of the same living organism, each generation destined to repeat the behaviour, with all its mistakes, of the generation before?

As Ros helped her sons pack for their journey, she remembered the painstaking preparations that Lilian always undertook when they had travelled; the endless lists, the boxes of provisions packed in the back of the car to save money, the careful budgeting for their time away. In this, at least, she was different, more carefree and more profligate.

The boys divided their last week between their parents and brought Ruffy back to Ros's house for their last night. Liz spent the evening in tears, which had the effect of keeping Ros strong. Ros held their plane tickets in her hand, Qantas round-the-world-tickets that would turn her sons from boys into men. London–Bangkok–Sydney–Bali–Vietnam–London: the modern teenager's rite of passage. She'd been most insistent that they fly Qantas – it was one of the only airlines that had a faultless safety record. Their planes never crashed. *Until now* the voice of fear threatened to whisper in her ear. It had been a difficult day; the envelope that had arrived in her hallway that morning had held her decree nisi. It was a time of endings, the end of her sons' childhood, the end of her marriage. Mike had phoned her at work later that morning.

'Are you sure this is what you want, Rosie?' he asked.

Ros's eyes stung when he said Rosie; it was his special name for her. But she pictured him held between Marie-Carmen's firm young Spanish thighs and understood there could be no turning back. 'Never turn back,' Lilian had always told her when she was growing up, 'keep moving forward. Always.'

When she'd arrived home, there had been a large bouquet of flowers waiting for her. *To the best mum in the world,* the card said. *Thank you for always being so look-afterish. We'll be fine and promise to stay alive. DON'T WORRY! Love from S & J.* Look-afterish was their word for Ros's motherliness.

She'd taken special care with the last supper, wanting to leave the boys with the taste of home in their mouths as they set off on the backpackers' holy grail to the land of Oz. She'd made baboo-tie, a Cape Malay recipe that her mother always used to cook and which was one of the boys' favourites. They fought each other for the layer of banana and flaked almonds that crusted the dish and the years and meals they had shared together seemed to compress. How quickly the time had passed from the day when she had brought her two small bundles home from the hospital, astonished by these miniature male creatures her female body had made. She'd never thought beyond the pregnancy and the birth and was overwhelmed that she had been allowed to take them home. 'Make the most of it,' older parents with grown children had told her as she gazed at the tiny faces of her sons, their small mouths working in search of her breast, 'it goes so very quickly. Before you know it they'll be leaving home.' The notion had seemed preposterous at the time. But, the cliché was true; they generally were. She looked at them, grown-up, with hair on their faces and under their arms and longed for the tiny babies she had once cradled and for the time when she had known at every moment where they were and with whom. How she wished she could still strap them in their highchairs and feed them mashed banana.

Jack finished writing a letter for Dogman to send to the council. It was a perfect example of officialese and demonstrated, once again, his talent for mimicry. He had twice read through the letter Dogman had received from the Noise Department as if to calibrate the tone of officialdom and had then sat down and handwritten, confidently and quickly, a response. He read through the letter to himself and gave a quick nod of satisfaction.

'With regard to the attached,' he said, infected by his own prose and waving the piece of paper in the air, 'I wish to refer you to the recommended course of action; delivery of the enclosed to the occupant of number forty-three, referred hereinto as Mr Terry Brice.'

'Ask him what he said to his dogs,' said Ros, 'they've been strangely quiet since he got that letter from the council.'

'Yeah and hurry up, bro, we're due at the Swan for a quick drink,' said Sid.

The boys gone for a final drink with their friends; Ros wound a soft white scarf around her neck, put on her coat and let herself out of the front door, Ruffy straining at the leash. Once again the dog led her confidently off down the road. Ros followed, her thoughts full of the times she had wheeled her boys in their double buggy through these same streets.

'Ooh, twins,' people used to say, peering into it, 'double trouble, aren't they lovely?'

Ruffy stopped outside a house on Thorpebank Road, number eighty-three, and pulled Ros insistently towards the gate. The houses gave directly onto the street, giving the impression of a child's drawing. Ros tried to pull the dog away, but she would not budge. A movement in the window caught Ros's eye and she looked up to see the silhouette of a couple entwined in the light of a lamp. The woman was young with long dark hair. She put her hand around the man's neck and pulled him down towards her, kissing him deeply. Ros looked away, embarrassed at being a spectator to the couple's intimate embrace, and tugged again at Ruffy's lead. The dog stubbornly pitted her body weight against the tension in the lead and continued to sit sentry. Ros's eyes were drawn back unwittingly to the couple as they finally broke away. She caught a glimpse of the man's face. It was Mike. He was smiling. She almost shouted out, a sharp 'stop that at once', as she'd used to when the boys were small and doing something they oughtn't. However, the memory of Steve/Pleasure4U enthusiastically thrusting into her naked body froze the words before they reached her lips. Ruffy stood still, her head held erect, one ear twitching in apparent outrage; or perhaps the outrage was Ros's own? Ros moved off briskly down the road, giving the dog no option but to follow.

On the Uxbridge Road, a man wearing a turban held in place by a jewel at its apex stopped her. The stone gleamed preciously, incongruous amidst the shabby kebab shops and Polish delicatessens that lined the busy street.

'You're thinking too much,' he said.

'Pardon?' said Ros, hesitating.

'You, your mind is always too busy, am I right?' He nodded encouragingly, his small dark eyes gleaming in the reflected light of a street lamp.

Why had she stopped? Did she feel he had the answer to an important question?

'Come here, let me look at your hand.' He took it into his own, which was surprisingly soft and warm. 'Very good.' He let go of her hand and opened a small zipped leather wallet from which he took a piece of paper. He quickly wrote something down and, before Ros could read what he had written, folded the paper up and placed it in her palm, curling her fingers around it. She was strangely compliant, had given herself over to him like a sleepy child allowing a parent to undress her.

'What number do you like between one and five?' he asked.

'Um, three,' she answered.

'What is your favourite flower?'

'Bougainvillea,' Ros said, recalling the wild splashes of colour she and Lilian used to admire on holidays abroad. Ros hadn't realised at the time how emblematic they were of Lilian's African life.

'Open the paper in your hand,' he said.

Ros unfolded the scrap of paper. *Three* it said, and underneath in small neat lettering, *bougainvillea*.

'How did you do that?' Ros was astonished.

He didn't answer; he had torn off another corner of paper and was writing again. Once more, he folded it up and placed it in her hand.

'Your mother is dead, yes? One year, maybe more.'

Ros nodded.

'And now it feels that everything is dying, am I right? Your husband also has gone, not dead, but not with you any more. He loves you. Open the paper.'

Ros did. It bore the letters, *L* and *M*.

'Mother,' the man said, pointing at the letter L, 'and husband,' he pointed at the M. 'Look at this.' In the zipped leather wallet, Ros could see a photograph of the man standing before her seated at the feet of a guru, an elderly Indian man with a long white beard. The photograph had been taken in India and the two men were flanked by a woman dressed in a sari and three squatting children who stared up from the sun-baked earth with wide eyes unaccustomed to a camera.

'How much you give me?' the man asked.

Nothing came without a price, Ros reflected, not even gum-baggley. She dutifully placed a few pound coins into the man's proffered wallet.

'That's all?' he asked, astonished that his wisdom should be so poorly rewarded. Ros made to move away.

'Wait,' he called, 'I tell you more things. You like sex, am I right?'

'Everyone does,' she called over her shoulder, quickening her step to increase the distance between them. 'Although not,' she reflected silently, 'with men who call themselves Pleasure4U.'

Chapter Thirteen

When Ros arrived home, she found Charlie and the boys kneeling on the living room floor. Charlie was teaching them Japanese folding, the art of folding a T-shirt in four moves.

'Lay the T-shirt flat, take a line from the middle of the shoulder to the hem, pinch the fabric with your right hand halfway down,' Charlie explained. 'With your left hand, take the point between neck and shoulder fold it in half to the opposite point on the hem keeping the pinch in your other hand, uncross your arms, shake the T-shirt and fold over, voilà the T-shirt is now perfectly folded!'

'That's brilliant, let me try,' Sid unfolded the T-shirt and started again. 'That's the best tip ever, man,' he said appreciatively, admiring the neatly folded T-shirt in front of him.

'Here's my modification for backpacks, once folded, roll into a sausage.' Charlie deftly rolled the T-shirt and poked it into Sid's backpack. 'When you want to wear it, simply unroll, unfold and you shall go to the ball!'

'Sid's right, this really is your finest tip ever,' Ros said, hugging Charlie. 'I can't believe you haven't showed me it before.'

'I only learnt it myself a few days ago. Amsterdam Rick, very resourceful man.'

'Not entirely meaningless sex, then?' Ros asked.

'Meaningless, but enjoyable and useful.'

Later, after Charlie had stencilled the boys' initials onto their backpacks for easy recognition, he gave them each a camera to record their journey and slipped substantial wodges of money into their back pockets when he thought Ros wasn't looking. He left shortly after, saying that he didn't wish to intrude on their last night together. Ros could see that wasn't the only reason as he clasped the boys to him, his eyes bright with tears.

'I saw Mike kissing,' she whispered to him as he left.

'We'll talk about it tomorrow,' Charlie said, touching her hand briefly.

Sid and Jack came and lay beside Ros on the sofa. She settled between them, an arm around each of them as they laid their heads on her chest. You had to have two children, she thought, one for each arm. How had Lilian managed with only one? And how did some women manage with none at all, with the awful loneliness of empty arms? The most complete happiness Ros had known was to have her small boys on her lap, their sticky arms around her neck, their warm bodies moulded into her own. Flesh of her flesh. How terrible it would have been never to have known this simple pleasure.

'Do you remember,' she said, 'how you would come into bed with me and Daddy and give us naked hugs when you were little?'

When small the boys, fresh from their bath, would run into their bedroom, shrieking, 'Nakey hug, who wants a nakey hug?' 'We do,' Ros and Mike would answer clasping the still-damp naked bodies to them, tickling them until they squealed, kissing their necks and squeezing their round baby bottoms.

'We'll always be your boys, Mum,' Sid said, kissing her, 'but naked hugs would be a bit pervy at this point.'

She'd wanted to keep them next to her, but they had gone to their rooms eager to carry out their final preparations. Ros wanted to talk to them, to tell them something important, although she wasn't quite sure what, and she remembered how Lilian had wanted to tell her something that last night in hospital. Children don't want to listen to their parents, she realised, especially when they're busy and excited with their own lives. She understood that the story Lilian was telling her now was undoubtedly connected to what she had wanted to tell her before she died and she dreamt of Lilian that night. It was a dream she'd had many times before where Lilian barely knew her and expressed little interest in her. She'd been away for a couple of years, but wouldn't say where she'd been. Ros woke in the grey dawn of Saturday morning with the bitter aftertaste of her dream. She stood in the kitchen quietly lining up her vitamins. What should she take for grief, she wondered, resolving to ask Hari if he had a special flower remedy to ease the ache that threatened to engulf her. PULL YOURSELF TOGETHER, she admonished herself, determined not to contaminate her sons' excitement at the adventures that awaited them with her misery.

Before they left, Ros made them all sit for a few minutes in silence, their luggage ready by the door. It was a practice that Lilian had taught her and which she, in turn, had learnt from her grandparents; an east European ritual that ensured the travellers' good luck on their journey and a safe return.

Mike drove them all to the airport, talking too loudly and too much as he always did when upset. She held her boys to her, inhaling them as though the memory of their scent could sustain her in the months to come and managing not to cry until they were gone from view. Jack was blowing, exhaling air through his lips in a series of short bursts to stop himself crying. He'd often done this as a child when he was trying to be brave, saying afterwards, 'I didn't cry, Mummy, I blew', and Sid, disentangling himself from a weeping Liz, had hugged Ros so tightly she couldn't breathe.

At the last moment, the boys looked at each other, then Sid, who had clearly been nominated as spokesman, put his hands on Ros and Mike's shoulders and said, 'Please will you and Dad try again while we're gone?'

Ros and Mike shuffled awkwardly as the boys always used to when the situation was reversed and they were being told to behave.

'It's something we're all just going to have to get used to,' Ros said quickly. 'This is between Dad and me. It's nothing that either of you have done, you do understand that?'

The boys had nodded and sighed.

'You know that we both love you very much? Nothing will ever change that,' Mike said, hugging them both tightly.

The automatic sliding doors of the departure lounge swallowed Sid and Jack up with a quiet whoosh and Ros turned to Mike and fell into his arms, broken. She felt as though someone had plucked her heart from her chest, thrown it on the floor and stamped on it. Their physical proximity soon unsettled them both and they drew apart.

'It's only for a few months,' Mike said, trying to comfort her. 'They'll be back before we know it.'

'Six months, Mike,' Ros said. 'Six long months.' Ros found she couldn't look at him without seeing the face of the young Spanish assistant as she had broken away from their kiss the night before, nor without remembering Mike's face, alight with the pleasure of that kiss. The boys' departure signalled an end for her and Mike to need to maintain such close contact. Apart from Ruffy, nothing would bind them for the next few months and news of their sons could be shared through email. A wave of desolation caught Ros in the pit of her stomach and threatened to overpower her. Why on earth did everyone pretend that gap years were acceptable? Parents spent eighteen years monitoring their children's every move and doing everything in their power to keep them safe and then blithely waved them off to travel alone for months to unknown and dangerous places. What kind of madness was this?

Back at the house, Ros tidied the boys' rooms. They'd left clothes in heaps on the floor, dirty coffee cups and papers strewn on every surface, palpable reminders of themselves and their lives. Underneath Sid's bed, Ros found Monty, the furry brown monkey that Lilian had given him when he was born. He was one of a pair; two monkeys that entwined each other, their long arms reaching behind each other's necks where they were held secure by Velcro. The other monkey was called Morris.

'Twins, like us,' Jack said once he could talk.

The monkeys were balding now, patches of fabric showing where fur had once been. Ros went to Jack's room and found

Morris wedged behind the headboard. She reunited the pair, carefully Velcroing their hands together, and sat on Jack's bed, the toys cradled in her arms, her sobs vibrating with the echo of the boys' lives spent growing up within this house. She felt a terrible stillness descending now that they had gone which threatened to suffocate her. Ros had not cried this hard since the days and weeks following Lilian's death. Ruffy put her paws on Ros's shoulders and licked the tears away before trotting off to the living room, stopping every now and then to check that Ros was following. She put her paw on Ros's chest and pushed her gently to encourage her to sit. Ros joined Ruffy in her customary position at the window to wait for the boys to return home. The dog didn't realise just how long her wait would be this time. As she sat quietly stroking Ruffy's head, Ros could imagine the two of them sitting expectantly side by side for the next six months.

'You know what they say, "*Partir, c'est mourir un peu*",' said Charlie, appearing at the door some time later.

'*Un peu?*' Ros said. 'It's more like a long, prolonged and agonising death.'

'Come on, we're going out to lunch.'

'How can I go out? Look at my eyes.' Ros held her face up to Charlie.

'Dark glasses,' Charlie said, picking a pair up from the mantelpiece and pushing them onto her face. He stepped back to appraise her. 'You look a little like a beetle in those, but never mind, better an insect than a lacrimonious matron.'

'That's not even a word; "acrimonious" or "lachrymose", you mean. I may be tearful, but I'm not bitter. Although, breaking up is hard to do.' Ros attempted a smile.

'Yeah, someone should write a song about it,' Charlie said wryly.

'They already have …' Ros began.

Charlie silenced her with a look.

'Lacrimonious should be a word,' he said, 'tears often are bitter.'

'So,' said Ros, 'here I am, my children abroad and my marriage over. I'm now a woman alone with her dog and even then not a whole one due to the need to share Ruffy with Mike. Still, at least I've got my gay husband.'

Ros and Charlie were on their second bottle of champagne – Charlie had insisted that nothing else would do – seated in a brasserie on Portobello Road. They weren't the only ones wearing dark glasses on this dull winter's day and blended in perfectly with the Notting Hill crowd they usually took pleasure in deriding. 'Bit sunny for you, is it?' Ros always wanted to say whenever she saw anyone in dark glasses on a grey day or at night. 'Too much glare from the moon?' Perhaps, like her, they were merely hiding eyes made red from crying rather than trying to be cool?

'Are you sure it was too big?' They'd been discussing Ros's disastrous encounter with Plezh and it was probably the fifth time Charlie had asked her the same question.

Ros swatted him with her napkin. An aeroplane passed overhead and she shuddered. She'd been trying hard not to think of her two boys somewhere in the sky, hurtling towards Thailand in several tons of steel. How did planes stay up anyhow and why hadn't she thought to find the pilot, make him have a blood test to ensure he was alcohol- and drug-free and tell him to be careful?

'The important thing is that you've lost your post-marriage virginity,' said Charlie.

'So has Mike,' Ros said. She told Charlie what she had witnessed the night before.

'Mike's simply having meaningless sex with a pretty girl to cheer himself up,' Charlie said. 'Anyhow, you've known he was sleeping with that Spanish girl for a while.'

'But seeing him with her like that was a shock,' Ros said. 'I mean, what if he's falling in love with her?'

'He's perfectly entitled to, Ros, you asked him to leave and filed for divorce. What do you expect him to do, weep over a photograph of you for the rest of his life?'

'Well, not necessarily for ever, but certainly a little sighing and weeping for a few years at least. Just because I don't want him doesn't mean I want anyone else to have him,' said Ros, 'especially now that I'm so obviously going to be on my own till the end of time. Pleasure4U has put me off men completely, and anyway, I don't think I can sleep with anyone else ever again.'

'Why on earth not? You can't let one bad experience put you off.'

Ros leant forward and whispered, 'This morning in the shower, I made a terrible discovery.'

'What?'

'Grey pubic hairs,' she said, the words coming out louder than she'd intended. She must have been more than a little drunk or she'd never have embarked on so delicate a matter in public at all, let alone so audibly.

'Ah,' said Charlie. 'Yes, I know the problem. What can we do?'

'You too?'

'I'm afraid so.'

Which was how they'd come to scour the nearby shops for hair dye and, purchases completed, had giggled like schoolchildren when they got out of the tube and saw the sign bearing the station's name: Shepherd's Bush.

'We can't really do this together, can we?' Ros said, when they had the dye open before them and had read the instructions.

'Why not? I won't tell, if you don't. First, we must rub Vaseline on our inner bits to stop the dye getting in.'

'Mrs B., you really are a wonder,' Ros marvelled, 'who would have thought of such a thing?'

'I am Mrs B. and Mr Tippy Tip,' Charlie said smugly, and they repaired to separate rooms to carry out the intimate Vaseline application.

Half-undressed and doing their best to preserve decorum, they pulled on the latex gloves thoughtfully provided by the dye manufacturers and, with their naked bottoms placed carefully on plastic bags, applied the black dye to their pubic hair. They sat, legs apart, for the next thirty minutes while the dye did what it had to do. Ros tried hard not to look at Charlie's penis. After so many years of seeing only Mike's, she'd seen a vast number in the past week or two, what with Plezh and naked yoga. She was, she felt, becoming quite a connoisseur. She got up, stooped like an old woman, walking with her legs apart, to prevent the dye from staining the inside of her thighs, and put the kettle on.

'So that's why old women walk like that,' Charlie said, watching her progress across the room. 'It's to keep the dye from running.'

They were suddenly overcome by the ludicrousness of the situation, still tipsy from champagne, both naked from the waist down, their most intimate regions slathered in dye and they laughed until it hurt.

Charlie looked at his watch. Fifteen minutes to go. The plastic bags were sticking uncomfortably to their bottoms.

'Snatch,' Charlie said.

'I beg your pardon?'

'I'm trying to think of some of the words I know for your thingy.' He paused. 'Fanny. Now you go.'

'Todger, one-eyed trouser snake, schlong, knob, willy, pecker,' Ros countered.

'Pussy, beaver, furry cup, minge, punani.'

'Cock rooster,' said Ros, remembering Plezh's name for his appendage.

'Quim.'

Then, the doorbell rang. Ros didn't know what to do. She jumped up and ran back and forth in an agony of indecision.

'Ignore it,' Charlie said.

But whoever it was had no intention of giving up and was leaning on the bell. Ros quickly fashioned knickers out of the plastic bag she'd been sitting on, tearing two holes through which to put her legs and, carefully hiding her body behind the door, opened it just wide enough to allow her head to peer round. Charlie hid behind her, shaking with silent laughter. Versace stood on the doorstep, a baby-sized doll in her arms. It was wailing loudly.

'Miss, it's driving me mad,' she said, holding the doll out

towards Ros. 'It won't stop crying. You take it. Please, I've got to go out with me mates.'

'How did you know where I live?' asked Ros.

'Me bruvva does the paper round for this street, innit. You've got to take it, Miss.' Versace was forcing the doll through the gap in the doorway.

'You can't just give a baby to the first passing stranger when the whim takes you, Versace,' Ros said, adopting the prim tone of the disapproving pedagogue and trying not to notice how 'whim' rhymed with 'quim'.

'I know, Miss, but it 'aint real and there's this like house party tonight and if I don't go, Aaron is going to get with Chanel.'

'Has this experience taught you anything?'

'Yeah, I 'aint going to have no baby anytime soon.' Versace thrust the baby at Ros.

Ros had no option but to take it. She resisted taking up the 'anytime soon' issue with the girl, for once the expression seemed absolutely appropriate and she had no desire to prolong the conversation; the thirty minutes were up and she needed to wash the dye off her love-rug and pronto.

Versace turned and scampered quickly down the path before Ros could change her mind.

'Look, darling, we've had a baby,' Ros said, shoving the crying doll into Charlie's arms.

They took it in turns to look after the doll in between rinsing the dye from their pubic hair, hair that was miraculously restored to the glossy chestnut of its youth. The dye left a nasty tidemark around the bath that proved as difficult to get rid of as the pink ring left by the Cat in the Hat, which could only be removed by Voom, a magic ingredient kept in the hat of little cat Z. Charlie dabbed bleach efficiently onto a white towel that had been similarly affected.

Versace had left a bag with nappies and bottles and finally, after a feed and nappy-change, the doll baby stopped crying. Ros placed it on the sofa, automatically arranging cushions around it so that it couldn't fall off and hurt itself.

'It's a doll, Ros,' Charlie said.

'Yes, but it's been programmed to behave like a baby and I couldn't bear to have its death on my conscience.'

To Ros's superstitious mind, the need to keep the doll safe had instantly and inextricably become linked to her sons' safe arrival in Bangkok. Illogical certainly, but she was a women who feared that sharp knives could fly out of drawers of their own volition and stab her and the boys to death while they slept at night. She remembered how Sid and Jack, when going through the Tamagotchi phase, had quickly tired of their computer pets' needs and that she had been forced to care for them and keep them alive, convinced that, otherwise, their death would be a terrible omen. In the end the batteries had run down and Ros had rationalised that the Tamagotchis' death was from natural causes and would not, therefore, have repercussions for her own or her sons' lives.

'Are you going to leave me at home on my own with a young baby?' Ros asked Charlie as he was leaving.

'I'll stay if you want,' he said.

Ros could see he wanted to go and she knew she couldn't put off confronting her empty nest any longer. Once he'd gone, Ros drifted around the house, uncertain what to do. The boys called her on landing, the telephone cutting into the silence and making her jump. 'You want tuk-tuk, one hour, five baht, cheap for you,' Jack trilled down the phone, proving beyond any doubt that they had indeed arrived safely in Bangkok. The conversation was brief; the boys were excited, eager for adventure. Ruffy, keyed up by the familiar sound of their voices, looked as dejected as Ros felt when the call was over. The dog sniffed the sleeping doll for a few moments before once again taking up her position by the window. Ros sat beside her, her hand on Ruffy's warm fur. A cold wind had begun to shriek outside, whipping around the building and causing the bare branches of winter trees to knock against the windows. So this was it then. Her boys had gone. That part of her life was over. How on earth was she supposed to get used to this? She understood how Lilian must have felt when she'd left home. It was something she'd never considered before; she'd been too busy at the time with her own feelings just as her sons now were with theirs. That was as it should be; it wasn't the child's job to take account of how great the parent's loss was. This was something children need understand only when they became parents themselves.

She phoned Jaime, but the call went straight to voicemail. She tried Ant's number but his new wife answered.

'We're just having dinner,' she said, 'can I get him to call you back?'

'Oh, don't worry, I'll see him at school on Monday, it was nothing important really,' Ros said. She sat still and watched the second hand of the living room clock. It moved very slowly.

Ros logged on to her computer. The usual emails were waiting for her:

A bigger penis can give you a tremendous boost!!!

An overall larger penis size also means a larger surface area!!! Ros wasn't entirely sure what the benefits of a larger surface area were.

88% of ladies want a man that is big, they say it's more fulfilling!!! Hmm, you'd have thought so, Ros muttered to herself, thoroughly irritated by all the exclamation marks, which should, she felt, be used sparingly at the best of times and never more than one at a time. She went onto StartingOver.

Sal, are you still on for Tuesday?

It was Jimmy. Did she really need to go on a date with a stranger?

I can sense your hesitation, Jimmy wrote. Please come. You won't have to do anything you don't want.

OK, but I'm really not sure why I'm on this site at all.

I'm so looking forward to meeting you. I feel mournful today.

Why? Ros typed, hoping he wouldn't tell her. She hadn't even met the man and the last thing she wanted was to be forced into a maternal role, offering succour and support. That was the trouble with men; all too quickly they turned women from lovers into mothers, and expected them to make everything better for them. Although, she supposed, women were often complicit.

It's OK, Jimmy wrote, as though reading her thoughts, I don't expect you to make me feel better. It's nothing I can't deal with and I won't bore you with it when we meet.

Ros felt relieved, despising herself for her meanness and suddenly eager to meet him.

All right, see you Tuesday.

Ros baby, do you want some more sweet Steve love?

Plezh popped up online. Ros quickly logged off. She'd have to deal with the Plezh issue sooner or later, but not now.

Sunday dragged slowly by. Charlie was away visiting his father in the country. Ros took Ruffy for his mandatory walks, pulling a coat over her pyjamas. She watched television with unseeing eyes, ate three bowls of cereal instead of meals, mechanically changed and fed the doll baby and wished the hours away. She thought of all the people who lived alone and for whom days turned into weeks without human contact and felt a frisson of fear that she had abandoned the companionship – however unsatisfactory – of her marriage. She was glad when the ten o'clock news started and she felt she could legitimately go to bed. She was just on her way when the doorbell rang. She opened the door to find Dogman on her threshold and realised that she'd been hoping it might be Mike.

'This is fer ya,' Dogman said, handing her a manila envelope. 'They put it through my door by mistake.'

This time the postmark was South African. The second instalment had been sent directly to Ros by the publishers with a form for her to sign authorising publication. The timing, Ros reflected, couldn't really have been any better. She got into bed and opened the envelope.

Chapter Fourteen

Lilian

I lay with Sipho in our secret place, the cavernous hollow of a giant baobab tree in a deserted piece of high veld outside Sophiatown. We weren't the only ones to seek refuge there; parrots, kestrels and owls nested with us and when, in mid-summer, we stayed beyond sunset, after the tree's gleaming white blossoms unfurled to begin their brief butterfly-lives, we had to share our quarters with the myriad fruit bats and insects which congregated to sup on the flowers' sweet nectar. After dark, lights glittered in the city below us combining with the blaze of the star-studded skies above to create the illusion that we too were suspended in the atmosphere.

I was in love for the first time and felt more at home in Sipho's arms than anywhere I had ever been. How could the expression of our feelings for each other be illegal?

Once, near the beginning, when we were so full of each other that it took every ounce of self-control not to touch, we were standing on the street after a political meeting. Sipho was standing very close to me and gently smoothed a lock of hair out of my eyes and behind my ear. We were so absorbed in each other that we failed to notice a policeman appear at our side.

'Is this native bothering you, madam?' he asked, roughly grabbing Sipho to push him away from me. 'Voetsak, kaffir.'

'No, not at all; let go of him at once,' I ordered. 'He's a friend of mine.' I turned to confront him.

'Oh, it's you,' the policeman said.

I looked at him; it took me a moment or two to recognise him. It was Keith du Toit. I'd lost contact with him but had heard from my mother on one of my increasingly rare visits home to Cape Town that he'd joined the police force.

'Sorry, Lilian,' Keith said, taking a step back and releasing Sipho as though he'd been stung. Despite my rudeness in not returning any of his calls, it was clear I still had some power over him.

'How could you, Keith? How could you join the police and enforce this regime?'

Keith shrugged, shuffling awkwardly like a reprimanded schoolboy.

'Ag man, don't start all that, it's a good job. When will you learn that the whites were born to rule and the blacks to serve?'

Out of the corner of my eye, I saw Sipho's expression harden.

'Never, Keith, that's when. I will never learn that.'

Sipho and I had walked away leaving Keith standing on the pavement. When I'd turned to look back, he was still standing in the same spot, watching us.

The experience had been unnerving and since then Sipho and I had taken more care. It was around that time that we made our nest in the tree. Saturated in African myth and fable, the baobab felt worthy to play host to our developing love for each other. The first time we went, Sipho and I were lying together, having made love, my head upon his chest, half-drugged by the hypnotic sounds of insects and our intoxication with each other.

'Do you know the story about this upside-down tree?' Sipho asked lazily.

'I know it's called upside-down because its branches are like roots so it looks like it's been planted head first.' I ran a hand down his taut stomach and admired the dark chestnut brown of his skin against the white of mine.

'There are many stories. One is that after God created the universe, each animal was given a tree to plant and when it was the hyena's turn, it planted its tree upside down. Others say it was the devil that planted it upside down.' Sipho stroked my hair and pulled me closer to him. 'There is yet another fable that claims that the baobab was one of the first trees to appear on earth and when the other trees appeared, it was overcome with envy because they were *taller, more graceful, more colourful and more luxuriant. So when the gods saw the baobab's jealousy they responded with anger and in order to punish it, they pulled it up by the roots and replanted it upside down.'*

'So the moral of that tale is, no doubt, to learn to be satisfied with the cards that fate has dealt you,' I said.

Sipho gave a bitter laugh. For those of us who lived in South Africa during those years, being satisfied was not an option. The baobab became a metaphor for the upside-down country in which Sipho and I lived and as such an appropriate place for us to celebrate our love for each other.

'Tell me your story,' I said to Sipho, 'you know mine. I want to be able to imagine you as a young boy.'

'What can I tell you? My story is the story of so many black boys and men living here today.'

'I want to know everything about you.' I sat up and looked down at him, at this face that had quickly grown so dear and familiar to me, at his big brown eyes and full soft lips.

'OK.' Sipho kissed me and sat up.

He rested his back against the cork-like bark of the tree and leant over me to get his cigarettes from the pocket of his hastily discarded trousers. He lit two and passed me one.

'My father came to Johannesburg from the Transkei to work in the mines. He was an ordinary man, very steeped in Xhosa tribal traditions and customs and he thought it was a waste of time for us children to go to school. But my mother was a strong woman and she insisted, working very hard at several jobs to make enough money to send me and my brother and sister. Anyway, when I was ten, my father was killed in a mining accident.'

I was struck by Sipho's matter-of-fact tone; aware that the death of a parent, while no less of a tragedy for an African child than for any other, was all too commonplace. Perhaps, I reflected, it was this tenuous hold on life that had given rise to the importance of the extended family in African life.

'My mother worked in the hospital as a midwife, but to earn extra money she used to do the washing for some families in Hillbrow *and I helped her with her work, fetching and carrying the clean and dirty washing back and forth. I could run faster than any boy in Sophiatown; my mother always used to say to me that every black boy living in this country should know how to use his own two legs in case he needs to get away fast. So, anyway, one of the houses where my mother worked, there was a boy my age. This boy was Harry.'*

'I didn't know that you and Harry had been friends for so long,' I said, astonished that neither Gloria nor Harry had thought to mention this fact to me.

'Oh yes,' Sipho said. *'Harry and Gloria became like my brother and sister. They would give me all their old books and Harry passed on his clothes to me. I was one of the best-dressed boys in Sophiatown. Harry's taste in books was very sophisticated even when he was quite young and, as a result, so was mine. We were already reading Lenin and Marx and having political discussions when we were fourteen. This was really my education. One day, Harry was sick and didn't go to school and later on, one of his friends told him that the headmaster had warned all the other boys about him at assembly. He said, "There is a boy here who is spreading left-wing views around. I must ask you not to listen to him." Before I met Harry, I thought, like most boys of my age, that the white man was superior to us. I remember one evening, it was late and already dark. I was standing in the street waiting for one lady to give me some washing to take to my mother when I saw a white man walking and three black men coming towards him. They came very close to this man and looked very intimidating. He took fright and ran away, looking back over his shoulder to make sure that they weren't following him. I realised then that we have something in us that can make the white man run and for the first time in my life I felt I had some power, that I was human too and my people had the right to a better life. I understood then that we blacks were watching silently; watching and waiting and that we would not always settle for this life that the white man has given us.'*

With the help and support of Harry and Gloria's parents, who were early members of the Communist Party of South Africa, Sipho had gone on to university and joined the youth league of the ANC.

Sipho and I had been living our secret lovers' life for three years. Only our most trusted friends knew of our relationship. By this time I had graduated from Wits and was working on the Rand Daily Mail, a left-wing newspaper. Although I still typed up documents for the ANC, I was finally typing for myself too and filing pieces on a variety of subjects. Sipho was working for Drum magazine reporting on the lives of urban blacks. We were never able to write as freely as we might have wished for fear of censorship and there was an ever-present danger that the publications for which we wrote could be banned.

'At least we are doing something useful,' Sipho said on one occasion when I was railing against the injustice of not being able to write the plain truth. 'One day people will read between the lines of these articles we have written and understand what was going on here. Good journalism, they say, is the first draft of history.'

With each year, more and more repressive laws were passed. Police raids were becoming increasingly common not only in the townships for petty violations of pass laws, but also amongst our circle of white political activists. All of us had learnt to listen out for the telltale sound of footsteps at night signalling a raid and we took care to hide any incriminating documents that might be in our possession. By now, Gloria and I were living in Hillbrow in converted servants' quarters in Lenny and Shirley's garden. They had married and now that I no longer presented a threat, Shirley and I had become friends. They'd bought a house with one of the most colourful and exotic gardens in Johannesburg and Shirley and I would often spend happy hours together tending the beautiful pansies that carpeted a large oval flowerbed in the centre of their lawn. Their house had become something of a headquarters and we had hidden leading activists in our spare room on more than one occasion during periods when they had been forced to go underground to avoid arrest.

The government had realised that whenever they banned organisations or publications, others would quickly mushroom to take their place and they had therefore adopted a policy of banning people instead. As a result, it was impossible for many of our banned *friends to attend meetings or meet with more than one person at a time.*

Harry had also married: Sonya, a beautiful ballet dancer from Aberdeen, my father's hometown in the Karroo. I had a dim memory of her as a child when I used to visit my grandparents: a small, slender girl, with disproportionately long legs, often glimpsed practising her arabesque on the stoep of her parents' house. They were leaving for England in order that she could pursue a career with the Royal Ballet, a decision that had cost Harry months of soul-searching. Lenny, Shirley, Gloria and I went with them to the airport to see them off.

'I feel terrible about going,' Harry said, 'as though I'm leaving a job unfinished.'

'It'll be useful having you there on the outside,' Lenny said. 'Who knows what will happen here – we may all be forced to leave soon.'

'I don't even know how I'm going to earn a living,' Harry said. 'The law they practise is different from ours.'

We knew that Harry felt that he had sold out. He was putting personal happiness before his political beliefs; a choice, he knew, that Lenny would never have made.

'It's your fault, doll.' Harry hugged me, joking in an attempt to alleviate his sense of guilt, while unable to wrest his gaze from his new wife. 'You wouldn't have me so I had to find someone else and look what happened.'

'I'm sure you'll survive without me, Harry,' I laughed, hugging him back.

Harry put his arms down alongside his body and turned slowly in a circle on one spot, his chin on his chest. After a few moments, he raised his head towards us quizzically.

'Chicken on a spit,' Gloria and I cried out together, our eyes shimmering with tears.

We stood in the airport by a large plate-glass window and watched Harry and Sonya's flight leave. The letters BOAC glinting on the side of the airplane were a tantalising signpost to a new life. I envied Harry and Sonya and wished that Sipho and I were on that plane beginning married life in a new country together, no longer forced to hide and dissemble.

*

It was February 9th 1955; Sipho and I had taken the not inconsiderable risk of staying at my place the previous night to enjoy the rare luxury of a real bed and a whole night together. That morning we had risen early, and on a whim decided to play hooky from work and to take a daytrip some twenty miles outside Jo'burg in my Austin Seven.

We drove through early morning rain, which the parched yellow land sucked up with greedy thirst, and stopped at a deserted picnic area where we concealed ourselves behind trees to set up camp. The rain had cleared and it was now a warm, late summer morning. Sipho lit a fire and we sat roasting mealies, which we swivelled in the flames on the end of long sticks. We ate them when cooked, burning our tongues on the hot kernels of corn, and followed them with mangoes, so succulent that the juice dripped down our hands and onto our arms. Sipho sucked it from my fingers and we lay back on a blanket, watching the dappled sunlight play in the breeze through the branches of the trees above us.

We were soon distracted by the sound of voices, and from the shelter of our hiding place I could see a family laying out their picnic on one of the tables in the whites only area. They were talking and laughing, a husband and wife and their two young children. Sipho watched my face carefully.

'Do you wish that was you?' he asked quietly.

'No,' I replied, 'on the contrary, I was thinking how far away from them I felt and how much closer to you.'

I felt queasy; the recently eaten corn seemed to turn in my stomach and the laughter of the children nearby sounded unnaturally loud. The arrival of the family had disturbed our peace and put our shadow relationship under threat. Sipho and I collected our belongings and quietly made our way out from behind the trees and to our parked car. He carried everything and walked several paces behind me in the hope that if the family noticed us, they would think that I was a white Madam out on an errand with her servant.

We were subdued on the drive back to the city, the picnicking family a reminder of a life Sipho and I could never share.

Once back in the car, Sipho echoed my unease.

'I feel like something bad will happen,' he said.

'To us?' I asked.

'I'm not sure. I just have a very bad feeling.' He rubbed his abdomen as though hoping to soothe the emotion he was experiencing. 'Sova singasemoyeni.'

I looked at Sipho quizzically.

'We are on the side towards which the wind blows. It means, we will soon know what is going on,' Sipho translated.

What neither of us realised as we drove back to Johannesburg was quite how quickly we would know. When we approached Sophiatown, a sight of devastation met our eyes. We had been active in the protest against eviction ever since the government had promulgated its plans to reclaim the land for the whites. Although Sophiatown was little more than a slum and many of its inhabitants lived in terrible poverty, it was also the heart and soul of black Johannesburg, it was where South African jazz was born, where black writers, doctors, lawyers and artists had made their homes. The residents weren't willing to relinquish it without a fight and when they'd received notice that the removals were due to begin on February 12th they began preparing themselves for a mass protest. But they were taken by surprise when, early that morning, two thousand policemen and soldiers, armed with guns and knobkerries, arrived in the township, rousing families from their beds and scarcely allowing them the time to load their possessions onto trucks before bulldozing their homes into oblivion.

The street where Sipho lived was in chaos; a small child separated from its parents sat crying at the roadside and others were screaming with fright; women were wailing, trying to rescue shoes, clothes and pots and pans from where they had fallen onto the ground; men were running to and fro, shouting to be allowed more time to organise their families and their belongings, one or two of them fetching a blow from the stick of an impatient policeman. The streets were crowded with open trucks carrying families, who stood holding onto their furniture and belongings as they were driven out of Sophiatown to be dumped like so much freight in Meadowlands some six miles to the south.

Sipho jumped out of the car and started to run in the direction of his house. I followed close behind. He ran straight past his yard and stopped in bewilderment before turning and retracing his steps. All that remained of the yard was rubble; the shacks had been razed to the ground. There was a strong stench of beer from the bulldozed site that had housed the shebeen. We stood leaden with shock for several seconds, before turning to run back to the car so that we might drive to Meadowlands as fast as we could.

Here too we found pandemonium; everyone appeared to be running around in search of family members.

'Hey, Joseph,' Sipho called out, seeing someone he knew, 'have you seen my family?'

Joseph jerked a thumb in the direction of the crowd of people behind us.

'Everyone is over there at the Native Resettlement Board's office, we all have to report there,' he told us, shaking his head wearily at the latest in a long line of injustices.

We hurried over to Vincent Street where, after running up and down the long queue, we eventually found Sipho's mother, Thandi. Her cheeks were wet with tears that fell in a soundless and continuous stream, like water from a leaking tap. She wiped them away absently with a large cotton handkerchief as though they were somehow unconnected to her.

'We have to wait here to be registered,' she said. 'Look, they take our home and in return they give each family two loaves of bread and a pint of milk.'

She indicated with her head in the direction of the office and we saw people emerging, bemused, bread and milk in their hands.

'Where are all our things?' Sipho asked; his face set in an expression of fury I hadn't seen before, an expression which transformed him into a stranger.

'They have piled everything up in front of our new house,' Thandi said quietly.

'I should have been with you when they came,' Sipho said. He turned to me. 'You should go.' His words were brusque and had a finality to them that chilled me.

He looked stricken, as though stripped of the last vestige of power over his own destiny. A man's home, however humble, is one of the things he holds most precious. In spite of the continuous police raids at all hours of the night and day, home was the one place where we still had some illusion of control. It is no wonder that all wars are fought for territory, either in an attempt to expand or protect it. This wanton destruction of their homes struck at the heart of Sipho's and his fellow residents' very sense of being. (The removals from Sophiatown continued over the following eight years until the Boers had recaptured all of the land. They built a new suburb there and named it Triomf, Afrikaans for triumph.)

'Let me help,' I said.

'Just go, Lilian, this is my world, not yours.'

I turned to go. I felt rejected, while understanding that this was not the time to seek reassurance from Sipho. He was angry and as the person closest to him, I must bear the brunt of some of that anger. It was unfair, certainly, but I had observed enough of the world to understand that this was how men could behave. I could feel tears forming and thought wistfully of the family we had seen picnicking earlier that day and wondered fleetingly why I had carved out such a difficult life for myself.

I didn't see Sipho for several weeks following the forced removal of his family from Sophiatown and when I called at Drum's offices, I was told he'd taken time off.

'Listen, he just needs some time to himself.' Gloria tried to comfort me.

'Maybe it's over, Gloria, maybe he meant it when he said this was his world, not mine.' I'd been playing our last exchange over and over in my mind. I went to bed each night with the dull ache of loss and awoke each morning full of hope that he would return. As the day progressed, the hope would trickle away to be replaced once again by despair and loss.

'Ag man, maybe it's for the best. What future is there for the two of you, really?'

She was right of course, but her words made me ache more. Never to lie in Sipho's arms again, or feel his lips against my mouth, his hands on my body, never to hear his voice whisper again in my ear? I was twenty-one and I felt that my life was over. I could neither sleep nor eat. I drove to Meadowlands and wandered around for several hours one Sunday afternoon hoping to bump into him. I didn't know his new address and the people I asked looked at me with suspicion and distrust. Eventually I felt too conspicuous on my own, gave up and returned home.

I lost myself in work, writing for the newspaper by day and drafting and typing documents for the ANC by night. One afternoon, I went to interview Gerry Vanderbilt, a prominent Afrikaans businessman who had recently spoken out against apartheid. It was rare for an Afrikaaner to take a stand against the government and the paper was keen to print his views in the hope that they might prove a clarion call for other less bold, Afrikaans anti-apartheid sympathisers. It was a good assignment for me and marked a shift in the editor's appraisal of my work. Too often, both as one of the few women on the staff and as the youngest, I had been called upon to report on Johannesburg's social and theatrical events and even to file pieces about fashion, something I would never openly have admitted to enjoying.

I pulled up outside Vanderbilt's substantial property in Orange Grove and parked my car. The air was full of the intoxicating scent of orange blossom from the trees that lined the driveway. My thoughts were full of Sipho and the pain in my heart had settled into a steady dull throb. I took a deep breath to prepare myself for the interview ahead and rang the bell. The house was strangely still. I rang again. No one answered. There were cars parked in the driveway. Looking around, I noticed that the front door was ajar and cautiously pushed it open. I entered the hallway and called out, 'Mr Vanderbilt, it's Lilian Block from the Rand Daily Mail.' Still no answer came. There was something unnatural about the silence; it sounded a discordant note of unanticipated interruption.

Tentatively, I went to the bottom of the stairs and called again up the stairwell. Listening closely, I could hear muffled voices. I started up the stairs and saw a single shoe lying on its side on one of the steps, hastily discarded as though its owner had been in flight. There

*was something portentous about this shoe, the image of which has
remained with me ever since. I advanced more quickly, certain now
that something was amiss and, guided by the stifled sounds I could
hear, made my way into the master bedroom. It was empty, but the
sounds were louder, voices calling and crying for help.*

'Where are you?' I called.

'In the cupboard.'

*A large double-fronted cupboard lined a wall. I advanced towards
it and tried the handle.*

'Where's the key?' I shouted.

'Isn't it in the door?' a voice answered.

'No.'

*After a heated exchange from within, a man's voice guided me
to a spare key in a nearby chest of drawers and finally I opened the
cupboard. The whole family was in there: Vanderbilt, his wife, their
two children, the cook and the maid. The maid was wearing only one
shoe.*

*'Your other shoe's on the stairs.' I knew she would be fretting over
the unwanted expense of having to buy new ones. 'What happened?'
I asked.*

'Burglars,' Vanderbilt said matter-of-factly.

*'There were three of them, bloody black bastards. You see what
happens when you give these bloody people sympathy?' his wife said.
'This is the thanks you get.'*

*'You can't blame them,' Vanderbilt said. 'People are hungry. Who
knows what desperate measures any of us might be driven to in
similar circumstances.'*

*'Ag shame man, you and your bleeding liberal heart. Your children
could have been hurt.'*

*'Ja, but they weren't.' Vanderbilt ruffled his children's heads.
'Now let's go and see what they took.'*

'How long were you in there?' I asked.

*'A lifetime,' said Mrs Vanderbilt. She turned to the maid. 'Here,
Sophie, take the children and give them some orange squash and a
biscuit.'*

'I make it two hours and fifteen minutes,' Vanderbilt answered, consulting his watch. Even though he was in his fifties and much older than his wife, he looked like a small boy who has enjoyed an exciting adventure. I warmed to him. Mrs Vanderbilt, on the other hand, reminded me of my mother.

Jewellery and cash had been taken and one of the burglars, either out of fear or as a mark of his contempt, had shat on the rug in the lounge. The irony of the gesture, if it was intentional, was that a fellow African was forced to clean up the mess and not the white man who had been burgled.

"Apartheid is avarice, man, and it can't go on,' Vanderbilt said later. We were sitting on his stoep drinking tea. 'This is a rich country, there's more than enough here for everyone. The white man has to realise this before it's too late, otherwise it'll end badly for everyone. Bloodshed, civil war, you name it and then the whites will lose everything they've worked for.' Gerry Vanderbilt leant back in his chair and pushed the tobacco down into his pipe. 'It's time we started working together to create a multi-racial society.'

'Aren't you afraid to talk so openly?' I asked.

'What can they do? I'm not politically active; I'm just an individual expressing his views. I've got plenty of money both in this country and outside it and a lot of important people are in my debt. If it all goes wrong here, I'll leave.' He shrugged and lit his pipe, sucking on it hard until the tobacco in the bowl glowed red.

'Anyhow, that's enough about me,' he said, 'tell me about you. Why's a pretty girl like you doing this job? How come you're not married and having babies? There must be a lucky man somewhere.'

I blushed. Liberal though he might be, what would Vanderbilt think if he knew the truth about my 'lucky man'? I felt a stab of pain as I thought of Sipho; it had been over a month since I'd seen him.

Vanderbilt looked at me consideringly.

'You look like a girl with a complicated life,' he said, pushing fresh tobacco into his pipe.

'Why on earth do you think that?' I said a little too brightly.

'I'm good at reading people,' he said. He leant towards me and added, 'Listen, if you ever need help, come and see me.'

LEADING AFRIKAANER SPEAKS OUT AGAINST APARTHEID
'Current Situation Will Lead to Bloodshed.'

These were the words below the masthead of the following day's paper. My first front-page headline. I went to the Waverley with some of my colleagues after work to celebrate. Gloria joined me there.

'I've got a surprise for you,' she said, coming up behind me and putting her hands over my eyes.

'Sipho?' I asked, my heart thrashing like a fish on a line.

'No. Keep your eyes closed.' She turned me round. 'OK, now you can open them.'

'Harry!' I shouted.

He lifted an arm and scratched at his armpit with the other hand.

'Monkey?' I suggested.

'Ja, monkey that's come home to the African jungle where it belongs,' Harry said. 'I couldn't do it, I had to come home.'

'What about Sonya?' I asked.

'Kaput. Finished.'

'Are you all right?'

'Listen, Sonya's a lovely girl, but my heart belongs here and it turns out I wasn't ready to give up on the struggle and settle for marriage.'

'What was England like?'

'Jesus, man, it's bloody cold, but terrifically interesting. You must go and visit, everyone should see it.'

'Let's,' Gloria said, turning to me, 'let's go on one of those tours and go to England and Europe.'

'Maybe,' I answered, thinking there was nothing to stop me now that Sipho had left me.

We went dancing after drinks, to a black jazz club we frequented. The band was playing Johnny Ace's 'Pledging My Love' and tears filled my eyes. It was Sipho's and my song, we'd danced to it the first time we'd gone out alone together to this very same club, the first night we'd made love.

'Come and dance,' Harry said, taking me by the hand and leading

me onto the dance floor. People slapped him on the back as we danced, welcoming him back, whites and Africans alike, many of them people he had represented whilst at the bar, defending them from the police's petty, unwarranted grievances against them.

'I missed you,' Harry whispered in my ear.

'I missed you too,' I said lightly.

'Listen, doll, I heard about you and Sipho. You know I love that man like a brother, but does it mean that there's a chance for me?'

Harry led me outside to the shelter of a jacaranda and lit us both cigarettes. All the elements had conspired to lend the night an air of romance: the moon was full, the air warm and the stars shone in clearly defined constellations. Harry took my chin between his thumb and forefinger and tilted it towards him. From inside, I could hear the last bars of 'Pledging My Love' fade to silence.

'Harry, you know how fond I am of you ...' I began.

He moved his thumb and forefinger from my chin to my mouth to hold it closed so that I couldn't continue.

'Don't say it,' he said.

'What?' I said with difficulty, gently pushing his hand away from my lips.

'The "but" that's on your lips. Let's not have any "buts".'

I wished I could forget Sipho and fall into Harry's arms. 'I'm sorry, but there is a "but",' I answered.

'The "but" of Sipho,' Harry sighed, shaking his head in resignation. 'I never should have shared my youth with that bloody man. You see how he repays my kindness? By winning the devotion of the girl I love.' I knew that he was joking.

'If there was to be anyone else, it would be you,' I said, meaning it.

When I got home late that night, I saw the glowing tip of a burning cigarette as I tipsily put my key in the lock. I jumped back in fright. Someone stepped out from the shadows outside our little outhouse.

'It's me, Lili,' Sipho said, coming into the glow of the lamp that hung above the door and taking me into his arms.

'Where have you been?' I asked.

'I took my Mom back home to the Transkei. They wouldn't give her permission to stay in Meadowlands; she didn't want to fight any more, so she went back to her village.'

'Why didn't you tell me?'

'Because I wanted to give you the chance to forget about me and find somebody else.'

I started to cry then, sobs of relief that erupted from me with the violence of water from a cloudburst. I beat at Sipho with my fists, hitting him on the chest over and over again.

'I felt so ashamed for you to see me put out of my own house like a dog,' Sipho said. 'How could I feel like a man after that?'

'But I love you, don't you understand how terrible it has been without you?' I said.

'I'm sorry, Lili, I'm sorry,' Sipho said, pulling me close to him. 'I love you, my girl, I'll love you for the rest of my life.'

'Never do that to me again, do you hear? Never.'

Chapter Fifteen

Ros hurried into the staffroom. She had stayed awake late into the night reading Lilian's story and had overslept. She had lost herself so entirely in Lilian's world that when she woke, she felt utterly disorientated. The transition from her mother's past into her own present had been both difficult and slow to achieve and, although late for work, she had sat in the kitchen, a hot cup of coffee in her hands, staring out of the window unseeingly. The images that passed before her were the ones that Lilian had described; now as firmly etched on the screen of Ros's mind as if she had seen them for herself.

Her thoughts moved to her early months with Mike, when they had been lost in each other, in a bubble of love that had separated them from the outside world. Mike made the bed into a tent by hanging sheets all around it and would touch and stroke her for hours, looking into her eyes with such love in his own that Ros felt sure nothing could ever change between them. 'I found you, didn't I?' he said, with wonder in his voice and Ros had known what he meant; she couldn't believe that she had found him too, couldn't believe the perfect contentment she experienced when she lay in his arms. 'You know this is for ever,' Mike had whispered, kissing her neck. 'You're mine, all mine,' Ros had whispered back.

Ros picked up the phone and dialled Mike's number.

'Hello,' Mike sounded sleepy.

'It's me.'

They were both silent. Ros wasn't sure what she wanted to say.

'Are you OK, Ros?' Mike's voice was gentle. 'They'll be back soon. Six months isn't so very long.'

'I know. You're right. It's not that, it's just, I've been sent this stuff Mom wrote about her life in Africa.' Ros started to explain, but soon became aware of a woman's voice in the background. Mike was not alone. 'Never mind, it's nothing,' she said and quickly hung up.

Mike wasn't hers. Not any longer. She'd known that of course, had brought the situation about, but being confronted so plainly with the proof that he was, or was about to be, someone else's made her ache with loss.

Without thinking, Ros dialled Lilian's number. The phone rang.

'Hello.'

'Mommy. It's me.' Ros paused.

'Darling ...' Lilian said.

'I miss you, Mom. I just miss you.'

The phone was still ringing without answer when Ros hung up.

At school, she found Jaime rushing around the staffroom, lifting papers and books and making a great show of searching for something while she tried to escape Peter Seers who followed in her wake determined to engage her in conversation.

'Have you lost something?' Ros asked.

'Yes,' Jaime answered, 'two things that are rather important to me, my mind and my waist.'

'Here, let me help you,' Ros said, turning a determined back on the Angel of Death and joining Jaime in her search. 'When did you last see them both?'

'I had my mind this morning before he came along,' Jaime tilted her head back slightly to indicate Peter who, having finally given up on her, was now attempting to talk to Sophie Bagshott and Emily Ball, whom Ros and Jaime had nicknamed the 'women in comfortable shoes brigade'. Ros and Jaime both instinctively glanced at the women's feet and exchanged a smile of satisfaction when they saw that the happy couple were indeed wearing quilted leather lace-up shoes with crêpe soles, thus adding substance to the euphemism.

'And the waist?'

'Yes, well, I haven't actually seen that for some time now,' Jaime said mournfully. 'Quite apart from the fact that the diet's not working, I'm getting that awful menopausal shape; if I'm not careful, I'll soon be a perfect cube, look.'

She held her hands to her sides and tried to squeeze them in where her waist should be. It had gone. Although a little plump, Jaime had, until now, always been shapely.

'It's not just that I don't go in at the middle any more, it's also this chunky part round here.' She patted the area below her breastbone and then grabbed the flesh around her stomach. 'I have too much substance and girth and I no longer have breasts, I have a bosom instead. I am beginning to understand the importance of structured foundation garments, a concept hitherto unknown.' She poked Ros in the stomach. 'Look at you, you skinny bitch, you have no need of such things. How do you do it?'

'Very little eating and separating from my husband,' Ros said.

'That's the most cogent argument I've heard for divorce yet and if that's what does the trick, I'm surprised there are any women of menopausal age still married. A husband or a waist? It's no contest, Tony will simply have to go.'

'I must warn you, being back out there isn't all it's cracked up to be,' Ros said, and she filled Jaime in on her date with Plezh.

'What do you mean too big?' Jaime said. 'Bigger than this?' She held up the half-baguette she'd brought in for her lunch.

'Not too far off,' Ros said.

'Ouch. That's put me off my lunch.'

'You shouldn't be eating wheat anyhow,' Ros said, 'didn't you know, it's the devil's work, makes you bloat, that's probably why your waist's gone. In the sacred world of gumbaggley, no wheat, no dairy, no alcohol, no caffeine ...'

'No life,' said Jaime.

'There is that, but you can live on a higher spiritual plane, yoga, meditation and the gratifying smugness that attends such a virtuous life.'

'Not likely since you told me about your naked yoga experience,' Jaime interrupted, surreptitiously tearing off a small corner of her baguette and popping it into her mouth. 'Anyhow, never mind that, tell me more about your night of passion – I can't believe you've kept it a secret for this long.'

'Well, it was all quite promising to begin with. The kissing started off quite well, but then his mouth turned into the nozzle on a vacuum cleaner; it attached itself to my tongue and sucked so hard I thought it was going to tear out by the roots.'

'Ouch again. Maybe it is better to have no waist and stay with your husband after all.'

'I still can't quite believe that I hopped into bed with some guy I met on the Internet,' Ros said.

'Oh, I can,' said Jaime, 'I mean, why not? Life isn't a dress rehearsal and all that bollocks.'

'Yes, but still, sometimes I think I have dissociative identity disorder, you know, that I'm several people, each of whom behaves differently, all living in the same body. I mean, that's what my mother was like and Mike too. So why not me as well? I've always had the ability to shock myself with my own behaviour.'

Jaime put her hand on Ros's arm. 'Do you wish you'd stayed with Mike?'

'Sometimes when I think of nice Mike,' Ros said, 'but then I remember angry Mike and how awful he made me feel. Do you think I should have stayed with him?'

'Oh no, it's not for me to say,' Jaime said. 'You can't change people and marriage is hard. After a while it feels like running a business with someone, you know, as though life is one long meeting. The laughter's not there any more, you're both busy and there's always a job to be done.'

'Can you think of anyone who's still really happy after years together?'

They were both pensive, as though flipping through mental

Rolodexes of married couples they knew. Eventually they shook their heads.

'You may as well go and find some more frogs to kiss,' Jaime said, 'there's always the hope that one of them could turn out to be the handsome prince.'

'That's the problem with marriage,' Ros replied. 'In the beginning, the frog turns into the handsome prince, but after you've married him, he turns right back into the frog again.'

'Perhaps it's because one stops kissing him.'

'Or because he stops letting one kiss him,' Ros said, remembering how hard it had been to get anywhere near Mike when he was angry.

'Nothing stops people getting married and divorced and married again though, does it?' said Jaime, eyeing Ant, who was pouring himself a coffee by the wall and picking flecks of paint from his hands. 'Everyone needs to believe in fairy tales.'

'Yes,' Ros agreed. 'What was it Voltaire said, if God did not exist it would be necessary to invent him? Well, if love doesn't last, it's necessary to believe it can.'

What had happened to Lilian and Sipho's love? Ros wondered. Had that lasted?

The bell rang for the first lesson and as Ros was hurrying down the corridor, Lola passed her.

'Now she tie him up,' she said cheerfully.

'Sorry?'

'My frien' Marie-Carmen, she tie this Miguel up to the bed for the sex. He like bery much, I think English man like this and the girl in the uniform too, no?'

The image of Mike tied up with a young Spanish girl straddling him made Ros think that her head might explode, splattering her brains onto the institutional green of the school's corridor walls. She restrained herself from asking Lola for further details in order to preserve her sanity and continued on her way. Versace ran up to her.

'How's the baby, Miss? Is she all right?'

Oh God, the baby! Ros had forgotten all about it.

'Hurry up, Versace, you'll be late for your lesson,' Ros snapped, avoiding giving her a direct answer.

She texted Charlie: *We are terrible parents, we forgot our baby.* Well, why shouldn't he shoulder some of the blame? She tried her best to concentrate on *Bleak House*. It wasn't easy. The image of the doll baby lying neglected and possibly dying at home was fixed and reinforced in her mind as they discussed Lady Dedlock's secret: the illegitimate baby girl she had had with her lover, Captain Hawdon.

'If I had a baby, like, I'd never leave it, I'd take it everywhere with me,' Chantelle said. 'That Lady Dedlock, she disgusting, man, she deserve to die for abandoning that baby, innit? She should of known it didn't die. Like, a mother would feel it, yano-whatImean?'

At break, Ros jumped into her car and rushed home, almost crashing into Charlie's car as it drew to a halt outside the house at the same time. He still had his wig on from court and they hurried into the house together where they found Ruffy in her basket, the doll baby held between her front paws as she gently licked its face. Ruffy looked up at them with an expression of contempt and when Ros tried to approach her to take the doll, she growled at her.

'She's never growled at me before, ever,' said Ros.

'It's our own fault,' Charlie said, 'we deserve to be punished.'

'But if we leave the baby with Ruffy she'll grow up to be a dog, like those children brought up by wolves who walk on all fours and only speak wolf-language.'

'Well, since she clearly faces certain death if left in our care, that may not be such a terrible alternative,' Charlie said.

'But what if Dogman's dogs also have a say in its upbringing? The child will become irrevocably feral.'

Ruffy got up and, taking the doll carefully between her teeth, walked past them, her tail held haughtily erect, and into the living room where she settled behind the sofa with her.

'We'll have to deal with this later. I've got to get back to school.'

'And I'm going to be late for my next case, which, ironically, is a custody battle; the father is claiming the mother is unfit and that the children should remain with him.'

'Lucky it's not us in court, I don't think we'd fare too well,' Ros said. 'What shall we do?'

'I don't know, this isn't really my area of expertise,' Charlie said, shaking his head. 'For possibly the first time in my life, I have no tips to offer.'

'I'll leave a bottle of milk out and we'll sort it later,' said Ros looking at her watch.

Ros filled the baby's bottle and thought about Sid and Jack far away in Bangkok without her. How could she have let them go? How could she have stopped them from going? Would anyone become a parent if they knew at the outset that one day they would have to let their children go? Sometimes life seemed too hard and too painful. Ros longed to get back into bed and pull the covers over her head. She contemplated calling in sick and taking the rest of the day off.

'Don't be ridiculous, Rosalind. You simply must pull yourself together; you have classes to teach. If teachers can't bring themselves to go to school, how on earth can they expect their pupils to?' Lilian's voice sounded loudly in her head. She was finding it harder and harder to remember Lilian as the mother she had known and thought of her increasingly only as a politicised young girl with a forbidden lover. Star-crossed lovers were a frequent feature both of literature and of life, Ros reflected. It was easy to see why they figured in literature; they made for a good story. When it came to real life, indubitably the illicit nature of such unions provided an added piquancy and, in Lilian's case, her love affair with Sipho was the clearest expression of her disapproval of the values and beliefs of the society in which she lived. Ros couldn't help feeling that her own life with its petty concerns was frighteningly banal by comparison. Were people only really fulfilled when they had something worthwhile to fight for?

Ros could never have imagined that her mother would have been quite so bold and independent; she thought of her with fresh admiration and felt that she had made a new friend. How odd that Mike knew so little of all this, that there were now parts of each other's life that they no longer shared. There had been a time when Ros would have known every detail about Mike, down to what underpants he wore each day. She felt further and further away from him, he was a once-familiar country that she had not visited for some time, growing ever more distant and blurred in her memory. Real knowledge of someone else was illusory, Ros reflected. Look how little she had known her own mother, never mind her increasingly unfamiliar husband.

Ros placed the bottle of baby milk near the edge of the sofa and left the house. She was walking back to her car planning to buy a big, juicy bone from the butcher to substitute for the doll baby when she bumped into Dogman.

''Ere, read this for us, will ya?' he said, holding out a letter to her.

Ros quickly scanned the piece of paper Dogman had thrust into her hand.

'Do you know someone called Deidre Southgate?' she asked.

'Yeah,' Dogman said and a flicker of something like shame crossed his face.

'Well, she clearly knows you, or knew you. It looks like she's left you a pile of money. This is from a firm of solicitors and they've been looking for you for some time. It doesn't mention the sum, but talks about a substantial bequest. Terry, I think you've just won the lottery.'

The power that words have to transform people is astonishing, thought Ros as she watched Terry. His face seemed to glow and change colour, his expression went from suspicion to disbelief before settling into one of wild joy.

'I'm sorry about Deidre,' he said, 'but she was very old and her memory had gone.' Terry looked wistful. 'Although I could have visited her more once she'd gone to that home.' He paused and looked at Ros. 'She was my aunt, well, great-aunt actually, and when I was little, she was my best friend. Blimey, who'd have known she had money tucked away.'

He put his arms around Ros and danced her round in a circle whooping with delight. Three of his dogs came running out of his front door like nosy neighbours to see what the fuss was about and soon added their voices to his. Ros was caught up in his happiness and felt tears pricking her eyes.

'I think, Terry, that you'd better learn to read before you miss any more opportunities.'

'What you on about, I told you I had somefink in me eye ...' Terry began.

Ros looked at him.

'All right then,' he conceded, 'but you'll have to teach us, I 'aint going to no classroom and doing it in front of other people.'

Ros was late and the traffic was terrible. She looked out the car window. A man overtook her, power walking on crutches, evidently intent on circumventing the park on her right. He had a leg missing. Earlier, a one-armed cyclist had passed her. Everyone seemed to be missing a limb today; she hoped it wasn't an omen. It was rare to see people with limbs missing, especially two in such a short space of time. The sight of sleeves and trouser legs neatly pinned where arms and legs should be had been a familiar one when she was a child; a tangible reminder of the two world wars that had formed the backdrop to her childhood. The fact that such a sight had become rare made Ros reflect, not for the first time, how lucky she was to be living in a country that wasn't at war and forced her to put her cares and concerns into perspective.

The perspective didn't last long, however, as her excessive lateness back to school meant that she missed the start of her lesson and found the Angel of Death in her seat, minding her class until her arrival.

'I covered for you,' Peter Seers whispered to her, standing up to meet her by the door. 'But unfortunately, Penny came by wanting to ask you something and knows you weren't here. She wants to see you in your office. Interesting thing about being late, you know,' he continued without drawing breath, 'more than twenty million hours per year are lost to lateness in the UK—'

'Does Penny want to see me now?' Ros interrupted him.

'What? Oh, yes, as soon as you got here, she said. Did you know, a recent survey found that people who are happy at work are more likely to be punctual and where the worker …'

The end of his sentence was lost to Ros as she hurried down the corridor. She found herself, if not in entirely good company, in company, nevertheless, when she arrived outside the Headmistress's office. Versace and Jaime moved over to make space for her on the bench.

'Now what, Versace?' Ros said.

'Smoking in break. You?'

'Late back after lunch.'

'How's me baby?' Versace asked.

'Actually, that's why I was late, I went home to check up on her.'

'She all right, yeah?'

'Fine, no thanks to you. My dog has turned into Nana from *Peter Pan* and won't let me near her.'

'I love that film.'

'You do know it was actually a book first?' asked Ros.

'Nah, I never knew that.' Versace picked at the peeling varnish on her thumbnail and shook her head in disbelief.

'Do you want the baby back?'

Versace shook her head vigorously. Ros turned to Jaime. 'What about you?'

'What baby? I certainly don't want a baby, are you crazy, mine are about to leave home.'

'No, I meant what are you doing here?'

Jaime looked embarrassed. 'Oh, that. Well …' she seemed reluctant to confess her crime.

'Well …' Ros said, making encouraging circling movements with her hand.

'I confiscated Versace's cigarette and then had a quick puff on it myself before putting it out. I didn't know that the prefect on break duty was watching nor did I know that the prefect in question was Martini to whom I'd given a detention last week for not handing her homework in on time. She shopped both of us.'

'Well, as they say, revenge is a dish best served cold.'

'Who's "they"?' asked Versace.

Ros and Jaime looked at her blankly.

'Who's the "they" what say that?'

'Oh, you know, people,' Ros said, waving an arm airily to include the world in general. She turned back to Jaime and looked at her incredulously. 'Jaime, you gave up smoking years ago and really, smoking a pupil's cigarette, what were you thinking?'

'I know, I know.' Jaime held her arms open to an imaginary audience and said, 'And that, ladies and gentleman, is why they call it a mid-life crisis.'

Versace was the first to be summoned. She took out her chewing gum and stuck it to the underside of the arm of the bench, pulled down her skirt and went in. She emerged a couple of minutes later, punching the air in victory.

'Yesss, result,' she said, 'suspended for three days. A nice little holiday, fink I'll go shoppin'.'

Ros and Jaime exchanged a look of disbelief. They couldn't understand the rationale behind the school's tendency to reward bad behaviour with a holiday. Surely detention would have been a more appropriate response?

'Why don't you take the doll baby with you on your three-day holiday and learn a little something about child-care?' Ros suggested.

'M-i-i-s-s,' Versace said plaintively. She hitched her skirt back up to the requisite bottom-skimming level, retrieved her chewing gum, popped it back in her mouth and ran off before Ros could say anything further.

'We appear to lack a certain authority,' Ros said, 'have you noticed?'

'D'you think I'll get suspended too?' Jaime whispered to Ros, her eyes suddenly full of fear. 'Or worse, sacked? Tony would go ballistic, I'd have to run away from home if I were.' At that thought, her face seemed to brighten.

'You'd better think fast. Why don't you say you took the tiniest of puffs for forensic purposes, to determine whether or not it was marijuana?'

'Brilliant,' said Jaime in the happy knowledge that the evidence had disappeared and the Head would be unable to see the perfectly ordinary filter-tipped cigarette which bore the mark of its brand clearly down one side.

Jaime was in the Head's office for some time. When she finally emerged, Ros anxiously studied her face.

'Quickly, tell me, what happened?'

'She said it was a somewhat unorthodox way of testing for drugs and that it raised certain questions about why I would recognise the taste of marijuana in the first place; she suggested that if I were so well versed, the smell should have been enough to tell me one way or another. I muttered something about teenage children of my own and tasting being the only sure way of knowing and she sort of bought it. God, look at me, I'm sweating.'

'You'd be a useless criminal; you've got guilt written all over you.'

'You say that, and yet, I stand before you a free woman with only a severe admonition to her name.' Jaime furtively slipped a Polo mint into her mouth. 'I'd better go, good luck.'

Ros looked up at the big clock above Penny Shield's door. Clocks were ubiquitous in the building, beating the steady rhythm of the school day. It was 2.06, only four minutes to the next bell, which meant her verbal *beasting* by the Headmistress would have to be brief.

Penny Shields looked up from behind her desk as Ros entered the room, took off her reading glasses and rubbed her eyes with her hand.

'I'm so sorry, Penny,' Ros began, 'I had to dash home and got caught in traffic – it won't happen again.'

'It had better not, Ros. Now I know you've been having a difficult time *personally...*' Penny said the last word so quietly it was almost inaudible, demonstrating once again her distaste for the intimate details of her staff's home lives.

Ros tried to intervene, but Penny, fearful that she might share further *personal* details with her, waved a hand in front of her face as though chasing away a bad smell.

'Let me just say this,' she said, 'teachers need to lead by example and I expect you to contain your own life and not let it disrupt your job here in the school. If there are any more incidents, I will be forced to reconsider your position as Deputy Head, which would grieve me as, recent behaviour aside, you are in all other respects a much-valued colleague. We'll say no more for now.'

She was right, Ros considered, as she made her way sheepishly down the corridor to the staffroom. She felt shrouded in disapproval, her own and Penny Shields's, and, irrationally, certain that she had somehow witnessed the scene, Lilian's too. She resolved to pull herself or her socks, or whatever it was that needed pulling, together or up. In any event, she would have to ensure that the seeping detritus of her personal life did not again impinge on her professional one. Although, in fairness, the whole doll baby saga was more a case of allowing her school life to impinge on her personal· one before ricocheting back, with unfortunate consequences, onto her school one. She wondered if it was as difficult for others to maintain order in their lives and prevent such chaotic spillage as it appeared to be becoming for her.

Back in the staffroom, Ros watched Mme Sauvage line up exercise books with Gallic precision. It was hard to believe that anything could ever take her unawares or deflect her from her purpose. Her orderliness was mesmerising and Ros came to herself several moments after the bell rang just barely making it to her GCSE English class on time.

It took Ros an age to get home; she met an obstacle in every road she turned into. It was quite apparent that the drivers of London's vans and lorries had drawn up an agreement to do all they could to impede her progress. Pedestrians were also in on the conspiracy as they crossed zebra crossings in apparent slow motion, just as people always did in the queue ahead of one at the supermarket checkout when one was in a hurry. As Ros waited for a white van to reverse out of a side alley – they really were always white – she watched an elderly black man walk up the road towards her. He looked to be in his seventies, about the age, Ros calculated, that Sipho would be. It's a lie that age cannot wither one, thought Ros looking at the man's weathered face as he drew near, when it so obviously does. No sooner has one ripened than one begins to decay. She briefly studied her own face in the rear-view mirror, noticing how the tender flesh on her upper eyelids was beginning its inevitable surrender to the laws of gravity.

The house smelt different when Ros came home due, in part, to the change of personnel. The twins' departure had meant the evaporation of that distinctive odour associated with the teenage boy that, for Ros, with its top notes of canine aroma, had come to mean home. She sniffed the air deeply as she closed the front door and was able to distinguish Charlie's cologne mingled with something altogether unfamiliar and yet distantly remembered. Entering the living room, she soon discovered its source. Ruffy sat in her basket by the sofa. She looked different: bigger and somehow misshapen. Ros looked more closely; the doll was no longer in the basket with her but instead Ruffy appeared to have acquired extra legs, eyes, ears … Ros approached the basket, Ruffy growled. A small puppy looked up at Ros with round, black eyes. The unique smell of poodle puppy permeated the air.

'What the …' Ros began.

Charlie coughed behind her. He was holding the doll baby and feeding it a bottle of milk.

'It seemed a fair exchange,' he said, 'a more suitable outlet for her maternal instincts and a reliable way of springing the baby from her grasp.'

Ros held up the carrier bag containing the bone she'd got from the butcher.

'I'd rather thought to get the same result with this,' she said.

'Clever,' said Charlie admiringly, 'I didn't think of that. Look, I was in the robing room after court and my opponent mentioned that she had a puppy that needed a home. When she said it was a standard black poodle puppy, it felt like fate and I couldn't resist.

Don't worry, I'll take it home with me when it's a bit bigger. I thought you could use the extra company for now.'

The puppy yawned, revealing a small pink tongue that contrasted sharply with the black of its coat. Ros was lost, overwhelmed by puppy love, the vexations of her day forgotten. She determined to return the doll baby to the PSHE teacher the following day. One new baby was more than enough, although judging by Charlie's unexpected preoccupation with the doll, she might have to give *him* the bone and take the baby when he wasn't looking.

Chapter Sixteen

When Ros woke the following morning, it was with the uneasy feeling of an impending ordeal. It took her a few moments to determine what it was: it was Tuesday and she was meeting Jimmy that evening.

'Wear leather to show him you mean business,' Charlie said on the phone when he rang to check on the puppy before she left for work. 'I'll be in and out all day on puppy duty, don't worry.'

'Wear a mask, or better still, a hood so he can't see your face, you look terrible,' Jaime said over morning coffee in the staffroom. She wasn't usually so abrupt, but an early morning encounter with her bathroom scales had put her in ill humour.

'Thanks, some friend you are.' Ros took out a compact mirror and studied her face, grimacing at the sight of the dark shadows beneath her eyes. 'I'm exhausted; I was up half the night with a crying puppy and wailing doll baby. What on earth am I going to do about tonight? I can't possibly go out looking like this.'

'Phone Charlie for a handy tip.' Jaime tipped powder into a plastic beaker, added water and shook it. 'Protein drink,' she explained. 'Meal replacement, I've given up food.'

'No wonder you're so crabby,' Ros said.

'What?' Jaime barked.

'Nothing.' Ros experienced a moment's pity for Tony.

'First, a face sauna and then cold tea bags on the eyes and a power nap,' Charlie said briskly when she phoned him.

'What exactly do you mean by face sauna?'

'Honestly Ros, have you learnt nothing? Boil some water in a pan, add some lemon juice and mint leaves, then put your face over it and cover your head with a towel. Do that for five minutes and then splash your face with cold water. Got to run, His Lordship approacheth.'

When she arrived home, the puppy and Ruffy were dozing in the basket. They looked so cosy that Ros had to fight the temptation to join them. That morning, she had returned the doll to Marilyn Jameson, the PSHE teacher, who had asked her where on earth it had been, saying it smelt funny; a little, if she wasn't very much mistaken, like dog food. She was right, Ros had thought, holding the doll to her nose and sniffing; Ruffy's assiduous grooming had indeed left its legacy: the unmistakable tang of dog breath. Fortunately, before Ros was forced to invent an explanation, Marilyn's attention had been deflected by the news of the death of one of her dolls due to neglect at the hands of a Year 10 pupil and she'd hurried away.

Ros followed Charlie's instructions. The steaming completed, she lay on the sofa with two cold green-tea bags on her eyes and instantly fell asleep. She awoke with a start at 7.15. She had only forty-five minutes to dress and get to town, which was why she had to slip into a public loo en route to remove one hold-up stocking; in her haste she'd forgotten to put the other one on. Under the circumstances, she quickly checked her face in the mirror to reassure herself that she'd applied make-up to both eyes and tried a little yogic breathing to calm down, doing a fast inventory to determine that she had two of all the other things that should come in pairs: shoes, earrings, legs, arms and breasts. All things considered, Ros couldn't help feeling this wasn't quite a textbook start to an evening out with a new man. Charlie's tips had proved effective though, Ros thought, scrutinising her face: she looked bright and glowing. Her red dress showed just the right amount of cleavage and, less being more, the black suede boots minimised the quantity of leg on display. (She'd read somewhere that the people who decided such matters had decreed you weren't allowed to expose breasts and legs simultaneously.)

It felt good to be out at night in the centre of London and Ros was unexpectedly pleased she hadn't lost her courage. It had been raining earlier and the bright façades of restaurants and bars were further illuminated by the headlights of passing cars, which swished slowly past on the wet asphalt and gave the streets a vivid, shiny appearance. The temperature had dropped, but despite the cold, people sat at tables outside Bar Italia on Frith Street, sipping their thick espressos and talking animatedly in cosy groups. As she passed them, Ros savoured her changed circumstances briefly and for the first time, with no children or husband waiting at home, she was free to do as she wished. Well, as free as a new puppy and a dog would allow.

She pushed open the door of the Coach and Horses and looked around. A small man with thinning hair and a wispy beard caught her eye and began moving purposefully towards her. His squinting myopic gaze and the questing movement of his head put Ros in mind of a ferret. She felt her heart sink. Plezh had had the looks but not the personality and Jimmy, whose personality had promised so much, clearly didn't have the looks. Why was it so hard to find everything in one man? What a pity the perfect partner could not come in kit form like Mr Potato Head, ready for assembly according to one's taste. Ros held her breath and prepared her expression hoping that in the course of the evening ahead, Jimmy's inner beauty would somehow find a way of transforming his outward appearance so that she would find him attractive. Just as Ros was masking her disappointment and preparing a friendly greeting, ferret man pushed past her and into the arms of the woman who had appeared behind her. Relief washed over Ros as she watched the woman respond enthusiastically to the man's embrace. What was, for Ros, a ferret in human form was evidently another woman's handsome prince. There's someone for everyone, Ros reflected. But if this man wasn't Jimmy, then who was? Ros turned her attention back to the busy pub and found herself looking straight into the dark eyes of one of the most attractive men she'd seen in a long time. Could the gods truly have bestowed such extraordinary kindness upon her; could this handsome black man seated alone at a table a few feet away be Jimmy? He looked back at her in an encouraging manner and rose to greet her. It *was* he. Ros felt a shock of pleasure. She had a sense of rights being wronged and circles completed. Was Jimmy to be for her what she suspected Sipho had been for Lilian? The man smiled and raised a hand, beckoning her to his table. As Ros moved towards him, her focus shifted; Jimmy became a blur, and the man seated at the bar behind him, his back to her, glass in hand, came into sharp relief. He looked like Mike, only healthier and younger-looking. Ros blinked, the man turned his head in her direction. It was Mike. She paused for a moment, frozen. The handsome black man was walking towards her. Ros turned and ran from the pub.

Of all the pubs in all the cities, she thought angrily as she ran up the street outside, my almost-ex-husband would have to be in the one I've picked for a rendezvous. What are the bloody chances?

What on earth would poor Jimmy think, she wondered; would he decide that she hadn't liked the look of him or that she'd seen that he was black and taken flight? She almost turned back, but the moment had passed and she no longer had the heart for a blind date. She wanted only to be home.

On the tube, Ros watched the man seated opposite her, slumped drunkenly in his seat, a tin of lager in his hand. He was sleeping, his mouth shaped into an incongruous pout as though inviting a kiss. It looked as though no one had kissed him for a very long time. Ros hoped that the world of his dreams was sweeter than that of his waking hours.

She logged onto StartingOver.com as soon as she arrived home.

`Jimmy, I'm so sorry I fled. My soon-to-be-ex husband was sitting at the bar behind you and I panicked.` Ros paused. What did she want to do? She began typing once more. `You looked gorgeous. Please can we reschedule? Love, Sal x`

She looked out at the puddle of light thrown onto the pavement from the lamp-post outside her window before getting up to pour a large vodka and tonic. After much cajoling and bribing with treats, Ruffy eventually allowed her to pick up the puppy, which lay nestled in her lap. She and Charlie had so far failed to reach agreement over its name. Ruffy was prowling around Ros's chair with the anxious air of a mother who has allowed a small child to hold her newborn baby. Ros knew how she felt and wished that Sid and Jack were safely back in her arms. She felt a gaping emptiness at her core and an urgent need to touch her sons. The silence began to close in on her. She phoned Charlie to fill him in on her latest disaster.

'Are you OK, Ros?' he asked.

'I'm fine.' Ros tried to sound breezy, but Charlie must have heard something in her voice because he offered to come over at once. 'I'm becoming one of those awful needy friends, aren't I?' Ros said.

'Yes, you are,' Charlie said.

'You're not meant to agree with me,' Ros protested. 'I only said that so you'd contradict me.'

'Don't worry,' Charlie said, 'it'll be your turn to look after me soon enough.'

A sudden bleeping sound alerted her to the fact that Jimmy had logged on. She waited to give him time to read the message she'd written a few minutes earlier.

You looked beautiful. I wanted to kiss you, Jimmy wrote.

So did you and so did I.

You should have stayed; we could have gone somewhere else.

I'm afraid I panicked. It was such a shock to see Mike behind you at the bar. God, I feel such an idiot, I'm so sorry. What unbelievably bad luck for him to have been in that pub.

Don't worry we can make another date.

When?

Well, I've got to go away for work for a few weeks, so it will have to be when I get back.

Ros felt suffused with disappointment by the thought that she would have to wait so long to see him again.

I saw my husband kissing a woman the other day, she wrote, feeling a sudden compulsion to confide in Jimmy.

How on earth did you see such a thing? Jimmy wrote.

My dog has developed the habit of leading me to her new haunts. She walked me to his new girlfriend's window.

How did you feel when you saw him?

Awful, as if the last fragile threads that bound us to each other had snapped once and for all. And angry, although without justification. I mean, it's not as if I haven't kissed someone else myself. God, why am I telling you this? It's not a very good way of flirting with someone, is it?

Do you like him, this man that you kissed? I feel jealous.

Oh no, complete disaster. Don't worry, it wasn't anything and I have no intention of seeing him again.

And your husband?

That's pretty much a disaster too. Ever since I saw him kissing that young girl, I realised that my marriage is absolutely over once and for all. I mean, I knew it was before, but that totally compounded it.

What drove the two of you apart? Jimmy asked.

His anger. I couldn't continue a life tiptoeing on eggshells. And you, what made you and your wife split up?

Funnily enough, anger played its part with us too. I was tired of feeling that I wasn't good enough for her and of having everyone tell me how lucky I was.

Yes, I can see that must be difficult. But why do men respond to situations with anger instead of simply admitting that they feel hurt or upset? Ros wrote.

Because everyone always tells us that big boys don't cry, Jimmy answered. Anger is the only emotion we're permitted.

I wish my husband had cried instead of raging. At least that might have allowed us to talk, Ros said.

People can change, they can learn to manage their anger, I'm sure of it.

She felt a warm rush of affection for Jimmy.

I found these xxxxs, she wrote, I think they belong to you.

You're right, I must have dropped them outside the Coach and Horses, Jimmy answered, when can I come and pick them up?

There are an awful lot of them. Will you be able to manage?

Hmm, I suppose if I try to pick up too many, I might go weak at the knees, Jimmy wrote.

Ros wondered if you really could fall in love with someone you'd never met. It was certainly beginning to feel like it.

Charlie came round a little later as Ros was switching TV channels mindlessly in the vain hope of finding something worth watching. She filled him in more fully on recent events.

'What incredible bad luck, Ros. Did Mike see you?'

'I'm not sure, he may have.'

'Won't he be wondering why you bolted?' Charlie asked.

'I never considered that. Do you think I should phone and give him some reason?'

Ros wasn't sure what explanation she could give him; she certainly didn't intend telling him the truth. A little later, she dialled his mobile number anyhow, trusting that something would come to her.

'Hello, Ros,' Mike said.

'Hi, um, I just wanted to say sorry for earlier, you know, when

I saw you in the pub. Ah, I thought you might be with someone and I didn't want to embarrass you, so I sort of panicked and left.'

It sounded plausible enough to her ears.

'No, no,' said Mike, 'that's fine, I mean, I was on my own having a quick drink.'

Ros could hear giggling in the background and a woman's voice. 'Come here, Mikey, if you goo' boy, I show you something ...'

'You're obviously tied up.' Ros, remembering what Lola had told her recently, thought this was probably literally the case, 'I'll talk to you another time.'

She hung up quickly, wishing she hadn't phoned at all.

'What I don't understand,' Ros was saying to Charlie, as they sat curled up on the sofa together, 'is if you like doing the actual, you know, fucking, why you don't simply do it to girls?'

It was a conversation that they'd had before. Charlie was very open about his sex life. In fact, Ros liked to tease him that he should be called 'everything you've ever wanted to know about gay sex but were afraid to ask', joking that some of the detail he gave one actually made one afraid to listen.

'I mean, you like girls. You probably spend more time with me and your other women friends than anyone else.'

Ruffy's ears pricked up at the sound of all the 'W's that had fallen from Ros's lips. She held her head alert for a few moments as if considering the possibility of a walk, but soon returned to grooming the puppy in the basket beside her.

'I like to think that our relationship is a bit more than the cliché of gay man with best girlfriend,' Charlie said.

'That goes without saying,' Ros reassured him. 'What I'm saying is, wouldn't it be easier if you slept with us too? Not me, obviously, but you know what I mean.'

'You like girls too, look at you and Jaime,' Charlie said, 'but that doesn't mean you want to sleep with her.'

'Yes, I see what you mean. So really what you're saying is that you're part girl?'

'I suppose I am in a way.'

'What do you say to those who think that attraction to the same sex is a form of narcissism?' she asked.

'I say they're not nearly as handsome as I am,' Charlie answered, holding an imaginary mirror in front of him and pretending to swoon at his reflection.

'But don't you see,' Ros said, 'that's the whole point, giving oneself to an*other*, the recipient should be other. The fact that a homosexual makes love to a person of the same sex means, in a way, that he's making love to his reflection and is the supreme narcissist.'

'Perhaps it's to do with the difference between men and women,' said Charlie. 'There's something inherently narcissistic about all men, straight or gay, and the fact that women can't have meaningless sex as easily as men could mean that they are less narcissistic, I suppose. Which sort of makes sense; if you think about it, they have to be; as the bearers of children, the future of society depends on them.'

'Very few men really try and get to know who you are,' Ros said.

'That's not true of me or our relationship though, is it?' asked Charlie.

'No, of course not, that's what I so love about you, the way we really communicate.'

'Well, I can't be narcissistic, then, can I? And anyway, I'd love to move beyond self-gratification, give up the promiscuous life, meet Mr Right and live happily ever after.'

Charlie got up to fetch another bottle of wine. The cork came out with a satisfying thwack. He laid it neatly beside the corkscrew, lined up the glasses and filled them. 'You're just like all women,' he said, handing her a glass, 'you can't bear to lose a good man to the other side and you want to save me.'

'That's not true and you know it. I'm simply trying to understand why you're impervious to our charms.'

'There you are, you see, you just want me to kiss you so that you can prove I'm not gay after all.'

'I certainly don't want you to kiss me.' Ros kicked him playfully.

They fell silent. The atmosphere had suddenly changed between them. They looked at each other and then looked away. Ros, who only moments before had been lying carelessly next to him, her legs resting on his lap, suddenly became aware of the warmth of his skin through his trousers. The smell of him was in her nostrils, not merely his cologne, but the scent of his body. She felt herself growing warm. It was too ridiculous; this was Charlie.

'Well,' she said briskly, getting to her feet, 'it's a school night, so I'd better get off to bed.'

'Me too,' Charlie said, looking at his watch. 'I'll come back and see to the dogs after work tomorrow.'

Their speech felt forced and unnatural. The possibility of sex had entered the room and taken a seat between them like an unwelcome guest.

'Night then,' Ros said, turning away at the same moment that Charlie moved forward so that they bumped into each other awkwardly.

They faced each other as Charlie steadied her with his hands and looked at one another; Charlie pulled her to him and kissed her. His lips were full and soft and they explored each other's mouths with their tongues. Ros instinctively moved into the kiss, pressing her body into his, and felt him hesitate. By any standards, it was a nice kiss, a good kiss, a passionate kiss even. But unquestionably it was a wrong kiss. They broke away and looked at each other wordlessly.

'Good kisser,' Charlie said, dispelling the tension, 'but please don't make me touch your breasts.'

Ros laughed and grabbed his hand, trying to bring it to her breast. Charlie gave her a quick hug.

'Fuck me,' he said. 'Actually, don't,' he added, holding up his hand to ward off the possibility. 'What I meant was, what was that all about?'

'Very peculiar,' said Ros, 'curiosity perhaps? Anyway, promise me this isn't going to make us weird with each other?'

'Of course not, darling; what's a kiss between friends?' Charlie hugged her. 'I'm obviously irredeemably a poof, I'm afraid, if I can resist you after such a lovely kiss. Pity, I do so love you.'

Alone in bed, Ros couldn't sleep. Thoughts of Jimmy, Mike and the kiss with Charlie had left her feeling restless. She felt an ache that she recognised as the sort of loneliness where you want somebody or something warm and alive beside you. What if this was it and she was destined to be a woman alone in a big empty nest for ever, forced to replicate her mother's lonely life? She went into the living room with the intention of coaxing Ruffy and the puppy into her bedroom for company. They were asleep on the rug, so closely entwined that it was impossible to tell where one began and the other ended. It felt wrong to disturb them. We're all animals seeking comfort and warmth from one another, Ros thought sadly as she went back to bed alone. She lay in the dark, listening to the distant rumble of the night bus that passed outside her window. Trying to imagine that her hands belonged to someone else, she ran them over her body caressing and searching until they came to her core. She stroked herself to a quiet climax and wondered whether Charlie might be doing the same in his bed at home. Was this the apotheosis of narcissism, Ros wondered, self-loving at its most literal, essentially a solitary and lonely pursuit?

Chapter Seventeen

Instead of comforting and relaxing her, orgasm had made Ros feel even more wakeful and she wandered around the house, sitting for a while in each of her boys' bedrooms before gathering the courage to climb up to the attic, unwittingly in search of the security of her own childhood, which, perhaps, she unconsciously hoped to find among the remnants of Lilian's flat and their life there together.

She opened a box of papers that had been taken from Lilian's office at the college where she had taught. Untouched since her mother's death, it was full of academic articles her mother had written, the margins heavily annotated in Lilian's distinctive hand. A person's handwriting is as individual as his or her DNA or fingerprints. Indeed, handwriting is the fingerprint of personality. Ros looked at a piece of paper covered with Lilian's looping 'Y's and 'G's, her distinctive capital 'I's and hasty 'R's. She was so clearly present in her writing: hurried, anxious, busy, wanting to get it all down before the thoughts eluded her. It was hard to believe that she was no longer here. A musty smell arose from the papers, enveloping Ros in the past. She leafed through them, through her mother's notes on George Orwell and E. M. Forster, her musings on Sylvia Plath and Shakespeare until she came upon an old page of rough paper torn from a notebook. Ros carefully turned the sheet of paper over; it was brittle and yellowing, on the verge of disintegration. On the reverse, she could make out the fading draft of what looked like a letter: here and there lines had been crossed out and rewritten. It appeared to be a note to Ros from Lilian after a fight between them.

Dearest Ros,

I'm writing this on the bus, so forgive paper and possible ~~p~~ wobbles in writing.

Something awful that I've always remembered is that Jenny Shapiro hasn't spoken to her daughter for over twenty years. I don't think that ~~could~~ should – could – happen to us, ~~I certainly couldn't bear it if it did, for reasons that you will, perhaps, someday come to understand~~ but someone has to make the first move to prevent such a terrible outcome, so here goes ~~even~~.

As you may know, I have a horror of not 'getting my due' and my horror extends to your not getting your due. 'Dues' frequently involve money in their tangible manifestation ~~and~~. Now as "Mommy and money" are a conjunction abhorred by you and the only way to avoid friction is for me to avoid ~~conversations~~ mentioning money, I get ~~very a little~~ very anxious that ordinary prudent and provident measures are neglected. As a consequence of this I bottle up my anxieties and then they explode catastrophically.

I dearly crave a discussion with you in which we can both unload our resentments, anxieties, bottled-up parts. Such sessions do help (have helped in the past) even if ~~you~~ the effect wears off. ~~The needs~~

Ros tried to think which year Lilian could have written this. She sat quietly and allowed memories to wash over her. Jenny Shapiro had been one of her mother's closest friends, although they'd fallen out a few years before Lilian's death. Ros had never known the reason and Lilian had been unwilling to explain. Ros hadn't even known that Jenny had a daughter of her own.

Ros and Lilian had fought often over financial matters. Her mother's anxiety about money had extended way beyond her compulsive adding up as she went along in supermarkets. Much of her thriftiness was understandable in the context of the era in which she grew up. Post-war shortages surely extended to South Africa too, after all. So, her uncontrollable preservation of minuscule portions of food in plastic containers in the fridge and hoarding of sachets of sugar and salt and pepper mined from cafés and restaurants on the rare occasions they ate out were, if irritating, at least explicable. 'It's the immigrant's mentality,' Lilian would say lightly by way of explanation. 'When you've started from scratch in a new country, there's always the fear that you'll lose everything, or that you'll have to move elsewhere and start over again.'

While Ros understood the roots of her mother's anxiety, she nonetheless found Lilian's preoccupation with Ros's own financial affairs intrusive. Particularly after she had grown up and become financially independent.

Tuesday, May 13th, 9am. Lilian had always been meticulous about dates and times; it was curious that she hadn't added the year. Ros closed her eyes and sifted through the years for a recollection of this particular occasion, like someone leafing through index cards in a library catalogue. It came back to her: it had been a few days before Mike had moved into her flat and Lilian had been trying to persuade her to ensure that he paid Ros rent.

'We're in love, Mom, for God's sake, we're planning to get married.'

'Well, why should he live for free when you've worked so hard to pay the mortgage on that place?'

'Are you suggesting he only loves me for my flat?' Ros said, suffused with sudden anger.

'That's not what I said at all; I'm merely suggesting that he should pay his dues. You always allow people to take advantage of you and you shouldn't have to support him.'

Ros had slammed her way out of Lilian's flat, fuming with the volatile rage only a parent can ignite in their child.

Ros couldn't remember now whether the letter or a version of it had been delivered, or how that particular row had resolved itself; but resolve itself it did. Their arguments always did, frequently ending in tears and hugs and Lilian saying jokingly, inevitably, 'You wait, you'll be sorry when I'm gone.' Tears pricked Ros's eyes at the recollection. Lilian had been right; the irritating fact remained that she so often was, if not always in the style – the way she said or presented matters – then usually in the content; Ros *was* sorry she was gone. She felt orphaned. She remembered their last row. As ever, it had been triggered by something trivial; in this particular case a chicken. It had been New Year's Eve; they were having a party that evening and Ros had too much to do and not enough help with which to do it.

'What is it, darling?' Lilian had said on the telephone. 'You sound panicky.'

'We've got fourteen people coming for dinner, Mike's in a foul mood and has shut himself away in his music room, the boys are fighting and the house is a mess.'

'What can I do to help?'

'Really?' Ros asked. She rarely asked Lilian to help her, experience having taught her that she'd have to pay for it later in one way or another.

'Of course, sweetheart, anything, just ask.'

'Well, could you possibly roast a chicken for me?'

'Is that what you're making for dinner?'

'No, no, it's for Ruffy.'

Lilian gave a contemptuous snort. 'Don't be ridiculous, I'm not roasting a chicken for a dog.'

'You asked me what you could do to help,' said Ros.

'But it's absurd to roast a chicken for a dog. Give her dog food for heaven's sake.'

'She's my dog and I need some chicken for her,' Ros said. 'Look, just forget it, OK? I don't know why I bothered to ask.'

'No, no, all right, I'll roast you a chicken, although I think it's preposterous.'

'Don't bother, I'll roast the bloody chicken myself,' said Ros, hanging up while Lilian's disapproving protestations continued to echo down the line.

Ros had roasted her own bloody chicken and made a bloody four-course meal for her guests, tidied the bloody house, done all she could to coax bloody Mike out of his bloody misanthropy and into good humour and persuaded the boys to reconcile their differences and tidy their bloody rooms. She had less than an hour before her guests were due to arrive and had never felt less in the mood for entertaining. The telephone rang just as she was stepping into the bath.

'It's ready,' Lilian said.

'What is?'

'Your chicken. Can you come and fetch it?'

'When?'

'Well, now, of course, since I've gone to the trouble of cooking it. I thought it was of vital importance that the dog should have a freshly cooked chicken.'

Ros held her lips together with her fingers to prevent the involuntary escape of irredeemable expletives.

'I'll pick it up tomorrow, Mom,' she said.

'You'll have to come now, tomorrow isn't convenient. That's the trouble with you, Ros; you always want everything on your terms. I'm also a person, you know.'

'Oh yes, I know all right, you've spent my entire life reminding me of that.'

Ros had hung up and within a few minutes guilt had driven her into her car and round to her mother's. Lilian had opened the door and wordlessly handed Ros a plate. On it sat the smallest roast chicken Ros had ever seen; a dog-sized bite of a chicken, little more than an *amuse-bouche* for Ruffy's eager jaws. A silly fight that had revealed so much about Ros and Lilian's relationship: Lilian's desire for control and Ros's need to assert her own personality; Lilian's implied and actual criticism and Ros's craving for her approval. And, it had been the last fight. Nine days later, the wishbone of the offending chicken still drying, forgotten on Ros's kitchen shelf, Lilian had died. Ros had pulled it with herself, whispering sadly, 'I wish you were still here, Mommy. I wish we hadn't had such a silly fight.'

The telephone rang early the next morning. Ros's eyes felt dry and scratchy from lack of sleep. Blindly reaching out to answer it, she knocked over the glass of water by her bed. Walking with liquids again, what would Lilian have said? Although, in fairness, she hadn't actually been walking, nonetheless the liquids had been walked, with the inevitable result that they had spilled, proving Lilian right yet again. The phone fell to the floor; scrabbling around for it, Ros finally succeeded in bringing it to her ear.

'G'day, Mum,' said Jack.

'Darling, how lovely to hear you! How was the flight?' Ros mopped at the pool of water on her, mercifully wooden, floor with tissues.

'No worries, we had a great time.'

The fearsome metal bird had lifted her sons back into the air, stamping its carbon footprints all over the sky like a giant with muddy seven-league boots and had deposited them safely in Australia.

'Hi, Mum, it's really cool here, so hot and sunny.' Sid took over.

'Cool and hot at the same time?' Ros teased. 'Did Grandpa meet you?'

'Yeah, yeah, it's all good.'

'Is he being look-afterish?'

'Yup, but not like you, of course.' Sid's voice sounded gruff and grown-up, as though he didn't want to be reminded of his and Jack's childish expressions now that he was, quite literally, a man of the world. 'Here he wants to talk to you,' he said.

Ros could hear noises in the background and reflected that her boys were now as far away from her as it was possible for them to be, right on the other side of the world in a different time zone, ending the day that she was preparing to begin. She longed to touch them, just as when they were small and she used to hunger for their soft baby flesh if she was deprived of them for more than a few hours. How had her father been able to leave her and settle so far away when she was a child? Was it different for men?

'Rosalind, how are you, my dear?' Her father's voice sounded older than she remembered.

'Hello, Dad, I'm fine. You?' Ros always felt stiff and unnatural when she spoke to her father, as though she were acting the part of a daughter in a play.

'Very well. Don't worry, we'll take good care of the boys.'

'Thanks. Listen, can I ask you something?' She paused, searching for the right words. 'The thing is I've got some papers and stuff belonging to Mom and, well, did she tell you much about her life in South Africa?'

'Very little, Rosalind, in fact, it was a subject on which it was extremely difficult to draw her. I always felt it stood between us.'

He sounded regretful and Ros mourned the lack of intimacy between them, which constrained her from questioning him further.

'Maybe I'll come over there and visit you too one of these days,' she said impulsively.

'I'd like that, my dear. I'd like that very much.'

Ros felt that he would have liked to say something more, but didn't know how.

'Oh, hold on,' he continued, 'Jack wants another word.'

'Mum, can you send my yellow T-shirt out, you know, the one with Lenin smoking a spliff on it?'

'Do you really need it?'

'Yeah, it's only like my favourite one, I thought I'd packed it?' It wasn't a question, but Jack's instantly acquired Australian speech tones made it sound like one.

'Are you eating properly, darling?' Ros asked.

'Yeah, yeah, don't worry,' Jack said.

Ros was pleased that she had been to Australia herself; it meant that she could picture Sid and Jack there, see them sitting in her father's garden under the lemon-scented gum tree, which would, at this time of the year, have shed its bark to reveal the smooth pale baby-skin of the wood beneath. The beauty of travel was that it extended the space inside one's head and painted the countries visited onto the map of one's mind, making them freely accessible. One had only to close one's eyes to be there.

Ruffy trotted into the room and looked at her reproachfully, a look that seemed to suggest that she could understand Ros's delay in feeding her, but what about the puppy? She hurried to the kitchen as the dogs criss-crossed in front of her feet in the way that pets do, almost tripping her up on the stairs in their eagerness for food. Like children, they found it difficult to defer gratification. Mind you, when she thought about it, most adults did too.

Ros had just concluded a skills' exchange deal with Dogman by the front gate: reading lessons in return for puppy sitting. Turning to hurry to her car, she bumped into something.

'I'm so sorry,' she said and immediately realised she'd apologised to a lamp-post. A blind man who, a moment earlier, had negotiated the lamp-post successfully, tapping at it with his stick, was passing with his guide dog and called out, 'Looks like you need my dog more than I do.'

Feeling foolish, Ros automatically bent to stroke the Labrador, thinking there were altogether too many dogs in her life already. The dog held itself erect and unyielding as if to say, 'Can't you see that I'm working?' Rebuffed, Ros turned away and hit the lamp-post again. This time she didn't apologise. She felt out of step with life, as though she were dancing with the wrong person or had lost her rhythm. She opened her car door and, stepping back, trod on something or, as it turned out, someone.

'Ouch,' Mike said theatrically.

'Sorry,' Ros said. She remembered their last conversation and added, 'What on earth are you doing here?'

'I've come to fetch Ruffy. It's my turn and I'm missing her.'

Ros looked at her watch. If she hurried she'd just get to school on time, if she lingered with Mike, she'd probably be late. Again. She'd failed to take into account the implications of the puppy for Mike's shared custody of Ruffy. This was a matter that required delicate handling and she would have chosen her words more carefully were it not for the fact that she noticed two things: one, Mike's moustache would soon be long enough for him to wax the ends and, two, more shockingly, he had a love bite. He had tied a scarf loosely around his neck, inadequately concealing the explicit proof of sexual engagement like a teenager who secretly desires to brandish his love trophy.

'You can't have Ruffy, Charlie has bought her a puppy,' Ros said brusquely.

'I can't believe this, Charlie and you have had a puppy together? Is it a boy or a girl?'

'A boy.' Ros laughed, she couldn't help it. It sounded too ridiculous.

'It's not funny.'

'You can come and visit her whenever you want,' she said.

'Honestly, Ros, that's just not the same. You can be so unbelievably selfish. You're not the only one who needs comfort at the moment.'

Ros remembered the girl's voice she'd heard in the background the evening before.

'It seems to me, Mike, that when it comes to comfort, your needs are being perfectly well met.' Ros pulled his scarf away from his neck, looked at him pointedly, turned, got into her car and drove off, leaving him standing on the pavement. She watched him in her wing mirror. He grew smaller as their distance from each other increased, the space between them a manifestation of the mounting emotional gap that separated them. She felt as if she didn't know him at all. She felt as if she didn't know Lilian at all either. When it came down to it, everyone was a stranger.

Ros entered the school building with a minute to spare. During her first lesson she confiscated the women's magazine that her pupils were covertly passing around and sniggering over, opened its pages and found herself looking up the skirt of a knickerless 'star' (it took little more these days than visibly going commando to be called a 'star').

'Copy this down,' Ros said, turning to the blackboard and writing, '"The ultimate result of shielding men from the effects of folly is to fill the world with fools". Does anyone know who said that?'

The class shuffled uncomfortably.

'Bob Geldof?' said Nathan, a usually attentive boy whose

concentration had been disturbed today by the sight of Versace's golden thighs crossing and uncrossing as she fidgeted at the desk next to his.

'No,' said Ros, 'anyone else?'

The class was silent.

'It was the philosopher Herbert Spencer.' She wrote his name on the board in capital letters and added his dates, 1820–1903.

'Yeah, well, how we meant to know that, Miss, that's like ages ago and we never studied that, it's not part of our course.' Versace was indignant.

Schooling had become so narrow, Ros thought; it was all about what the curriculum required a pupil to know in order to pass exams, rather than about getting an education.

'What do you think past societies would say about ours if they could see it,' Ros continued undeterred, waving the magazine she still held in her hand, 'a world full of Paris Hiltons, Coleen whatshernames, Victoria Beckhams and Jade Goodys, people who are famous for being famous?'

'McLoughlin,' Versace said.

'Pardon?' asked Ros.

'It's Coleen McLoughlin, well, Rooney now 'cos she's married.'

'That's my point; you know their surnames and everything there is to know about all these so-called celebrities. What do you think past societies might have said about ours?' Ros repeated her question.

'They'd say it was full of fools,' said Nathan, hoping to redeem himself.

Ros smiled at him encouragingly.

'Fing is, Miss,' Versace said, 'maybe them celebrities 'aint fools. Maybe there's like summink going on that we don't understand, right, like it all means summink? You know like you should use your brains to understand stuff, but what if, like, you know how we've got electricity and like two hundred years ago they never done and like they didn't know it existed and if someone told them it did, they'd have fought they was mad like or a witch or summink? Yeah? Well, what if in a hundred years they discover there's summink else apart from yer brain, that means like you believe in God like when you never fought you would, but you had like a … pashonga or summink … and your pashonga understood summink like what yer brain didn't. Looking back at us, yeah, they'd fink we was crazy for not knowing we had a pashonga, innit?'

'You mean that there may in fact be a point to all these pointless magazines full of pointless celebrities but we can't see it; either because we haven't got a pashonga or because we don't use it?' asked Ros, writing the word SOMETHING on the board in big letters to show that it ended with a 'g' and not, as was popularly believed, with a 'k' and that there was a 'th' worthy of consideration in the middle.

'Yeah.' Versace looked pleased with herself and looked around the room as if inviting her fellow classmates' approval.

It was an interesting proposition and looking back on her life, Ros felt that there had doubtless been any number of occasions when she would have done well to listen to her pashonga rather than her brain.

'What if we used to have a pashonga and now we don't?' asked Ros. 'I mean, if we used to recognise folly and now cannot and that's why our society is deteriorating so rapidly?' She looked up at the clock and saw that only a few minutes remained of the lesson.

'I want you all to write two to three pages of A4 in point 12. Use this quotation from Herbert Spencer as your starting point. Is our world full of fools? What are the things that might make someone think that it was? How might life be different if we did indeed have, as Versace suggests, a pashonga? Have fun with it, play with some ideas, give your imagination free rein.'

The class gave a collective groan. The bell rang, Ros smiled and walked briskly out of the room, peripherally aware that at least two of her pupils were giving her the finger as she left, while Versace protested loudly, 'It's not my fault' in answer to her classmates' complaints that she should never have mentioned a 'bleedin' pashonga' in the first place.

'I'd like to have a pashonga if it could make me understand why on earth I'm still married to the same man,' Jaime grumbled to Ros in the staffroom. Ros had been filling her in on her previous lesson.

'What's he done now?' Ros asked.

'Existed,' said Jaime. 'The very fact of his living and breathing. When he coughs I want to hit him and the way he hums drives me insane.'

'That's a little extreme,' said Ros. 'Although if you're not allowed to dance, he shouldn't be allowed to hum.'

'Precisely. The humming is another of his tools of control: he hums when he's talking in order to hog the airtime so that no one else can speak while he's thinking how to finish his sentence.'

'You're right, that is annoying and should be punishable with a lengthy prison sentence,' Ros agreed, noticing that Jaime had allowed a few wisps of hair to curl at the side of her face. Clearly, the worm was turning. When she pointed it out to her, Jaime said, 'Yup, I've turned into an exploding doormat. It feels good.'

Jaime poured boiling water onto the powder in her mug and stirred it, vainly trying to smooth the lumps that formed.

'I think the meal replacement drinks are making me a little irritable and my breath smells like a wrestler's armpit. But, I have lost seven pounds in four days,' she said.

'Well done, that's great; but it seems to be a choice between being fat and jolly or thin and grumpy.'

'Except one never really is jolly when one's fat. Anyhow, I don't care how vicious and smelly it makes me, I'm not giving up till I'm thin.'

'Well, you are, I mean, you're giving up food,' said Ros.

'Ha ha, skinny cow, I hate you.' Jaime leafed through the magazine that Ros had recently confiscated.

'You know what's most pernicious about all this "celebrity" gossip?' said Ros.

Jaime didn't respond, she'd been sucked into the pages of the magazine, forced to grapple with the thorny problem of whether or not one was allowed to wear a miniskirt over the age of forty. (Only if one wore it with 60 denier opaque tights, apparently.)

'It's the fact that one finds oneself actually caring,' Ros continued. 'I see Jennifer Aniston on the front cover and find myself worrying about how she's doing, whether she'll ever find love again and if she'll manage to have the baby she so dearly wants before she's too old. It's too absurd for words, I don't even know the woman.'

Jaime laughed. 'Oh, look,' she said, turning the page, 'Victoria Beckham wears flip-flops. Now that's what I call news.'

'Why is it, do you think, that other eras always seem so much more vital and meaningful than our own? Look at my mother battling apartheid in South Africa in the fifties. Or think of artists in the first half of the twentieth century, for example, like Pollock, Picasso, Kandinsky,' she continued. 'They were all so interesting, vibrant and experimental. And what about the Bloomsbury Set? What have we got? *Big Brother.*'

'Yes, true, but if you'd lived then, you wouldn't be living now,' Jaime replied reasonably.

'God, look how thin that model is,' Ros said, looking over her shoulder and pointing at the opposite page. 'Half these girls are serious drug addicts, why don't they just caption it: "Heroin, mmm it's so more-ish" and be done with it? Or "Lose weight with Class A Drugs, we did!"'

'You're a little waspish yourself, today,' Jaime said, eyeing her curiously.

Ros filled her in on recent events.

'You just have to get back on the horse,' Jaime said.

'The trouble is there seem to be rather a lot of them – horses to get back on, I mean. Children leaving, the almost-ex husband shagging someone young enough to be his cliché, gay best friend kissing thing, a whole new dog in my life, mother speaking from beyond the grave. I feel a little overwhelmed.'

'Wait till you read the rest,' Lilian's voice interrupted loudly in Ros's ear, right on cue as though she were sitting next to her.

'Why couldn't you have just told me?' Ros said.

'Told you what?' said Jaime. Ros must have spoken aloud. 'Are you all right, Ros? You look a bit peculiar.'

'Fine, fine; I was just thinking of something.'

'You seem rather stressed. Come to an exhibition with me tomorrow night,' Jaime said. 'Tony can't come, you can be my husband instead.'

'OK, I won't kiss you when I arrive then.'

'No, of course not, don't look at me either or listen to a word that I say.'

They shared the short cheerless laughter of women who know what it is to be married for a long time.

'Perhaps you need more therapies to relax you. Yoga or meditation or something,' said Jaime.

Ros's memory of her last yoga class with its swaying genitals and unfettered breasts came back to her. It wasn't an experience she was anxious to repeat and she'd been considering taking up Pilates instead. In truth, she felt a little gumbaggley'd out. She remembered that she had her neck appointment later that afternoon and was in two minds whether or not to keep it.

Jasmine Thompson wasn't a good advert for her profession. Her head seemed to rise directly from her shoulders. In truth, the woman had no neck at all.

'Now I know what you're thinking,' Jasmine said.

'No, no, honestly, I wasn't looking at your ...' Ros paused, her own neck reddening with shame at the realisation that her surprise was so transparent. She couldn't bring herself to articulate the word 'neck' when Jasmine was so cruelly without one.

'You're wondering how this little ruler can tell me what I need to know,' Jasmine said, holding up a metal rod in front of Ros's eyes.

'That was a close one, Ros.' Ros could hear Lilian laughing and turned her head quickly in the direction of the sound. She glimpsed her mother's face at the window, blinked and, when she opened her eyes again, saw only the branch of a tree brushing against the glass like a whisper.

'Look at me, please,' Jasmine said.

Ros brought her head round to face her.

'This is a spirit level,' Jasmine said, holding up a glass tube mounted on a piece of elaborately carved dark wood. 'If the bubble of air doesn't sit in the middle, it's likely to mean that your neck needs realigning.'

It didn't and her neck did, of course. Jasmine made Ros lie down, checked her heels to see whether they were in alignment and, after asking Ros to turn on her side, made minuscule adjustments to the position of her head, which, she assured Ros, would make all the difference.

Ros had never liked being held around the neck and had sometimes wondered, in a whimsical non-believing sort of way, whether in a past life she might have been strangled. She remembered José's assertion of his former existence as a warrior princess. People only ever recalled themselves as kings, warriors or princesses; illustrious figures who were now demeaned by the lowly status of their twenty-first century incarnations. It appeared that few, if any, had lived previous lives as petty criminals or chimney sweeps.

Earlier in the waiting room, Ros had flicked through an out-of-date magazine from the many artfully piled onto the highly varnished coffee table in front of her. Out of one had fallen a newspaper article; it was dated February 12th 2003. A single sentence, highlighted on the page, caught Ros's eye:

When someone has something important to say, they will find a way to say it.

Ros settled back on the sofa on which she was sitting and began to read. The piece was about a woman who had made a pact with her husband that whoever died first would send the other a message from beyond the grave to settle once and for all the question of whether life continued after death. Soon after, the woman had died unexpectedly of a brain haemorrhage at the age of sixty-eight. Her husband began receiving messages from her via their friends and acquaintances. She told him to get the roof fixed (it turned out several tiles had come loose and presented a danger) and to prune the roses (she had been particularly proud of her rose garden). She also accurately described her death and that of her mother who had died in the Blitz. She explained that the more open a person was in life, the more he or she would get out of the afterlife.

Ros baulked at the religious undertones of this, the veiled implication that the less one sinned, the more one would be rewarded. But as she lay on Jasmine's treatment table, she realised that her very presence in Wimpole Street was a direct consequence of a message from her mother via a medium. She considered further the article and its relevance to her own recent experience. What was it that Lilian really wanted to tell her and why had she waited so long to tell it?

Ros slapped at a tickle on her arm, and looking down saw a smear where she had unwittingly squashed a small spider. For all she knew, it could have been an Egyptian prince in a former life and, with difficulty, she resisted the urge to apologise to it. 'Perhaps,' she mused ironically, thinking of Lilian's persistent voice in her head, 'I was Joan of Arc in a previous lifetime and have retained a gift for hearing voices.'

As Ros paid Jasmine's bill, one hundred and twenty-five pounds, she marvelled that her mother, with her obsessive regard for economy, could have been the instrument of such extravagance. Clearly, money, like time, had no meaning in the afterlife.

Chapter Eighteen

`Am I going mad?` Ros was on the Internet talking to Jimmy. She'd told him about Lilian, the manila envelopes, the spooky occurrences, everything. Jimmy had coaxed the story out of her, interjecting with thoughtful questions and prompts when she hesitated. Ros was touched by his interest and sensitivity; he felt at once kindred and deliciously unknown. It felt easier to discuss Lilian with someone she hadn't actually met; the care needed to write rather than to speak about it all helped Ros articulate her own response to what she had learnt about her mother. They'd been on the Internet for over an hour. The dogs were dozing contentedly at Ros's feet and she felt happily cocooned in cyberspace and marvelled that she could feel so completely at ease with a handsome man she had merely glimpsed once in a pub.

`What pains me most is the fact that she never talked to me about this phase of her life,` Ros wrote.

`Parents have to preserve boundaries with their children,` Jimmy answered, `in order that the child is allowed to remain the child and not forced into becoming the parent. Perhaps she thought it would damage the balance of your relationship.`

`Why? I would have respected her for taking a stand against apartheid and enjoyed hearing about her relationship with Sipho.`

`You don't yet know what happened, what the outcome of that relationship was,` Jimmy said.

`That's true and I'm almost dreading the next`

instalment. I'm still surprised; my mother was always so vocal about asserting her right to exist. When I was growing up and guilty of the child's usual gross egocentricities, her repeated cry was, 'I'm also a person.' It used to irritate me when she said that, I mean, of course she's a bloody person, I used to think, everyone's a person, why did she have to go on about it? But now, having raised children of my own, I can sort of see what she meant.

A person's a person no matter how small.

Ros's fingers froze on her keyboard; she stared at the words that Jimmy had typed in astonishment.

Why did you just say that? she asked.

It's from a Dr Seuss book, *Horton Hears a Who*.

I know that, I just can't believe you quoted it. That's what we used to call the boys when they were tiny because they were such people from the very second they were born. We called them both A Person's a Person, or A P's a P for short. That's so amazing that you should say that.

Well, they have just made a movie of the book, Jimmy wrote. You know, perhaps this story of your mother's is her way of showing you how much of a person she was. Maybe she wanted you to understand something about her.

But then why couldn't she simply have told me rather than leave it till after she was dead?

Perhaps there's a reason for that.

It's so great talking to you, Jimmy; I can't wait finally to meet you, said Ros.

Are you actually divorced? Do you think there is really no chance for you and your husband? he wrote.

Sometimes I wish we could have tried harder to make it work, Ros wrote, but he has a real anger problem and won't admit it. Until he does, there's nothing I can do. Anyhow, he's seeing that young Spanish girl now.

Ros was meditating, or at least trying to. She sat cross-legged; the acrid smoke of the incense that burned in front of the Buddha made it hard to breathe. Sharonananda was murmuring incantations, inviting them to look into a still lake.

'There is no wind or disturbance on the surface, look closely at the water, hold your gaze and you will see to the bottom,' she intoned monotonously.

Ros felt she was on the brink of a sudden insight into the world. The whole of life, she reflected, was a process of growing up. But just as one felt one was getting somewhere, reaching some sort of understanding, one found oneself on one's deathbed, uttering the words, 'Oh, now I ...' and just failing to complete the sentence before one died. She remembered Lilian saying how wasteful human experience was since no one was able to learn from the mistakes of others. Ros tried not to fidget; her legs were beginning to ache. Sharonananda's name must be Sharon, she thought, with 'ananda' added on. 'Would I be Rosananda?' She quite liked the sound of that. At least it wasn't naked meditation; that really would be a step too far. Although, now she came to think of it, hadn't John Lennon spent much of his time naked, meditating and doing yoga? The difference was that he had done it on his own or with Yoko.

Ros couldn't silence her inner dialogue with its inane musings and now the tip of her nose was itching. She opened her eyes. She was in a large carpeted room in the basement of a Buddhist Centre in South Kensington surrounded by meditating strangers. They sat facing a large bronze Buddha, which smiled at them. Ros couldn't help feeling there was something smug about its smile. The strangers were motionless, no doubt able to see all the way to the bottom of their still lakes while Ros's view had been obscured by the seething waters of her turbulent mind. She envied them their stillness. The door opened and a latecomer tiptoed into the room. He took a cushion from the cupboard and sat down. There was something familiar about him. Ros looked at him more closely. He reminded her of someone. She closed her eyes again trying to shift her focus back to meditation. Sometimes one has to close one's eyes to see clearly; it came to her at once, the latecomer was Robbie, the old boyfriend her mother thought she should have married. When she'd known him, Robbie had had a luxurious head of dark hair. Now, opening her eyes again, Ros could see the little that remained of it was grey and closely cropped. He looked up and their eyes met. Robbie's widened in recognition and he smiled and gestured to the door with his head, indicating that they should talk after the class. Hair loss aside, he'd aged well. His build had remained slim and athletic and his face had held its form instead of collapsing into the jowly multitude of chins, which Ros had observed to be the sad fate of so many middle-aged men. Had Lilian sent him to her? Ros wondered. Even as she thought it, she chided herself for being ridiculous. She really must get a grip or she was in danger of actually embracing naked yoga and changing her name to Rosananda.

With a flash of lucidity, Ros realised that Robbie represented a resource hitherto unexplored, a rich seam of gold in the seemingly arid rock of life after marriage: past lovers. The possibility of the alluring Jimmy was one thing, but how much safer would it be to return to a land previously travelled? The journey to it was so long in the past that any fresh visit would feel like a new adventure yet without the dangers of the unknown. Ros was taken aback by her current persistent sexual urges. She'd lived long enough in a marriage where sex, certainly towards its end, was only ever intermittent. Throughout the many dry seasons, she'd enjoyed close physical intimacy with her sons. Unusually, her boys had remained affectionate even throughout their sometimes-difficult teenage years and cuddles with her children, although obviously not sexual, had nonetheless satisfied her hunger for skin. Her recent separation both from Mike and the boys had created a yearning in her that felt akin to physical starvation. It wasn't so much the act of sex she craved, as the need to lie in someone's arms or to have them lie in hers, the need to touch and be touched. Ros closed her eyes and tried to remember what sex with Robbie had been like, marvelling at the fact that even when a relationship with someone is over, one still possesses knowledge of the most intimate nature about them. For instance, Robbie, she recalled, never wore underwear. She opened one eye slightly to look at him and glanced unwittingly at the bulge in his trousers. Looking up, she saw that he was looking at her, deeply and penetratingly. Ros blushed; she recognised his expression: he used to look at her in just such a way during sex when he was at the point of orgasm, his eyes wide open, frank and challenging. She could almost smell him, could almost feel the heat of his body on hers.

They went for a drink after the class. Robbie went to the bar without asking her what she wanted and came back with a spicy Bloody Mary.

'You see,' he said, 'I remembered.'

Ros smiled. What else did he remember about her? She had no doubt that the intimate memories she had about him were echoed by some of his own about her. We scatter small parts of ourselves as we journey through life, she thought, pieces that are stored by others and about which we may have no memory. She could feel herself beginning to blush again. They exchanged salient information. He was divorced, three children: two girls and a boy.

'To divorce,' he said, raising his glass to hers, 'less money, more sex.'

It was just what Ant had said when he'd divorced, Ros remembered, but then he'd remarried and had both less money and less sex once again. He wasn't the best advertisement for changing partners. Was there really such a thing as a happy marriage? After the first wild rush of dopamine that attended new love had flooded the brain sending one into a state of feverish ecstasy, it invariably settled into the chemical indifference that transformed both partners from boyfriend and girlfriend into husband and wife. Love junkie was the correct term for serial monogamists or even for polygamists, thought Ros. They were little more than addicts looking for their next fix. Would Robbie give Ros the dopamine rush she realised she herself was craving?

Robbie fixed Ros with a meaningful look and she felt herself flushing once more. She appeared to have become a teenager again.

The divorce, or rather the demands of an avaricious ex-wife, had brought Robbie out of retirement and into a new career as a hedge-fund manager. This meant nothing to Ros for whom the term conjured up only rows of neatly cut green hedges, which soon morphed in her imagination into Edward Scissorhands-style elaborate topiary as he tried to describe to her what the job entailed. After his lengthy explanation, she surmised that it was something to do with money and making more of it. In fact, an awful lot more, if the vintage Maserati he got into after they left the bar were any indication. Ros wasn't sure at what point she had agreed to return home with him but she followed him in her car and soon found herself both in his bed and in his half-remembered embrace. Less money, more sex. Robbie was right (although he seemed still to be getting plenty of both). It felt wonderful to be touched and Robbie's lovemaking was satisfying. The memory of pleasure shared all those years ago was aroused and recharged by his once-familiar body moving in synchrony with hers. Robbie kissed the nape of Ros's neck. She shivered.

'I love that,' she said.

'I know,' Robbie answered, 'I remember.'

Ros felt touched that he'd carried this memory of her pleasure zones.

'I also remember that you like this,' Robbie said, tracing a path with his tongue down her stomach and in between her thighs.

On the crest of a wave of pleasure, Ros felt intense relief that she had had the foresight to dye her pubic hair. Robbie liked to make love with all the lights on. It felt natural for them to be together and Ros was surprised that she hadn't felt embarrassed about revealing her post-childbirth body to this man who had known her in her prime. It had also helped finally to expunge the image of sex with Plezh, an image that had been playing over and over in her mind. She'd been wondering whether part of the blame for the awfulness of that encounter had lain with her. Had she simply forgotten how to do sex? As Ros lay in Robbie's arms afterwards, waiting for their breathing to regulate, she felt reassured by the pleasure she had both given and received.

'You should have married me, Ros, when I asked you to all those years ago,' Robbie said, running his hand up and down the side of her body.

'Why,' said Ros, her skin responding with goose bumps, 'so that we could be getting divorced now?'

Robbie laughed, 'Maybe it would have been different for us and we would have stayed together.'

Ros tried to imagine how life with Robbie might have been. While she could just about envisage it, she couldn't begin to imagine having had children other than the ones she had, which meant ultimately that she couldn't imagine having married anyone other than Mike. Sid, Jack, Mike were the family cake she had made, and Mike, whatever their relationship now, was an integral ingredient. No wonder breaking up was painful, how could you extract the flour or the eggs from a baked cake without ruining it?

'Remember when I proposed?' Robbie said.

'Yes,' Ros answered.

Robbie, prosperous even then, had whisked Ros away for a weekend by the sea. They'd gone to Whitstable and stayed in that charming hotel on the seafront that resembled a 1950s picture postcard. Ros tried to remember its name.

'The Continental,' Robbie said, watching recollection flicker across her face.

'Of course.'

On the Saturday night, they'd gone to the famous seafood restaurant nearby ('Oyster Fishery Company,' Robbie prompted. 'Of course,' said Ros again) and Ros's attention had been caught by a couple at the table next to theirs who sat in total silence for the duration of their meal. Ros monitored them closely and observed that they didn't exchange a single word with one another. If asked, would they have said they'd had an enjoyable evening out? Ros wondered. Was talking less important to others than it was to her? It had occurred to her then that her and Robbie's conversation often faltered, leaving gaps that, left untended, could develop into unbridgeable chasms. She didn't want a marriage like the one they were witnessing at that mute table next to theirs. So when her food came, rather than delight at the diamond ring she saw lying on the half-shell where an oyster should have been, her instinctive response had been a longing for the sweet soft flesh of the shellfish instead. She'd fleetingly contemplated quickly swallowing the ring in order that she might sidestep the issue of Robbie's proposal.

'You rejected me kindly,' Robbie said.

'Did I? I hope so.' She kissed his chest. 'And look at us now, all these years later, *à la recherche* ...' Ros said.

'Hmm?' said Robbie

'You know, us, *à la recherche du temps perdu.*'

'What's that?'

'Proust, you know, in search of lost time, memory lane, come on, you must have heard of that.'

'Oh, right. You always were literate, Ros. Don't you remember, I never have time to read and when I do, I only read non-fiction or emails.' He turned her face towards his and kissed her.

Suddenly Ros did remember. She also remembered that this was another reason why she hadn't married him. She hadn't been able to imagine a future with someone who didn't read books, who couldn't share her literary and, in consequence, internal emotional landscape. This fact, combined with the realisation that they didn't really have very much to talk about in general, had led not merely to a rejection of his marriage proposal, but to an end of their relationship as well. None of this augured well for a future with Robbie now, but at the very least, meaningless sex with him felt a little less meaningless than it would have with a total stranger, than it had with Plezh. Robbie turned the television on, reminding Ros of yet another reason their union had been doomed: post-coital sport on TV.

'Goodness,' said Ros, just as she had to Plezh in similar circumstances and all too recently, 'is that the time? I have to go.'

'It's late, Ros, stay,' Robbie said, his eyes fixed on the television screen.

'No, I can't, I've got a puppy at home, I shouldn't have left it on its own this long as it is.'

So, once again, Ros had exchanged the bed of a man she'd

recently had sex with for the seat at the wheel of her car in the chilly early hours of empty London streets. She entered the house quietly and stood at the kitchen window looking out into the garden beyond. The puppy excuse had been a lie. Ruffy and Puppy (now its official name) had both gone to stay with Mike. He'd insisted on his custodial rights and the only way to enforce them had been for him to take the puppy as well.

Arriving home, Ros wished that Lilian were still alive and that they could have enjoyed one of those rare nights where they sat talking in the kitchen until the early hours. It was curious that she so rarely thought about those occasions and that her recollections of her life with her mother had been all too frequently focused on the negative aspects of their relationship. Ros could acknowledge now that she'd been furious when her mother had died, irrationally believing that it was somehow Lilian's fault. She knew that rage was part of grief and marvelled only that it had taken her this long to realise it and to begin the process of forgiving.

'Where on earth have you been? I've been worried sick.' It was Charlie. He'd woken her up ringing her doorbell. 'I was phoning you all evening and didn't know where you were.'

'I was out having meaningless sex with an old boyfriend,' Ros said smugly.

'That doesn't count, that's nostalgic sex, not meaningless sex. Everyone does nostalgic sex.'

'It was weird; he remembered all this stuff about me. Sexually I mean.'

'Ah,' said Charlie knowingly, 'best sex.'

'What do you mean?'

'You were obviously his best sex; that's why he remembered. Everyone always remembers every detail of their best sex.'

'Really? But I couldn't remember all that much about him. Doesn't best sex have to be mutual?'

'Course not. Do you know nothing? One man's best sex can be another man's poison. Or woman obviously in your case.' Charlie nodded; kindly acknowledging that heterosexuals can have sex too, while simultaneously managing to indicate that the pleasure of heterosexual sex was as nothing when compared to the heady delights of homoeroticism.

'It was perfectly nice and enjoyable, but not firecracker sex.' Ros felt secretly pleased to think that she might be Robbie's best sex.

'Look at you,' Charlie said, 'you look as though you've just been told you came top in chemistry. Did you? Come, I mean?'

'Stop it,' Ros said, hitting him, 'we don't all have to share every detail like you, you know. But, yes, thank you for asking, I did. Not like with Plezh who rolled over the moment he had, leaving me unfulfilled. Such rude behaviour.'

'You should do what I do in such circumstances,' Charlie said.

Ros looked at him questioningly.

'You say, "All those who've had an orgasm, put up their hands." Then when you don't put your own up, they are shamed into doing something about it.'

Ros hugged him. 'That's why I love you,' she said, 'you are so ridiculous.'

'Why didn't you phone and tell me where you were?' Charlie said.

'The whole point about being a soon-to-be-divorced empty-nester is that I don't have to account for myself,' Ros answered. 'Although, as it happens, I did phone and I left a message on your voicemail.' Ros noticed that Charlie looked shifty.

'Oh, my phone must have been turned off.'

'You couldn't have been *that* worried about me then,' Ros said. 'OK, who is he?'

'This gorgeous man I met at work.'

'What do you mean at work? In court, where?'

Charlie looked sheepish and remained silent.

'Who is he, Charlie?' Ros had unwittingly adopted her let's-get-right-to-the-bottom-of-this teacher's voice.

'He's the sperm burglar's brother,' he answered quickly, turning to busy himself at the sink rinsing the dogs' bowls so that he didn't have to meet Ros's eyes.

'Charlie! Isn't that unethical?' Ros was shocked.

'The case is over, the sperm burglar won her maintenance, although thanks to me she got considerably less than she'd hoped for, and Archibald is the most delicious man I've met in years.'

'Archibald?'

'He can't help his name, Rosalind,' Charlie said.

'Rosalind is a beautiful Shakespearean name. Methinks this leap to his nomenclatorial defence suggests this could be more than meaningless sex, my lord,' Ros teased.

'We'll see.'

'For God's sake, don't introduce him to Puppy with the words, "Kiss Mummy", will you?'

Charlie laughed. He had once gone back to a date's house full of the expectation of carnal bliss. On entering the front door, the man had scooped up the small ball of fur that had hurled itself at his legs, kissed it on its snout, allowing the chihuahua to lap at his mouth with its small tongue and squealed these very words to the dog, holding it up to Charlie's face in order that it might indeed kiss Mummy. While these two small words encapsulated the man's longing for family, for Charlie, rather than heralding a happy beginning, they were the two bullets that precipitated a summary ending and he'd fled. He and Ros had laughed for ages about it afterwards.

'Does Archibald kiss better than me?' Ros asked.

'He's more bristly, which, as you know, is just the way I like it.'

This easy banter dispelled any residual awkwardness remaining from their unlikely kiss.

'Why is it that one can never find everything all in one person?' Ros asked, as they sat curled up together on the sofa. 'Your brain, say, with Mike's disposition before he became Angryman, added to his sexual technique. Why can't I have that all rolled up into one perfect man?'

'Because as flies to wanton boys, are we to the gods ...'

'... They kill us for their sport,' Ros finished for him.

'Mind you,' Charlie said, looking at Ros, 'Mike had two out of three, which is not bad going.'

'Yes, but had is the operative word; he didn't retain it.'

'I wonder if Archibald could be everything in one?' Charlie mused. 'That's what's so nice about the start of a relationship, isn't it? The belief that this person could be *the one*.'

'That's the definition of *the one* when you come to think about it,' said Ros, 'the person who combines all the qualities you want in one package. No wonder it's so hard to sustain long-term relationships; such an idealistic expectation is bound to be thwarted.'

'Let me labour under the illusion for a while,' Charlie said, getting up and kissing her on the forehead, 'it's been a long time between dreams for me.'

So much for meaningless sex. Everyone, it seems, is searching for love. As Ros let Charlie out, she picked up the junk mail on the mat. A now familiar, brown envelope was concealed beneath the local free newspaper. It was late. Ros sat down, opened it and began to read.

Chapter Nineteen

Lilian

Our lives returned to normal, or as normal as lives like ours could be. Over the following year my mother became ill, necessitating several visits to Cape Town. I sat by her bed as she lay dying and mourned the fact that we had never been close and that I had never truly experienced a mother's love. I felt sorry too that, for her part, she hadn't known the love of a daughter and made a vow to myself that, when the time came, I would be a different sort of mother. My father seemed older, shrunken and ever more inaccessible to me during my mother's illness. Josiah cooked my favourite dishes and Diana made a fuss of me and gave me a beaded necklace that she had made specially.

'In order to be happy, Lili, you must learn to leave the past behind,' she said.

The three of us often talked quietly into the night about politics and I told them of my involvement with the ANC in Johannesburg.

'Be careful, Lilian,' Josiah said, 'these people will not rest until they have everyone who is against them locked up.'

Diana looked at me closely. She'd always been able to tell when I was keeping a secret and I wished that I could tell her about Sipho and my relationship but I couldn't bring myself to burden her with it; I knew she would fear too much for me.

After my mother died, my father sold his business and moved to Johannesburg with a speediness that surprised us all. I didn't flatter myself that he did this to be near me, his only daughter, but wonder today with the gift of hindsight whether in fact my presence in

Jo'burg formed, at least, part of the reason for his move. Diana and Josiah were forced to return to their townships and I sent them money whenever I could. My father bought a house in Joubert Park and soon started keeping company with a wealthy Jewish widow called Marcie. After the first wave of grief, he seemed liberated by my mother's death and more at ease with himself and with Marcie, who became his second wife. (Is it the fate of everyone to return to their roots as they grow older?) He was more at ease with me too and our relationship improved, although not enough for me to reveal to him the intimate details of my life.

The day in December 1956 when one hundred and fifty-six people were arrested, Gloria, Harry, Lenny, Shirley and me amongst them, for what became South Africa's famous treason trial, was also the day when I discovered something that would change my life for ever.

The police had come, as was their custom, in the early hours before dawn. A noise had disturbed me and, getting up, I'd seen shadows pass to and fro in front of the frosted glass of our front door. We'd taken to keeping the curtains tightly drawn, allowing no chink through which our movements or those of any guests could be distinguished, aware that we were increasingly kept under surveillance. I crept into Gloria's room to wake her and give her time to hide any documents that might incriminate her. Those that I had been working on were already hidden under a floorboard in the lounge. Secreting them had become a ritual that I observed nightly before going to bed, like brushing my teeth.

I answered the peremptory knock at the door. There were two of them. They pushed past me and, after ordering Gloria and me to sit, proceeded to rifle through the papers on our desk, throwing anything they deemed suspicious onto a pile in the centre of the room. Next they went through our collection of books. The elder of the two, a sandy-haired Afrikaaner with a moustache, pounced on a History of Russian Ballet, *a book that Sonya had given Gloria for her birthday a year or two before.*

'Hey, look at this Commie literature, this is the sort of stuff we're

looking for,' he said gleefully to his companion, adding it to their growing pile.

He went into my bedroom and over to my chest of drawers.

'Not in there,' I said sharply as he made to open the top drawer. 'That's where I keep my underwear.'

The policeman paused, caught between embarrassment and a determination to do his job. Professionalism won out and he continued his search, pulling out my underwear with unnecessary force, angry that I had shamed him.

'You think you're so smart, girlie,' he said, 'but we've got your initials all over illegal documents.'

Fear flared in me. It appeared my old varsity habit of initialling my work had finally caught up with me. I took care to erase any inadvertent initialling of ANC documents, but obviously I had not been vigilant enough. I experienced a strong desire to vomit and running from the room made it to the lavatory just in time. I retched over the bowl until nothing was left inside me but bile. Standing up, I looked at my face in the mirror. It was pale and tinged a sickly yellow; I felt faint. I could see the shelf reflected in the mirror behind me; on it sat a packet of tampons. I made rapid calculations in my head. With all that had been going on in our lives, I couldn't remember when I had last menstruated. I realised at once that I was pregnant. Snapshots of the past few months flashed in my head and I knew exactly when conception must have taken place.

One early spring afternoon at the beginning of August, Sipho and I had made love in the baobab tree. It had felt particularly intense and joyful and as we had lain together afterwards, I'd had a waking dream that I was back in Cape Town in my favourite rock pool; the water flowed into empty hollows, forcing sand between the toes of my bare feet and causing the sea anemones to flutter and weave. It had been a particularly sensory dream and I'd experienced a rush of adrenalin. I felt sure that that was the moment when Sipho's sperm began their determined journey within me to fertilise my waiting egg. If I were right, I must already be over four months pregnant.

My first response to this discovery was intense joy followed immediately by a blend of fear and despair so bitter I could taste it.

'I'm pregnant,' I whispered to Gloria as we were led out to the police car.

'Are you sure?' Gloria asked.

I nodded. She took my hand and we sat in silence throughout the drive to Marshall Square police station where we found many of our closest friends already gathered. Indeed, there were so many familiar faces crammed into the station that it felt like a cocktail party. In the chaos, Harry pulled us to one side and whispered, 'They're charging us with high treason; they say we're part of a national conspiracy to use violence to overthrow the government and replace it with a communist state.'

'Are you serious?' I asked.

He nodded.

'No talking,' a policeman said, appearing at Harry's side and pulling him away roughly.

Gloria and I looked at each other in disbelief. It was, of course, nonsense; many of those arrested weren't communists and never had been. No doubt the state thought that this would be a convenient catch-all to silence all those opposed to the system. What they hadn't anticipated was that in the months and years of the trials that followed, it would offer a unique opportunity for people who had previously been banned, and therefore forbidden from meeting and speaking to each other under the Suppression of Communism Act, to meet daily to plan their future political tactics. The irony amused us.

In the police station mêlée, while women were being separated from men and blacks from whites, Gloria must have told Harry of my situation and he in turn told Lenny, because instead of being charged with treason, like the others, I was sent home the following day. I found out later that Lenny, who shared my initials, LB, had asserted that the initialling of documents meant that he and not I had drafted and typed them.

'I was being charged, as it was,' Lenny told me later after he'd been bailed, 'and there didn't seem much point in you having to go through all that in your condition. Anyhow, I feel a certain sense of responsibility for having got you into all this in the first place.'

'You didn't make me do anything I didn't want to do,' I said.

Lenny smiled. 'Ja, look at the mess your fast typing almost got you into.'

I nodded sorrowfully, remembering the train journey from Cape Town to Jo'burg; it felt a lifetime ago.

Sipho laughed his rich warm laugh and bent to kiss my stomach when I told him my news. But by the time he'd raised his head for his eyes to meet mine, they were sombre and his smile had vanished.

'Every man wants to give a baby to the woman he loves,' he said, stroking my stomach and drawing my head onto his shoulder. 'A baby is the greatest gift of love.'

He had so far managed to avoid arrest: we had always been careful to deflect attention from him in the knowledge that any repercussions were liable to be more severe for him than for us. Additionally, he was too important a point of contact between his community and ours.

'What can we do?' I asked.

'Let's leave this place and go away together. We'll go to Swaziland and then go somewhere from there.'

'Would you really abandon the struggle and leave?'

'I would leave for you alone anyway, but for you and our baby, I won't hesitate,' Sipho said.

'When can we go?' I asked.

'I think it would be better to have the baby here and then go,' Sipho said, instantly decisive.

It was one of many qualities I loved him for. Looking into his eyes, I marvelled that it was possible to love someone with such intensity and that I had been lucky enough to find such a love.

'My mother will come up and deliver the baby,' Sipho continued, 'and then we will wait a few weeks after the birth to travel. It's too dangerous to go away with you pregnant without knowing where we'll be for you to give birth.'

'But won't that be dangerous?'

'Lili, at least it's a danger we know. I won't risk anything if there's any chance you or the baby will come to harm.'

The remaining five months of my pregnancy were difficult ones,

*but not for any medical reason. I had to hide my expanding girth
and lie low. It was bad enough to be unmarried and pregnant, but
to be pregnant by a black man was against the law. My friends
were caught up in the treason trial and, although now out on bail,
they spent their days preparing their defence and, like a child that
has been overlooked for the school team, I felt irrationally left out
and strangely envious. I had told the editor at the paper that I had
glandular fever and he gave me easy assignments that could be
carried out from home. Sipho visited me whenever he could, cycling
over on Zakhele's bicycle, which still bore the scars of the day he'd
been knocked off it in the rusting dents on its mudguards. Our
escape to Swaziland had been planned for six weeks after the birth of
our baby.*

*Sipho was concerned by the fact that others knew about my
pregnancy, not merely because of our situation.*

*'In Xhosa custom,' he explained, 'an expectant mother thinks it
is bad luck to let anyone, apart from her husband and very close
relatives, know that she is pregnant.'*

*Sipho's mother, Thandi, arrived in Jo'burg to look after me and
prepare for the birth. Lenny and Shirley had somehow arranged
a pass for her, saying that she was working for them as a maid. I
had met her only once before, on the day of Sipho's family's forced
removal from Sophiatown. When she arrived, she cast a professional
eye over me and put her hand on my belly.*

*'Uneenyanga ezingaphi?' she asked. 'How many months pregnant
are you?'*

'Ndineenyanga ezintandathu,' I answered.

Thandi laughed, delighted that I had answered her in Xhosa.

'Six months, very good; the baby is growing just fine,' she said.

*I went into labour in the early hours of May 10th, 1957. Sipho sat
outside and in between my contractions I could see the tip of his
cigarette glow hot and red as he chain-smoked throughout that long
unforgettable night. Thandi tended to me. I didn't have the luxury
of painkillers and she gave me a piece of cloth to bite on to prevent
my cries of pain from becoming too loud and attracting unwelcome*

attention. Gloria sat by me and wiped my forehead, passing an ice-cube over my dry lips every now and then.

A wave of pain engulfed me, so strong that for a few moments I couldn't breathe. I felt as though I was being borne up on it, buffeted from side to side and then, suddenly, it reached a crescendo, a point where physical pain was no longer of any consequence and I was aware only of Gloria's voice next to me exhorting me to breathe and of taking deep breaths in and out, in and out and bearing down, pushing and breathing, pushing and breathing until I was beyond pain, in a land I'd never visited where all that mattered was this moment, breathing in and pushing down hard as I breathed out. I pushed and pushed and then, as my womb emptied in a rush, there was instantly no need to push any more. I caught sight of Thandi's face and saw a look of wonder pass over it. The miracle of birth. However many times she had seen it, and I knew it was many, that moment when a baby enters the world for the first time, crumpled and looking as old as time, was as full of wonder for Thandi as the first time she had witnessed it. Thandi lifted the baby in the air, her professional eyes moving over it quickly, calculating, assessing and, with a quick nod of satisfaction, she laid it on my stomach. I reached for it and instinctively drew it towards my breast.

'Hello, my darling,' I said as if I'd known this tiny creature all my life, stroking its matted black curls and looking at its small face and perfect body, touching the velvet of its creamy brown skin.

Gloria kissed my forehead and bent to kiss the baby's head, tears coursing down her face. The baby filled its small lungs with air and furiously gave voice to its complaint at being forced from a warm home and into this unknown world.

'Ngumntwana mni? *What sex is the child?*' Sipho's voice made me jump, coming through the fly screen at the open window behind my bed.

'It's a girl,' Thandi said, 'nkosazana, *a princess.*'

'To hell with Xhosa custom,' Sipho said, 'I'm coming in.'

Thandi shook her head disapprovingly.

'He shouldn't see the baby until after ten days when the belly-button is healed,' she said firmly.

'These are unusual circumstances,' said Gloria quietly.

Thandi hesitated and then nodded and, taking the baby from me, swaddled her expertly in a small cotton sheet.

Seconds later, a smile walked into the room, a gigantic white smile with Sipho attached to it. He took the baby from his mother and brought her back to me, laying his arm around me so that the three of us were enclosed in a circle.

'Nkosazana,' he said, 'shall we call her that, Nkosa for short? She symbolises the meeting of black and white, she is the princess of a new tribe.'

I distantly registered Thandi's look of doubt and concern, a potent reminder of the gravity of our situation. I was, after all, the white mother of a black child in apartheid South Africa. I buried my face into Sipho's neck, inhaling his familiar odour, which was, for me, the smell of home, and our daughter opened her big brown eyes and solemnly regarded us, not with the unfocused sight of the newborn, but with a penetrating look that seemed to imply she understood everything.

'My girls,' Sipho said, laughing with pleasure.

Chapter Twenty

Ros put the pages down and wept, her body racked by loud sobs of loss and longing. Not only was she not her mother's first and only child, she had a sister she had never known. After a while, her tears subsided and she sat quietly, dimly aware of the ticking of the clock on the mantelpiece.

She got up, fetched her laptop and retreated into a corner of the sofa with it, tucking her legs beneath her. She had the impatient urge to talk to Jimmy and fill him in on the latest developments in Lilian's story. She logged onto the dating site.

Jimmy, is that you?

Ros was delighted to find Jimmy online so late. She explained about Lilian and the baby, summarising as best she could.

What happened after she'd had her? Jimmy asked.

I don't know yet. I'll have to wait for the next instalment.

Are you going to tell your ex about this?

I don't know. You're the only other person who knows so far.

Don't you think you should tell him?

Why? He's my ex, or soon-to-be ex. Anyhow, I'm sure something bad happens, after all, if it were something good, I'd have known I had a sister, Ros wrote.

You have to find out, you must track this Gloria down or phone the publishers. You can't give up the race when the finishing line is in sight, Jimmy answered.

Ros sat back with a start. First Dr Seuss and now this: once again Jimmy had said something that was part of her and Mike's private lexicon. In fact, this phrase was one of Lilian's that they had appropriated. Ros remembered only too clearly the first time Lilian had said it. She had been studying for her O levels and with just two weeks to go before her exams began, she'd run out of steam and simply couldn't be bothered with it all any more. Lilian had found her in her room, lying on her bed, listening to Capital Radio and reading a magazine. She could even remember what song had been playing: 'Bad Girls' by Donna Summer, because as she lay there, she'd thought, I'm sick of being a good girl, fuck O levels, I'm going to be a bad girl instead. Lilian had come in without knocking, violating Ros's highly developed teenage sense of privacy. Had she entered a moment or two earlier, she'd have caught Ros smoking too. Ros was relieved that she'd had the foresight to spray her deodorant in the air to mask the smell of tobacco, although she hadn't had time to turn the radio off, hide her magazine and pick up *Animal Farm*, the book she was supposed to be studying. Lilian, assessing the situation with a glance, had sat on the edge of her bed.

'You know what you remind me of?' she'd asked quietly.

Ros rolled her eyes and sighed. 'No.'

'An athlete who's running a race,' said Lilian, 'he's out in the front, winning is a certainty, but just as he sees the finishing line, he stops and says, "Oh, fuck it, I can't be bothered."' Lilian paused and stroked Ros's hair off her face. 'You're almost there, darling, you can't give up the race when the finishing line is in sight.'

Ros wasn't sure whether it was her mother's unaccustomed use of the F-word, or the power of her metaphor, but she'd held this image ever since and both she and Mike had used Lilian's words to refocus their sons' attention in times of need.

Ros shifted on the sofa, rearranging her legs; she had pins and needles in her right foot. She stood up and walked around the room, stopping to examine her face in the mirror. The evening of her date with Jimmy came into her mind and she replayed it, closing her eyes in order to concentrate better. She opened the pub door and walked in, but this time the sight that met her eyes was refracted, as though she were looking at the scene through a different lens; this time, the handsome black man in the foreground was blurred and Mike, sitting at the bar, was in sharp focus. One's brain decides what one sees, Ros reflected, and there are numerous ways of looking at the same thing. She was reminded of the pictures she sometimes showed her pupils, magical 3D pictures, which, if you looked at them long and hard enough, yielded an image not immediately apparent to the eye, a hidden image, that emerged only if one let oneself go and was prepared to believe in an alternative, buried reality. The night of her date with Jimmy, Ros had looked at the picture incorrectly and, in recollection, she understood that she was seeing it correctly now for the first time. Mike was Jimmy and Jimmy was Mike. Did he know? Had he known all along that Ros was Sally, even before seeing her walk through the pub doors? Should she challenge him? She returned to the sofa and picked up her laptop once more.

You're right, she wrote, I will finish the race.

Will you tell me what happened? asked Jimmy.

Do you really want to know? Ros teased. This was fun: knowing, and Mike not knowing that she knew.

Of course I do.

Maybe you're right, maybe I should tell my ex-husband, after all, he knew my mother very well.

Yes, I think you should.

There was a silence between them. An indicator on the screen told her that Jimmy was typing. It kept flashing on and off. It was as though he typed something, erased it and began typing again. Finally his message popped up.

I have the feeling that things aren't over between the two of you.

Oh, they're over all right, wrote Ros, he's seeing that young Spanish girl now.

I'm sure he'll come to his senses. Any man worth his salt knows you should never sleep with a woman under the age of forty.

Oh, come on, Ros answered. All men want to shag twenty-three-year-olds. Otherwise, why do so many trade their wives in for younger models?

Those are the men who aren't worth their salt. Women under forty may look good naked, but they don't yet know what they're about and what they want. The older woman is ultimately far more fulfilling, Jimmy said.

I'll let Hugh Heffner and Peter Stringfellow know, and my ex-husband come to that, Ros joked, continuing, So, when shall we meet? How, she wondered, would Mike deal with that?

Unfortunately I have to stay away for a couple more weeks.

Ros suddenly tired of the game. She wanted to think about Lilian and her baby. Even now, she was only half concentrating on Mike/Jimmy's words, her attention drawn once more to the pages lying beside her. How old had Lilian been when Nkosa was born? May 1957. She'd have been twenty-three. The scent of Ma Griffe, her mother's perfume, briefly stirred her senses and a small shiver ran through her.

Ros phoned Charlie.

'Jimmy is Mike,' she said without preamble.

'What? Ros, do you know what time it is?'

Ros ignored him. 'Jimmy. You know that chap on the Internet I've been talking to? And when I went to meet him Mike was there? He's Mike.'

'Are you sure?'

'Yes. He keeps saying Mike-like things and it's too much of a coincidence.'

'Does he know you're you?'

'I don't know. But anyhow, never mind about that. That's the least of it. It turns out I have a sister.' Ros wondered whether Nkosa was still alive. 'Or at any rate, I had a sister. I mean, my mother had a baby before me.'

'I'll come and stay over,' Charlie said, sounding concerned. 'I'm not working in the morning.'

'I'm not sure I know who I am any more,' Ros said.

Charlie had made her a cup of tea and was sitting next to her. He'd been reading Lilian's story.

'I wonder why she didn't tell you?'

'That's what I keep thinking. But you know, there was always something held back and elusive about her. I never felt I could quite reach her and her mood used to change so quickly. At least now I can begin to understand why. She always used to say that it was so wasteful that human beings could never benefit from each other's experiences and had to make the same mistakes for themselves. But the truth of it is that even if we don't learn from them, we all feel the ripple effect of the lives of others. Even though I didn't know her secret, I always sensed there was something private about her that removed her from me and denied us an ease and intimacy we might otherwise have had.'

'No one exists in a vacuum,' said Charlie, 'and difficult and painful experiences always impact on others.'

Ros thought about her great-grandparents, Meir and Rebecca, and the relatives they had lost in the war. Just as the Holocaust reverberates down succeeding generations, she reflected, so the current turbulent climate in South Africa is a result of a generation dealing with the pain and injustices of the apartheid system that their parents and forebears endured. A system, it now turned out, that had implications for Ros's life today. When would she know the rest?

She didn't have to wait long; the morning's post arrived unusually early and brought the final instalment.

Chapter Twenty-One

Lilian

For the first few weeks after Nkosa's birth, we cloistered ourselves in the garden house and the day-to-day task of looking after a small baby lulled us into a false sense of security. Our friends kept close watch to ensure our safety and Sipho came every morning and evening before and after work. Thandi, whose pass had not been renewed at the end of her first month, despite Lenny and Shirley's best efforts, travelled in from Meadowlands each day to help. She ran the daily risk that is the plight of so many Africans, of being stopped at random by police and asked for papers she did not possess. Twenty thousand women, Gloria, Shirley and I included, had all marched to Pretoria with the Federation of South African Women the previous year to protest against the pass laws. The authorities' refusal to renew Thandi's pass was doubtless petty revenge for Shirley's involvement in anti-apartheid politics. The state had many ways of making our lives difficult. Now too, of course, with the treason trial hanging over so many, the authorities were constantly on the lookout for any further ammunition they could find to use against us.

At first I was grateful for Thandi's help. Nkosa was her first grandchild and she could hardly tear herself away each evening.

'Give me our baby, I will take care of her,' she said repeatedly. 'It will be much safer for her to be with me in the location; after all, she is a black child. Next door to me is a woman who has also given birth, she can feed Nkosa along with her own baby; she has plenty of milk.'

Her words unsettled me. I couldn't contemplate allowing another woman to breastfeed my baby. While I had anticipated my child being rejected by the white community, I hadn't anticipated that she might be so completely appropriated by the black one. For me, Nkosa was neither a black baby nor a white one; she was simply Sipho's and my baby, our daughter, a fact that I had to ask Sipho to remind his mother of on more than one occasion.

'She only wants to help us out,' Sipho said.

I looked at Nkosa's face and marvelled at the complicated ancestry I saw mirrored in it. The generous space between her upper lip and nose reminded me of Grandpa Meir, while the arc of her eyebrows matched Sipho's and the shape of her eyes were my own. As I fed her, I admired the curve of her cheek, her small jaw working to draw the milk from me, and considered the beautiful woman she would one day become. Our love child, a child forbidden by law and born out of wedlock, Nkosa was a child created entirely by the love her father and I had for each other.

When exactly did the nightmare begin? Distress has fractured memory and left only flashes of recollection, which, their threads hanging loose, have entangled and lost some of the intricacies of their connection one to another.

It is night. It has been a difficult day. Earlier, I was carrying Nkosa, cradled in my arms, from the lounge to the bedroom when a sudden sound from outside jolted me. I am ever fearful of the police, particularly since I am in possession of some dangerous documents, and although they are hidden beneath the secret floorboard, their presence in the house combined with the special vulnerability and fearfulness of the new mother are making me more than usually jumpy. My sudden movement caused the hot tea I carried in my other hand to spill onto my baby's tender, newborn arm. A moment before, she had been sleeping peacefully and now she was screaming, her small red face crumpled with a suffering that I alone had caused. Thandi took Nkosa from me with a look that implied I was not fit to be a mother.

'You must never carry hot liquid when you are holding a child,' she shouted, sending me to the garden to cut a leaf from the aloe that grows under Lenny and Shirley's dining room window, its scarlet flowers extending like red-hot pokers towards the sky. On my return,

Thandi briskly extracted the gel-like flesh from inside the leaf and applied it to the burn on Nkosa's scalded skin while I held her to my breast and fed her, hoping that my milk would be a healing elixir and help to assuage my terrible guilt. Thandi was even more than usually reluctant to leave and, sensing my distress, Sipho decided to risk staying the night. Thandi encouraged him: it was clear that she didn't trust me alone with Nkosa.

It felt luxurious having Sipho to myself. Gloria was out and it was the three of us, a family together at home like normal families, a dream that we wanted to enjoy for the short time we held it.

'I'm not sure your mother likes me,' I said to Sipho. 'Isn't it odd, it's something I never considered,' I continued. 'I mean, I was so busy thinking about us hiding our predicament from the white community, it never occurred to me that your mother might not be happy for you to have a child with a white woman.'

Sipho looked troubled. 'Nothing in this life of ours is perfect. In many ways, my mother is a traditional woman. She wants only the best for me and for Nkosa. In time, she will grow to love you too.'

I have finished a night feed, have kissed Nkosa's warm neck, wondering at my possession of this creature, this person that Sipho and I have created together, and wished I could be all nose to fill myself with her sweet baby smell. Her arm is bandaged, the burnt skin beneath bubbled into a large blister, a terrible reminder of the earlier accident. I move her gently from my breast where she has fallen asleep, drunk on mother's milk, and lay her gently back into her crib next to us before returning to bed. The moon is full tonight and shines in through the window and I lie bathed in its light, briefly at peace. Something temporarily obscures the moonlight. I tense, instantly alert. There it is again, shadows moving quickly and seconds later, a sharp knock on the door. Sipho wakes up, he puts his finger to his lips. We hear the front door opening, followed by a loud voice. It is Gloria's. She must have returned home after we had gone to bed.

'She doesn't live here any more, I'm here on my own,' she says loudly, warningly.

'Well you won't mind us having a look then, will you?' a voice answers her with a strong Afrikaans accent. The sound of boots

treading heavily on wooden floors; a voice that sounds familiar although difficult to place. Sipho and I lie in the dark, afraid to move while the search goes on. We consider the options: flight through the window is impossible; we can see the light of a police car outside and the silhouette of a policeman within. Sipho, on hands and knees, so his shadow cannot be seen from outside, takes Nkosa from her crib and brings her into the bed with us. There is nowhere for us to go, nowhere to hide. Sipho gets up and starts to dress. It will be better if we are not discovered in the same bed; that, after all, is a criminal offence.

We hear a voice saying, 'I'll take a look in here.'

The door of the bedroom opens. There is a man at the door; his head turns, I see the familiar face of Keith du Toit, elevated to the rank of sergeant if his uniform is anything to judge by. He comes in quickly and shuts the door behind him.

'Lilian,' the word is whispered.

Keith takes in the scene before him, looking slowly from me to Sipho and then to the baby I have quickly taken into my arms. His expression changes to one of distaste, even revulsion. When Keith regards the people I love in such a manner, the force of the rage that mounts within me leaves me breathless. Sipho sits next to me on the bed and puts his arm around me as if to protect me from the wave of Keith's aversion. Keith turns, is about to leave the room, his mouth beginning to form the words that will end all hope for us. He looks back at us and Nkosa opens her eyes and yawns. She turns her head, her mouth working, instinctively rooting for my breast. Something extraordinary happens to Keith's face. It softens, he smiles, looks at us again, this time with different eyes. It is as if, in that instant, Sipho and I have witnessed his soul awakening.

'You have to get away from here,' he says, his voice so low it is barely audible. 'Your name is on a list and they're going to arrest you.' Keith takes a pad out, scribbles a number on a piece of paper and hands it to me. 'Here, phone me tomorrow.'

I pause.

'Take it, Lilian, I'm trying to help you.'

Sipho nods almost imperceptibly and his hand tightens on my shoulder. I take the paper.

With a final look at us, Keith leaves the room and closes the door, saying loudly, 'There's nothing in there, boys, no need to search.'

Later they leave, taking Gloria with them, and I go into the lounge to phone Harry to tell him what's happened and where he needs to go to bail Gloria out. I stand on the threshold, immobilised by the sight of a missing floorboard and an empty cavity beneath the spot where it once lay. The floorboard is propped against a nearby wall, discarded. The papers it concealed were very early discussion papers about the path that lay open to the ANC if we were unable to achieve change through peaceful means. They intimated the eventual possible need for armed struggle against apartheid if all else failed. The papers are gone. Even Sipho doesn't know about these papers, which had been entrusted to me by members of the ANC executive. (Gloria told me later that the police had been specifically looking for these documents. I can only assume that an informer had apprised them of their existence; someone who was perhaps listening in the shadows when the papers were given to me for safekeeping, or someone who was present at the meeting where they were drafted. Who knows? In a society where so many live in poverty and in need of favours, it is always possible to buy information.) The floorboard, Gloria told me later, was discovered accidentally: a meticulous policeman listening to the sound of his feet as he walked the boards first in one direction, then in the other, until a variation in sound aroused his suspicion and led him to discover the loose board and change the course of my life for ever. I phone Harry again quickly, notifying him of the seriousness of the situation. Gloria will doubtless be charged with harbouring the documents.

Five days later, I stood at the railing of the Union-Castle liner, sailing back on the same shipping line that had brought Grandpa Meir from Libau to South Africa, although I was doing the journey in reverse and not travelling as far as Lithuania; I would be getting off in England. I watched the familiar shoreline, the almost-flat Table Mountain with bluish-green peaks flanking it. It was so familiar and dear to me. I could even see the square box of the cable car, suspended in the air swaying precariously as it took its cargo of people to the mountain's summit. That's something I never did, I thought, when I imagined I had all my life to live here. There was never any hurry, and now I'll never do it. I knew that I was unlikely to return and that if such a possibility did arise, it wouldn't be for many years to come. I pushed my hair back firmly behind my ears, tucked my blouse, damp with leaking breast milk, into my skirt and stood up straight. Tears coursed down my cheeks.

It's almost too painful to reflect on the events that led to my departure from South Africa without my child and the man I could think of only as my husband. After the police raid, we had run away to Meadowlands. Thandi had taken charge and, made conspicuous by the colour of my skin, I had been hidden in a small back bedroom. When I had crept out the next night to telephone Keith, he had told me to get out of the country as quickly as possible by any means I could. The police knew that the documents had been entrusted to me and not to Gloria and were determined to find me.

'Why are you doing this, Keith?'

'Don't you know?' he asked.

I thought of all the times I had caught him looking at me, an expression of longing on his face as though I were the answer to a question he hadn't yet managed to formulate. His overt desire for me used to make me feel like a bird being pursued by a cat; I realised now that I had got it the wrong way round: I was the cat and he the captured bird I had unwittingly toyed with.

'Yes,' I answered. 'I suppose I do.'

We paused awkwardly for a little while, the silence stretching tautly between us.

'Thank you,' I said, quietly. 'Listen, I have no right to ask you for anything more, but you're a good man; please be as kind to others in the future as you have been to me.'

I could hear a sigh at the other end of the telephone. Keith hesitated and said, 'Bye Lilian, look after yourself and let me know what you decide to do.'

I heard a soft click as he replaced the telephone in its cradle.

Where could I go? Swaziland was no longer an option: Keith had told me that the police suspected I would use that route and were on the lookout. Southern Rhodesia did not present a long-term solution either – although more lenient, it would never tolerate us as a family. Keith had told me that the authorities knew that I had given birth to a black child, although, mercifully, they didn't yet know who the father was. Sipho and I weighed up our options. They were few. If caught, I would be imprisoned and the possession of the hidden papers was likely to ensure a lengthy prison sentence, which would see me separated from both Nkosa and Sipho. I had to find a way for us all to leave the country. The problem was that we didn't have passports and it was hardly likely that we would be given them.

I lay in Sipho's bed listening to the sounds outside, the comings and goings to a nearby shebeen, the echo of drunken laughter, someone whistling in the distance. How strange it felt that life could continue as normal for those around us, when we were facing such a crisis. Exhausted by all that had happened, I was on the point of sleep, that moment where reality and dreams fuse and become indistinguishable from each other, when the words that Gerry Vanderbilt had spoken to me the year before sounded loudly in my head.

'If ever you need help, come and talk to me.'

Was he a lifeline that could lift us to safety? We had no option but to ask him. I woke Sipho.

'Who is this man and how do we know we can trust him?' Sipho said.

'What other choices do we have?'

Sipho traced his forefinger around the contours of my face as though committing me to memory and sighed.

The following evening, under cover of dark, Harry came to collect me by car and drove me to Vanderbilt's house. Vanderbilt had seemed unsurprised by my story. We were in his lounge and he got up to get the drinks from the sideboard.

'Ag man, you're not the only girl or boy to get involved with a native,' he said, fitting a new cartridge into his soda siphon.

I must have winced because he added quickly, 'Sorry, I know you people don't like that term, I don't mean anything by it.'

'I think of him only as a man,' I said quietly, 'my man.'

Vanderbilt spritzed soda water in three short bursts from the *siphon into each of our whisky glasses. The sounds punctuated the silence as though finalising something.*

'You must go to England. It won't be as easy as you imagine there, but it'll be a helluva lot easier than it is here.'

'We haven't got passports,' I said.

'I can get you passports,' Vanderbilt said, with the assurance of a man who knows how to do deals, 'but this has to be done quickly.'

'I'm still not sure why you're doing this,' I said.

Vanderbilt busied himself with the glasses on his sideboard. 'I was married once before,' he said, 'and had a daughter. She'd have been about your age now.'

I went over to him and took his hand.

Vanderbilt was as good as his word and it was all done so quickly that I barely had time to register the events. Thandi wanted to take Nkosa back with her to the Transkei, and have us send for her when we had established ourselves, but that was out of the question. Finally, after much discussion, we persuaded Thandi to come with us and Vanderbilt obtained papers for her as well.

The day before we left Jo'burg, Sipho and I were sitting in his bedroom in Meadowlands, Nkosa asleep in a small makeshift cot in front of us.

'We can do this,' he said, looking at me intently, 'we can win. We can all get out of here and be a family together.'

He got down on one knee in the narrow space between the bed and the wooden crate that served as a chair and took both my hands in his.

'Lilian,' he said, 'when we are all together in England, will you be my wife?'

I felt him push something into my hand and opened my palm to find a ring made of black, green and yellow beads; the colours of the ANC flag, the party that had first brought us together. (How else could our lives have collided?) I held out my hand.

'Put it on my finger,' I said, 'and let's make this our wedding and think of ourselves as husband and wife from this moment on.'

Sipho looked at me.

'I'm sorry,' he said.

'For what?'

'For loving you when it's brought you nothing but trouble.'

I held his face in the palm of my hands once more and kissed him. 'Don't ever be sorry, I'm nothing without you,' I said. 'Ndiyakuthanda.'

'I love you more.' Sipho smiled with pleasure as he always did when I spoke Xhosa to him.

He placed something smooth into my hand and curled my fingers around it. I opened them to see a fiery green stone lying in my palm: an African opal.

'The fire of Africa,' Sipho said, running a finger over the stone in my hand. 'It will burn for ever, like our love for each other. We will make this into an engagement ring for you when we are in England.'

He drew my head onto his shoulder. 'We have done everything the wrong way round, Lili, first a baby, then a wedding ring and last of all an engagement ring.'

'The wrong way round, but with the right man,' I answered, kissing him.

We consummated our 'marriage', seeking comfort in each other's bodies, almost overpowered by the emotion we felt and, fearful of our uncertain future, we wished that the night could last for ever. Afterwards, we lay together silently, and I watched the clock next to the bed, willing its hands to stop moving in order to hold off morning for as long as possible. Time never obeys the dictates of man or woman, however desperate they are, and daylight arrived all too soon.

I had told my father I was taking a trip to England and determined to tell him the truth in a letter once I arrived. Harry had given me his ex-wife Sonya's number and written to her explaining that we were coming. I phoned Keith once more to thank him for his help and to tell him we were leaving. Sipho and I travelled to Cape Town with Nkosa and Thandi. We were to stay with one of his cousins for our final night in Africa and Diana, my old nanny, travelled at my request from her township some fifty miles away to see me. I quickly explained everything to her.

'My baby, my poor baby,' she said, taking me in her arms and rocking me as she used to when I was little and had hurt myself. I longed for the time when Diana used to solve my problems by dabbing crimson Mercurochrome onto my cuts and grazes or by placing before me a steaming mealie with the kernels expertly sliced off with a sharp knife, as only she knew how. Myself a new mother, I was in need of a mother of my own more than ever and Diana was the closest I had ever had to one. One creates patterns in one's life without being aware of them and it is only with hindsight that an understanding about the inevitability of certain events grows. In the light of my love both for Diana and Josiah, my 'alter' parents, perhaps it wasn't so very surprising that the man I loved so passionately was also an African?

We woke early the following morning and made our way to the dock. The Athlone Castle gleamed white against the deep turquoise of the Atlantic Ocean and for the first time, almost as though I hadn't dared to believe it until it was within my grasp, I felt a flicker of excitement at the new life that was opening up before us. When we arrived at the quayside, I had to go up one gangway, Sipho, Nkosa and Thandi another. Apartheid was in force even at sea and blacks and whites had separate quarters. We had yet to work out how I could feed Nkosa while on board and I had spent many hours expressing milk into bottles to ensure she had enough to be going on with until we found a way. The official opened my passport and compared me to the photo in it. I was travelling under a false name and my heart was beating so loudly I felt sure that he would hear it. But he soon handed the passport back to me and languidly waved me on. To my right, further down the length of the ship, I could see Sipho and Thandi with Nkosa in her arms approach the front of their queue. Once on board, I stood by the railing in order to keep them in sight, my lips working, soundlessly incanting, 'Let them through, let them through, let them through.' At last they were being seen, their papers examined, the uniformed official standing aside to allow them to board. I realised that I had been holding my breath and was just about to exhale when I saw policemen running towards them, shouting.

'Officer, hold those natives, do not let them board.'

This was the moment that divided my life for ever into before and after, a moment from which I could never hope to recover. Sometimes, when something or someone is broken, they can never be repaired.

One of the policemen made straight for Sipho and, putting his hand on his shoulder, pulled him back so that he fell into the line of people behind him. Thandi with Nkosa still cradled in her arms was quickly surrounded and absorbed by the crowd of Africans waiting on the quayside who bore her away and out of the police's grasp. She looked back once, finding me with her eyes and cried out.

'I will keep her safe.'

How can I describe the intense pain I felt, how once again, as when Sipho had been knocked from his bicycle all those years before, the world began to move in slow motion and sound became distorted?

In the distance, I could see Sipho being led towards a van. A policeman opened the back and grabbed both his arms to throw him inside. Sipho twisted round to look back at me, his lips forming a final kiss as he sought to reassure me. The policeman turned to follow his gaze and looked straight at me. It was Keith. His face wore an expression of triumph: if he couldn't have me, neither could Sipho. I had misjudged him and this horrifying betrayal was my punishment and Sipho's too. My rejection of him had soured his love for me into hatred and I was paying the highest price imaginable – the loss of those dearest to me. I felt as though my heart had been torn from me and I could taste the sharp bitterness of fear in my mouth. How I wished then that I had allowed Keith to arrest me the night he had found Sipho and me together. I could hear a terrible sound; the keening of an animal in agony and some part of me recognised it as my own voice. I tried to get off the boat, thrashing my way through the passengers that surrounded me, their faces grotesque masks of horror as they witnessed my distress. Strong arms held me back and I must have lost consciousness as, when I came to, the gangplank had been lifted and the ship was moving away from the shore.

I never saw Sipho, Nkosa or Thandi again.

Chapter Twenty-Two

Charlie came into the living room.

'What's going on, aren't you going to work?' he asked.

Ros didn't answer. She didn't even hear him. She sat, her back to him, looking without seeing out of the window and towards the street beyond. She felt suspended in the world that her mother had inhabited fifty years before and didn't feel able to return from it. She forgave Lilian everything, regretting only that she was part of her mother's 'after' and had not shared her 'before'. How could anyone be expected to survive such loss? Ros was struck by the baldness of Lilian's language as she had described this terrible event. 'I never saw Sipho, Nkosa or Thandi again.' It reminded her of a woman she had seen on the TV news when the tsunami had engulfed parts of Thailand killing her young daughter. 'Then a wave came and took her,' the woman had said, her simple words starkly at odds with the shocking grief in her eyes.

'Ros.' Charlie touched her shoulder, making her jump.

'There's no more, that's the end. I don't know what happened after that,' Ros said.

'What are you talking about? Are you all right? You look awful,' Charlie said.

'Hmm?' Ros said absently. 'Do you think one has to know one's mother before one can really know oneself?'

Charlie knelt down on the floor in front of Ros. Ros saw Sipho's face as she imagined he must have looked when he knelt in front of her mother and asked her to marry him. Sipho. Where was he? Ros had to find him. Him and Nkosa. She remembered her dream about a policeman finding a body hidden beneath her floorboards; Lilian's fate had been sealed by a policeman finding documents beneath hers. Where was it that she had once read that the dead visit us in our dreams?

'Ros, Ros, Ros ...' Charlie was saying her name repeatedly. 'You're as white as a sheet.'

Ros looked at Charlie. 'You have to help me find them.'

'Why don't you tell me everything,' Charlie said, 'but first let me make you a cup of hot sweet tea. You look like you're in shock.'

Charlie was just setting the mug down next to Ros when the doorbell rang, startling them both. Some of the hot liquid spilt onto Charlie's hand and Ros gave a cry of alarm disproportionate to the incident.

'It's OK,' Charlie said soothingly, 'I'm fine. Now who on earth can that be?'

Mike stood on the doorstep with Ruffy and Puppy. His face was gaunt with fatigue but oddly smooth and clean-shaven. Ros noticed absently that any vestige of a moustache was gone.

'Ruffy wanted to come home,' he said.

Ros knew the real reason for his visit. After her last Internet conversation with his doppelganger, Jimmy, Mike no doubt wanted to come clean about his identity. He would also want to know the outcome of Lilian's story. In a detached kind of way, Ros wondered how he was going to play things.

'How can I help you, Mike?' she asked unkindly.

'There's something I want to tell you.' He busied himself taking off the dogs' leads and went into the kitchen to give them something to drink, calling over his shoulder, 'I've been doing anger management. I go to meetings at that church where you saw me the other week.'

Charlie looked at Ros. 'Shall I leave you two alone?' he asked.

'No,' answered Ros. 'Stay!'

Charlie, Mike, Ruffy and Puppy all froze. Despite her turmoil, Ros couldn't help smiling at their collective obedience. She could hear the world coming to life outside her window. The early morning sounds of rubbish carts and the click-clack of heels on paving stones as people made their way to work. She felt detached from it all, as though she inhabited a parallel universe of the bereaved. It was as though Lilian had come to life and died all over again. Ros longed for her boys with an acute visceral ache that made it hard to breathe, and she wondered what could have happened to Nkosa. Happiness turns on the pinhead of our actions, whether intentional or accidental, thought Ros. How quickly and easily people's lives can become sad.

All at once, she had an image of her grandfather on his one visit to England when Ros was seven. He'd presented a forbidding figure and had patted her awkwardly on the shoulder, declaring her a 'nice-looking girl' as though she were in no way connected to him. She remembered trying to hug him and finding his body made up of awkward, sharp angles that didn't mould to the shape of a young child's embrace. He was not at all like the kindly grandpas of the books and films she knew.

Ros recalled a snatch of conversation, overheard when she was supposed to be in bed but had been hiding instead behind the living room door, peeping in at her mother and this strange grandpa with his funny South African accent.

'It's nice to meet my granddaughter, Lilian,' he'd said.

'Really,' Lilian had answered, 'I didn't think my daughters were of particular consequence to you. They never have been in the past.'

'I have tried, Lili,' her grandfather said and his voice had sounded sad. 'We've looked everywhere, but no one knows anything.'

Why's Mommy being so mean to Grandpa? Ros had wondered before the sound of Lilian getting up had sent her scampering off to bed. And why did she say 'daughters' when there's only me? She'd fallen asleep and thought no more about it.

She hadn't seen her grandfather after that visit but each year, on her birthday, she received a card from him, signed Grandpa, his writing growing perceptibly frailer over the years until, somewhere around her sixteenth birthday, the cards had stopped coming.

Ros marvelled at the way in which new information created a

pathway to old, releasing memory as though turning the key in a canal lock and allowing the water to flood through. She wondered what else might be buried inside her head and how she might access it.

She looked up to find Mike and Charlie looking at her expectantly with the kind of eagerness Ruffy displayed when waiting to be fed.

'Sit!' Ros said automatically, pointing at the sofa opposite her.

Charlie and Mike obediently sat at once and in unison. Ros took a deep breath and began.

'Let's go and search the attic,' Mike said, jumping up as soon as Ros had finished, 'there may be other clues there.'

Men always needed to fix things, to take immediate action, when what Ros really wanted at that moment was the physical comfort of a hug. Charlie was the one who provided that, instantly and intuitively. It made Ros think that every woman should have two husbands, a straight one and a gay one, to satisfy all her needs. Was that the purpose of eunuchs in ancient courts? she wondered irrelevantly. Not, of course, that Charlie behaved in any way like a castrated male.

'I have to go to work and I want to absorb everything I've learnt before finding out any more,' Ros said, looking at her watch.

'Of course,' Mike said, immediately contrite. 'Let me come back later and help you.'

Ros said nothing.

'Please,' asked Mike.

'Actually,' Ros said, 'I'd like both of you to help.' She wasn't sure how much she wanted to be alone with Mike. The state of their relationship was not currently her priority. In a curious way, she felt that she were mourning the loss of Jimmy, a man with whom she had felt a strong affinity and who, it appeared, had never really existed.

Ros felt better when she got to school. She needed the routine of everyday life to secure her after all that she had learnt.

Jaime was admiring her reflection in the staffroom mirror. Newly highlighted ringlets framed her face, which appeared slimmer and younger-looking than it had even the week before. She turned on seeing Ros's reflection join her own and cha-cha-cha'd her way over to her.

'You're turning into Richard Gere in *Shall We Dance?*,' Ros said.

'Well, since it appears to be impossible to live one's life without turning into one cliché or another,' Jaime answered, 'one may as well choose one's cliché and if mine is the crime of a middle-aged love of dancing, then, let the music play on.'

'Too true,' said Ros, thinking of her newly single, empty-nester state and how it had propelled her into a life of reckless questing.

Was it only genuine tragedy that enabled a person to lift their life above cliché, Ros speculated, thinking about Lilian and Sipho. Sometimes, there was a terrible price to be paid for flouting convention. Was Tennyson right about it being better to have loved and lost than never to have loved at all? What would Lilian have said?

Ros brought Jaime up to date.

'What I don't understand,' said Ros, 'is that if Mom wanted me to know I had a sister, why didn't she just tell me instead of making it so damn complicated? Pictures locked away in the attic in a suitcase I might never have opened, instalments by post from America and South Africa, strange messages from mediums, odd no-neck neck-women. I mean, if she can do all that then why not simply say, "Ros, you had a sister"?'

'I think,' answered Jaime, 'that is your brain working, trying to reason and look for a logical explanation. If ever there were a situation where you should be using your pashonga, this is it.'

'I suppose. It's just curious. It's completely changed my view of my mother. I mean, I thought I knew her and now I discover I didn't at all. It's as though I have to replay the whole of my life with her in the context of this new information and reassess everything. I can't even begin to think how painful this must have been for her.'

'So is she still talking to you?' asked Jaime, 'In your head, I mean, like you say she has been.'

'You think I'm insane, don't you?' Ros answered. 'No, perversely, she now seems to have gone rather silent.'

'Your future happiness may well depend on your ability to leave the past behind,' Jaime said.

'Yes, O guru,' Ros said, 'you're probably right, but I think I first have to resolve it before I can leave it behind. I have to find out if my sister and Sipho are still alive.'

Ros gathered her books and hurried off to her *Bleak House* class, leaving Jaime nibbling on a meal replacement bar, which, in an effort to eke out her meagre rations, she had cut into minuscule squares. Ros was struck by the madness of a world where half the population was starving and the other half imposed starvation on themselves to compensate for their prior excess. Surely there had to be a better way to share things around?

Matt was reading the chapter from *Bleak House*, where Lady Dedlock reveals to Esther that she is her illegitimate child. Ros, who was sitting at her desk enjoying the sound of Dickens's words coming out of the mouth of this bright inner city boy, was forced to hide her face from view, her forehead in her hands, so that the class couldn't see the tears spilling from her eyes. How ironic that Ros should have been teaching precisely this book all term, ignorant of the story that lay hidden at the heart of her own family. She recalled the assignment she had set her pupils all those weeks before.

'Find someone real or imagined that you think you know and see whether new information about their lives or circumstances changes the way you think about them.'

Little had she realised at the time how relevant this was to become both for her and for her relationship with Lilian. That was the problem with life, all too often it imitated art, but, unlike art, it rarely concluded with all its loose ends neatly tied together.

Ros made her way across the crowded playground, assailed by snippets of conversation from passing pupils. It wasn't merely the violence of their language, but the strangeness of the terms they used and the absence of any grammatical principles that confronted her.

I really am turning into my mother, Ros thought and for once, instead of being horrified by the thought, she felt comforted.

She looked down at the opal ring on her finger and brought it to her lips. She looked at her hand, the hand of a middle-aged woman, the skin now delicate and thinning. It could have been Lilian's.

'Come, we go park.' A loud voice broke into her reverie.

Ros turned and saw that Dwayne, a boy in Year 11, had addressed the words to Versace. He wore his jeans low on his hips, the crotch suspended at knee level. Ros, whose own sons favoured this same fashion, couldn't understand how anyone could bear to have their movement so restricted.

'There are two things every girl should know,' Ros said, falling into step with Versace who had thrown Dwayne a brief contemptuous look before moving off in the direction of the school building. 'The first is never to go out with anyone who doesn't know how to use prepositions and definite or indefinite articles.'

'It's all right, Miss, I ain't gonna go park with him.'

'To the,' said Ros.

Versace looked at her blankly.

'To the park. Preposition followed by the definite article, implying you know which park he has in mind, otherwise it would be **a** park, indefinite article, meaning any park.'

'Yeah, right, I'll remember that. What was the other fing?'

'Hmm?' Ros said absently.

'You said there was two fings a girl should know.'

'Ah, yes, never put anything into your mouth that hasn't been boiled,' Ros said.

'But that would mean like you couldn't eat raw fruit and vegetables and that's good fer ya, innit?'

'Good point,' Ros said thoughtfully. 'I might have to revise the second thing, but the grammar one should be adhered to.'

Who was talking, Ros or Lilian? Ros was no longer sure.

'You're funny, Miss, you make me larf, you do.' And, as if to prove her point, Versace giggled.

'Where are you from?' Ros asked her.

'White City,' Versace replied disingenuously. She knew exactly what Ros was asking.

'No, I mean before, you know, your family.'

'Oh, that, yeah, well like me mum's white and me dad's parents was from Africa.'

'Which part?'

'Nigeria.'

White mother, black father, just like Nkosa. Ros suddenly wanted to stroke Versace's beautiful brown face. I could have had a sister just like you, she thought.

Mike and Charlie were in the attic sifting through Lilian's papers while Ros was examining the photographs taped to the lid of the suitcase. She noticed that something was lodged in a tear in the lining and, reaching in, she pulled out a tiny black and white photograph, bleached sepia with age, of her mother with a baby in her arms and Sipho by her side. A family. Lilian and Sipho both looked so adult in spite of being in their early twenties. But then, Ros reflected, people did in those days. They went from childhood to adulthood seemingly overnight, replicating the costumes and customs of their parents as soon as they left school. It was only baby-boomers onwards who refused ever to grow up.

Ros became aware that Mike had stopped moving. She turned to look at him and found him standing as though frozen, an envelope in his hand. She went to take it from him and he instinctively held it out of reach. Their eyes met and Mike silently handed it to her. She turned it over in her hand and read her mother's handwriting:

Sipho Nyathi/Prisoner No: 41202
Number Four Prison
Old Fort Complex
Constitution Hill
Johannesburg, South Africa

An official stamp covered the upper part of the envelope with the stark words:

DECEASED
RETURN TO SENDER

Ros sat down, the envelope held fast in her shaking hand. She brought it up to her face once more and examined the postmark. March 2nd 1958, some eight months after Lilian left South Africa.

'Why don't you open the letter?' Mike said, putting his arm around Ros. 'It might tell us something more.'

Ros opened the letter carefully, trying not to tear it. The glue had lost its stickiness over the years and it opened easily. The letter was short and she scanned it quickly before reading aloud.

Dear Sipho,

I hope that you received the parcel I sent you a few weeks ago and that the contents have helped with your comfort. H. has told me how things are with you and that a great deal of interest is being taken in you and your friends. We are doing everything we can here to help and I hope that once this is all over, we will be able to meet as planned. There is so much more to say, but this isn't the place; that song of Johnny's sums it all up. I wish I could say more, but there are so many others between us. Do please get word to me as soon as you can. I worry constantly. Yours always, L.

Charlie took the letter from Ros and read it to himself again. 'Censors,' he said.

'What do you mean?' asked Ros.

'Here, look,' he pointed at the letter, '"there are so many others between us." The prison authorities would have read the letter first and blacked out anything they didn't want the recipient to read. I wonder what Johnny's song was.'

Ros thought hard. It rang a bell. She went down the attic ladder and returned moments later with Lilian's pages, leafing through them until she found what she was looking for.

'Here it is, Mom mentioned it when Sipho disappeared once

and she thought their affair was over. The song was Johnny Ace's 'Pledging My Love'. It was their special song.'

'Forever my darling our love will be true, always and forever I'll love only you,' Mike sang, holding Ros's gaze until she looked away.

The three of them were silent. In the distance, Ros could hear the church bells in Coverdale Road strike the hour. They struck seven times and each toll seemed to deepen the pain of loss brought by the discovery of Sipho's death. Ros felt that she had lost someone very dear to her.

'Now what?' she asked quietly.

'Now,' Charlie said briskly, rolling up his sleeves, 'we know Sipho's surname and we begin our search for Nkosa Nyathi.'

Chapter Twenty-Three

A month had passed since that evening in the attic with Charlie and Mike. A long month of searching with still no word from Gloria. The publishers hadn't been able to offer any additional information. Although Ros hadn't found Nkosa, she felt happier than she had done for some time. Lilian was right; people really did need projects. A few weeks earlier, Ros had received a postcard from her old school friend Debbie. It depicted a fifties-style mother, hair neatly coiffed, dress cinched tightly at the waist and bore the caption My Mother Was Right About Everything. On the back of it Debbie had scrawled,

> *Mine wasn't, but yours was. Right that is. Sorry not to have been in touch sooner, I'm living in Singapore and just heard that your mother died. I've always remembered her, she told me I could do and be anything I wanted. I always thought you were so lucky to have a mother like that. Will let you know when I'm next in England – it's been far too long. Much love, Debbie.*

Ros had pinned the postcard above her desk where she sat most evenings and weekends working at her laptop. Lilian hadn't always been the easiest of mothers: her nature had been challenging, uncompromising and she had been, like all human beings, fallible. However, Ros felt more ready now than at any other time in her life both to recognise her mother's strengths and to heed her advice. Even in the most mundane decisions, she could hear Lilian's counsel in her head and frequently paid attention to it.

Perhaps it *was* possible to learn from the experience of others after all. Was it, she mused, because Lilian was dead? Was one more receptive to learning from the experiences of a dead parent than a living one because it allowed one to honour them in some way? Or was it that with the knowledge of Lilian's earlier life she had finally been able to solve the puzzle of her? For the first time, Ros could see Lilian as a person who had had a past, rather than simply as a parent whose sole purpose had been to give *her* life. She understood finally what Lilian meant when she used to protest that she was also a person.

In addition to the discovery of Lilian's returned, unopened letter to Sipho, the sad proof of his untimely death, they'd found an unfinished letter from Lilian to Ros written a week before Lilian had died, proof that her mother had wanted her to know about her early life. A first draft scribbled, in accordance with Lilian's waste-not-want-not approach to life, on a piece of cardboard that had once formed part of a box of tissues.

> *Darling Ros,*
>
> *I'm sorry you didn't enjoy a closer relationship with your father. One day, when you know my story, perhaps you will understand why I wanted you for my own. It was grossly selfish of me, but I lost my first daughter; I wasn't going to lose my second. I'm afraid our experiences sometimes cause us to behave unwisely. I should have been more generous both to you and to your father. Poor man, his only crime was falling in love with me. I should never have married him; I was incapable of loving any man after losing Sipho. But I'm so glad I did, otherwise I wouldn't have had you. I've never stopped looking for Nkosa. Perhaps one day ...*

The letter had ended mid-sentence. Ros didn't know whether Lilian's certainty that Nkosa was alive was based on fact or on a mother's intuition, but it had given Ros hope.

She had largely abandoned gumbaggley since her search for her sister had begun, apart from a surprising new habit of practising yoga on her own and in the nude in the privacy of her bedroom.

Ros wasn't sure why, but she found naked yoga both soothing and a useful way of confronting who she really was, although she still couldn't comprehend how people could possibly do it in public. Although, in truth, Ros wasn't always alone either: both Ruffy and Puppy liked to watch her, often taking their place beside Ros, their paws placed neatly side by side in front of them as all three of them stretched back effortlessly into the downward dog pose.

Naked yoga aside, Ros was entirely focused on finding Nkosa and all else appeared trivial by comparison. From time to time, she still talked to 'Jimmy' on StartingOver.com. In spite of the fact that she knew he was Mike (although he still didn't know she knew, or at least hadn't admitted to knowing), their aliases allowed them to talk to each other with a freedom and intimacy that eluded them face to face, when the baggage of all their years together seemed to overflow to create impenetrable chaos. She realised now that she'd always held herself back when they were together. A reticence learnt from her mother perhaps, which now that she knew its origins, she felt released from.

The only other thing that mattered to her was checking to ensure that Sid and Jack fulfilled their promise to stay alive. Lilian's loss of her child exacerbated Ros's perennial fear of losing her own. Although the boys emailed only intermittently, she spoke to them on the telephone every few days and was able to chart their progress from Sydney to Cairns by Greyhound. Sid's abandoned girlfriend, Liz, had been all but forgotten and the boys (Jack included, who seemed finally to have gained some part of the sexual confidence that Sid had always had) were cutting a swathe through the female backpackers they encountered and whose nationalities Ros was easily able to discern by the modulations in Jack's accent. The last time they'd spoken, Jack had told her 'zat we are 'aving a merveilleux time, really fantastique'. Ros had wondered whether the job of UN interpreter might be another he could consider. It would be steadier than either espionage or acting.

Ros hadn't even minded when in a new and complex arrangement, Ruffy and Puppy, whom none of them dared separate, had to be shared on a rota system between the three of them, Ros,

Mike and Charlie. It was the consequence of having two husbands and not living with either of them. Ros had even learnt gradually to enjoy the time on her own at home, although her use of the Internet in trying to trace Nkosa bordered on the obsessive.

Dogman, whose life was virtually unchanged in spite of the fifty thousand pounds he had inherited, was a frequent visitor, initially coming twice a week for reading lessons, a skill he acquired with surprising speed and efficiency. He now visited more regularly and had taken on the unofficial role of research assistant in Ros's quest to find Nkosa. He was also a surprisingly good cook and, with a diligence that never ceased to touch and surprise her, made sure that Ros ate. When off duty, he was often to be found on a park bench beside a tall, wide, oak tree in Ravenscourt Park ostentatiously reading Heidegger's *Being and Time*, his ferocious dogs, apparently becalmed by his new learning, coiled neatly at his feet.

'I'm not sure I understand what it's about,' Dogman had told Ros when she'd asked him about his choice of reading matter, 'but I can read all the words, well, almost all.'

'Don't worry, I don't think anyone really understands it, but why don't you read something a bit more, I don't know, enjoyable?' Ros asked.

'Nah,' he said, 'philosophy's a babe magnet, know what I mean? Girls love it; they think you're really clever and unthreatening. Lots of 'em come and sit on my bench and start talking to me. I've done very well with Heidegger. Mind you, some of the girls talk a bit too much during sex. I might give Sartre a go next.'

Ros, Charlie and Mike had done all they could to find Nkosa. They'd read all of Lilian's papers, which bore witness to her own ceaseless and unsuccessful attempts to trace her lost daughter. Ros had been disappointed to hear nothing further from Gloria in spite of her promise to be in touch. The publishers had given her Gloria's number, but no one ever answered her phone. They'd placed adverts in South African newspapers, written letters to the High Commission, and searched every Internet site available, from lostsiblings.com to genesreunited.com. So far, everything had drawn a blank and they had recently engaged the services of a private detective based in Johannesburg to help them. It appeared that Lilian had cut herself off from her South African friends after Sipho's death. It was as though the only way she could continue had been to lock the past away as firmly as she had locked away her photographs in the small suitcase in the attic. Her visit to South Africa two years before her death had been her final attempt to find Nkosa. It too had proved unsuccessful.

One afternoon, Ros sat in the attic looking again at Sipho's now familiar face staring out at her from the small photograph. It was as though she hoped he might speak to her. She experienced a sudden and urgent need to return to Clare Voyante and, as she stood up, her shoulder caught the shelf above her, causing Big Mouth Billy Bass to fall to the ground. Dislodged from its wooden mount, the fish finally broke its long silence and began to sing.

> *In every life we have some trouble*
> *When you worry you make it double*
> *Don't worry, be happy*

Ros picked it up astonished, and, turning it round, saw that there were no batteries in it at all.

'Ah, there you are, dear,' Clare Voyante said, opening the door to her as though she had been expecting her.

'Did I phone you?' Ros asked, no longer able to remember what she might or might not have done. Big Mouth Billy Bass had confused her badly and she'd immediately got in her car and driven straight down the M1 to Milton Keynes.

'She told me you were on your way. Come and sit down.' Clare Voyante led the way, murmuring, 'Yes, yes, I'll tell her, all in good time, dear, don't take on so.'

Ros could only assume that Lilian was in her ear.

'Why didn't she tell me before?' Ros asked as soon as they were settled in the white room.

'She's saying, don't worry, she wants you to be happy.'

'Yes,' Ros said shortly, 'Big Mouth Billy Bass already explained that to me.'

Clare Voyante looked puzzled and seemed on the point of asking for an explanation when her face contorted and her voice changed.

'African sisters,' she said. As before, her voice sounded like Lilian's.

'Yes, I know I've got a sister,' Ros said. 'But where is she?'

'You must find her,' the voice said.

Clare Voyante looked disorientated. She shook her head and said in her own voice. 'She's gone, dear.'

'Damn, I need some answers.' Ros felt frustrated. Clare Voyante had been her last shot.

Ros picked up the small straw basket that she had found in the suitcase and which now lived on her desk. She had long ago realised that it was the same tickey basket Lilian had bought on her train journey from Cape Town to Johannesburg. She opened it and took out the black, green and yellow beaded ring she had found inside it; Lilian's wedding ring from Sipho. Ros turned it in her fingers, feeling the smoothness of the small beads and wishing that each one could form a path to lead her to her sister. Their research had yielded some facts: Sipho had been charged with treason two months after Lilian had left South Africa. He had died in custody and the cause of death was recorded as being due to 'multiple causes', a common euphemism for police brutality.

The phone rang, breaking into Ros's thoughts. It was Charlie and he sounded excited.

'Good, you're there. What are you doing?' he said.

'Nothing much.'

'Don't move, I'm bringing someone to see you.'

'Is that Mike I can hear in the background?' Ros asked.

'Yes,' said Charlie. 'We'll be round in ten minutes.'

What were they up to? Ros stood and wandered round the living room, restlessly waiting for them. She picked up the photograph of Lilian in Cape Town and looked hard into her mother's eyes, finally able to meet her gaze. She kissed the glass and returned it carefully to the mantelpiece. For so long, Ros had felt pity only for herself for having lost her mother when she'd felt too young to do so. Now, at last, she felt sorrow for Lilian whose life had ended too soon, before she'd had the chance to forgive herself and to find the daughter she'd never wanted to lose.

The doorbell rang and Ros hurried to answer it. Charlie and Mike stood on the threshold and as she opened the door, they moved apart to reveal the woman who stood behind them.

'Let me look at you,' she said, taking Ros's face between her hands. 'I can't believe it, you look just like her.' The woman drew Ros towards her and embraced her. 'I'm so happy to see you,' she said. Her voice held the strong trace of a South African accent, the cadences of which reminded Ros sharply of her mother.

'This is Gloria,' Mike said simply, stepping forward to stand at Ros's side.

Gloria was still beautiful; she wore an African print cotton dress with beaded jewellery, which chimed with Lilian's description of her. She was the same age as Lilian would have been, seventy-three, but moved with the agility of someone much younger and held herself very erect. Resting in her embrace, Ros was made aware of how much she missed the company of people Gloria's age. That was the unforeseen consequence of losing one's parents; one lost an entire generation.

'She wouldn't see us,' Gloria said a little later when they were all sitting around the kitchen table with a drink. 'After Sipho died, Lilian found any contact with the rest of us unbearable. I never understood it, I thought we'd be the best ones to comfort her as we'd known them both so well, but it was her way of coping; it was almost as if she had to close a door on her past and pretend that none of it had ever happened. She sent me a photograph of you when you were born.' Gloria traced Ros's jawline with a finger. 'We did keep in touch now and then by letter and in the final two years of her life, when we were writing our books, we emailed more and more often.'

'What happened to the baby, to Nkosa?' Ros asked.

Gloria sighed. 'Thandi took her back to the Transkei, to the countryside. She must have changed their names as we haven't been able to find them – I think they might have gone to Swaziland later. Gerry Vanderbilt did all he could to help, but in the end he had to leave Africa too.'

'What happened to the others?' Ros asked. 'Harry, Lenny and Shirley?'

'Harry died a few weeks ago,' Gloria said sadly, 'of cancer.' Her eyes filled.

'I'm so sorry,' Ros said.

'That's why I haven't been in touch.' Gloria cleared her throat and wiped away her tears. 'I'm so sorry it's taken so long. I felt terrible about it, but I had to look after Harry. I was about to make contact when Charlie found me and arranged for me to come over.'

Ros looked gratefully at Charlie.

'I hoped for ages that Harry and your mom would get together,' Gloria continued. 'He'd always been in love with her and Sipho was like a brother to him. When he saw there was no hope, he went to America, to Boston, and eventually married someone else; so did I. We left South Africa in nineteen sixty-one after the treason trial collapsed.' She looked thoughtful and added, 'And after Sharpville. Lenny and Shirley came here, to England. They tried to see Lilian. In fact they did actually meet up once or twice, but it upset her too much and after that she wouldn't respond to their invitations. They moved back to South Africa when Mandela came to power and took active roles in his government. I can give you an address for them, they're still there and living in Jo'burg.'

'Why did they kill Sipho?' Ros asked.

'I don't think there was any special reason,' Gloria said. 'I'm afraid it happened quite frequently. The police would question prisoners for hours and beat them to try and get information from them. All too often we would hear that someone had died from multiple injuries or had committed suicide. Everyone knew that it was just a euphemism for police brutality and murder.'

She was silent for a few moments. They all were.

'He was a wonderful man, Sipho; something set him apart. He was the kind of man who had greatness in him. If we hadn't been childhood friends, I think I'd have fallen for him myself.'

'I wish I'd known him,' Ros said, feeling a sudden pang of sorrow that Sipho hadn't been her own father.

'She never forgave herself for staying on that boat and leaving Sipho behind,' Gloria said, adding suddenly in Xhosa, *'Isala kutyelwa siva noolopu* – a person who will not take advice gets knowledge when trouble overtakes him. That's what Lilian's cook, Josiah told her; she always remembered that, although she disagreed with him: it was following the advice of others that meant she left South Africa. She felt guilty about it for the rest of her life.'

'Why did she never tell my father?' Ros asked.

'There was a terrible stigma about having a child with a black man even in this country,' Gloria said. 'Your mother was always a brave woman, but I think losing Sipho and Nkosa made her lose her courage. That's why she never told you either.' Gloria took Ros's hand in her own. 'Was I right to send you the book?' she asked.

Ros nodded. 'Of course you were. She tried to tell me the day she died.' Ros remembered the last time she had seen Lilian. 'She said she wanted to tell me something and mentioned her book. I thought she meant the book she was reading and didn't stay to listen.'

Ros could hear the blare of the television set from Chris's shop over the road and, through the window, could see Chris settling into his armchair in front of it. She found this a reassuringly familiar sight in a world that had, over the course of the past few months, changed irrevocably.

'Nkosa was my imaginary friend,' Ros said suddenly. Mike, Charlie and Gloria looked at her. 'It's just come back to me. I had an imaginary friend from Africa that I used to call Kosi. It must have been her. I wonder whether Mom told me about her when I was small or if I saw a photo or something. I remember Mom and I had a big fight one day and she told me I was too big for imaginary friends. I couldn't understand why she was so angry. It makes sense now.'

Gloria stayed with Ros for the rest of the week and between them they formulated a plan for Ros to visit South Africa. She had decided to take three months' leave from school to go and see her mother's homeland for herself and continue the search for Nkosa. She would arrive back in England in time for Sid and Jack's return and the start of the autumn term. It was to be her own mini-gap year.

'Great idea, Ros,' said Charlie when she told him. 'Mike and I can take care of the dogs between us. By the way, what does he think about it?'

Charlie topped up Ros's drink. They were sitting in her garden, their peaceful enjoyment of the early summer evening punctuated by the sound of Dogman mowing his lawn next door.

'I haven't told him yet,' Ros said. 'But I've told the school and when I said that I had very personal reasons for needing some time away, the Head agreed to it immediately.'

The lawnmower stopped and Dogman's head appeared over the garden wall.

'Sartre's a winner,' he said, giving Ros the thumbs-up. 'I'm off out on a date, see you later.'

'I've also got a bit of news,' Charlie said when he'd gone. The affected casualness of his tone made Ros immediately suspicious. 'Archibald's moving in and we're going to try for a baby.'

'How?' asked Ros.

'We've got a surrogate.' Charlie looked sheepish and couldn't seem to meet Ros's eyes.

'Who is it, Charlie?'

'Hmm,' Charlie pretended not to hear.

Ros took him by the arm and turned him towards her. 'Who's the surrogate?'

'Oh, um, it's Angelique, Archibald's sister,' he said.

'The sperm burglar?' Ros was incredulous.

'You mustn't call her that any more,' said Charlie, 'she's sort of my sister-in-law now. It means both Archibald and I will be the baby's blood relatives.'

'God, Charlie, has she agreed to do it?'

'Yes, although she says she will have to come to terms with actually being given sperm rather than having to steal it, and that usually when she has a baby, she gets a house but since we're family, she's prepared to make an exception.'

Ros shook her head incredulously. 'The world's gone mad.' She thought for a while and added, 'Can I be godmother?'

'Of course,' said Charlie.

Mike wanted to go with Ros to Africa when she told him her plan.

'I have to do this alone,' Ros said.

He looked forlorn and Ros had the urge to pull his head onto her shoulder and stroke his hair. They were in a café around the corner from the house having supper. It was the first time they'd gone out together, just the two of them, since separating and it felt strangely like being on a date. The irony was that their divorce had been finalised the week before.

'Eh, Jimmy,' Ros said, putting on a Scottish accent and holding up her Bloody Mary, 'cheers.'

Mike's head snapped up with alarm. 'Why did you call me Jimmy?' he asked too quickly.

'No reason.' Ros feigned innocence. 'That's how Scottish people greet each other isn't it? I was merely being Scottish.'

Mike shifted uncomfortably in his seat and opened and closed his mouth. Ros was about to tease him that he looked like a goldfish. He ran his hand through his hair compulsively as he often did when agitated. Ros took pity on him.

'I knew her smile in an instant; I knew the curve of her face,' she sang. *'It was my own lovely lady, and she said, "Oh, it's you."'*

'How long have you known?' Mike said quietly. 'The Piña Colada song,' he continued without waiting for Ros to answer, 'I'd forgotten that's how the lyrics went. How ironic that that was the song I chose and how extraordinary that it should come true.'

'I knew that night when I first found out I had a sister,' Ros said. 'What about you, have you always known?'

'No, not in the beginning, but I realised that night in the Coach and Horses.' Mike took her hand, 'Ros ...'

Ros shook her head. 'I'll be back before you know it and then the boys will be home too.'

They sat in silence for a few moments as though unsure what to say or do next. Next to them, a young couple sat entwined, their eyes full of each other, at the beginning of their journey together.

'Do you ever wish you could start again, Mike?' Ros asked.

'Yes,' Mike answered, following Ros's gaze, 'of course.' He took her hand. 'But, the one thing I'm absolutely sure of is that I'd want to start again with you. There are lots of things I would have done differently. Not let my anger get out of control for one thing, not have hurt you, not have fucked it all up so badly.'

'It takes two,' said Ros, 'it must have been awful feeling that you were never good enough, and somehow I must have made you feel that. I'm sorry.'

'I'm sorry too,' Mike said. 'I liked being Jimmy and meeting Sally; she was different to you, more vulnerable and fragile. You're always so on top of everything.'

'Are you serious? Don't you realise that's all an act to prevent myself from unravelling? You see, that's the problem with marriage: one loses the art of conversation and assumes that the other person is inside one's head and understands everything.'

Ros looked at the man who had until recently been her husband and, for the first time in years, could see the face of the young busker she had fallen for.

'Do you remember when Sid's braces came off and Jack said his teeth had come out of prison?' Mike said.

'I'd forgotten that.' Ros laughed. She was aware of how much she and Mike shared – the whole of their children's lives for one thing. 'I miss them so much. But you know, I feel better about them having gone now. I mean, at least we were fortunate enough to have them, to grow and nurture them together until the time came for them to leave home, rather than having had them snatched away from us like Nkosa was from Mom. Although painful, their going away now is part of the natural order of things.'

They fell silent again.

'Every stage of life is difficult, isn't it?' said Ros. 'I keep waiting for the easy part and it never comes.'

'It's only difficult if you think it is,' Mike said. He reached out and stroked the side of her face with a finger. 'I've missed you, Ros. My own lovely lady. Although, I always think of you as a girl.'

'Do you? I rather like being a girl.'

Mike moved closer to her. 'Can I come home with you to-night?'

'How many times do I have to tell you,' Ros said, 'I never sleep with a man on the first date.'

Mike was about to protest that wasn't strictly true, what about that bloke she'd told him about when she thought he was Jimmy, but instead asked, 'Not even the man you're going to marry?'

'No,' Ros said, shaking her head firmly, 'I won't become your wife again. That's the trouble with marriage, you stop being girl-friend and boyfriend and become husband and wife, each wanting to change the other instead of accepting them for who they are. Perhaps I am my mother after all and simply bad at being a wife. She froze my father out and I did the same to you.'

'It's time to let Lilian go and to stop comparing yourself to her,' Mike said quietly.

'I know and I think now that I understand her, I'm finally ready to.' Ros leant her head on Mike's shoulder. 'I have a question,' she said.

'Go on.'

'Why were you even being Jimmy in the first place when you had Marie-Carmen?'

Mike looked embarrassed. 'Marie-Carmen was just ...'

'... meaningless sex?' Ros finished for him.

Although the love bite on Mike's neck was long gone, Ros needed any residual memory of it to fade before she could seri-ously contemplate any sort of future with him.

Chapter Twenty-Four

Ros was hurrying across the playground. It was her last day at school and she was leaving for Africa in a week. She'd spent the past few days reassuring her pupils that they'd be fine without her. In truth, she felt guilty for abandoning them at this late stage in the school year, especially her GCSE and A level students. But she'd helped Penny find an excellent replacement.

'It won't be the same without you, Miss,' Versace said, catching her up as she was about to enter the main school building.

'It's you who has to do the work, Versace, not me,' Ros explained. 'And you are more than capable of it. I have to go to Africa to find my sister.' Ros surprised herself by telling Versace some of Lilian's story.

'Oh yeah,' Versace observed casually when she'd finished, 'me dad's got loads of bruvvas and sisters in Africa he never knew he had. I hope you find her, Miss, and I'll see you next year. Because of you, I've decided to stay and do me A levels after all.'

Ros instinctively took Versace by the shoulders and kissed her on both cheeks. 'I'm very proud of you,' she whispered in the girl's ear. 'You've got an excellent brain.'

'Me pashonga's not bad, neither,' Versace said, smiling broadly and allowing Ros to see that she'd had a small diamond placed in the centre of one of her front teeth.

Ros turned to go.

''Ere, Miss,' Versace called her back, 'you should go onto the Internet like my dad done. African Sisters or summink.'

Ros hesitated. It rang a bell but the memory eluded her. She walked towards the staffroom – would she miss school? she wondered. She'd felt so energised since making the decision to go away that she doubted it. The break in routine would do her good.

Ros saw Lola outside the staffroom.

'How's your friend Marie-Carmen?' Ros asked, feigning casual interest.

'Las' week, she no bery goo',' Lola said, 'this Miguel he throw her away, he wants for to pick up again his wife.'

Ros felt irrationally angry with Mike on Marie-Carmen's behalf. 'I hope she'll be OK,' she said.

Lola looked serious. 'Firs' she bery sad, she get drunk and forget to put out the cigarette so is a fire.'

'Oh my God, is she all right?' Ros asked.

'Bery goo' now, she have new man. Is fireman, bery bery handsome.'

A fireman! Ros felt a momentary pang of envy. She and Marie-Carmen shared a remarkably similar taste in men.

'Where are you, Jaime?' Ros teased, pretending to look for her friend under a pile of biology textbooks in the staffroom.

Jaime laughed, or rather a very slim woman with a mass of wild curly hair did. Her friend was barely recognisable. She'd lost two and a half stone, found her waist, turned her matronly bosom back into breasts and developed a passion for salsa dancing.

'I still can't believe how fantastic you look,' Ros said.

'Me neither,' Jaime said.

'What does Tony think?'

'Who?' Jaime said with feigned bewilderment.

'Oh no, you haven't left him, have you?'

Jaime shook her head, laughing, 'Tony's fine, he's coming round to it. He says it's like having a new wife. The truth is, he can't keep his hands off me. Watch out, A of D approaching.'

Ros turned and, seeing Peter Seers over her left shoulder, made a great show of gathering up papers and files.

'Isn't Jaime beautiful?' Peter said, his eyes shining with devotion.

'She certainly is, but she always was—' said Ros.

'Was Keats right about beauty being truth?' Peter interrupted Ros. 'I do have a feeling of truth when I look at Jaime,' he continued without waiting for an answer. 'I feel I could find the answer to everything if only I looked at her long and hard enough.'

'That's quite enough of that, Peter,' Jaime said, blushing with pleasure in spite of herself. 'I'm a married woman.'

Peter nodded sadly. 'I know,' he said and abruptly stopped talking.

Ros and Jaime exchanged looks of astonishment; the Angel of Death had finally been silenced.

'Right, I'm ready,' Ros said. 'Jaime, come and see me off.'

Peter mutely watched them leave the room; his expression reminded Ros of Ruffy's when she put the Good Boy chocolate drops away in the cupboard.

They collided with Ant who was coming into the staffroom just as they were leaving it. Ros bent to pick up the book he had dropped, *Welding for Beginners*.

'There's this one thing I'm trying to persuade her to do—' Ant began.

Ros held up her hand. 'No explanation necessary,' she said, 'I just hope that whatever it is proves pleasurable enough to have warranted such effort.'

Ant smiled; a secret sort of smile that implied that it almost certainly would. Ros and Jaime spent the rest of the journey to the school's front gates trying and failing to guess what sexual act could possibly be worth welding for.

Once home, Ros burst through her front door and rushed to her computer. African Sisters. That was the message Clare Voyante had given her on her last and, as she'd then thought, fruitless visit. She typed the words in and a list of options came up. An address caught her eye: Africansistersunite.co.uk. A first glance suggested that the site was geared towards volunteer projects for women in Africa. *Africa needs her sisters*, read the strap line at the head of the page. *We are looking for volunteers amongst women more fortunate than their African sisters to help put an end to poverty and illness.* A menu to the left of the page offered a variety of African countries. Ros clicked on South Africa. Her eyes skimmed the web page. There were various projects on offer, opportunities to see the country and to help with HIV orphans in schools and townships. In small lettering at the side of the screen, she found the words she sought. *Lost Siblings.* Ros felt a rush of adrenalin. She put both hands to her head in lieu of finding wood to touch, crossed her fingers, took a deep breath and clicked on the letters.

An hour later, Ros got up and went to stand at the living room window. She looked out onto the street. She had searched through countless lists of names and photographs. Nothing. Nothing for her anyhow. She had posted her own photograph and a message nonetheless and now she was back to where she'd been before hope had flooded her: back to waiting and wanting.

Perhaps she should do some volunteer work while in South Africa? At least then her visit would fulfil some other purpose and in some karmic way she might be rewarded with finding Nkosa. Ros opened the web page again and clicked on the project to help HIV/AIDS orphans.

Volunteering is the perfect way to see things outside and greater than ourselves.

A group of children smiled out at Ros from the screen. In their midst, with her back to the camera and only her jaw visible, stood an African woman, her head swathed in bright orange cloth.

Nkosa Butshingi is looking for volunteers to help build a school for these children.

The woman's surname was unfamiliar, but the curve of her jaw was unmistakable.

And finally ...

As she was about to leave the house for the airport, Ros logged on to StartingOver.com for the last time.

Bye, Jimmy, she wrote, you were right about my ex, he is unfinished business. I don't know whether it will work out for us long term, but now that he's working to bid farewell to Mr Angry and I am finally coming to terms with my mother's death, I want at least to explore the possibility.

Good luck, Jimmy wrote, I really think you should give him another chance. I'm sure he's a decent guy who simply lost his way.

We'll see. Perhaps you should make another go of it with your wife too. Bye.

I hope meeting your sister makes you happy, Ros. 'Jimmy' dropped the pretence. Just remember, I'll still be here and waiting for you. I love you.

Ros smiled. 'We'll see,' she said quietly, 'one thing at a time.' She shut down her computer, picked up her suitcase and stepped out of the front door.

Ros could feel Lilian by her side all through the night flight to Johannesburg. She'd felt her presence only intermittently over the preceding few months, but now she was back in earnest, accompanying Ros on her journey to her homeland. 'Careful of my lipstick, careful of my hair,' her mother's voice sounding softer and gentler than Ros had remembered it previously, less forbidding and more loving. Ros felt that if she turned her head she would see her, but Lilian was too quick for her, seeming to vanish as soon as Ros moved and leaving only the faintest scent of her perfume in her wake.

'Nearly there, nearly there now,' her voice seemed to whisper.

Ros wasn't sure whether she was awake or dreaming. Some passengers slept, others sat quietly, their faces illuminated by the flicker of images on the screens they watched.

Nkosa was meeting her at the airport. When they landed, Ros ran the length of the long corridor that led to passport control, not caring what her fellow travellers thought of her.

As Ros entered the arrivals lounge, she found herself directly in front of a face that she knew. A beautiful woman of fifty stood before her, her hair caught up with brightly coloured batik fabric twisted around her head making her look every inch an African princess. Ros looked at her and recognised instantly that Nkosa was a black version of herself; her face was Ros's own.

'Come here, baby sister,' Nkosa shouted as soon as she saw Ros, holding her arms wide and giving a rich laugh of happiness, which, Ros was sure, could have been inherited only from Sipho, her father. 'Come and let me hug you.'

Ros's face was buried in Nkosa's neck as she held her, eyes tightly shut. She opened them again and, out of the corner of one, thought she caught sight of Lilian, or someone who looked very like her: a cloud of auburn hair, a head looking back for one final glance, and the woman left the terminal and disappeared from view. It seemed as though she'd evaporated because Ros could no longer see any sign of her.

Was it her imagination or had Lilian really been with her all these months guiding her into her sister's arms? Or, was this manifestation of Lilian who had seemed to haunt her, this mother without, really the mother within; had she absorbed Lilian within her in the way one does after a loved one dies, reluctant to relinquish them? There is no division, it seems, between the past, the present and the future; they are inextricably linked. All of us,

Ros reflected, are the story so far of our lineage and our lives are partially determined by what has preceded us.

'Come, baby sister,' said Nkosa, stroking Ros's shoulder as she hugged her, 'we have a lot of catching up to do.'

As Nkosa withdrew her hand, Ros caught sight of her arm. Above her wrist an old scar was faintly discernible – Lilian's sad legacy and the outcome of walking with liquids. Enclosed in Nkosa's embrace, Ros felt whole for the first time. Whatever else happened, whether she and Mike got back together or not, she finally knew who she was. A wife, a mother, a daughter and, most delightfully and unexpectedly, a sister.

Acknowledgements

I'd like to thank my mother, Leonie Lichtenstein, who died too young and whom we miss so much. Lilian's story is not my South African mother's, but I hope its spirit honours her and my father, Edwin, and some of the things they stood for. Thanks are also due to Sir Sydney and Lady Felicia Kentridge, Margot Light, Edna O'Shaugnessy and Lewis Wolpert for sharing their memories and knowledge of South Africa with me.

Grateful thanks to my husband, Simon Humphreys, for his scarcely credible forbearance, his charm, his wit and his singular grace (he wrote that bit), and my children, Oscar and Francesca, who have always been people no matter how small. Also to my brother, Conrad Lichtenstein, my friends, Deborah Bangay QC, Simon Booker, Richard Denton, Peter Grimsdale, Claire Ladsky, Melanie McGrath, Shyama Perera, Andrew Singer, Colleen Toomey and my very own secret gay husband, Adam Wide. And to Jochen Encke who looks after me.

Thanks to Kate Mills, my editor at Orion, who has been consistently inspiring and patient, and to Susan Lamb, the Queen of paperback publishing and Juliet Ewers and Jon Wood. Also to Clare Alexander, my incomparable agent, who keeps me on the path of writeousness (sic) and to Sally Riley at Aitken Alexander who ensures that my books have a life in other languages. To my Swedish publisher, Marika Hemmel, thank you for the fish.

A mention for the Andalusian village of Pinos del Valle, with its mountain views and blue skies, where much of this book was written, and for my friend, Sabrina Broadbent, who sometimes joined me there to work on her own book; and finally, I'd like to remember the late Miriam Makeba who did teach my mother to dance the *kwela* in Johannesburg in the 1950s and whose music supplied the soundtrack to my childhood.

Olivia Lichtenstein. London, January 2009